A New World

Emma Gilman

Venture Press—Colorado Springs, CO
ISBN: 979-8-3306-7918-8
Title: *A New World*
Author: By Emma Gilman
Digital distribution | 2024
Paperback | 2024

This is a work of fiction. The characters, names, incidents, places, and dialogue are products of the author's imagination, and are not to be construed as real.

Published in the United States by New Book Authors Publishing

Dedication

To my mom,

Who dedicated everything to me.

You made this possible.

Prologue

Everyone is broken. Leaders lead on broken foundations—like crumbling concrete and displaced nails in the structure of a home, ready to collapse. And it is impossible to build a future on something that is destined to fall. Followers follow on broken ideals, only looking in the dark for a string of light or a bit of hope to point them in the right direction. But what happens if there *is* no hope left?

I contemplated this revelation while standing under the high vaulted ceiling of the church—the church that confined me as a child and still confines me today. The white stone of the interior was consuming and suffocating, the high beams running across my head seeming as though they might come crashing down. The rows of stark white pillars created a hollow feeling—like the room would continue and never end.

The wooden benches were filled with families, every child hushed and placed obediently next to their parents. Women sat adoringly with their hands folded in their laps, their petite palms wrapped in useless lace gloves. Meanwhile, their husbands straightened their ties and looked to the priest as if he was their savior. The priest's words were taken in loving accord by the people of the church, and it felt as though we were under the control of everything he proclaimed. The priest was an old man with graying hair and hunched shoulders. Beyond his dying stature, his eyes were drooping and tired. Quite frankly, he looked as hopeless as the rest of us, if not more weathered from the years of his testimonies.

I'd come to realize that hope can destroy you. Working tirelessly to convince someone to believe what you believe has the power to drain every ounce of faith within you until you are nothing more than a broken follower yourself, searching for yet another light.

"We are all one in the church," the priest's voice registered clearly among the fog in my mind, and I looked at the man in reverence.

Yes. Yes, we are. We are a broken, incomplete people. Together, yet unchanged.

"Now take the bread and the cup, and repent for your sins," he said this almost accusingly.

I swallowed the dark plum wine and chewed solemnly on the stale bread, the fibers cracking uncomfortably between my clenched teeth. The contents had no flavor, no texture. But despite how plain they were, tears brimmed in my eyes as the mush of bread slowly glided down my throat.

"Forgive me," I whispered, not knowing to whom.

Chapter One

Two months had passed since I'd left the circus. Two months I had spent in Axminster, wishing I was traveling cross country on a rambunctious train where only a few hours were spent with eyes closed every night. Instead, I slept alone, staring up at the ceiling of my childhood bedroom, wondering what it would feel like to sleep next to Joseph in the aftermath of our nuptials.

The wedding had been set for the 26th of July. In exactly one month I would stand before Joseph and relinquish my dreams along with my autonomy. I would belong solely to him with no other responsibilities but to be his wife. And I was terrified.

Hot beads of tears rolled down my cheeks, but I allowed them to fall freely in the emptiness of my room. This room was not a sanctuary—it never had been. The sheets on my bed were pulled too tightly around my ribs and the sunlight streaming through the shutters was pasty and dull, not vibrant as it had been in the open fields of the circus. Every piece of furniture and decor was too perfectly placed, and the air was stale and bitter. I was slowly suffocating in a reality I couldn't escape— a puppet on my mother's strings, and I couldn't possibly cut myself loose.

And on those dreadful nights, when I couldn't erase the image of Joseph standing at the altar waiting for me, I opted to read through Mr. Monte's letter, comforted that everyone was safe from the perpetrator and the menace of Mr. Young.

To ease my aching heart, I imagined what I would be doing if I were back with the circus—eating garlic roasted chicken and scalloped potatoes with the crew, dancing until midnight with mugs of ale jumping feverishly in our hands, and maybe even practicing with Toulouse. I imagined Charlotte's laughter and Olive's incessant attempt to sneak a sip of alcohol from Wilman, who couldn't leave his post at the bar. The thought of Evelyn smacking the girl's hand made me laugh, and the sound echoing off the walls of my empty bed chamber reminded me how alone I really was.

Finally, I thought of Cassius's eyes. I thought about those golden irises and the way his eyelashes fluttered softly on his cheeks when he was dreaming.

This is for you.

I closed my eyes and hoped that he would receive my message somehow, across the cavernous space separating us. He was rescued by Mr. Monte for a reason, and I had to ensure that wasn't in vain.

The last performance of the year...

A darkness had fallen over the circus. The candlelight had been blown out, whisking tendrils of smoke around the room. A drum beat steadily in the circular chamber of the tent, reverberating off the walls until every other human thought and characteristic was lost and replaced with complete devotion. Hearts beat with the drum, every sense taken over; and hands clapped with the rhythm as the audience recognized too late that they'd lost control. There was no turning back. A loud roar echoed throughout the room and instinct would have provoked them to cover their ears, but no one could seem to move in the trance that had befallen them. Their stares were fixed on one thing and one thing alone—a pair of eyes like gems flickering wickedly in the darkness, amid a terrific mane of golden fur. The lion slowly stalked toward them, his impeding eyes speaking for the circus.

And they asked, "Can you hear me?"

The audience fought to block out the sound of dancers shouting and plumes of fire raging past their ears, just so they may hear that lucid voice once again.

"Wake up," it whispered.

Wake up. And in a moment, everything flashed by in a blur. Nimble women kicked their legs into the air, a man struck a lion with a whip, and a jester flew by on a unicycle. It was too much, too fast, but they couldn't look away. The audience emerged from their trance just in time for the performance to conclude. No sooner had the candles been lit and the introduction given, and the crowd was filing out. The experience was breathtaking, although most were too mesmerized by the magic to notice the faults in the performance and what was really transpiring when the curtain was drawn.

"Charlotte, what da hell were ya doin'? You were in my way through da entire dance!" Josephine screamed as soon as the curtain was drawn.

"Don't get me started, Josephine. Your ears blocked my face the entire show!" Charlotte bickered back.

"Ya know I can't control it. Maybe if you weren't trying to be in da spotlight all da time, we wouldn't have dis issue!" Josephine threatened within an inch of Charlotte's face.

Charlotte grabbed onto Josephine's long earlobe and began to pull on it. "Maybe we should just tie it back to your head. Maybe then your balance wouldn't be thrown all over the place, huh?"

"Ladies! Ladies stop! What's going on here?" Mr. Monte raced into the fray and grabbed Josephine to pull her back. Meanwhile, Cassius wrapped his arms around Charlotte's waist and held her in place while she wriggled. Both women attempted to reach one another even still, flinging their hands wildly through the air.

"Josephine won't get out of my way! The performance was ruined tonight!" Charlotte whined.

"Oh, shut up, Char, you're just upset that you weren't in the front!" Josephine spit back at her.

"Hey!" Mr. Monte erupted, his low voice echoing through the room like a roar of his own, making everyone fall quiet. All eyes watched him as he let go of Josephine and ran his hands through his hair. He'd gained a few silver strands in his coarse brown hair, the length had reached his shoulders, and his beard had grown out over the past few months.

He looked rather disheveled. Tired. Older. "This is not who we are." He finally looked at the crew with tears brimming in his eyes and anger pulsing through the vein in his forehead. "Since when do we bicker and fight and take our anger out on one another? We're a team—a family!"

The room was so silent the only thing you could hear was the sound of miscellaneous feet stepping in the sand, the grains sifting over one another.

Charlotte spoke up quietly, embarrassed by her actions. "We haven't been a family for months. Not since Juniper left."

Mr. Monte's lip curled, and he spouted, "Juniper's gone, and she isn't coming back. You all better get used to it." Mr. Monte threw his coat over his shoulder and began to walk away.

Suddenly Hugh spoke up and stopped Mr. Monte in his tracks, his usual confidence overridden with confusion. "I thought you were going to bring her back. You told us she would come back." His voice was small, pleading almost.

Mr. Monte's face fell, and he ran a defeated hand across his mouth. Shuffling back and forth, he debated what to say. He'd failed his team, but he wouldn't give them false hope—wouldn't lie to them.

"I tried." Mr. Monte shrugged hopelessly. "I tried and it didn't work." Without another word he stormed out of the tent.

While the red and white tent flapped in the breeze, the performers slowly began to crumble. Anyone who'd just seen their performance would be fooled. They had put on their smiles, lifted their chins, and did the only thing they knew how to do—perform.

But behind the curtain, it was clear that the circus was falling.

Very, very quickly.

Chapter Two

Mr. Monte...

In the last two months, I'd lost everything. The performers, the energy, the love. My crew was no longer enthused by their work or excited to make families smile. The magic was gone. It disappeared the day Juniper fled. All the stress caused by the killer and by Mr. Young's arrival had finally sent the circus over the edge.

The performers were scared.

But I was to blame as well for the change in the circus. I was once bright and cheerful; but I'd become angry and revenge-seeking. For months I've wanted to do something, anything, to regain the hope we held last year. I tried endlessly to get Juniper back. I sent letters day and night, hoping she might convince Mr. Young to let her go—to let all of us go. But we were fastened to him by chains too strong to break. We were overpowered. Mr. Young held the future of the circus in his fingertips. And one wrong move from Juniper and we would be lost forever.

I blamed myself for this every day. Why couldn't I secure Juniper a home like I could the others? Why couldn't I protect her?

Beyond the pain I felt for disappointing Juniper, I had to deal with my other stars. I tried to keep their hopes up, even if it meant lying to them, but it wasn't working. I couldn't count the number of times I had said, "I'm working on it," or "She'll come back to us."

We'll be okay, I told myself every day, but I couldn't see how. Morale was lower than it had ever been, and excitement was dwindling. This happened once before with Penelope Plume's death, but in the midst of darkness, Juniper emerged and brought that light back to us. She promised the future of the circus and made our bond unbreakable.

Somehow, I had to rekindle that. No matter how defeated the performers were or how lost they felt, there was still hope. Mr. Young couldn't break us so easily.

Juniper...

I took a deep breath before stepping out of the glossy charcoal carriage in which my family and I were traveling. *They're not your real family. Your* real *family is behind you, where you* left *them,* my subconscious informed me. I was welcomed by a hoard of voices screaming in my ear.

Upon arriving in Axminster, I thought the people would have been angry that I joined the circus to begin with. I presumed they thought of me as a foolish little girl seeking an adventure. If only they knew the circus was much more than a silly adventure.

But they weren't angry with me. They had bright smiles on their faces, hands shooting out of the crowd and waving newspapers in the air smeared with my name. They were clapping, cheering…for me.

"Juniper, will you sign my copy? My daughter loves you!" a woman in an expensive scarlet dress screamed over the crowd, scrambling toward me.

I remained frozen, paralyzed; my expensive carriage boots planted in the cobblestones underfoot. I had just abandoned my friends. Why were they cheering for me?

"Please Juniper! I'd love your autograph!" A little boy ran up to me and clung to my floral, silk gown, ripping the seam on my bodice.

I stood there motionless, unable to form words.

"Juniper, Juniper, Juniper!" the crowd cheered as though I were a star.

My mind was running too quickly to comprehend anything. There were too many voices, too many people. My mouth was dry, and I coughed on the lump in my throat.

Suddenly a barrage of guards came rushing down the street to hold back the crowd.

One of the officers grabbed my arm roughly, making me wince as his fingers dug into my biceps. "Miss, it would be safer if you got back in the carriage. Return straight home. The city is running rampant with your fans. I must say, I'm one myself." He smiled sheepishly and ushered me back into the carriage where my family sat, appalled.

Mr. Young had his hands folded on his lap and narrowed his eyes at me, annoyed at the attention I was receiving.

"See what you've done, Juniper? You've encouraged the masses to follow a poor, immoral group of people. How unfortunate." My mother shook her head before pulling out a Georgian fan and waving it at her rosy face. "No one has any sense of decorum anymore. All because of you," my mother spat before hiding her face behind the floral fan.

I wanted so badly to curse at her. I wanted to tell her how angry I was with this entire situation. She wouldn't have to put up with this if she'd let me stay in the circus. This was her fault. But it was also my fault. Because of who I was and where I'd come from, the dream of being in the circus was too far out of reach. I was a fool to think I could have ever belonged there.

As I sat on the bench in front of my bay window and watched families make their way back from Sunday chapel, it occurred to me that Axminster had not changed since I left. But I had changed too much to belong here. Sitting in a tight day dress with a rose-colored print, I could barely breathe through the corset pressing against my ribs.

I wished I was in a pair of breeches and a loose poet's shirt. I wished I could feel the sun on my back and the wind rushing through my hair as I flew through the air on the trapeze. But instead, I was contained as a prisoner in high walls, my dress serving as shackles. I couldn't bring myself to come out of my bedroom for an entire week. My mother brought three meals a day and I picked at the food mindlessly, but how could I eat when there was a life out there for me to be living?

And despite how much I missed the circus, there was something I missed more.

Him.

So much so that I thought my heart might just combust into a million pieces. But instead of dwelling on the fear that I might never see him again, I opted to think of everything distasteful about him.

In my time away, distanced from those who made me truly happy, it was easier to remember all the things that went wrong, rather than the things that went right. I thought back to when Cassius and I first met and how sickly he was. Drunken, rude, and reckless, sleeping with different women every other night.

I thought back to when he called me Prune, my mother's cruel nickname, just to mess with my head, never knowing how it truly hurt me. He constantly led me to think we could be more than friends, and then kept me at arm's length. He was confusing and manipulative. He picked on me because of my status and made me feel as though I would never belong. I thought of how difficult he was to talk to—how difficult he was to love.

When I drifted through the field of sunflowers surrounding my house, I forced myself to hate his harsh words instead of remembering how kind he could be. I distracted myself with his reluctance to love me, rather than focusing on the pleading in his eyes when I left him. It was easier to hate him if I couldn't be with him. I had to convince myself of that.

I took a deep breath and brushed the invisible lint off my dress. I could do this. I could live without the circus. I could move on.

I had to.

Suddenly a knock sounded at my door. I jumped slightly, but remained silent, hoping whoever was on the other side would figure I was resting. But of course, in her usual invasive manner, Colette peaked her head inside. Today, she didn't wear the same sad smile and weary eyes. Her lips were pulled back to reveal her pearly white teeth and her cheeks were blooming after being in the sun all day. She almost looked like she belonged in the circus. She would be tan and beautiful. Strong. Free.

It seemed my every thought reminded me of the circus.

"Something's waiting for you downstairs," she cooed, like we were sixteen again, waiting for a secret lover to come sweep us off our feet.

Something or *someone*? For a moment I imagined Cassius or Mr. Monte standing at my door. Did they come to rescue me? I jumped from the bench resting in front of my window and raced down the stairs, holding onto the wooden banister, and picking up my dress to keep from tripping.

I despised these clothes with a passion.

Finally reaching the foyer, I looked around with hopeful eyes, finding the entryway and the living room empty. My smile faded as my attention shifted to a large woven basket with a red ribbon plastered to the front, sitting on the dining room table amidst the clean china and cutlery. I approached the basket warily and peeked inside as if something would jump out and bite me before finding a load of goodies inside. Handmade trinkets, freshly baked goods, a beautiful scarf with my name embroidered in gold string, and lastly, an envelope with my name on the front. I plucked it from the masses, and eagerly ripped it open.

I thought for a moment this might have come from the circus to thank me for my time there, but the things in the basket were far too expensive

for them to afford. And the contents of the envelope proved me right—
a single check in the amount of $500 made out to me.

In fanciful letters on the memo line of the check, someone had
written, *For your dowry.*

I turned around abruptly, my face a mess of confusion.

My mother answered my question before I even had to ask. She
spared a moment to look away from her newspaper, her eyes amused.
"The one good thing that came from you running away with the circus
is that your community can celebrate that you're back where you
belong." My mother smacked her hands on her lap and laughed. "This
dowry will help you when you are a married woman. You'll have more
money than you know what to do with."

My jaw shook. I could hurt someone if I was given the chance. Really
hurt someone. I gripped the side of my dress, so as not to make any rash
decisions.

"You think this is funny?" I stepped toward her, and her smile
faltered. "The people are paying me because of my desertion, not
because I am talented or beautiful. Sure, I made a name for myself, but
they're only paying me because I have rightly returned to them to fulfill
my obligation as a lady of society. It's a bail, mother, and now they own
me. Don't you see that?"

"It is better *they* own you than the circus." Her eyes returned to the
newspaper article on her lap as though I was no longer in the room.

I clicked my tongue against the roof of my mouth. "As my mother, I
thought you'd understand that it's better if *no one* owns me." Gripping
the check, I ripped open the front door and launched down the
cobblestone pathway that led from our home into the city. I didn't know
where I was going, but I had to get away—away from that stuffy house,
away from my insistent mother, and away from my sister who just follows
like a little lamb. I shouldn't be angry with her, but I was. She was so
easily controlled by our mother, having no free thought of her own.

Before I knew it, I'd made it to the heart of the city. The chapel
loomed in front of me, and the bell rang loudly at noon, startling me.
The full sound resonated in my ears, and when it stopped, I continued
to hear a low humming in the back of my head. The sun reflected off the
stained-glass windows, making the fountain in the center square
shimmer. While examining the thin check in my hand, I had the desire
to rip it to pieces, but I hesitated.

Five hundred dollars? What need would Joseph Young have with
$500? Mr. Young and his rapacious family were richer than anyone

could possibly fathom, which is why I understood the real reason behind the community offering me a dowry. It wasn't because they truly wished my marriage success, but because I had threatened everything they stood for by running away with the circus, and my return had finally restored their reputation.

I certainly didn't need it. With this amount of money, the circus would be well taken care of. *The circus.* Suddenly the guilt disappeared, and I knew what to do to make this right. If I couldn't be with the circus, at least I could help them financially.

I raced to Axminster Primary Bank, pushing past a barrage of people amidst the crowded streets. It took them a moment to gather their bearings, but when they recognized me, they began to shout my name and endless commands.

"Sign my copy!" A woman waved me over, as though I were her servant.

"Juniper!"

"Miss, my son would love to meet you!" A man with a cane pointed at me.

Ignoring their comments wasn't so hard this time around because I had a purpose. The people chanting for me, racing after me, and sending me gifts had no effect on me.

Finally, I made it to the bank, finding solace inside the large, colosseum style architecture. The building was made of rich grey stone, stretching high over my head into a dome. As a child, I came here often. My mother thought that frequent trips to the bank might force us to see the advantage of marrying into wealth.

It didn't work.

"Next up!" a woman with greying hair yelled, waking me.

I stumbled over to her. "How can I get this money to someone else?"

"We'll have to deposit it and issue them a new check. Who is it going to?" she asked kindly with warm brown eyes and a soft smile.

It seemed to be the first ounce of kindness I'd received since returning to this city.

"Monroe Beringer, with the circus."

For a moment I wondered if she'd ask me for an autograph, but she only studied me curiously. After disappearing behind a large oak door to search through her records, she returned and said, "It appears Monroe Beringer has an account with the Bank of Hewe. We will send a check there immediately."

"Thank you," I said, and turned to walk away.

Suddenly, she blurted out, "Why did you leave?"

It was the first question anyone had asked me since I'd arrived. And although I knew exactly what she was referring to, I was afraid to answer. "Pardon me?" I feigned confusion.

"You left the circus before the last performance of the year—the most *important* performance of the year. Why?" Her brown eyes widened in sadness, as if she had been looking forward to seeing it.

Her question struck me. *Why?* My breathing hitched and my head began to pound. All at once, the noise in the room silenced and I felt my heart beating rapidly in my chest. But before I could break in front of this stranger, I shook my head and answered as quickly as I could. "I'm getting married." I forced a smile, pulling my cheeks back until it was almost painful.

The look she gave me was anything but happy. She didn't look surprised, just disappointed, as if she understood that's all our kind was good for. Despite my rebellion in the last year, I'd come right back to the place I started. To this woman, I was no different than when I'd left.

I think there was a small population of the wealthy that looked up to me because they wanted change. But I couldn't give that to them. I was no rose. I was no star. I was just a woman bound for a husband.

I dipped my head in her direction as my hands began to shake. "Thank you for your help."

Turning over my shoulder, I moved quickly through the bank and into the sunlight, out of the claustrophobic room. Taking a breath of fresh air, my lungs still felt clouded.

The woman at the bank wasn't very fond of me, perhaps because she was genuinely disheartened that I had left the circus. But even those who were only praised me because I had abandoned the circus and returned to them, not because I was ushering in a new world where the poor had a place among the wealthy. They didn't love my efforts. No, they loved my obedience—my loyalty to them. And standing on the steps of Axminster Primary Bank, with hundreds of people milling about, calling out my name, I realized I'd never felt so alone.

Cassius...

I must have stared at my bedroom wall for two hours the night she left before my skin started to crawl and my blood began to boil. When things were beginning to feel right, when she really got to know me, she left. And I couldn't help but think that this life was too much for her. That *I* was too much for her. And she did exactly what I always thought she would. She chose the easier option. She chose a wealthy man who would give her anything she ever wanted.

I had nothing to offer her. I always knew I'd never be good enough for someone like her—someone so beautiful and passionate and full of ambition. She wanted the most out of life, and God, she deserved it. I was a fool to think I could give her that.

I paced restlessly and groaned at my inability to change the situation. At my end, I grabbed the first thing I could reach and launched it across the room. The sound of a crystal drinking glass shattering on the far wall suddenly broke my fixation, shards bouncing at my feet. My chest heaved up and down and I felt relieved to release some of my anger, but it wasn't enough. I wanted to forget that I ever trusted Juniper Rose with my secrets—with my heart. I wanted to forget I ever knew her, but that was impossible. No amount of forgetting could ever change the way I felt about her.

I stumbled to the corner of my room where a cart of rum sat faithfully. Throwing the cork and with no need for a glass, I brought the bottle to my lips. The alcohol slid gracefully down my throat and soothed my roiling stomach. And after downing a few heady gulps, it was difficult to think of her absence.

I sank slowly down the wall, jaw quivering, hands shaking. I took a deep breath and tucked my knees into my chest, desperately holding onto the bottle of liquor, yet the tears didn't come. I had cried them all out after I lost my sister. Now, I just felt numb. When I lost grip of the bottle and it dropped to the ground, I watched the amber liquid slowly sink into the grains of wood before I drifted off to sleep—my only reprieve from life without her.

Mr. Monte...

"Where is my lion tamer?" I shouted at the crowd of performers, searching for the boy with hair as black as ink.

No one spoke a word, afraid that if they told the truth, it would upset me further. So, they mindlessly fiddled their fingers while I looked at each of them accusingly.

Suddenly a head poked up and Charlotte stepped forward. Bowing her head low to whisper in my ear, she said, "It's happening again. He doesn't look too good."

And immediately my anger evaporated and was replaced with concern. My eyes dropped to the floor, and I left the room with less pep in my step and a heavy weight on my shoulders.

When I opened Cassius's bedroom door, the sight of my boy sprawled on the floor with a discarded bottle at his feet broke my heart. It was almost more than I could bare, seeing Cassius in the same state as when his sister was killed—curled in on himself, like a child afraid. Taking a seat beside him, I shook his shoulders until he woke in a daze.

"Cassius, it's time to practice," I told him, hoping that giving him something to do would provide a distraction.

Cassius shook his head, his eyes red and puffy.

I leaned in closer and whispered as a father would, "Your friends are waiting for you."

Lacking the strength to respond, Cassius just laid his head back down and closed his eyes. If I couldn't hold everything together for him, maybe I could just hold *onto* him. I set a hand on his shoulder.

"I'm here. I'm not going anywhere," I reassured him.

This had happened before. Cassius lost his way when Penelope died. Everyone did, but he had taken it worse, since he'd lost his best friend and only remaining family. He drank constantly, he was plagued with terrible nightmares every night, and he refused to eat. He lost weight and started erupting in fits of anger. I thought it unfixable at the time, but he got through Penelope's death and grew stronger because of it. And he would get through this trial just the same.

All I could provide was my support and love.

"My boy, we got through this once. We can do it again."

Cassius looked up then and his jaw quivered. "We shouldn't have to. Why do we always have to get *through* things? I'm tired." His eyes were rimmed with red and full of exhaustion as they drooped to the floor.

In one respect, I was alarmed to find Cassius giving up so easily, but in another respect, I understood. He'd been through more than anyone should have to go through in their young life. Most everyone he loved had been taken from him, and this loss forced him to respond from a place of great pain. To not acknowledge that would be cruel.

The past six years had been hard for the circus, and now with Cassius broken once again, we needed a miracle. I knew I had to do something, but what I wasn't sure. I wouldn't let the circus come to ruin, and I wouldn't let Cassius destroy himself. So, I got up off the floor, grabbed Cassius by the shoulders, and shook him awake.

He slowly peeled his eyes open.

I leaned in close and said, "I promise you; things *will* get better. You just have to have hope, okay? And in the meantime, leave the rest to me."

Cassius sat there quietly, unable to form a response.

But a simple nod prompted me to leave him to rest. My first thought was to march into Axminster and force Mr. Young to change the terms of his bargain, but that was futile. No threat would change his mind. Not unless I had a better deal to offer him. And I didn't. So instead, I ventured to my office to write to someone who might be able to help us.

Dearest Monroe,

I trust this letter finds you well. I hope your mother is feeling better and that her sickness was fleeting. And I'm sorry to distract you from being with your family, but I have pressing news. I need your help, Monroe. Without Juniper, the morale in the circus is dropping rapidly, and I don't know how to fix it. Cassius is on the brink again and it's worse this time, for some reason. I'm out of options. Please come back.

Your dearest friend,
Edward.

The day after Juniper left the circus, Monroe received a rather mournful letter explaining that his mother had fallen ill. Smallpox. And it was taking her by storm. His mother had always been a fighter, but it didn't seem like she was strong enough this time.

People were fighting smallpox every day but the likelihood of survival without the advancements of medicine or simply being able to afford basic health care was killing much of the population. And knowing this, Monroe had gone to take care of his mother. He'd been gone for two months, and he'd be gone even longer if a funeral was necessary.

What was strange was that he wasn't answering my letters. I understood he was busy, but Monroe loved the circus, and even in his absence he would do everything he could to help. But he wasn't. I hadn't heard a single word from him in the past two months.

I brought the letter to my lips and swiped my tongue across the film, sealing it tightly. He would receive this, and he would answer it. He had to. Otherwise, we might be in big trouble.

I gave everyone the day off so I could think clearly. Before Monroe returned, I needed to boost everyone's spirits. So, I put my mind to the heart of the circus. Whenever I was feeling down, I would march into the dining room, grab myself an ale, and watch people dance. Seeing how free the performers were always made me feel better.

And with this idea, I turned to face my performers and said, "My friends! I have a request to make. Cassius is feeling down, as you all know. Everyone has been for the past few months, but I want to help. So, I propose we all venture into town!"

"And why would taking a walk help?" Hugh asked in judgement, the golden hoops in his ears shaking.

"Silly boy, we aren't going for a walk. We're going to grab a drink!"

It took three performers to pull Cassius out of his bed and into the city. He looked haggard. A light stubble had begun to grow on his chin, and the bags under his eyes were like deep purple bruises. His hair was longer than usual, curling around his ears and tickling the nape of his neck. He looked sickly, but at least he could walk.

The group trudged with melancholy toward the city, their heads hung low. I thought getting away from the train for a time would raise their spirits, but I was wrong. They needed something stronger.

I burst through The Boiling Pot, the most famous brewery in Isleburry.

"Ah, Mr. Monte, my favorite customer!" a burly man with a belly hanging over his belt exclaimed. He had thin ginger hair hanging in odd curls and his hands were meaty, making a pint of ale appear small in his grip. He was the kind of fellow that made the entire room light up just by smiling. He was genuine, loving, and drunk most of the time.

"Bjorn!" I yelled and clapped the man on the back. "It's been a long while, but I'm hoping you can help me and my crew out! We need a drink. The strongest you have."

The man chuckled heartily, making his belly bounce. "I think I can help you out."

The performers grabbed a seat without hesitation, but they were silent, mindlessly sipping from their glasses. But by the haze in some of their eyes, I could tell they were slowly letting loose. I eyed Bjorn and flicked my hand, motioning for him to bring one last round to the table. He did so willingly, appearing just as interested in seeing if I could turn this group of lazy slugs into a band of true hellions, as everyone presumed them to be.

By the end of the next round, I turned to Victor—a flame thrower—and began a funny tale. "Do you remember when you first joined the circus and almost set the dining room on fire?"

He laughed heartily before reminiscing with me. "I just wanted to smoke my cigar in peace. Was that too much to ask? How was I supposed to know that the floor would be caked in a layer of alcohol?"

"Witnessing a bunch of men and women dancing in a circle and stripping off their clothes wasn't proof enough of our drunkenness?" Hugh asked, slapping a hand on his knee.

Victor sighed but a smile remained on his face. "I had no idea what to think when I arrived here. The circus is a madhouse," he defended himself.

"Fair, but you're as daft as they come!" Flint exclaimed with a proud smile.

The other men joined in on the laughter, but before Flint could look back to Victor, the flamethrower was already on top of him. Victor pummeled Flint's head, rustling his hair playfully, as though they were brothers.

The other men cheered Victor on while Flint writhed on the floor. The women just snickered and continued to drink, betting on the better man. Flint slipped from Victor's grip and turned to wrestle him, but Flint was no match for the hulking flamethrower.

So, I broke up the brawl before things could get out of hand, and the men clapped each other on the backs as if nothing had happened.

"You've got no room to talk of masculinity or smarts, Rye! You looked like a scared little girl the first time Evelyn lifted her skirt," Victor poked.

"That's because she's eighty years old! That's like watching my grandma undress!" Flint gagged and Evelyn proceeded to slap him over the head with her slipper.

"Well, I wouldn't be put off by it. Your grandma is one fine lady," Victor gushed, and Flint punched him hard in the shoulder as a warning to watch his tongue.

This was the first time I had heard any of them *really* laugh in months. I'd never started a family of my own, because I never needed to. This was my family right here.

"What about that time I fell off of the white stag and almost got trampled by an elephant?" Charlotte asked.

"No way, that doesn't compare to the time Cassius got a chunk of his calf bitten off by that insane bird!" Piper and Olive announced together.

"Oh my gosh, what was its name? Reena was it? That was the only animal I've ever wanted to get rid of." I held my stomach in laughter, but I spotted Cassius on the far side of the room, looking out one of the dirty glass windows in contemplation. Was he even listening to our conversation? "Right Cassius?" I prodded in an attempt to include him.

He turned abruptly to the group, caught in the middle of a dream. "Huh?"

"Do you remember Reena? She practically pecked your eye out!"

"Oh yeah, she was wild." His voice was monotone as he fixed his eyes on the table.

Gus looked at me at that moment and I knew exactly what he was thinking. I gave him a wink before he stood and walked over to Cassius to whisper in his ear. "She wasn't the only wild girl you've encountered. Remember Stephanie?"

Cassius immediately spit out his drink and eyed Gus.

Maybe bringing up another girl would upset Cassius. Everyone knew he was head over heels for Juniper before he knew it himself. Maybe this would send him back over the edge.

But it surprised me when a smile spread across his face. "The one who followed us to the train?" he asked.

"Followed *you*. She was obsessed with you," Mila snorted.

"She was waiting by your bedroom door. I think she would have eaten you alive had we not dragged her to the police!" Gus yelled.

Cassius began to chuckle, unable to contain himself any longer. His shoulders shook lightly, the whites of his teeth gleamed in the faded yellow candlelight, and his eyes crinkled sweetly. There he was.

I watched happily as light filled my boy's eyes for the first time in months.

"You're just irresistible, man!" Hugh jumped up and grabbed Cassius by the shoulders.

Then every man in the room was grabbing at him and jostling him around. Cassius closed his eyes in amusement, tilted his head back, and smiled.

This was family.

Chapter Three

Juniper...

The weeks that passed were nothing short of mundane. Every day was the same—so similar it was difficult to remember what day it even was. They blended into one another like watercolors on a canvas.

My mother reintroduced our old routine to me, and it felt as though I'd never left. Every morning I would venture to the church to help organize fundraisers—bake sales, gardening days, town clean up— anything to help fund the growing church in Axminster. Then, I would return home and pretend to listen to the talk of business affairs between my mother and Mr. Young that preceded every extravagant dinner.

My guilt in participating in these lavish dinners and expensive shopping sprees was assuaged, knowing I sent that check to Monroe. In some small way, I was able to help the circus, which meant I still had a place in their lives.

I so badly wanted to return to them. I hated more than anything that I was plucked from that life so soon. What if they thought I had deserted them? Surely, they knew I was protecting them, not just fleeing to a better life, away from the trials of the circus. That thought brought me back to something Cassius had said long ago— *'You do not belong here. You will* never *belong here. I'd run back to your city before you embarrass yourself if I were you.'*

I never wanted to run. I wanted to stay and flourish. I wanted to be consumed by the circus. And when I was with Cassius, I wanted to be consumed by him. He was fire—a burning passion spreading uncontrollably, and yet he was ink—a dark mystery sometimes cold and vacant. He was a roaring sea of desire, and I was but a small boat, unable to pull myself out of his storm. But he was also kind and gentle. He had spent years alone, pushing others away, but somehow, he had allowed himself to trust me. And I had up and left him!

"Ugh!" I groaned out loud, raking my hands through my hair. My mind was running wild and I couldn't stop it. Why did any of this have to happen? Couldn't I just be with Cassius, the man that I—no, I did not love him.

Did I?

The time I shared with him made me question who I was, and he made me think about what it truly meant to work hard for something you love. He made me fearless. And I did love him for it. I loved every bit of him—the troubled and the good. I loved that he tried to find happiness, despite his dark past and the pain that lingered in his heart. I loved the temper that revealed his passion, his gentleness toward the circus, and even more his kindness toward me. He was often distant, but when he let his guard down, I came to understand who he really was—a boy who was afraid to give his heart to anyone out of fear of being abandoned.

But he was mine. Even if I married Joseph, and even if Cassius found a new love, he would still be mine, because we had shared something *real*. We shared a love that wasn't easy, but it was everything.

Thinking of him with someone else physically hurt. If I could just see him one last time, I'd confess what I truly felt, but there was nothing I could do. It was summer now, and my mother was planning my wedding in every spare moment she had. All I could do was stall until I had an actual plan of getting out of this arrangement.

My mother called me quickly into the living room, and with her typical disregard for my state of mind, she proclaimed, "It is tradition for mothers to pass down their wedding bands for their children to use. Mr. Young and I arranged it for tomorrow." My mother's clipped tone left no room for argument, and she returned to her agenda that was chock-full of meetings.

"I'm not going to that." I stood my ground.

My mother set down her planner, unfazed. "And why not, Prune?"

I hated that name, and after years of allowing her to speak to me that way, it was time I said something. "Stop calling me that," I retorted.

She deflected my response with a huff, and the lines on her forehead grew prominent in exasperation. "You know better than to speak to your mother that way."

I gently took a step forward, unfazed by her comment. "I also know better than to allow others to make decisions for me."

I smirked. We could play this game all day long.

"What on earth are you talking about?" My mother rested her hands on her hips, her dress swaying lightly across the wooden floor.

I heaved a sigh of frustration, my nostrils flaring. "I should be able to make my own decisions, Mother. I don't need anyone telling me who I must love and who I must spend the rest of my life with!"

"Not this again," my mother groaned, returning to her seat on the sofa.

I had been protesting my marriage to Joseph since the day I learned of it. I couldn't go through with it. I wouldn't! It went against everything I believed in. "Yes, this again!" I raised my voice. "We will talk about this every day until it's clear to you that I will not marry him!"

My mother smiled cruelly. "Then you can tell your friends in the circus that Mr. Young will be stopping by to warn them of their destruction. I'm sure they would love to hear from you," she sneered.

I turned for the stairs and quickly fled to my room. The air around my mother was unbreathable, but in my empty room, it was worse. It felt like the walls were rumbling. My ears were humming, and the floor was vibrating under my feet, as though it might not hold me up for long. My mother was right. Mr. Young would force me to marry Joseph by the end of July unless I had something to use against him. It was June already and that meant I didn't have very much time to figure out what that was.

I had sent out a letter to Charlotte and Cassius in desperation, yearning to hear from someone…anyone, but I never heard back from them. Mr. Monte did write to me, urging me to ask Mr. Young to free me, but nothing I had done or could do would change Mr. Young's mind. And when I had no good answers to give Mr. Monte, he stopped sending letters. I hadn't heard from anyone in a month. I had lost all connection to the only thing I'd ever loved.

And with no response from my friends, I couldn't urge myself to move most days, laying up in my bed for hours at a time. When the sun faded and the moon brought out the stars, I'd watch them sparkle, thinking of the performers shining on the stage as I fell asleep. They ran through my mind one at a time. Charlotte—that beautiful blonde dancer with ringlets of hair pinned all over her head. And then Olive, with her skin matching her name and her giggle irresistible. And dear Mr. Monte, hair down to his shoulders, a clean top hat, and always with his arms splayed out to the audience. Flint with his contagious smile, riding atop a gallant horse and Gus in his hazy room with a deck of cards in his hands. And finally, I pictured Cassius—his lovely deep-throated laugh, his warm caramel eyes, and his lean arms as he gently stroked Abbas.

I couldn't seem to separate dreams from reality as the hours dwindled by and morning crept closer. In the dark abyss of sleep, I slowly watched through a sheen of fog as Cassius stepped closer and closer, as if he was trudging through thick mud, his steps lagging. His dark hair waved in the wind, like a crow's feathers.

His eyes were mischievous orbs of gold, shining through the darkness, and his smile grew from a small grin to something twisted. As soon as I closed my eyes in comfort, he reached out and gripped my neck. Hard. I gasped, trying to wrench his hands from my throat. And when I managed to open my eyes, Cassius was no longer in front of me. The killer was dressed in a black cloak, and he grew taller the longer I stared. His head was covered in darkness; his body too big for me to fight against. I screamed as loud as I could, although there was no one to call for, no one to save me. The killer slowly lifted me until my toes left the floor.

This was a dream. It had to be. There was no way for the killer to find me now—the only plus-side of being in Axminster.

"Wake up, Juniper."

A voice echoed in the back of my head, but it didn't sound like mine. I recognized that voice, but I couldn't place it.

"Wake up."

My body lurched forward, and I gasped for breath, grappling at my throat until I realized that the killer's hands were no longer there. My hands darted around in search of him, but he would blend in too much in the pitch-dark room. Finally, Colette burst into the room to find me with my hands over my ears.

"Make it stop, make it stop," I cried, shaking my head back and forth. Every time I closed my eyes, I saw the killer, his hands dragging my dress up my hips, and those empty gray eyes. "Make it stop."

That was the first dream I'd had of the killer, and in the months to come, they never did go away.

Colette tried to pull me back to my bed, but I couldn't stand the feeling of her skin on mine. Her fingers were clammy and quick, only reminding me of his cold fingers that night, climbing up my thighs. She left me alone after I stopped crying. I couldn't sleep and I wouldn't dare try, so instead, I watched the clouds drift over the night sky, as though they were waltzing with one another.

I smiled as another dream washed over me, and without even realizing it, I began to sing, "Ho, hey, the circus has arrived, it's late now, come and play outside." My voice was soft, and it broke often. This didn't sound like a song of freedom. It was more like a song of mourning. "You'll never know how far you'll go. Take a chance, beat your fate, kick the dust, clap your hands, say your name out loud," I gasped a little, my voice shaking. "Here comes the crowd. The circus has arrived." I blinked as tears fell down my cheeks.

I wished for a moment that I could forget about the circus—forget that any of it ever happened. It'd be easier that way, instead of having to remember what I lost.

In the blink of an eye, the sun was shining, and a bird was pecking at my window. Irritated, I opened the glass and a sweet breeze wafted through. In the distance I could hear people faintly shouting and carriages rattling along the cobblestone streets. It was a busy day in Axminster. And when my feet led me to the center of town, I understood why. A newspaper article announced the circus's last show before their summer break.

Oh, how I wish I could be there. I would love to see Charlotte's dazzling smile and Evelyn's weathered hair. And Olive…golly, do I miss that little girl. And Cassius…

I imagined him in his teal suede vest and black poet's shirt with his hair soaked in sweat and that signature curl dangling in front of his eyes.

I couldn't forget them, no matter how hard I tried. Without realizing, I walked up to a vendor's stand.

"I'll take one," I remarked quickly, hoping no one would notice me.

I handed the vendor three gold coins, and he offered me the paper in return. I read through every line, eager to know what they were doing without me, and what they would be up to this summer.

As I stood in a throng of people eager to get their hands on their own paper, I realized that the circus was moving on without me, and I was waiting for something that was never going to come. They weren't going to fight to bring me back. They weren't going to demand that I return. How could they? Mr. Young was too powerful. I would make myself miserable if I didn't accept the situation and move on. This was the life I had been given. Maybe, just maybe, I could make something out of it instead of dwelling on the past.

I swallowed hard and headed home. As I followed the path lined in wildflowers, I looked down to the newspaper in my hands.

It was time to say goodbye.

So, I took one last look at the photo of the circus. I gazed at their smiling faces and their hands joined together before letting the newspaper fly away in the wind.

When I opened the door, I was welcomed by my mother standing in the foyer.

"Juniper! Thank the Lord." She rushed over to me, her little hands moving feverishly by her gown. "I've just started printing out some place cards for the wedding. I need you to look over the guest list and make sure we've remembered everyone."

I looked at the table covered in expensive parchment and quills of every shape and size. I hadn't realized choosing a font was such an important requirement for my wedding day. But there was no running anymore. So, I sat down compliantly and said, "Sure, Mother. I can do that."

Her head flicked up and she looked at me as though she didn't even know me. And she didn't. Her reckless daughter had been traded for an obedient girl. But she shook her head nonetheless and plastered a smile on her face. "Good, good."

I spent the entire afternoon approving the guest list, making place cards for the two hundred guests (which I thought was rather excessive), and selecting the flowers for the centerpieces. By the time the sun was falling, the pollen from the flowers was beginning to make me queasy, and my mother's incessant excitement wasn't helping either.

My mother stopped me as I stood from the dining table. "Where do you think you're going? We still have to pick out the fabric for the tablecloths!"

I sighed and said with as much respect as I could muster, "I just need some air. I'll be back soon." I hated my mother now more than I ever did growing up because she stole my happiness, my passion. She took it all away to protect her precious reputation. Whatever she wanted, she got.

I closed my eyes and drank in the warm air around me.

"You okay?" Colette emerged from the dining room to stand with me in the greenhouse.

I just nodded my head, continuing to look forward. What could I say? I couldn't explain my situation anymore because it wouldn't change anything. It was hopeless to dwell in the past. So instead, I focused on the future. "I just can't believe it's happening like this."

Colette read my mind and nodded along with me. "I always thought I'd be married before you."

"Well, you're on your way." I smiled and nudged her ribs, which made her giggle.

William had recently taken his relationship with Colette a step further. He put a down payment on a small house not a mile away from our own. Close to family and to town, she'd have the perfect life with William. Now he just had to ask for her hand in marriage.

Collette turned suddenly. "You know, I can't really imagine you with Joseph," she admitted. "He's too…"

"Clean?" I asked.

"Yes," Colette started laughing and before I knew it, I was too. I held my stomach to stop the ache from spreading as we joked about his perfectly gelled hair and pressed attire. I hadn't laughed that hard in a long time.

But suddenly her smile faded, and she became serious. "You don't have to go through with this." She grabbed my arm tightly.

"Yes. I do." I squinted, trying to see what she was getting at. I couldn't run back to the circus. Mr. Young's deal specifically required me to marry his son, and that's what I would do.

Her eyes sank to the floor. "I'm just worried. We don't know the slightest thing about Joseph. Sure, we played with him as kids, but it's been years."

For some reason I trusted that Joseph would be kind to me. He'd be a good husband—probably better than I deserved. The only problem was that I didn't love him. I shoved the thought away. "It's not Joseph I'm worried about. It seems like Mr. Young has more in store than he's letting on."

Colette frowned and pulled me in closer, "What do you mean?"

I shook my head, "I don't trust him. There's something he's hiding from me. Even *if* he's being truthful, he holds the circus over my head. There's no way out of this, Colette."

Her cheeks suddenly flared red. "It's not fair!"

Her exclamation took me by surprise. I knew she disagreed with my mother's ways and with Mr. Young's, but she'd never expressed it openly. She'd always been more comfortable sitting quietly on the sidelines, watching things unfold.

"Nothing has ever been fair." I shook my head. "We're Roses. Everyone expects too much of us. And I'll detest their preoccupation with status for the rest of my life, but that's the way it is."

And by the look on Colette's face, she was even more shocked to hear I'd given up so easily. I was always a fighter. I fought for a different life, for a different love than that of my sister and mother. But when all of that was stripped from me, I didn't see a point in trying so hard anymore. It just hurt too much.

I squeezed her hand to reassure her. "I should go back before Mother decides to chain me to the table." I rolled my eyes jokingly before heading back into the dining room.

My mother spoke up when she heard my small steps enter the room, "Do you think we should invite the Lancasters?" She flipped a pen in between her fingers, debating.

I put on a smile and sat down with folded hands. "I'm sure they would love to join the celebration."

Chapter Four

Mr. Monte...

While in the city of Isleburry, I made a quick stop by the post office to check if I had any mail delivered. I wasn't expecting Monroe to write back, but it would sure ease some of my worries. When I offered the clerk my name, he handed me two small envelopes. I snatched them eagerly, finding one addressed from Monroe himself. I tore into the letter, completely disregarding the other.

Edward,

I'm sorry for my absence. My mother is not healing the way we expected. I don't know when I'll be returning. I know you need me, and I so badly want to be there to help, but my family is taking this very hard. I understand that Mr. Young must be dealt with. I'll think of a solution while I'm away, and when I return, we'll make a plan to retrieve Juniper and return her to where she belongs. I promise.

Write to you soon,
Monroe

I scanned over the letter twice, three times. It wasn't what I wanted to hear, but it was better than silence. I tucked the letter back into its envelope and inserted it into my vest pocket. In the struggle to secure it to my person, the second letter fell to the floor. I'd almost forgotten about it. Flipping it over, I found an unexpected name on the front.

Juniper Rose.

My breathing hitched and I ripped open the seal. I'd written to Juniper many times, but she had nothing to offer me in return. Now that she was writing out of the blue, it led me to believe she had something that would help us. I scanned through the letter as quickly as I could.

Mr. Monte,

I have good news! When I returned to Axminster, many in my community were delighted to see me. They adored my work in the circus, but even more that I had come home to marry into a prominent family. To celebrate this, they contributed generously to fund my dowry, but rather than take this money into an already wealthy marriage, I chose to send it to you. I trust that this fine sum of money will change the circumstances for the circus.

With love,
Juniper

Earlier this morning, I thought the circus was doomed, and now there was hope. Thank you, Juniper Rose.

The Axminster Publication

July 26 is a day to celebrate indeed!
The adored Rose family will join with the
prestigious Young family through the matrimony of
Juniper Rose and Joseph Young.
This couple has committed to forever, despite their
separation while
Miss Rose was a performer in the circus—proof that
their
bond cannot be broken by distance.
Here's to this lovely couple and the future of
propriety!

"There. You're all set!" My sister gently grabbed my shoulders and turned me toward a full-length mirror.

A translucent piece of tulle hid my eyes, making the world appear blurry. I ran my hands down the soft white fabric that extended to the floor. My wedding dress was very conservative. Plain white, with no lace or diamonds or buttons. The sleeves ran all the way down to my wrists and the neckline up to my collarbones. It was fitted at my waist, but the rest of the dress ensured there would be no wandering eyes.

I was a modest woman now, fully reformed following my wild days at the circus. Although I had detested thinking about my wedding day, or who I would be marrying, I had always dreamed of the gown I would wear. In my childhood, I envisioned a ball gown—nothing too lavish, but grand enough to feel like a princess. It would have a simple neckline and the voluminous skirt would have threads of diamonds all throughout the billowing tulle. I wanted to shine in the sunlight. But this dress I saw in the mirror just felt...plain.

My sister placed a diamond encrusted pin in my hair to hold the tight bun to the nape of my neck. "You look beautiful."

"Thank you." I grasped her hand tightly, not in an endearing way, but more for life support. I was getting married. I was finally doing what my mother always wanted.

I took one more look at myself, unable to comprehend it.

"Juniper! Are you ready?" My mother barged into the dressing room and her hands flew to her mouth. She remained quiet for a long while, making me feel as though I'd forgotten something or done something wrong. But she surprised me by saying, "You look breathtaking—the very vision of all that I dreamed for you."

I swallowed the lump in my throat, unsure of what to say. It was foreign for my mother to compliment me. "Thank you, Mother," I answered quietly.

She straightened the veil over my eyes, linked her arm through mine, and led me out of the room. I wound down endless hallways toward the front of the chapel where I would officially take Joseph's hand. The walls twisted and turned in odd ways, making me queasy.

For the first time in my life, I missed my father. I was just a girl after all. This was supposed to be the most memorable day of my life, and he wasn't here to walk me down the aisle.

A small tear fell from the corner of my eye, unnoticed by my mother and sister who flanked me. I wished I was anywhere else. The hallway was too tight, and I was inhaling sweaty, strained air because of the veil covering my face. I couldn't breathe.

As we neared the aisle, two hundred guests stood to their feet and placed their hands over their hearts in awe.

The air was knocked out of me, and the walls pressed in, their white stone drowning me. Every face in the room became blurry. I felt claustrophobic, trapped. There was no way out of this now, that much I understood. And then the music started—a soft melody from a string quartet. It sang to me quietly, before being accompanied by the large organs at the top of the church. They rang out loudly, reverberating off the colosseum walls and into the steeple.

My mother and sister began to walk me toward the altar where Joseph stood.

I looked around frantically, searching for an escape route. I couldn't do this. I couldn't marry a stranger. This wasn't supposed to happen.

Suddenly my mother's grip on me tightened, her nails digging into my palm, and I was sure crescent moon-shaped indents would appear. I yelped and looked down at her. I wanted to fall in front of her and beg.

Let me go. Please.

But she wouldn't hear a thing.

I clenched my teeth to ignore the sting in my palm and turned my head forward. Mr. Young and his wife stood in the front row, smiling lovingly. I tipped my head to him, finalizing our deal—to remind him that I would owe him nothing more in the future.

And then I looked to Joseph. He turned to me at the very moment the organs hit their last note. His eyes were breathtakingly blue, and he looked regal in the black suit he wore, fit with a long waistcoat and a white sash across his chest.

My mother handed me off, giving my hand one last pat.

I looked to my sister in desperation, but all she did was kiss my cheek and take her seat.

Joseph took my clammy palms in his own and I began thinking about what it would be like tonight, after our wedding. Would we travel somewhere for our honeymoon or remain in Axminster? What will I do when he takes me to his bed?

While the priest spoke, images of Cassius popped into my mind— running a loving hand down the cheek of his lion, singing along to the song of the circus, and wrapping his arms around my waist, dipping me in a low bow and kissing me deeply. I couldn't stop the tears from falling.

Maybe the crowd thought I was absolutely in love with Joseph. The newspaper reporters would capture photos of me and write about how happy I was to marry this man—how fortunate I was. But in reality, I knew that I would never forget Cassius. Until the day I died, I would be thinking of him.

"Do you, Juniper Rose, take this man to be your lawfully wedded husband?" the priest turned to me and asked.

This is for you Cas. This is all for you. "Yes, I do," my voice broke.

He turned slowly to Joseph. "You may kiss the bride."

The entire room leaned forward to watch. Joseph closed his eyes and leaned forward, his lips warm, soft, and gentle, not rough with passion. I was unable to close my eyes or comprehend how I'd made it here. This felt wrong. So terribly wrong. I tried to pull away quickly to get the taste of him out of my mouth, but he grabbed me, hard. This wasn't like Joseph. Something wasn't right.

I tried to pull away again, but his fingers sunk into the skin on my arms. I yelled out in pain, but no one seemed to hear a thing. The crowd simply continued to clap. What was wrong with them? Why didn't anyone say something to stop him?

"It is with great pleasure that I announce to you—Mr. and Mrs. Young!" the priest shouted with jubilation.

The entire room erupted, clapping their hands, with smiles beaming across their faces.

I looked at my mother and sister, and they were smiling proudly alongside Mr. Young and his wife.

Joseph pulled me toward the front of the church to exit, but the thought of going home with him made me want to scream. This was not where I belonged. I belonged with the circus!

Sensing my struggle, Mr. Young came to stand next to me and gripped my elbow. "Stay put," he growled in my ear.

In a moment of fear, I acted. I pushed Mr. Young and Joseph and ran. I burst through the double doors, and a blinding light poured over me. Suddenly I was looking down on myself, through someone else's eyes, and the image started to darken around the edges, like a vignette.

And then I was gasping, awake in my bed with sweat pouring down my temple. My chest pumped up and down, and I placed a hand to my heart, thinking it might leap out of my chest.

It was just a nightmare, I tried to convince myself. I got out of bed and opened the window, letting a cool breeze waft over my heated face.

The dream was so vivid, so real. It seemed like a sign. In the circus,

Hugh had been able to read the future and determine what images would come to pass. Was this similar? Had I seen something that was likely to happen? If that was what my wedding would look like, I knew one thing—I wouldn't be going through with it. By the way I was treated by Joseph and Mr. Young, I knew I would be sentenced to a life of unhappiness if I married Joseph.

Then and there I decided. I wouldn't marry him, and I wouldn't stay in Axminster. I had to find my way back to the circus.

I intended to stay in bed all day and determine a plan to get back to the circus, but I was sadly interrupted. I expected it to be my mother or Colette knocking on the door, so I was surprised to see Joseph's face on the other side. I sat up straight, alarmed after just seeing him in my dream. I knew the Joseph in my dream was different from the real Joseph.

My time with him in the past few months had shown me that. Walking through the city, having dinner with him, and spending quality time apart from our parents made me realize he was nothing like his father. He wouldn't harm me in any way. He might even cherish me and love me. But I couldn't return the favor and that was all that mattered. He deserved someone who loved him completely and I couldn't give him that.

He slowly entered my bedroom, putting his hands in his pockets. "I'd like to show you something. My father said it might ease your mind with the date approaching."

I was so tired of Joseph listening to his father. Couldn't he think for himself? "And do *you* think it will?"

"No, not quite," he answered honestly. "I think it might scare you more than he intends, but nonetheless, I think you should see it."

What must he be talking about? With the mystery looming, I quickly dressed and followed Joseph out of the house.

He refused to tell me where we were going, but the ride must not have been more than ten minutes, and when we trotted up a dirt road, my breath was taken away. In front of us was a modern masonry home. The walls were built of dark red brick, and the windows were crystal clear, surrounded by black shutters. The long dirt path leading up to the house was lined with a black picket fence and a grand arrangement of trees and flowers in the front yard. It looked like it had its own arboretum.

And when I saw a small swing under the canopy of two large oak trees, I was giddy. I could lose myself here.

With anticipation, I asked, "What is this place?"

He smiled at his hands and said softly, "It is to be our home." The innocence in his eyes made me sad.

I turned away from him and looked around the place once more, trying to imagine us creating a life together here. In the mornings, I'd wake up next to Joseph. We'd drink tea together and I'd make him breakfast. Then he would go to work, and I would clean the house until he returned. This house wouldn't be filled with love or a family. It would be filled with an obligation and nothing more. I couldn't imagine us every being happy here.

I resorted to avoiding the subject and said, "It's lovely." And it was. The interior was gorgeous, but not overwhelming. I was expecting the most extravagant furniture, but it was beautifully modest. The walls were made of dark oak. To my left was the living room and inside were cocoa-colored loveseats and a dark grand piano on a plush Indian rug. Above the entryway was a chandelier, casting warm light into the open foyer. And to my right there was a long dining table—too long for two people. A grand staircase led to the upper-level right in front of me, the stairs wide and glossy.

I climbed the stairs quickly and found the master bedroom. The four-poster king-sized bed was surrounded by a black canopy and donned with soft turquoise silk covers. This would be our bedroom. But there was no grey fur blanket like on Cassius's bed. There was no mass of pillows that I loved to sink into. And there was no *him*.

I left as fast as I could, escaping down to the kitchen. Besides the fact that I was to live with a stranger, I think I liked the house. It was warm and cozy.

On my way to the front, I noticed that the hallways connecting each room were rather small. It reminded me of the cramped interior of the train cars in the circus, the candlelight making shadows dance on the walls.

"What do you think?" he asked when I met him in the front entryway.

"It's not too shabby," I shrugged my shoulders and he laughed. I noticed it was the first time I had ever heard him laugh. He always seemed so serious.

As soon as we opened the front door to leave, we were met by photographers and journalists.

"May we get a photo?" a man yelled.

"Is this a pre-wedding gift?" a woman asked, putting a microphone to my lips.

I felt absolutely bombarded. I stepped back and Joseph offered to grant them a photo, but nothing more. He positioned himself next to me and I followed. Until I figured out how to get back to the circus, it wouldn't hurt to play the part. Joseph suddenly wrapped an arm around my waist, and I flinched from his touch. A flash of him holding my arm in place as I tried to run away from him came back to me.

He asked a question that shook me awake, "Is this okay?"

"Yes," I whispered uncomfortably.

He still smelled too much like soap. I remembered the men in the circus always smelled like the earth. Not dirty, but rather close to nature. They were hard working—as real men should be—and their physiques were proof of that. I suddenly thought of how Cassius smelled. Like smoky alcohol and sweet bales of hay.

That was when the photographer yelled, "Smile," and before I knew it, a white beam flashed, and the photo was taken. I'd had the goofiest smile on my face thinking of Cassius.

But it did not come without consequences. The following day, paperboys screamed through the streets. News was spreading fast, and from more than one source. Shopkeepers and vendors alike held baskets of the latest news article, fresh from the post. The image of Joseph and me and our soon-to-be home had spread across the country. I almost looked happy in the picture. That hadn't been my intention, although I wondered what the circus must be thinking of me.

Cities all over the world were going berserk with the news and as a result, people had started asking questions. To clear the confusion, reporters arrived on the front steps of the Rose household. Invited in welcomingly by my mother, they settled in front of me, prepared to put the world's questions to rest.

"So, Juniper, I'm sure you can't wait for your big day!" A reporter with grand monocles hovered a pen over his notebook in anticipation.

When I figured out that he was waiting for me to answer, my words stumbled out awkwardly, "I guess you could say that. I'm more nervous."

"Nervous? Why?"

Well, how would you feel if you were forced into an arranged marriage and ripped from your true home? I wanted to ask, but I couldn't. Although my mother was not home right now, she would pummel me to death if this was ever published. So instead, I held my tongue and answered with, "It's a big day for a woman, but I'm sure it will be a lovely event. My mother has basically planned to have an aquarium put into the entrance of the church," I joked lightly.

The reporter laughed along with me before moving onto the next question, "The world wants to know how you've dealt with the drastic change from being in the circus and returning to Axminster. Would you like to speak on that?"

Finally, a question I could answer. No one had brought up the circus since I returned home. They'd rather I forget it entirely. I thought about saying something my mother would be proud of to keep up appearances, such as, 'I'm happy to be home after my time away. I think I'm finally ready to settle down.' But neither of those answers were true. Now was my chance to be honest. And on the off chance that anyone from the circus read this, they would understand how I felt. As a bonus, I might just put my mother's knickers in a twist.

"It is a sad feeling, leaving something so important behind, but I think everyone must make sacrifices, and this was mine. I loved the circus with all my heart, and I would encourage everyone to take a risk and try something new, because you never know what you might find out there in the world. I'm going to miss it greatly."

All he did was nod his head and scrawl my words down in his notebook. Then he looked up at me seriously with a crease in his brow. "A lot of people thought your actions were reckless when you ran away from Axminster. Now it seems people are more open to the ways of the circus since you joined their ranks. Why do you think that is?"

I paused to think for a moment before answering, "I think people are open to change. Apprehensive, but open. And I think everyone just needed a push to have their minds altered. I'm glad I gave them that push because I believe that the circus and the less fortunate are worth fighting for. The people of Axminster and beyond watched one of their own join the circus and saw how much light it brought to my life. The world was afraid to believe in the circus at first, but I think they've come to see that being of lower class in no way decreases your talent or worth as a human being."

"I agree." He continued to scribble. "Well, thank you for your time, Miss Rose. I hope to see you again soon."

"You as well," I answered, and meant it. This reporter was the first in Axminster to be interested in hearing about my journey.

I watched him shut the door and climb into his carriage. As I reflected on our conversation, and with the plan of my departure brewing, the tension in my shoulders was beginning to slowly fade away.

Chapter Five

Cassius...

The morning after the circus had tarried at the bar, Mr. Monte woke me with a startle and forced me to practice, even if I was walking around only half sober. It was a struggle to put myself together every morning when I knew I'd only fall apart again that same evening. It was most difficult when I was by myself, left to my thoughts, so I tried to surround myself with as many people as I could. But there were days when it felt like everyone was against me—like there was no one I could trust.

One afternoon I was lying next to Abbas after an exhausting routine. Mr. Monte insisted it would awe the crowd if we could convince them that I'd been bitten, but I hadn't figured out how to piece it together yet. I brushed my hand through Abbas's golden fur, and his warm skin was a comfort. Closing my eyes, I suddenly remembered Juniper practicing with Abbas all those months ago. She was terrified of his ferocity, but because of that fear, we discovered how to trust one another.

I sighed and Abbas grumbled in response, as if he understood what I was thinking.

"I know, boy, I miss her too." I looked to the top of the tent, where white met red in a twisting illusion.

Suddenly, shouts arose from outside, so, I decided to cage Abbas for the day. When I walked outside, I found the other performers retreating to the train with hushed voices.

I marched over to where they stood, and when they saw me, everyone went quiet.

"What's going on, guys?" I tucked my hands in my pockets and stared at the sea of nervous eyes.

"Oh nothin', we were all just about to grab a bite," Hugh exclaimed, averting his eyes to the floor.

They were hiding something from me. The way they coddled me for months after my sister died taught me to understand when they were being overprotective. Suddenly, I felt like a kid again, excluded from playing with the older kids at the foster home.

I found Olive in the middle of the group with her hands folded behind her back. "Olive, I think Evelyn is taking a nap. She surely won't stop you from taking a sip from my flask," I prodded her.

"Olive—," Charlotte tried to stop her but before the words left my mouth, Olive raced up to me, uncovering a newspaper in her hands.

"Thank you," I snipped and snatched the paper from her.

When she realized what she'd done, she sank into the crowd, riddled with embarrassment.

It didn't take long for me to find what they were looking at. On the front page was a life-size picture of Juniper and Joseph Young in front of a large house and suddenly my heart sank. I hadn't seen Juniper since she left. I had visualized her so many times, but my imagination never served her justice. It frightened me to think that I might be slowly forgetting her.

I didn't realize the wedding preparations were happening so quickly, although it made sense. It was the beginning of July. It had been three months since she left, yet it felt like just yesterday she looked at me for the last time.

She would marry him soon. Was this their home? And why did she look so happy? The smile on her face appeared genuine.

I took my eyes off the paper, not able to look at it any longer. I wanted to rip it to pieces. And my friends were hiding it from me, as though I couldn't handle it. Maybe I couldn't, but I didn't want their pity.

I unclenched my jaw and took a deep breath to calm my anger. "You thought I wouldn't find out?" I asked, eyeing everyone in front of me.

A multitude of heads sank to the bright green grass below their feet.

"Cas-" Charlotte stepped forward, making me take a step back.

"Don't *Cas* me, Charlotte," I spat out her name. She and I used to be close—a little too close. I distracted myself with her when the lonely nights came, but she wasn't just a plaything anymore. She was a friend. And now she, as well as all my other friends, were hiding things from me. "I don't need to be lied to anymore. Juniper did enough of that for all of you." I started for the train before Gus spoke up.

"You think she lied to you?" he asked with a curious tilt of his head.

I whipped around to face them. "She lied to *all* of us. All that talk about 'finally belonging' or 'feeling at home' was a lie. I'm sure she considered returning to Axminster—to *civil life*—the entire time she was here. Why wouldn't she? She had everything."

"Then why would she risk *everything* to come here?"

I'd never seen Gus angry before, but the look he gave me was threatening.

"She left to save us. You know that," he drilled, stepping closer and closer to me with each word.

I shook my head, unable to think about what was true and what wasn't. Deep down I knew she left to help the circus, but that hurt almost more than if she'd left willingly. She was halfway across the country, soon to be married to another man, and I couldn't be with her. It was easier to convince myself that she was just the spoiled woman I always assumed she was.

Before walking away, I looked up to Gus. "I don't know anything anymore."

And with that, I stormed into the train. When I reached the privacy of my chamber, I took a moment to calm the anxiety coursing through me—to stop the shake in my hands. The lights were too bright, and the recent conversation still echoed in my mind, far too loud for me to think of anything else. I covered my ears with my hands, closed my eyes, and tried to figure out what was truly bothering me. What would fix this perpetual hopelessness?

I wanted to start over. I wanted to tell Juniper how much I cared for her. Did she know how much I missed her? How much I needed her? And if she did, would she have stayed? It was selfish of me, but even if it meant the downfall of the circus, I wanted her back.

I couldn't shake my anger. I had two options: either beat Mr. Young to a pulp or offer him a better deal, but who was I kidding? I didn't have that power. I never had any to begin with. I was just a kid off the streets, and though I was given a home and a family, it didn't change the fact that I was next to nothing. I was poor. And the poor weren't given second chances.

Juniper...

A thud came upon our door and my mother eagerly hopped to grab the Sunday paper, which included all the gory details of Axminster's wealthy socialites. She trotted back inside with gargantuan gift baskets on either arm. It had become routine by now.

Gift baskets were delivered every week to our house, filled with delightful but unnecessary goodies, such as orange and cardamom truffles, soft fabric fashioned into thick wool blankets, beautifully crafted wide-brimmed hats for the women in the household to enjoy, and always a dainty dowry check amongst the towering monstrosities.

My mother kept her eyes glued to the paper while hostilely tossing me three checks and leaving the gift baskets on the kitchen table. I picked through each envelope, already allotting time this afternoon to run the checks to the bank.

Contentedly, I laid my head back on the veranda and closed my eyes. I listened to the wind ruffle the pages of Colette's book and my mother delicately turn the pages of her newspaper.

Suddenly she threw it upon the ground, startling me awake. She looked at me with vengeance in her eyes, her nose flaring.

"What the hell is this?" She waved the newspaper in the air. "'*The world was afraid to believe in the circus at first, but I think they've come to see that being of lower class in no way decreases your talent or worth as a human being.*'" She quoted my words. "What is wrong with you?"

"What do you mean? I did as you asked. I let the news take pictures of me for everyone to see. I'm a star now!" I smiled at her, as if this was everything I'd ever wanted, but she sensed my sarcasm the moment the words left my mouth.

"You ridiculous girl, you think this is funny? The entire world will join the circus if you continue praising them!" she hissed at me.

"Why shouldn't they?" I shrugged my shoulders calmly. I was done being angry. My mother wasn't worth the effort. "Why shouldn't they?" My voice softened even further. "The performers are the most hardworking people I've ever met. They are a selfless and joyous people."

My mother huffed out a laugh. "They are reckless, lazy gypsies who search for the easy way out of hard situations, and you are lying to yourself and everyone else if you think otherwise." She clicked her tongue.

"Last time I checked, you don't have control over what I say or do anymore. I am a grown woman. I can take care of myself."

A smile spread across her face, and she paused to study me for a moment. "I have control over everything you do. Don't forget that I'm the one who made this agreement with Mr. Young in the first place." She began to walk away and when she reached the door, she looked over her shoulder. "I almost forgot. Mr. Young and his wife are hosting a dinner party at their manor for close relatives and friends. I'll see you there on Tuesday."

I sighed when she closed the door. Great. Another gathering where I'd have to get dressed up, cinch my corset, and pretend to love Joseph and the life I'd been given. And in that moment, when I walked upstairs trying to figure out what to wear, I realized that my mother was right. I hadn't even thought about refusing her two minutes ago at the mention of dinner. She had absolute control over me.

Cassius...

When the evening came, I retired to doing the one thing that scared me the most—being by myself. I couldn't trust any of my friends, but I didn't want to think about Juniper, so I took to drinking, but even that didn't help.

After downing a few glasses of stale ale, I found myself pulling open the top drawer of my bedside table to retrieve the news article, staring long and hard at Joseph. I wanted to punch him in the face. I wanted to mess up that perfectly gelled hair. I wanted him to know what it felt like to hurt.

And when I turned my attention to Juniper, my shoulders relaxed. She looked beautiful—thinner than usual, but still beautiful. I wanted to know why she was so happy. As much as I tried to convince myself that she was a selfish prude, it was clear to me when she walked the tightrope that she loved the circus. So why did giving it up make her so happy? I wanted her to be miserable like me. I wanted her to miss me like I missed her. But she'd moved on.

A figure walked through my door without knocking, and I tried to shove the newspaper away as quickly as I could.

"Hey, man." Gus came to stand awkwardly at the edge of my bed. "I wanted to apologize for earlier-"

"Did Charlotte send you here? Did she feel bad for hurting my feelings?" I asked in a mocking tone.

"No, she didn't. She was the one who told me to let you figure it out yourself." He fixed a glare on me this time. "Look, I didn't come here to pity you or say sorry. Quite frankly I'm not sorry. I know that Juniper saved us, and I think you know it too."

I looked down to my hands, contemplating this. I know she did. But that didn't mean she didn't change her mind once she returned to Axminster and realized what she'd been missing. She could be truly happy now. I should want her to be happy, shouldn't I?

For the first time, I revealed my fear to Gus. "In the brief time Juniper spoke of Joseph, she detested the idea of marrying him, but what if that's changed? What if she really does love him?"

But Hugh was honest with me when he said, "I don't think Juniper would trade this for the world. You saw the look on her face when she was forced to leave. She would have done anything to stay here with us. But, if she has gotten used to her life in Axminster again, then it isn't our concern. It's her choice Cassius, and we can't change that."

He was right. I couldn't force her to love me. If she'd truly moved on, then that was that. It was over. But still grasping, I argued back, "And if she hasn't? What then? We can't just let her bear this burden alone. We have to fight back!"

He nodded his head, as if he'd thought this over many times, and when he looked up at me from under his burly eyebrows, his eyes were glossed over. "There's nothing we can do. Look at us," he chuckled. "We're just a group of foster kids."

If I could change anything in this world, it would be all of our beginnings. We didn't deserve this. No one did. It wasn't fair to be destined to a life of worthlessness just because of the families we were born into—something that was beyond our control.

Gus was right. There was nothing we could do to change Mr. Young's mind. And it made me angry enough to burn Axminster to the ground. My heart began to beat faster and faster—so hard against the walls of my chest that it hurt. I grasped at my shirt, trying to make the pounding stop until a sharp pain seized my chest. But when I closed my eyes, everything seemed to calm. My breathing slowed and I realized something had to change. I had survived the loss of my sister. I could survive this.

So, I made the decision then and there.

Turn it off.

I'd done it once before. I'd forced myself to forget every painful thing that had happened to me and just live, because it was easier that way. So, I closed my eyes and decided to just forget. Forget about Juniper, forget about Penelope, forget about being nothing in the eyes of society. And I sighed, feeling the weight lift from my chest. It might mean I'd forget what it feels like to love, or to hate, or to mourn, but at least I wouldn't have to work so hard anymore.

Gus smiled and clapped me on the back. "All I know is that you are Cassius Plume. You are every woman's dream."

I nodded my head. I was *Cassius Plume*. I'd forgotten myself because I was wrapped up in a silly love affair. But that wasn't fun. I remembered real fun—drinking until I couldn't stand, dancing until my feet hurt, and finding pleasure in random, beautiful women. *They* were fun.

And for a moment an image of Juniper flashed in my mind. Her eyebrows were pulled together as she laid a hand on my cheek. She wouldn't want this for me. But she wasn't here.

So, I pushed her out of my head and stood to meet Gus. "Let's have some fun, shall we?"

Chapter Six

Tonight was Mr. Young's fancy dinner where we'd eat caviar and sip expensive champagne like one big happy family. Did they know there were people starving out there? Beyond their fine porcelain plates and goblets of wine, there were people that were cold and frail. And I'd known them personally.

One of my maids stood on my left side, and another on my right, holding strings in their hands. They had me hunched over my vanity, my knuckles white from gripping the wooden frame.

"Pull!" a woman named Talia yelled and both of them pulled at the same time.

I gasped, holding a hand to my stomach.

"One more, honey," she said warmly, grasping my shoulder.

When they pulled again, I could scarcely breathe. It reminded me of when I fell on my tailbone as a child, knocking the wind out of me. I straightened my shoulders and took as big a breath as I could, feeling lightheaded and queasy.

"Small breaths, Miss. Small breaths."

I felt physically sick with the amount of pressure on my ribcage. I remembered the days when I would walk freely in a loose shirt, taking full, easy breaths, and now I was restrained, captured, chained. I would always be caged in this place, surrounded by people who thought looking beautiful was a woman's only value.

The look in Talia's eyes was remorseful. I was the richest girl in Axminster, with too much fame—none of which I wanted—and a maid with next to nothing in her pocket and calluses on her hands felt sorry for me. For a moment, I felt connected to the lower class—like they didn't just see me for my money, but as a real person. Their sympathy reminded me that even though I had returned to high society, I was still thought of as the girl from the circus. She wasn't gone—not in their minds, and sure as hell not in mine. That only made my motive to escape this life even more dire."

With that thought in mind, I spun away from the mirror and marched down the stairs.

It was only a short ride to Mr. Young's estate and when we walked up the long flight of stairs to the entrance, I didn't feel nervous. I knew who I was and who I would always be. I wasn't a puppet for my mother to play with, and I was not a little girl Mr. Young could manipulate. I was Juniper Rose—the darling tightrope walker of the circus.

I dug into a lamb chop roasted in garlic butter and rosemary, thin sprigs of asparagus sprinkled with lemon zest, and red potatoes drizzled with olive oil and seasoned with herbs de Provence. Shoving a rather large portion in my mouth prompted my mother to give me a withering glare across the table.

"So, Juniper, did Joseph show you the house today?" Mrs. Young inquired.

I lifted my hand and covered my mouth to appease my mother before answering, "Yes, he did. It was lovely!"

She seemed to believe my enthusiasm. "I'm sure you will be able to start a family easily there. There are three bedrooms and bathrooms. How exquisite!"

I choked on my food, garnering a few concerned glances. Start a family? We weren't even married, for heaven's sake. Could these people slow down?

"I have to admit, that is not something on my radar at the moment." There was no point in lying to them. It was fair to warn them of my intentions and desires. I didn't know if I wanted children. I'd never really thought about it before.

Mrs. Young took her usual persnickety tone when she said, "Oh, well I'm sure you'll change your mind once you and my son start your life together. Bearing children is one of the greatest gifts God has given us."

I breathed out slowly and my mother took the silence as an initiative to jump into conversation with Mrs. Young to change the subject. "So, Patricia, where did you get that fabric? Monica's Dress Shop is looking rather dreary these days."

I looked down to my plate, sifting through the conversation we'd just had. If I did marry Joseph, which I wasn't planning on, would he want to have children? I couldn't even image the idea of us being intimate, let alone starting a family. And I didn't want to be used by my husband for breeding purposes. But suddenly, warmth spread through my palm, and I looked down to find Joseph's hand entwined in my own. I had the urge to rip away from his grasp, but he looked at me as though he understood my worry.

I smiled gently back at him.

"It's from Caesar's Boutique, right down the street," she exclaimed, and my mother held her hand to her chest in astonishment. Caesar's Boutique was one of the most expensive stores in Axminster. "It humbles me to admit that this fabric was more expensive than anything I've allowed myself to indulge in before." Mrs. Young looked up to her husband for permission, and he nodded his head.

Mrs. Young smiled and continued, "And I can afford something like this because Mr. Young has been offered a position as an investigator in The Axminster Guard."

The Axminster Guard was a force of men who fought crime throughout the city. An investigator was the lowest position, but everyone had to work their way up the ranks.

Mr. Young took over for his wife, "As you all know, I am very concerned about truthfulness and loyalty. In my time as a landholder, I've experienced a myriad of fraud, embezzlement, and general deception. And petty crime has continued to increase in this city, as I'm sure all of you have seen in the weekly paper. I am tired of allowing thieves to take what they want without paying like everyone else."

Mr. Young looked at me all of a sudden, his eyes glistening in the dim candlelight. I was sure he was associating the circus with the many thieves in the city, which made me want to crawl across the table and stab my fork in his eye. The circus performers were no thieves. They were hardworking outcasts who had to fend for themselves.

He continued proudly, "So, I applied to become an investigator, and I just received word today that I will begin training next week."

Everyone in the room clapped and clanged their champagne glasses together in a toast.

Even Joseph grabbed his father's shoulder and said, "You'll make great changes, Father."

It seemed the whole room was buzzing with excitement, and only I could see the truth. Mr. Young was not an honest man. He did not want to safeguard helpless people. He just wanted to punish those only trying to survive. He was selfish. And my family and everyone else was being lied to.

After the merriment ended and we'd had our fill of champagne, my family and I excused ourselves.

As I descended the stairs of their estate, Joseph jogged to catch up and called out my name. When I turned, he asked, "What do you say we go for a walk?"

I looked to my mother, who was smiling like a silly schoolgirl. I'm sure her stomach was doing summersaults at his noble request. My mother and sister nodded and hopped into a carriage, leaving me with a patient Joseph.

"I'd love that," I said politely. Although I was nervous to be around him, I didn't want to be crammed in a stuffy carriage with my nagging mother.

The night was beautiful. It was warm outside, with a gentle summer breeze washing over my face, and the stars blinking gently up above. It would be a crime not to indulge in it. Beyond the fresh air, I wanted to speak freely with Joseph. He was very kind at supper in offering me his hand. We had been put in an unexpected arrangement, so the very least I could do to ease the discomfort between us was to get to know him.

We walked around the Young's lavish estate, passing by a large granite fountain spurting water into a glistening basin. So many things had changed. Just a few months ago I was walking through tight train cars, drinking dry ale, and walking a tightrope. Now I was walking the perimeter of Mr. Young's estate, hand in hand with a practical stranger.

"What my mother said about our relationship was completely inappropriate, and I apologize," Joseph said in the darkness.

He didn't seem to waste any time, which I appreciated. He was straightforward—just what I needed in this predicament.

"It's alright," I whispered.

"No. It's not. But I'm sure questions about our future will continue to arise, and I don't want you to be put in an uncomfortable position answering them."

I listened intently while he spoke. Joseph and I had barely exchanged words since I moved back to Axminster. There was always a silent agreement between the two of us—a mutual understanding that we needn't grow closer. Until now.

"So, here is what I propose." He stuck a pointed finger in the air, which made me giggle, before continuing to say, "Are you a good liar?"

I held a hand over my heart, as though it were blasphemy what he'd just asked. "How rude of you to assume I'd indulge in such a sinful act!" I exclaimed.

When he saw the appalled expression on my face, he laughed.

Thank God. He had some sense of humor in that perfectly coiffed head of his.

"I didn't assume, Miss Rose. I *know*."

"Oh, is that so?" I didn't know Joseph was such a confident man, but it was rather nice bantering with him.

He nodded quickly, sure of himself. "We've all lied. And it doesn't matter how good you are because it's our inherent nature." He shook the seriousness away by saying, "Plus, I think this will be a good lie."

Interested to see where he was going with this, I indulged him. "Alright then, let's hear it."

Placing his hands behind his back and resuming his leisurely walk, he proclaimed, "In the future when anyone asks about our plans for starting a family, we shall say we are unsure."

"Unsure?" I burst out laughing. "That is not a word you use to describe your plans with your partner!"

He looked exasperated, as if to say, *how should I know, I've never done this before!* "Well then, what would you say, if you think it appalling to appear indifferent."

I pondered his question, thinking back to the time I shared with Cassius. The late-night kisses, finding each other's warmth in the dark, and those crisp summer mornings waking by his side had made me feel so giddy. I felt loved and protected—like nothing I ever did would change the way he felt about me. More than that, our love was easy. I was so full of joy, always excited for what the next day would bring with Cassius.

Realizing I'd taken too long to form an answer, lost in my memories, I quickly turned to Joseph. "I would say you and I found the courage to become one in every way possible and that we'd like to enjoy our time together before starting a family. They'll be none the wiser."

I did not intend to share with him my plan on leaving Axminster and refusing his hand. Although he deserved to know, I couldn't have Joseph whispering in his father's ear.

He stared at me for a moment, surprised, and I wondered if he knew that I was thinking of someone else. Did he know that every time I woke, my first thought was of Cassius, and that when I closed my eyes, I prayed to God I might see him again?

Despite what he thought, he smiled and strung my arm through his. "Well then, Juniper. I think we've formulated a rather believable lie."

I nodded in acknowledgement before noticing that he'd led us to a black gate with a sea of trees on the other side. "What's this?"

He stopped in his tracks. "It's my father's arboretum. I saw you glancing at the garden of our soon-to-be home a few days ago, and I thought you'd appreciate this."

The garden was my favorite thing at the house his family bought for us, but I didn't think he'd noticed. I dipped my head toward my shoes before finally admitting, "You're not as bad as I thought you'd be."

"Is that so?" he repeated my words from earlier. "What did you think I would be like?"

"A proper, entitled man who expects everything to be handed to him." I shrugged my shoulders and looked up nervously, worried I had offended him.

But he surprised me by huffing out a laugh and placing his hand on his stomach, as if it pained him. "Well, I am glad to have proved you wrong. I must say, you're rather blunt, Juniper Rose."

I smiled sheepishly, feeling as though I was beginning to make a friend. "I don't like to waste time, Joseph Young."

"I've come to notice that." He laughed and ran a hand through his glowing hair.

Joseph and I were more similar than I originally thought—both trapped in a life we didn't want by our insufferable parents who refused to break free from societal norms.

We began walking through the arboretum, spotting oak trees and weeping willows. The varying leaves seemed to shimmer beautifully underneath the stars as night took full bloom.

In the comfort of a large willow, its leaves curling over us, I thought about what Mr. Young had revealed tonight. "Do you think your father will make a good investigator? Do you think he is an honest man?" I asked Joseph.

The question came out of nowhere, surprising him, but he answered quickly, "Frankly, no. But I think he's determined at whatever he sets his mind to. He won't let anything escape him or go quiet, as most other men do."

Go quiet. Those words reminded me of something and, as we walked, I tried to remember what, but it seemed to be locked far away in my memory. When we had covered the entirety of his estate and arrived at the carriage that would take me home, the stress of his presence had evaporated. I didn't have to pretend anymore, like I did with Mr. Young at his magnificent parties. I felt safe with Joseph.

Wait. *Safe.* That's it! Mr. Monte's letter.

The perpetrator's attacks have stopped. Since you left, everything has

gone quiet. *I do not know if he will be gone forever, but for now, you are* **safe**. *We all are.*

If Joseph really believed that his father would do everything in his power to end crime, then maybe he could help me. Mr. Young could find the killer that threatened the circus and put an end to him. Although the killer was gone for now, it didn't mean he'd be gone forever.

"Is everything alright?" Joseph asked, sensing my quietness.

I lifted my head up from the floor and smiled. "Yes. Yes, of course."

And it was. I finally had a way out of Axminster.

The next few days were good. I spent a lot of time with Joseph to keep up appearances. Plus, he was good company amid the loneliness. I learned a lot about him. Things that stuck out were that he'd always wanted a wife but believes in love unlike his father, he detests being forced to do things he doesn't believe in, he loathes feeling out of control, and he loves writing for pleasure and drafting little stories for others to enjoy.

In fact, one of his favorite memories as a child was writing short stories and performing them for his family.

I told him about myself as well, even the parts that were hard to talk about, like the circus and my love for walking the tightrope. I told him about Mr. Monte and his wonderful teaching, little Olive's incessant desire to steal someone's drink from under their nose, and Charlotte's shocking beauty.

I left Cassius out of the picture because I didn't want to hurt Joseph. I hoped that, by the end of the day, I had convinced him to believe in the circus as much as I did. Nonetheless, I no longer felt afraid of our relationship. Even after all this was over and I returned to the circus, maybe we would remain friends.

The next afternoon, the scorching heat confined us to the house. A knock sounded upon our door and my mother jumped from the loveseat to answer. We weren't expecting anyone today.

I heard many words exchanged but I couldn't determine who the voice belonged to until Mr. Young came strutting into our living room, laid his top hat on one of the free chairs, and sat on the plush sofa I was occupying. He could easily make himself comfortable, that much was clear.

I greeted him kindly before my mother spoke up. "Would you like some tea?"

"That won't be necessary. I won't take up too much of your time." He waved his hand in the air to decline. "I was hoping to speak with Juniper." My mother looked at him with a smile, moving to sit down. "Alone," he finished.

I looked to him suddenly, wary of what he might ask. What had I done?

"That'll be just fine." My mother extended her hand to my sister to show her out of the room, and as they hurried, their day dresses swished stiffly like the pages of an old book. Before I knew it, they had disappeared, and I was alone with Mr. Young.

He took a deep breath before turning to me. "After the discussion we had at dinner last night, we have all been concerned. We want to know if it is in the foreseeable future that you will start a family."

Joseph's words came to me then, *are you a good liar, Juniper?*

Our lie might work with the public, but certainly not with Mr. Young. And even more than that, I was done pretending. Sure, it would keep Mr. Young off my back, but soon enough, I'd have to admit my intentions. It might as well be today. "I do not intend to sleep with your son and start a family, because I do not intend to marry him."

He stared at me for a long moment before laughing and bringing a hand to his stomach to compose himself. "Oh, but you will." His face turned serious. "What do you hope to accomplish by refusing me again and again?"

I couldn't seem to form any words. An image of Cassius had appeared in my head, and it wouldn't go away. His eyes were bright, and he was filled with passion—more than Mr. Young could ever muster. Suddenly all the anger I had pushed away came surging up.

"Why do you want me and Joseph to start a family so badly? Why are you so intent on selling off your heirs, like Joseph, so your name will spread like some king?" I asked in anger, my voice rising.

"It's all about my legacy. The more I am known, the more people pay for my services. And not only my services, but my friendship and my loyalty. In the past decade I've gained respect from individuals across the entire country, and by creating a bigger family, I can ensure that my business will continue to prosper through them when I'm gone," he stated matter-of-factly.

"So, this is about money then?" I scoffed in disbelief.

"It always is." He smiled.

"But it shouldn't be," I claimed with the utmost conviction. "There is so much more to life." I shook my head, remembering how content I was in the circus. "There is friendship, devotion, hard work, and love. I've learned how to live for other people and take into account their happiness instead of my own. But you live only for yourself, and I feel sorry for you." I nodded my head repeatedly.

His eyes seemed to search inside mine, attempting to find my motive. The only motive I had was to unearth the deception in his family and his workplace and expose it to everyone else.

"And where might you have learned so much? The circus?" He leaned closer, and I could feel his warm breath brush across my cheek.

"Yes," I answered plainly.

"Well, despite what you learned in that pig pen, you are in Axminster now, and you will be required to follow my rules. You will do whatever I ask. You will marry my son and you will raise a family. Otherwise, your friends will be left to fend for themselves."

"It is my body, and I will decide what to do with it." I stood my ground and did not dare look away from his daunting eyes.

"How can I convince you?" he asked with clear desperation. I'd never seen Mr. Young out of control, asking for someone else's help. It was pitiful.

At first, I wanted to scream at him and tell him that he never would, but I rethought my decision. Joseph believed his father would eliminate crime in this city, and I had to trust Joseph on this, because he'd never lied to me before. I realized this was my chance to discuss the terms of our deal. He was the one who arranged this agreement, but I was determined to use it to my advantage. "You can help me find the killer that threatened my life and so many others in the circus. You're going to be an investigator after all. This can be your first job."

He scoffed and turned away from me, "I will not help that group of vagabonds. It goes beyond my morals."

"You don't have morals." I probably shouldn't have said that, given that I wanted Mr. Young on my side, but I couldn't help myself.

"I've already done my share. I've promised to ensure the future of their business. Why would I risk anything else for them?"

In the past few months, I'd been so angry about so many things that were out of my control. I felt helpless and useless all at once. And now I had the chance to make a difference. "You promised to *protect* the circus until the day you die. Those were your words. And if you don't find the killer, then you are going back on the terms you stated, which means the deal is off."

"The deal is off when I say it is off," he growled.

I had to think of something else, and quick. If he wasn't concerned with his word, then what was he concerned with?

His reputation and his money.

"I know you're a businessman who likes to make deals, but bribery betrays the honesty required by The Axminster Guard. If I were to tell them you used bribery to force an entertainment company to work under your command, I'm sure they would reconsider your position, wouldn't they?"

Mr. Young looked at me with fire in his eyes. "You wouldn't dare." He looked honestly scared. His eyes were squinted, and his shoulders were hunched tensely as he leaned closer to me.

Finally. Now he knew what I was capable of. I would not sit around and allow him to control my life any longer. I would protect the circus at any cost. "One phone call and your career as an investigator could be over before it even begins. If they find out what a corrupt businessman you are, there's no way-"

"Alright, alright!" he yelled, stopping me mid-sentence. He looked over his shoulder, worried that my family might have heard, but they didn't show. "What do you want me to do?"

I smiled deviously and leaned in close. "Here's your first assignment, Investigator Young. Find the man that killed Penelope Plume."

Chapter Seven

Mr. Monte...

The circus had spent the past week brainstorming ideas for our first performance. It being the first of the year, and especially after the great loss of our rose, this performance had to be spectacular—different.

"How about we begin in Turnstead and weave our way through the northern kingdoms? We can start our show in the opera house in Plum District. We'd have a full house!" Emma, one of the dancers, offered the idea.

"That sounds great, but what is the theme for our performance? It can't be an ordinary show where we ride around on unicycles and tell fortunes. This one has to be different!"

Charlotte jumped up from her seat and exclaimed, "What if we engage the crowd in our performance, maybe connect them with the animals? Cassius could use an audience member to help tame the lion."

I liked the idea of engaging the crowd, but it wasn't enough. We needed more.

"We could change our costumes. Liven it up a bit," Olive offered.

"This isn't some masquerade ball that we're dressing up for. It's a performance." Gus diminished her idea immediately, and the little girl went to sit back down glumly.

Wait. That's a good idea. "But it could be, Gus. Imagine it. We welcome everyone, no matter what kingdom they come from to join us in Hewe for a Masquerade Ball. And in the heat of dancing, we whip out our show," I exclaimed.

This could be our best idea yet. But no wealthy patron would attend this masquerade ball unless it was hosted by someone of equal title. We needed someone with wealth and popularity to announce this masquerade ball in their name. Only then would we draw the audience we needed.

"What if we contact Gisèle Perrault and her husband? If they send out the invitations, everyone from the rolling hills of Culchester to the white waters of Isleburry will come! If this works, we will perform at their estate, disguised in masquerade attire before we surprise them." I then pointed to Emma to reinforce her idea. "We'll begin in Hewe and move through the northern kingdoms."

"But why would Gisèle host a party in the middle of July? She'd have to have a good reason," Gus brought up.

I thought it over. "They're rich. They never need a reason."

Suddenly Olive ran to me, wrapping her arms around my leg. She looked up at me with excitement in her eyes and said, "I've never been to a ball before!"

I giggled and tucked her head into my hip. "Well now, my dear, you will not only attend one, but you'll be the main attraction."

"I love it!" Charlotte exclaimed, jumping up and down.

All the dancers started talking about what kind of ballgowns they'd wear and what masks they'd conceal themselves in before I briefly interrupted them, "It's final, then. I will start creating costumes with Valetta and warn Monroe of our plan. This will be ostentatious!" I clapped my hands, hoping everyone would jump at the chance to begin practicing, but they seemed uneasy about something.

"Is Monroe coming back?" Olive looked up at me from where she still clutched my leg.

I sighed, unsure of what to tell them. I was their leader. I was supposed to give them answers or at least peace of mind, but I didn't have any. I rubbed my hand through her silky hair. "He will. I'm not sure when, but he'll come back to us."

Olive's head sank but before the mood could be dampened, Charlotte leapt over to Olive. "Maybe Monroe will be back in time to see our first performance. We should start practicing so we can surprise him. He's going to love it." She encouraged the little girl.

Olive cheerfully exited the room, hand in hand with Charlotte. Everyone followed the pair and made their way to the tents in the field. As bodies passed me, I searched for Cassius, and finally stumbled upon a head of black curly hair standing next to Gus. He was talking fervently about something, moving his hands quickly in a passionate manner. As I approached him, he doubled over in laughter over something Gus had said. I knew he had begun to feel better the night we traveled into town, but today he looked like a whole new man. He was laughing. My boy was laughing.

He turned suddenly to see me standing there. "Mr. Monte, Gus and I have an idea. What if he and I burst into the masquerade ball, appearing as thieves who've come to disrupt an opulent evening? Everyone will be frightened until they realize we're a part of the show. We could be the ones to reveal that the circus is in their midst!" His eyes were glowing with excitement.

I was stunned. I'd never seen him this passionate about the circus before. "I think that's a great idea."

Juniper...

The following week, Mr. Young came to me with reports of killings in the last decade. Today, he brought quite a surprise.

"I found a multitude of newspaper articles in the archives at work," Mr. Young offered. "Some of them have pictures of killers they never found, but most detail clues about their motives. I thought if you read through them, you could tell me which one sounds most like your perpetrator."

I began to leaf through the pile of files, my eyes already tiring. "I can look through them, but I doubt he'll be in here."

"Why is that?" Mr. Young asked.

"Because last year we had reason to believe he was a part of the circus—an inside performer who had access to me. Therefore, the city most likely wouldn't have been involved in any of the investigation. We need to look specifically at six years ago. There was a murder in the circus, and it was covered up as an accident. Look in the archives for something that goes along the lines of that."

He nodded his head and leapt up to search. Suddenly he stopped before the door and turned to me. "How do you know all this?"

My head sunk. How could I explain this easily? "The woman that was killed six years ago was Penelope Plume. Her brother was my friend in the circus, and he's been looking for the killer for a long time."

Mr. Young looked almost sad for a moment. But then I reminded myself that he was doing this for selfish reasons, not because he was concerned with helping my friends.

Despite his motives, I felt more driven than I had in the past three months. Cassius lost his sister. She was raped and committed suicide because of it, and the paper claimed it was an accident. Cassius had to live every day knowing that the man that killed her was still out there, along with the guilt that he couldn't protect her. And last year the killer had come for me. He haunted my dreams almost every night, so much so that I was afraid to walk alone in the streets after dark. And it must have terrified Cassius just the same to know that the killer was back.

It was time to find this man. Not just to protect myself and everyone else in the circus, but to honor Penelope and Cassius. He deserved to know who the killer was. He deserved to see him serve a lifetime in prison for the atrocities he committed.

My mother asked what Mr. Young had been doing here earlier in the morning, and I feigned that he was helping me prepare for life with a businessman. Joseph was to follow in his father's footsteps, and Mr. Young was teaching me to be a helpful wife during his business meetings and transactions, as Mrs. Young had done for him.

And she believed the lie without a doubt. It was so easy lying to her. All I had to do was tell her something she wanted to hear.

I think Joseph would have been proud to see just how accomplished a liar I was.

And when Mr. Young appeared later that night with a stack of newspaper articles in his hands, my mother was none the wiser. I took him up to the abandoned study that used to belong to my father, and we got to work.

"What'd you find?" I asked eagerly. I hated to say this, but investigating a crime was invigorating, especially because I had been a victim myself.

"Not very much, but I think it's a start."

He whipped out the first newspaper, which read '**Penelope Plume, darling of the circus, has a terrible accident!**' There were ten other articles just like it.

"Every one is the same," Mr. Young announced before flipping the page to a picture of Penelope atop the tightrope, her toned arms lifted to the sky, and a breathtaking smile on her face. No matter how many memories Cassius shared with me, he couldn't possibly do her justice. She was beautiful, glimmering with passion and pride.

"Penelope fell from the tightrope—"

I stopped him immediately, "There's no way someone as accomplished as Penelope would fall so easily. She'd been walking the rope for over five years, and she knew the ways it bent and twisted." I shook my head. "This was no accident."

"Then what was it?" His eyes flickered dangerously in the candlelight used to illuminate the room.

It felt wrong revealing such a terrible thing to Mr. Young. This secret belonged to the circus and to Cassius. And it felt like a betrayal to tell dear Penelope's story to such a cruel man. But if this would help us find the killer, then it was the right thing to do. "It was a suicide." I cast my eyes onto the desk, unable to look at Mr. Young.

I continued to explain, "From what I know, the killer raped Penelope and it sent her spiraling. She was threatened more and more—she was stalked, physically harmed, and emotionally drained—until one day it drove her over the edge. She killed herself. And everyone called it an accident."

Mr. Young listened intently. "We're not going to find anything in these then." He slammed the newspapers on the table. "If we want the truth we need to go straight to the source. I suggest your friend in the circus, Penelope's brother, may be able to help us."

"No, no," I insisted. The idea of seeing him so soon made my stomach spiral. It felt like ages since I had laid eyes on him. I wanted so badly to touch him. I wanted to feel his warmth again—his sturdiness. But as much as I longed to see him, I wanted to protect him from reliving this terrible trauma. "He wouldn't speak about it to just anyone," I said in an effort to dissuade him.

"Then you go to him," he added tersely.

I looked at him gravely, a fire coursing through my veins. "You don't get it. I left them. I could never ask such a thing after what I did—after what *you* did."

Mr. Young had no idea how his actions affected people. I couldn't just return and act like everything was normal. I left before the final performance of the year when they needed me. I didn't want to admit it, but I was afraid to see Cassius for fear he would cast me away—that he hated me for what I'd done.

Disregarding my insults he asked, stumped, "Then what do you propose we do?"

I thought for a while, letting my mind wander back to my time in the circus. When I came face to face with the killer the first time, it was in the middle of the night, when he attempted to do the same vile things to me as he had done to Penelope. He attempted to rape me because he wanted revenge. His words returned to me quietly.

"You deserve to feel what she felt." he spat at me. "What they both felt!"

"They?" I asked dumbfounded, frozen on the ground before him.

"Katriane!" he roared.

For so long, I'd wondered who he was talking about. A woman by the name of Katriane was the reason the killer was after every tightrope walker, and we had to discover why. I relayed this information to Mr. Young.

He stood quickly in the small office, his face cast in shadow in the dimly lit room. "There must be hundreds of women named Katriane in the world. Is there anything specific that would help me narrow my search?" he asked.

I thought for a moment. "If this woman is of such importance to the killer, she must be his lover or a family member or a close friend. Just look for a woman by the name Katriane who was involved with the circus. That's all we have."

"Alright, I'll start there and let you know if I find anything." And with that he exited the room.

I spent the night wondering what Mr. Young might find. Was Katriane the killer's lover? Was she his mother? And why was she the reason he was now hurting me? I knew two things to be true:

1.   The killer was a member of the circus.

2.   Katriane was connected to the circus in some way, and the killer was using Penelope and me to avenge her.

Whatever his reasons, I wouldn't rest until he was brought to an end.

Chapter Eight

D

ing-dong.

    The doorbell rang in a sing-song kind of tune, prompting my mother to rise, wipe off some invisible lint on her corset, and saunter to the door.

"Good morning, Ms. Rose. I have a special delivery from Gisèle Perrault." A delivery man clad in a fine navy suit extended his arm toward her, holding a cream-colored envelope. He must have been a personal servant of Gisèle's, for he was wearing black silk gloves and beautiful attire. Her estate was enormous, and her staff were obviously fitted according to her reputation.

As soon as I heard her name, I leapt up from the couch, tripping on the end of my dress. The last time I'd seen Gisèle was at her estate when the circus performed for her as a congratulations on her recent engagement. I had told Mr. Monte it would benefit us to connect with the wealthy because it would invite a more diverse audience to our performances.

I came to stand next to my mother, eager to tear into Gisèle's letter.

"Gisèle? I haven't heard that name in years!" my mother exclaimed, taking the letter from the delivery man. Our family name was scrawled in fanciful cursive across the front, a golden wax seal closing the back. "Thank you, Sir." My mother tipped her head at the man.

Once she closed the door, Colette and I eagerly fidgeted by her side.

I wanted to scream at her to open it faster, but she took her time in acknowledging the pretty lettering on the outside. Finally, I snatched it out of her hands and tore it open for all our sakes. Inside was an invitation:

A masquerade ball? My first thought was that this party might actually be fun. I wouldn't be required to talk to any esteemed families if they couldn't see my face. It would be a night of dancing without the pressure of formalities. But my second thought was that Gisèle was never a woman to party. Sure, she enjoyed being surrounded by friends and family, but she never enjoyed huge crowds. Even as a little girl, she detested the large gatherings her family arranged. So why was she throwing the biggest party of the year?

In any case, I was going to see her.

I remembered with fondness the night we performed at her estate. It was such a fun night, filled with endless drink. My distant friend had finally seen my talent and love for the circus despite my own mother refusing to witness it. It was the first time I had introduced the circus to wealthy life, and the first time I regretted it. The performers seemed so ashamed of their simple life, made so obvious by the opulence of the evening. Cassius, of all people, took it the worst. He'd gotten mindlessly drunk, embarrassing the entire circus in the process. I remembered him shouting at me in a solitary room, his eyes glazed over and dark.

I shook the image from my head and looked over Gisèle's letter once more. "It says here we must RSVP a month before the event occurs. I'll contact her immediately." I was so excited to see Gisèle and reminisce about old times. I hadn't seen her in a year, after all.

"Oh, no. We're not going to this." My mother laughed haughtily and took the invitation from me.

"Why not?" I exclaimed in frustration. "Gisèle has been a lifelong friend to all of us."

My mother scoffed. "Gisèle was also the woman who allowed the circus into her home." Shaking her head, she finished with, "She is no friend of ours."

"How could you say that? Her family was always there for us, and we have no good reason not to go."

My mother raised her eyebrows in defiance before tearing the invitation in half. "I will not enter her home if she believes in something so preposterous."

My hands flew to my mouth, containing a yelp. Gisèle was my friend and the last connection I had to the circus. I wouldn't let my mother ruin that.

"You and Colette can sit here all you want, but I *will* be going to the ball." I turned around and immediately ventured to my room to find parchment to write to her quickly.

Gisèle,

I am writing to RSVP to your invitation, although I regret to inform you that my family will not be joining me. It seems very grand, but I'm sure it will be one hell of a night. Do you remember when the circus performed for you? I must say, that was one of the most memorable nights of my life. I hope you remember it as fondly as I do. I cannot wait to see you!

Sincerely,
Juniper

I sealed the letter and sent it immediately. Not a week later, she responded.

Juniper,

I am so thrilled you are coming! Lionel insists that it will be the biggest event of the year, which makes me nervous. I do remember when the circus joined us on the night of our engagement—what a splendid performance. It saddened me to hear that you left the circus, and I'd like to know more. Let's catch up. It's been too long.

With kind regards,
Gisèle

Going to Hewe to catch up with an old friend? Getting a break from my maddening family? Nothing sounded better.

Choo Choo! The train came to a halt at the station. After two hours of sitting on a leather seat reading the latest news in the paper, my bum was aching. Outside the glass window, the city of Hewe was buzzing with energy. It was one of the biggest cities in our realm, and one of the most exciting. It housed the most famous entertainment industries in the world.

From opera to ballet, it had everything you could ever desire. The city was like a show itself. Performers bustled around in full costume—large day dresses and exquisite top hats of varying rich colors. The whistle of the train and the trot of the carriages on the cobblestone streets was a music of its own. The city was everyone's stage, and I just happened to be its latest performer.

I hopped into a carriage. "To the Janvier Estate!" I ordered the driver happily, folding my hands atop my lap.

The man whipped the horse and we were off. Before long we had exited the constraints of the city and emerged into the open country, where horses grazed freely. Across rolling hills laid various estates and mansions with tall glass windows, articulate gardens, and immaculate interiors. This was where the wealthy resided. One of my happiest memories as a child was spending a week every summer with the Janvier family.

While I was reminiscing, we reached the front gates, where a man in a crisp top hat, suit, and black cane was awaiting our arrival.

"Welcome, Miss Rose," he said in a deep voice.

He ushered me up the long flight of stairs and past gargantuan statues of men and women, and hedges of the brightest emerald. I'd been here many times, but my mouth still managed to fall open.

When the man who welcomed me opened the front doors of the estate, Gisèle was waiting for me with her husband by her side. Men were usually the lead in marriages these days, but Gisèle's confidence overshadowed Lionel's in the way she rushed to me.

"Oh J, how I've missed you." She wrapped me in a breathtaking hug, practically breaking my ribcage.

"I missed you too," I managed to squeeze out while my face was squished into her shoulder.

She quickly pulled me away, giving me whiplash. "What are you doing? In Axminster, I mean. What happened to the circus? And who the hell is Joseph Young?" She took my hands in hers, and the whites of her eyes were bulging in surprise.

Gisèle was the only wealthy person I knew who was as interested in the circus as I was. My head dipped to the ground, and I opened my mouth to speak, but nothing came out. There was too much to say, and I had no idea where to start.

Gisèle sensed my uneasiness and led me down the hall, adorned with at least three chandeliers. "Lionel, would you ask Genevieve to put on a pot of tea? Juniper and I are going to retire to the garden for some quiet."

Her husband nodded smoothly and walked away to find a servant.

We emerged into the beautifully clean air, the birds chirping softly and not as annoyingly as they did in Axminster. The sun was shining so brightly that it was almost blinding, but the warm afternoon rays were a comfort. The grass was vividly green and surrounding us was a large field filled of wildflowers and a wall of ivy climbing up the exterior of the home. Gisèle quickly sat me in a cream-colored chair opposite her own with a small tea table between us.

"Tell me." Gisèle squinted while rubbing my hand. No one had touched me so affectionately in months. Since Cassius, actually.

In Axminster, no one dared hug me. My sister was affectionate enough, but she was giving all her attention to William. I didn't blame her. I would do the same if Cassius were here.

I began to talk about someone else to get Cassius out of my head. "Joseph Young is the son of Stanford and Patricia Young. I thought you might have heard of him. Mr. Young is a famous businessman in the entertainment industry. He surely has influence here in Hewe."

"Oh, I've heard of him once or twice," Gisèle joked. "I didn't know he had a son."

And that's when I began my story, dating all the way back to when our families met, and leaping forward to Mr. Young's self-serving deal that forbade me from continuing in the circus.

"Let me get this right." Gisèle pointed her finger at me while tendrils of her hair blew gently in the wind. "Your mother made a deal with Mr. Young to marry you to his son just because she wasn't fond of the idea of you joining the circus?"

I nodded and rolled my eyes. I couldn't believe it myself. "She even attempted to sue the circus when I fell, alleging they were 'using unsafe equipment.'" I quoted her with a scoff.

"No offense, but your mother is a lunatic." She huffed and leaned back in her chair.

I shrugged my shoulders and a small smile spread over my face. I quickly pinned my hair back as it had begun to stick to my neck in the summer heat. "None taken. I mean, my mother always wanted me to marry rich, so I should have seen it coming."

"But you're an adult, Juniper. How long will you let her control your life?" Gisèle asked.

I was taken aback at first. Since I had made the decision to run away to the circus, I thought I was free of my mother's influence, but it seemed I wasn't. I blamed Colette for always abiding by my mother's rules, but I was no better than her.

To sort out the mess in my head, I said, "If it were up to me, I'd flee to the circus all over again, but I would be dooming them. I must think about everyone else, not just about what I want."

She nodded her head slowly, but before things could get too grim, I changed the subject. I wasn't here to dwell on the past but rather to see a good friend. "Tell me, who thought of throwing a masquerade ball, you or Lionel?"

She smiled excitedly. "You think Lionel could come up with something like this? It was my idea—I thought we all could use some levity and I miss dressing up like we did as kids."

I laughed, "You're personable, Gisèle. Why would you want to hide behind a mask?"

She looked up from her hands, a small smirk playing on her face. "Maybe it's not me that I'm trying to hide."

I looked to the vast field behind her, pondering her mysterious comment. What could she have meant by that?

Before I could become too curious, she added, "I feel people might enjoy a night where they don't have to mingle with someone who's richer or more well-known than they are. I just want everyone to have fun."

Something didn't make sense. I shook my head then, realizing that I wasn't back at the circus trying to figure out some mystery. I was with Gisèle, my childhood friend, and throwing parties was what her family had always done.

I cleared my throat. "I, for one, think this is the best idea you've ever had. I detest going to parties. They're all the same. My mother always introduces me to some viscount or diplomat in the hopes of joining our families. And when that doesn't work, she repeats the cycle all over again. This idea actually seems…"

"Fun?" she asked.

"Yes," I laughed. "Fun."

We sat in silence for a minute or two before Gisèle leapt up without warning. "This talk is very dull. I say we go into town!" She grabbed my hand, practically ripping me from my seat, and pulled me through her lavish home.

Lionel emerged from the kitchen with a kettle and two teacups on a tray.

We passed him in a flourish, the smell of lemon chamomile wafting into my nose. I briefly turned around to smell it again while Gisèle tugged on my arm harder.

"Sorry, dear," Gisèle yelled back to him. "We're off to go shopping!"

He just shook his head and sighed, still holding the rejected tray of tea.

A servant with greying hair took the tray from him. "Women," he sighed.

The last thing I heard was Lionel's rich laugh before the door slammed shut.

Gisèle didn't waste any time. She hopped into an ornate carriage; one of many in her possession, and ordered, "To Nettlewood Street!"

And we were off. Trotting through the city, riding past museums, bakeries, and vendors advertising sundries, like Venetian fabrics from across the sea and the newest styles in women's fashion. I braced my arms against the polished window and leaned my head out of the carriage to smell the sweet aroma of the city bakeries. Closing my eyes, I took in the sound of bustling carriages, and when I opened them, we rounded the corner and passed the biggest opera house I'd ever seen. A gasp escaped my lips.

"Eustachio's Opera House," Gisèle exclaimed with a tone of wonder as she witnessed the disbelief in my eyes. She launched into telling the story of the establishment with pride—as though living in Hewe granted her some hold over the histories that were made here.

"Eustachio is some man from across the sea who decided to build an opera house in his name. Quite conceited if you ask me, but it has become the main attraction of the city. The most famous dancers, singers, and artists come from all over the world to perform here. Those who really know the history of Hewe call it 'Le Joyau de la Ville,' which translates to 'The Jewel of the City.'"

White stone so pure it almost looked translucent climbed high into the sky. The top of the architecture was crafted into a dome, the tip hoisting a small statue of a woman holding her breasts, her face lifted high. A beautiful arch framed the entrance of the building with eight flights of stairs leading up to the wide double doors. It looked magical on the outside, and I couldn't even imagine the detail on the inside.

Peeling my eyes from the opera house, I gazed into the street, where children frolicked with their mothers and fathers close by, and all of them dressed in colorful attire. Laughing, jumping, and chasing after each other, the children seemed so free. So filled with wonder.

"If this is what you live amid every day, you would love the circus." Everything passed in a blur, but I memorized it as best I could. If I ever settled down, it would be here. Not in Axminster, with Joseph and my family living as neighbors, and most likely not with the circus. When I grow old, I want a nice house in Hewe where I can admire the city in its fullest potential. And I would bring as many circus performers as would fit.

"Oh, I know I would," she answered delicately, staring at the passing streets with me. Her eyebrows curved upwards, and a smile tugged at her lips. Despite living in Hewe her entire life, it appeared Gisèle was still enthralled by the city's magic.

She showed me down Nettlewood Street—the fashion district in Hewe—which was packed with eager buyers, and shops that were bigger than any in Axminster and filled with the most exquisite fabrics. When the day was over, I had fallen in love with Hewe all over again.

I had five or six bags on my arms, their strings digging grooves into my skin. Part of me was glad to be with Gisèle doing such things. Before, when I belonged to the circus, I would have felt guilty for buying such extravagancies while the rest of them were barely surviving. For a long time, I felt like a fraud—like I didn't belong there. And that went away quickly enough, although there was a part of me that was always different from the other performers—a part of me that would never quite understand them. And Gisèle made that part of me feel respected instead of judged.

Back at the carriage after a long day of sight-seeing, I turned to her. "Thank you for showing me the city. Especially Eustachio's Opera House," I sighed contentedly. I had never seen something so wonderful. "Maybe the circus will perform there one day, once the world has settled the debate between the upper and lower classes." Considering that idea seemed out of proportion. "Maybe," I repeated doubtfully.

Gisèle smiled genuinely with a glimmer in her eyes. "Well, they may not be too far away from that endeavor," she said mysteriously.

"What do you mean?"

Had they been given an offer to perform there this year? Were they finally building their name as we had tried so hard to do last year? But how did Gisèle know before I did? Wouldn't Mr. Monte have written to me first if he had such great news?

Gisèle shook her head. "As smart as you are, Juniper, I thought you would have suspected something much sooner."

She gently grabbed my biceps to stop me in my tracks. And the excited smile she offered convinced me that something was brewing.

"They are the very reason I've encouraged wearing masks at this year's ball." When my perplexity persisted, she groaned and revealed something I wasn't prepared for. "Juniper, the circus is the main event of my masquerade ball, but I couldn't have them wandering about in plain sight, now could I?"

My heart dropped to the pit of my stomach. "What?" That was the only word I could manage to utter.

The circus was coming to Gisèle's masquerade ball. Why? I couldn't comprehend the fact that I would finally see them again in a month's time. Mr. Monte, Charlotte, Olive, Evelyn, Gus, Hugh, Flint, Cassius. They would all be standing in front of me. Every night I dreamed of seeing them again and imagined what I'd say, but I never thought I'd be given the chance. Now, all that I had imagined would come true. I would be able to tell them how painful it had been not seeing their smiling faces every day and how devastated I was to leave.

I would hug each and every one of my friends until their embrace was memorized in my mind. That made me think of Cassius. I couldn't wait to feel him around me again. I imagined grasping his broad shoulders and nuzzling my head in his neck. His curly hair would tickle my forehead and then he'd kiss me, as though no time had passed at all. The taste of his lips I'd never forgotten—something close to bitter alcohol, but there was a sweetness mixed in there. I couldn't quite explain it, but it was warm, seeking, and fresh all at once.

I hadn't realized I was crying until Gisèle reached up and brushed the tears from my cheeks. I was addled, but managed to clear my throat and question, "What are they doing at your party? Only wealthy people are invited."

She tilted her head in humorous shame. "Come on, Juniper. You designed this plan." Her eyes brightened at that. "You always wanted Mr. Monte to attract wealthy audiences. That's why you contacted me. Think about it. Every wealthy family in our region is invited to a party at my home. Does that sound like me? Why would I host a party full of dukes and viscounts, or the most famous celebrities and entertainment moguls?"

My eyes widened. "Because you believe in the circus, and you're the only person Mr. Monte would ever trust to help them." I took a deep breath. "The masquerade ball is just an excuse for them to perform, isn't it?"

She nodded slowly as I put the pieces together.

I laughed and shook my head. Mr. Monte was a master of deception, a true showman. He and the rest of the circus had guaranteed a spot among not only the biggest crowd, but the biggest financiers, and no one would guess.

I almost leapt up and shouted my thanks to the heavens, but instead, I threw my arms around Gisèle.

"Thank you," I cried into her shoulder. She had always believed in the circus, and her hope offered more to them than even the richest supporter. She had no idea how much she was doing for them. For us.

Suddenly I began to think about what might really transpire in a month's time. Would the magic of being near the circus prompt me to seize the opportunity to return with them? Or would I remain at Joseph's side where my mother had ordered me to stay?

How long will you let her control your life?

Gisèle's words whispered in my mind, over and over, prompting me to change my circumstances.

Mr. Monte...

"Straighten your shoulders Gus, you look like a withered crone slumping on a cane," I ordered, slapping Gus's shoulders with a stick.

He immediately straightened, wincing.

Cassius looked over from his position in the new waistcoat Valetta had trimmed for him. "Don't you think this is child abuse?"

"The wealthy also do not speak unless spoken to." I slapped the back of his head for speaking out of turn, and Cassius immediately broke formation to hold the back of his temple.

That afternoon I had called the performers together to train them in etiquette. I was going to make tea and crumpets to really make a fuss, but I didn't have the funds for that right now. I wasn't hurt by the fact. After our performance at the masquerade ball, we would have more money flowing into our pockets than we'd ever had before. Every person in attendance would pay five gold coins to support Gisèle's favorite cause—which happened to be the circus—something the wealthy wouldn't be informed of until later.

"First order of business is getting you all trained in proper etiquette. It doesn't matter if we are wearing fitted suits and fine gowns, the wealthy will recognize us in a matter of seconds unless we know how to blend in. Everyone, find a partner."

I walked around the room, watching as pairs joined together. Men grabbed hastily at women's waists and gripped their dainty hands lazily.

"You're grabbing her bum as if you're going to throw her into bed. A little respect would be encouraged." I moved Edwin's hand onto Elain's ribcage.

He sighed as I walked away, grateful to have missed a beating. And then I turned around and smacked his back with the stick, watching him jump slightly while the others chuckled. "None of you are actually related to me by blood, so it doesn't count as child abuse."

The entire crew bellowed with laughter.

I quirked a smile and placed my hands behind my back. "You are all well versed in how to have a good time, but do you know how to waltz?" I asked.

The room shuffled awkwardly, and a sea of heads dipped to the floor all at once.

"I'm not asking you to shovel manure all day. It's not going to kill you. Pick up your heads." I turned on a soft medley and the sound of a violin picking its strings filled the room.

Dear God, help me, I prayed. This was going to take a lot of work.

Upon returning to Axminster from my lovely visit with Gisèle, I began searching for a ballgown. Sure, I had attended my fair share of evening balls, but never a masquerade ball. They were vastly different.

To an evening ball, one would wear a floor-length dress, not blooming in fabric or color. Modest, but beautiful. Concealing. But to a masquerade ball, one would wear something of the utmost flamboyance. Skirts with long trains and tulle bursting from the waist. Colors of glittering hues—azure, olive, and rose. And of course, gems and rhinestones and lace were a must. Necklines always plunged deeply, reaching the point of inappropriateness.

Masquerade balls are a chance to show off how wealthy you really are, and luckily, I am one of the wealthiest women in Axminster. More important than that, I would finally see my friends again. I would see Cassius. And it wasn't conceited of me to want to look my best.

I hopped from boutique to boutique, searching for something of the right caliber. The chapel and the market were located in the Upper District, while the fashion industry laid in the Lower District. And I hadn't found anything worthy until I stumbled across Loretta's Boutique.

A bell jingled overhead when I entered the small shop. The walls were a dark steel, the metallic base creating a vast contrast to the magically colored dresses hanging on the many mannequins.

"Welcome in!" a spritely woman announced, her blonde hair swishing around a set of small ears. She worked busily, marking a checkbook, before looking to me. "Is there anything I can help you find?"

"I need something out of this world," I chuckled. "Do you think you have anything of that sort?" I held out a finger, a sack of gold coins swinging playfully on the end of it.

"Juniper Rose." She took off her glasses to get a better look at me and leaned back on the counter casually. "Darling of the circus turned married woman. I can only guess that you've come looking for a gown for Gisèle's ball?"

Due to my surprised expression, she added, "About ten other women came through here today for the very same reason. Almost every gown worth wearing is gone." She sighed dramatically before looking up at me with a twinkle in her eyes and a smile playing on her lips. "Almost. I was waiting for you."

I let out a sigh of relief. It seemed having a reputation came in handy.

I followed her to the back of her store where a heap of fabrics laid carelessly. She pushed back a dark curtain, and we entered her design room. There, a few mannequins were scattered across the room, posed in a striking manner.

"Here we are." She stood in front of a gown so large it took up half the room. The train must have been seven feet long. The entirety of the dress was made of gold metallic flower petals. When Loretta brushed her hand along the skirt, the metal *clinked* delicately on the floor, like the sound of heels clicking on marble.

The dress had a plunging neckline which curved along the breasts and dipped down to the naval. The bodice was made of a single plate of gold, the metal swirling as though it were melting, and attached to the sides of the dress, hanging halfway down the biceps, were off-the-shoulder sleeves made of see through lace, golden flecks embedded into the fabric.

I laughed to myself as the metal flowers clicked against one another, and I realized what this dress reminded me of. The petals on the billowing skirt were strong and protective, the bodice the same, like a plate of armor. The entire dress was made of gold—the safety blanket for the wealthy. But the swirling bodice was a warning that gold would one day melt, leaving the body exposed.

It was a work of art, how the materials were formed to wrap something so delicate in protective, unyielding power.

"Would you like to try it on?" Loretta inquired, snatching me from my thoughts.

Not able to take my eyes off the silhouette before me, I smiled. "No. It looks exquisite."

I followed Loretta to the counter where she packaged the dress and matching shoes.

"That will come to two hundred even." Loretta was tiny behind the counter, and she swelled with excitement, thrilled that someone had purchased her prized creation.

I knew the feeling all too well.

I handed her the bag of coins and took the box from her. As I began to walk away, I heard the cash register open. Exiting the store, the bell jingled once again, and I voiced calmly, "Keep the change."

Chapter Nine

The following morning our maid, Kathryn, made tea and crumpets for us to enjoy. Such niceties I had missed in the circus, although I shouldn't have. Colette left her unfinished biscuit on her plate, which would be thrown away later. Her carelessness—all of ours—continued to remind me that there were people going without, and we were throwing away our share.

A dull thud echoed on our door while a low male voice exclaimed, "mail," almost inaudibly from the other side.

My mother hopped up eagerly to fetch it before settling back down in her seat, laying a napkin across her lap. Her eyes roamed over the paper for what must have been thirty seconds before she slammed it down on the table. Peeking over at the source of her outburst, I saw myself on the front page holding two large bags, exiting sneakily from Loretta's Boutique. I sank lower in my chair, trying to prepare for her lecture.

She huffed out a sigh and brushed back her dark brown hair graying at the roots before reading from the newspaper, "'*Juniper Rose was spotted exiting one of the most notable boutiques in the Lower District. We have reason to believe Miss Rose will be attending Gisèle Perrault's masquerade ball. Her longtime friend has been a supporter of the circus since last year. Will Gisèle continue to aid the circus in other ways? And will Juniper help in Gisèle's efforts, despite her vow to marry Joseph Young? We'll have to wait and find out.*'"

My mother didn't bother looking at me. Instead, she stared at her empty plate, chewing thoughtfully on her cheek. "I think this speaks for itself," she said as she threw the paper onto the kitchen table.

"Mother, you know reporters twist the truth all the time." I attempted to mend the situation before it could get out of hand.

"Then what were you doing at Loretta's Boutique? Searching for a new necklace? We all know that doesn't sound like our prune." My mother rolled her eyes in my direction, unable to look at me.

My mother wasn't the type to talk calmly about a situation when she was angry. Instead, she was degrading, and she made me feel like a child again.

There was no point in lying. "I was shopping for a dress for Gisèle's party."

My mother smiled, holding all the control as usual. She picked up the newspaper and turned to a more interesting page, commenting quietly, "You will be returning it tomorrow." Before I could disagree with her, she continued, "You will not be associating yourself with Gisèle after she blatantly allowed the circus into her *home* last year."

"Oh, give it a rest," I groaned and rolled my eyes.

When would she drop this? When would she realize that those who encouraged the circus weren't in company with the anti-Christ, sent to doom us all? She didn't have to like the circus, but she sure as hell didn't have to shame those who did.

But then she grabbed me. Hard. Her filed fingernails bit into my biceps as she tugged me toward her.

"Mother," Colette warned, standing from her seat at the table.

I winced in pain as her fingernails clawed into my skin. An image of an old dream resurfaced—Mr. Young forcing my compliance on my wedding day. His touch had hurt just as much, but I knew now that Mr. Young was not the one controlling this situation. It was my mother and it always had been.

Her eyes were dark and wide as she seethed an inch from my face. "I don't know what you hope to find in the circus, but it is time to let it go. *Now*. Enough shaming our family."

I leaned forward even closer, trying to mask the fear racing through me. I wouldn't be threatened by her. "I could care less what happens to you. Even if for some reason I were to hinder our family name and turn the world against you, you would still have enough money to last you a lifetime. You have everything you'll ever need." I sounded more confident than I felt.

I wasn't sure if she could sense how terrified I really was, but when she dipped her feet into something, she wasn't getting back out of the water.

Before I saw it coming, my mother's hand flew up and slapped me across the face. My cheek burned a bright red as tears pooled in my eyes.

Her nostrils flared. "I was lenient when you ran off to the circus. I labeled it as a childish act I thought you would outgrow, but I see now that you haven't. I will make things a lot harder for you if you cannot learn to grow up. Do you understand?" Her face shook with her teeth clenched.

I stared at the tablecloth, not daring to meet her eyes as I cried, but she gripped my chin, turning my eyes to hers. My jaw wobbled and I hated myself for allowing her to see it.

"Do. You. Understand?" she asked again, with more force.

I nodded sheepishly. "Yes."

Colette watched from across the table with tears in her eyes.

Suddenly a knock sounded on our door and I jumped. I quickly wiped the tears from my face and sniffed away my fright. My mother put on a hearty smile, the switch in her emotions so terrifying.

This is what her life was made of. Lies. She spent every day pretending to be someone she wasn't. She acted strong, content even, when she was hurting just as much as the rest of us. The truth was, she was a sad, lonely widow with no ambition, I was a girl who adored something most thought unrealistic, and Colette was in love with a man who wasn't filthy stinking rich but could make her happy. That was the truth. And instead, my mother was determined to keep up this façade, failing to realize that those lies were tearing our family apart more than the truth ever could.

"Welcome!" my mother announced, her cheery voice posing to hide the miserable family behind her. Her smile appeared genuine, only from the hours it was practiced in the mirror. How did she manage to do that? Everyone seemed to read my face, knowing exactly what I was feeling before I even knew myself.

"Good afternoon!" The entire Young family entered our home with bright countenance.

I greeted them at the door, doing my best to hold back my tears. Joseph and his mother made their way to the table where Kathryn was currently placing more crumpets on a crystal platter.

I was about to join them before Mr. Young grabbed my hand. "We need to speak," he said quietly but urgently.

In the anticipation of Gisèle's masquerade ball, I had almost forgotten about Mr. Young's mission. Had he found something? My heart was racing as I followed him to the conservatory in the back of our home. If anyone noticed our absence and came looking for us, it would appear as though we were just enjoying the garden and some fresh air.

"I found something you'll want to see." Mr. Young continued to scan the greenery while his detached posture masked the seriousness in his voice. He slipped a folder from inside his jacket and said, "Take a look."

As he handed me the folder, I realized I needed to sort out my priorities. Sure, seeing the circus at the masquerade ball would be thrilling, but the investigation of the killer was more pertinent. I ripped the folder from his hands and sorted through the newspaper articles he had printed. I found one that jumped out to me with the name Katriane printed in the headline.

`Katriane Beringer takes on the rope once again, completing not a double, but a triple!`

I scanned through more stacks until I found another article with more information:

```
On October 24, Katriane Beringer mis-stepped and
  fell to her death in front of a stadium full of
    people. She was the picture of grace for over
      ten years, and she will forever be missed.
```

Katriane died? That must be why the killer was seeking revenge on Penelope and me. Katriane fell to her death while walking the tightrope, but did he believe that we deserved the same fate? But how was the killer connected to Katriane?

Wait. Katriane Beringer. *Beringer*. I knew that name!

"Juniper, this is Monroe Beringer," were Mr. Monte's words.

"Oh, my God!" my voice echoed in the small room.

"What, what is it?" Mr. Young asked fervently, hushing me in the process.

I surveyed the room to see if anyone had overheard. Then, I pulled him in close and whispered, "I know someone in the circus who is related to Katriane! He may know something about her death. I have to go talk to him."

I was ready to leap out the front door and never see this place again. Was Monroe Katriane's brother? Her father? I had to find out what he knew.

I brushed past Mr. Young in an attempt to leave, but he grabbed me hurriedly and said, "What's going on?"

This was my chance to go back to the circus and protect my friends— my chance to see them again, not just for one splendid night, but for good. If I played my cards right, I could make my stay permanent.

So, I cleared my throat and announced, "Monroe Beringer works in the circus, and I believe he may be related to Katriane. He must know something about her connection to the killer."

"And if he doesn't know anything? If he refuses to tell you?" He placed his hands on his hips, crinkling the dress shirt under his suit.

I answered without even thinking, "Then let me draw the killer out. If we can't get information from my source, then we need to take matters into our own hands. Let me go back to the circus. We'll announce my return and draw the killer back out of hiding. He'll come looking for me, I'm sure of it. And when he does, we'll be prepared to bring him to an end."

Mr. Young mulled this over for a long time, struggling to find an answer. He looked through the glass doors of the conservatory, hoping no one could witness our heated conversation. "And are you going to randomly return to the circus without notice? What are they going to think after you were ordered to wed my son?"

I shook my head, trying to put all the pieces together. "Gisèle Perrault is hosting a masquerade ball. No one knows this, but when I saw her last week, she told me this party is a way for the circus to perform in front of a large crowd of wealthy men and women. They're going to be at the party, and I think *I* should be as well. I'll contact Mr. Monte and let him know beforehand. And when I perform with the circus at the ball, a newspaper will be published the next morning, signaling my return. The killer is bound to make himself known before the next performance."

I thought further on Mr. Young's question. Having no answer for my delayed marriage to his son, I resorted to threatening him instead. "As for your son, if you don't help me defeat the killer, I won't marry him. Our deal will be off, as I warned you before." Shrugging assuredly, I stared at him, my gaze unfaltering. "You decide."

Mr. Young nodded slowly. "How will I know that you will come back?"

The only thing I could offer him was the truth. "You don't," I answered, trying to hurry our conversation before my mother sought us out. "If you fail to do this—if you fail to let me go—your word will mean nothing. But if you *do* let me go, I'll know that I can trust you to take care of them. That's all I want. So, trust me when I tell you that I will return if you keep your promise," I pleaded.

Mr. Young sighed, thinking over my proposition long and hard.

"Juniper, lunch is ready!" Colette appeared from behind the doorway and beckoned us to return to the dining room.

Mr. Young began to walk away.

No. I had spent months trying to find a way back to the circus and out of this deal. Now that I had one, I wasn't going to wait any longer. I needed an answer now.

I grabbed his arm and lowered my head to look into his downcast eyes. "What will it be?"

He looked deeply troubled, but suddenly his face calmed, and he straightened the vest over his clean white button-down. "You will return to the circus tonight to draw out the killer. I will organize a fleet of officers to be with you at all times until he is locked behind bars. And when he is contained, you will return to Axminster and marry Joseph, is that clear? No more blackmailing one another or threatening my job. Find the killer and get out, and I will continue to protect the circus."

I rethought his offer. I had no intention of coming back to Axminster to marry his son, but I couldn't tell him that. I would have to think of a convincing reason for staying in the circus, but until then, he didn't need to know. "We have a deal." I extended my hand for him to shake.

He grabbed it forcefully and shook it once before pulling my body into his own. He whispered roughly in my ear, "Don't do anything you'll regret. I could still just as easily burn the circus to the ground. You remember that." He quickly let me go and walked into the dining room with a cheerful expression.

His threat meant nothing to me. Tonight. Tonight, I would return to the circus to find the killer.

Chapter Ten

Mr. Monte…

"Positions, everyone!" I clapped my hands, and the performers began to station themselves around the tent. "Dancers, take the center. Let's run the beginning, shall we?"

I must have watched the opening act a dozen times before finally feeling content with it. But just as we were about to begin it once again, a postman emerged into the tent and hurried over to me with a small letter in hand.

"Express delivery for Mr. Monte," he proclaimed with a questioning tone.

My confusion matched his own. Express delivery? Whatever the message, it must be important. Express delivery was expensive, used only by those with enough wealth to throw away over simple matters like mail, or someone with urgent news. I took it from him eagerly and tore open the edges. Inside it read:

Mr. Monte,

I have reason to believe the killer remains a threat to the circus, but I have a solution. I want to finally put him to an end, for Cassius's sake, and for all of ours. But in order to do so, I must return to the circus to draw him out. A little birdy told me the circus would be attending Gisèle's masquerade ball. Surely, it would be a lovely surprise for the rose to return as well, would it not? If you accept, I will gladly perform with the circus again. But do me a favor? Keep this a secret. I don't want anyone knowing I've come back until after the performance.

Sincerely,
Juniper Rose

My dear Juniper continued to save us every day. It was a good idea to continue looking for the killer, and not only would we surprise the audience with a performance at their masquerade ball, but we'd surprise them with the rose of the circus returned to her rightful place.

But that meant I needed to get her on the rope. She'd been out of practice for months, and in the eyes of a showman, that might as well be years.

I made quickly to the outskirts of the city, concealing my face under a hood. If word spread that I had indeed run away in the middle of the night to the circus, my mother would find me before I could even board that train. This was my only chance at escape, and I had to make it count. My mother wouldn't be able to stop me, so long as I was far, far away before she realized I was gone. Luckily for me, Mr. Monte planned my entire escape down to a tee. He instructed me to follow his step-by-step plan just yesterday:

1.   Wilman will be waiting for you on the deck of the third train car as we wind our way through Axminster. I'll instruct the brakemen to slow down due to a shortage of coal, but we won't be able to stop the train completely.
2.   Once you enter the train car, Charlotte will be waiting for you. The main hall is busy and crowded, so Charlotte will take you the back way to her room, where you'll stay until you're revealed at the ball.
3.   Finally, if you are to perform with us, we must get you comfortable on the rope. We must be careful of our whereabouts since you insist no one knows you've returned. Therefore, we will not be able to train until the sun has fallen. I hope you haven't forgotten everything I taught you.

I was going back home. I didn't care if I had to train from dusk until dawn because I'd finally feel the rope under my feet again. Soon, I would see my friends; better yet, I would see Cassius.

I wish I didn't have to keep my presence a secret, but I wanted it to remain a surprise for many different reasons, the first being that if the circus wasn't surprised to see me at the ball, then how would hundreds of other people be? And second, there was a lingering worry that my friends would be angry I left—that they'd question my intentions once again. I couldn't help but wonder what I'd missed in the months I was gone. Was I the same girl as when I left? What if too many things had changed?

But I was *still* a performer. That's what I'd always be, and I hoped they'd all realize that come performance night. Regardless, there was no sense dwelling on that now, so I busied myself following Mr. Monte's plan dutifully, leaving no room for mistakes.

That night I made it to the edge of the cornfield bordering the perimeter of the city. Hiking my bag onto my shoulder, I waited impatiently for the train to arrive. I couldn't comprehend how it had come to this. I was to be married in less than a month and by sheer power of will, I managed to slip away.

Once we found the killer and brought him to justice, I'd have to find a way to stay with the circus. I needed a logical reason, no, a religious or constitutional reason that my family wouldn't dare interfere with. I wracked my brain while I stood on the outskirts of the city, the chilled summer breeze causing gooseflesh to rise on my arms. But nothing came to mind, and I took a moment to settle my thoughts. For now, I had to focus on finding the killer. The uncertainty of my future would have to wait until later.

As if I'd thought it into existence, the train slowly came into view. It blared loudly, echoing far and wide across the region, the bright headlights cutting through the dark sky like a beacon. It emerged from of the tree line at a rapid pace, and I skipped across the field to meet it at the railway. The wheels slowed only slightly, triggering fear to set my feet moving faster. I expected it to slow down far more than it did, but it seemed the closer it came, the faster it sped. I kept running toward it, fearful of missing my only opportunity.

The train would not stop. It would not turn around for me. This was my only chance.

I pumped my legs faster and looked around manically, searching for help, anyone to take me from this blasted city and into freedom.

There, in the darkness, I spotted a black shadow standing on the platform of a train car.

Wilman.

I ran as fast as I could, driving my arms back and forth to gain momentum. Wilman just stood there with steel in his eyes, as if he knew I didn't need his help.

I ran faster, my cheeks flaring red, sweat beading on my forehead, and my lungs burning. When I finally managed to reach him, Wilman held out a hand. I thought for a moment what would happen if I missed it and the train entirely. It would hurt. If I fell, I wouldn't get back up. And the train would be too far out of reach.

That prompted me to make my next move correctly. I kept running, only slowing down slightly to jump for Wilman, and placed my foot on the steps leading up to the platform. When he hauled me over the edge, I rolled onto my back and gasped for air as the midnight breeze whipped at my hair. Watching the stars flick by, I laughed softly to myself, at the recklessness of what I'd just done. My giggle soon turned into hysterics, and I clutched my stomach in pain.

When I managed to contain myself, I looked up and saw a faint smile on Wilman's face, his full cheeks pulling back to reveal gangly teeth.

"Welcome back, Juniper," he said.

Step one, complete. On to step two.

Wilman carefully peered into the train car, finding it empty for the moment.

We had to be quick.

He rested a hand against my lower back, leading me inside. I wish I had longer to take it all in—the dark interior of the train lit by a few candelabras scattered along the walls, how the floorboards creaked, how the smell of manure from the animal pens drifted from the back of the train, the way shadows danced along the walls and laughter spread through the halls. All the doors were closed, my friends only a few feet away. Would it be so bad to let them see me, just once, so that I could witness their smiles, their laughter, their happiness?

"Come on, Miss. Can't be turnin' back on ya word now." Wilman led me forward and pulled at a panel of wood to our right.

The panel flicked open, along with four others—a space only wide enough to squeeze through. Anyone could come walking down the corridor, and my cover would be blown. So, I took one last fleeting glance into the train car, knowing I would walk freely in it in a matter of weeks. I took a deep breath and turned away before crouching low and stepping through the hidden panels. Wilman crawled in behind me, his beer belly making it difficult for him to push through the opening.

When I crawled inside, the light leaked out of the world. Wilman boarded up the panels once again to hide our trail, and we were left in darkness. I shuddered as my imagination suddenly filled with the image of a man dressed from head to toe in black, his eyes soulless pits. My breath came out shaky as I blinked rapidly, trying to clear him from my head, that killer. He was so tall, that's what I remembered. Hulking, practically.

I shook my head. I had many dreams of the killer in my time in Axminster, and no one was able to wake me from them until I was lurching out of bed, running to the toilet to throw up the contents of my dinner. Over and over, night after night, it was the same routine. And the only nights I slept peacefully were the ones when I blacked out from pure exhaustion.

To calm the nervous trembling in my hands, I closed my eyes, remembering a time when Cassius had shaken me out of my nightmares, grasping onto me to tether me to the world. He had been my lifeline in the months that followed the incident, when the killer and I had come face to face for the first time. And right now, Cassius was so close, and I still couldn't reach him.

I heard footsteps approaching down the hall, outside the wall we were stuck behind, as if someone had been listening to the thoughts in my head.

"It was a great idea, but I understand why Monte refused our act. He'd allow us to take risks if it were any other night, but he's not going to allow anything unexpected in this performance under such high stakes."

I knew that voice. It was low, gruff, laced with maturity. *Cassius.* But his voice had changed in the time that I was away. It sounded distant.

He was just out there. I reached forward and placed my hands on the wooden boards concealing me, wanting to be nearer to him.

Another male voice answered him, "And for good reason. If anyone were to discover us, it would ruin the entire evening and our return for the performance year!"

Who was he speaking to?

Just hearing him was enough to pull me out of my head and forget the trauma that plagued me. I sighed, listening to his conversation with the mystery man, until their voices faded completely. Without notice, a different voice filled the space around me.

"Juniper?" The voice was high-pitched, light, and jovial.

I couldn't see, but I knew exactly who that voice belonged to. "Charlotte?" I gasped when she pulled my body close to hers in a bone-crushing hug.

"I'm so glad to see you! When Mr. Monte told me of your plan, I thought he was drinking again," she whispered.

I huffed out a laugh. I was sure my idea sounded preposterous. "I can't believe I'm here either!" I exclaimed, but lowered my voice when Wilman sent me a warning glare.

My eyes had adjusted in the darkness, so much so that I was able to spot Charlotte's small frame in front of me, clad in her usual silk dress, the edges cut to reveal her long pale legs.

"How *did* you manage to escape Mother Almighty?" she asked.

I snickered, preparing to launch into a full-blown story before Wilman cleared his throat.

"That's a story for anotha' time. You know da drill. Get to Charlotte's room and get some rest," he ordered.

Charlotte giggled and I bid him farewell, mentioning my thanks, before she led me away, all the while holding my hand tightly. We wound down the halls, twisting and turning, which led me to question how she knew this route so well. Mr. Monte must have had a lot of faith in Charlotte's ability to conceal me.

I wouldn't want anyone else doing the job.

Within a few minutes, the secret passageway had opened into the hallway once more, right outside of Charlotte's room, and she snuck us in quickly. After she locked the door, she began jumping up and down like a little girl.

"Tell me everything," she whispered, her little arms shaking by her side.

And so, I did. I was so grateful to have someone to confide in, after months of being secluded and alone. In Axminster, there had been no one to talk to. Possibly Colette, but she didn't understand my yearning to return here as Charlotte did. No one could without experiencing the wonders of the circus for themselves.

She listened intently, gasping and throwing out curses when the story called for it. And when I finished, I felt my shoulders relax and the tension leave my body. Things had happened that I didn't like to remember, but in the end, I'd made it here.

Charlotte was not angry that I left and did not once speak of that night, and I realized then that the other performers would feel the same.

I heaved a sigh of relief.

I was home.

Diana Rose...

"Juniper, it's time to get up!" I yelled from downstairs while flicking a piece of hair from my cheek. This summer heat was unbearable.

My patience was growing thin. We were already late to meet the Cordova's at their sprawling vineyard, and I wouldn't tolerate her laziness. The Cordova family was well-connected and talented, and they were offering to help with the decorations for the wedding.

"Juniper!" I yelled again but heard no feet moving. I grudgingly stomped upstairs, hiking my dress high enough so as not to get dirt on the hem. This inability to rise in the morning was not what was expected of a punctual lady.

I opened her bedroom door, prepared to rip the covers off her bed, only to see that they had already been pulled back in a mess. She had risen, which surprised me since I had received nothing but grief from her in the past few months. She wasn't keen on doing anything I wished or anything relative to her wedding.

But then I spotted the window pushed wide open and the drapes fluttering lightly in the breeze, allowing in the crisp morning air.

My heart started racing. I ran over to her bed, looking underneath for the brown duffel bag she used when she left before, and I found it to be missing.

"Colette!" I screamed.

She rushed down the hall, clearly worried. "What, Mother? What's wrong?"

I turned around with my nostrils flared and my hands bunched into fists at my side. "Call William."

"Mother, what's going on?" she demanded with more vigor.

"Your sister is gone," I took a deep breath before erupting, "again!"

Amid the chaos, I managed to gather William and the entire Young family to discuss the situation.

I cleared my throat, mortified beyond measure, before I began. "Juniper has left again. I am guessing she fled to the circus, although I am unsure why." I bowed my head regretfully, despising the way the Youngs looked at me with such confusion and disappointment. This was an embarrassment to our family, and I didn't need anyone looking down on us after we had finally started to rebuild our name.

The room began to spin, and I was taken back to a similar moment in time. The day my husband left us, a swarm of good friends and family had arrived at the house. After expressing their sympathy for our family, they mingled with one another, eating from the dainty platters of food Kathryn made that morning.

It felt like a funeral. But there was no remorse in the air, only hushed whispers of disdain and judgement, and withering glares from those I counted as my friends. That day, I had not only lost my husband and the sole supporter of my family, but also the support I so desperately needed from my community. I had lost their respect simply because I was alone. And if I wasn't worthy of a husband, then what was I worthy of?

Taking me from the past, Mr. Young suddenly looked up from his seat at the table and said, "I may be able to shed some light on the issue." He wrung his hands together nervously, already knowing how furious I would be with his involvement in this. Regardless, he continued, "Juniper was ready to refuse your hand, Joseph, and I was nervous that she would completely change her mind come your wedding day. So, I took matters into my own hands, and I asked her what I could do to convince her to marry you. She requested that I find a supposed killer that has threatened the circus for the last six years, and who may still be at large."

I rubbed my temple as a migraine began to form. Of course, she did. Anything to save that damned place.

Mr. Young looked at me with raised eyebrows, as if to ease my nerves. "I am willing to do anything to ensure my son's future, which is why I agreed to her terms. I had been investigating the case for a month, when I came upon some mysterious information only one man can clarify. Unfortunately, he resides with the circus. She had to go to him directly if we were to find the killer. And once we *do* find him, she has promised to return to Axminster and marry my son. There is nothing to worry about." The pitch of his voice raised in dismissal.

"You daft imbecile!" I screamed, not caring what the others thought of my outburst.

I had spent my life protecting Juniper, and in the past year, everything had fallen apart. I thought maybe we were beginning to mend things when she returned, and now Mr. Young had messed everything up. "You let her walk right back to the place she loves more than anything! There's no way she's coming back now."

Mr. Young thought on the idea for a moment, appearing seriously concerned, before his face lit up. He splayed a hand in front of him to calm me. "Our deal is still intact. If she doesn't return, I'll burn the circus to the ground just like we talked about!"

I mulled it over and nodded my head in agreement. Maybe Mr. Young had his wits about him. I couldn't believe Juniper was in that horrendous place again. They were corrupting her every single day, and one day I feared she would be too far gone. There was only so much a mother could do. It would be easy if she didn't rebel and fight against me, but then again, easy is not what I signed up for. I was a mother, and a mother's job was to make hard decisions for her children, whether they liked it or not. One day Juniper would see that I did what was best for her.

One day.

The circus wouldn't win. I wouldn't let them. That group of vagabonds had nothing to offer her but scraps. Juniper deserved the world, and I would not allow her to settle for less.

After all, we were beautiful ladies from the wealthiest district in Axminster. We got everything we wanted.

Juniper...

I spent all day holed up in Charlotte's room, but after twenty-four hours, I was bored out of my mind, picking through Charlotte's jewelry to kill time. The train had reached its stop on the outskirts of Hewe where we would train for the masquerade ball at the Janvier Estate. I was mindlessly searching through her closet and all the small lacey dresses, thinking of what Cassius might think of me in them, when something scuffed on the floor behind me. I turned to find a white envelope that had been slipped under the door.

I plucked it off the dark panels of wood and tore open the seal. It read:

Ready for your first lesson?
~M

When the sun had fallen and I was allowed to meet Mr. Monte in secrecy, I jumped into a leotard, pulling the tight fabric high onto my hips, and relishing the sound of it snapping on my skin. I made quick work of following Charlotte down the same dark corridor, listening for any voices I might recognize. I heard none, guessing that most of the performers had retired early for the night to get a jump on training the next morning.

I jumped out of the train, bidding Charlotte farewell, and ran to the towering red and white tent in the distance, its tip reaching to the glimmering stars.

Come back, it called to me. And I answered, sprinting through the field and then pushing inside the flaps of the tent.

I was reawakened. I stepped into the light and took in a breath of that finely ground sand below my feet, a scent so familiar and overwhelming I wanted to cry. The tightrope twisted daringly, reaching from one end of the tent to the other. I could practically feel myself bending and turning along with it.

Get me up there, I wanted to scream. That is, before I spotted Mr. Monte standing across the room with his hands tucked into his pockets.

"My dear, Rose. Welcome back," he said so softly it brought me to tears.

Before I knew what I was doing, I was running to him. He chuckled as I slammed into his body, his shoulder-length brown hair tickling my cheeks. I sobbed into his shoulder, my body racking with the weight of the past months. How had I managed to leave this behind? How did I pick myself up every day when this is what I was missing?

"I missed—," my voice broke as I tried to form the words I so badly wanted to say.

"I know," Mr. Monte reassured me. "I know, but all that matters is that you're back. I hope you haven't forgotten everything." He winked and motioned to the tightrope looming above us.

I shook my head playfully. "You know, it's funny. When I was in Axminster, I dreamed that one day I would come back here, and I wanted to be prepared when I did. I didn't want to lose my technique on the rope." I looked up to it, mesmerized. "Every night I ran through routines in my mind. Jumps, turns, twists, even just walking. I would close my eyes and imagine all of it, hoping I would remember how to do it if I got the chance to return."

Mr. Monte smiled brightly. "Let's see if it paid off, shall we?"

I nodded once before approaching the platform. It was as if I had never left. I taped the bottom of my feet with a sticky white tape before climbing the long ladder. When I came to stand on the platform, I took a deep breath, the long nights of imagining this moment finally coming true.

And the adrenaline racing through me was addicting. Despite the fear of heights and the fear of falling, the excitement led me to take one step forward, the rope bending beneath my weight.

This time I wasn't nervous about what would happen next—about what would happen with the killer, with Cassius, with my family. I was on the rope again and I couldn't worry about anything else. I took step after step, curling my toes around the rough rope, until I reached the other end. I attempted a few spins, but I didn't go as far as to leap or jump. The very first thing I learned here was to know my limits and not ruin an achievement with a failure.

Throughout the night as the moon arced across the sky, I spent hours with Mr. Monte. He gave me little hints on how to make my legs straighter and how to appear more elegant, but he was pleasantly surprised with how I'd retained my skill in the months I'd been away.

And when it came time to get a few hours of sleep, I was saddened. I was so eager to continue that it made my hands itch. But he promised me we would continue to learn many more tricks for the ball.

It was then that I realized that I had time. *We* had time.

Chapter Eleven

After practicing with Mr. Monte for the first time in months, I felt rejuvenated. But I was weary of hiding in Charlotte's room all day. What was I supposed to do until midnight when I could finally practice again? Before I blew my own brains out due to boredom, I received another letter.

Come to my office. It's time we talk about the reason you're really here.
~M

Mr. Monte's tone was serious, apparent in his words. Before I arrived at the circus, I had informed him of my intentions to draw out the killer, and now he wanted to know the steps we'd be taking.

After weaving quietly through the train while everyone was out in the sun practicing, I took a seat in front of Mr. Monte who was leaning back in his chair, contemplating, with his ankle folded atop his knee. I could see a small curve in his cheek from where he nervously bit the inside of his mouth, but finally, he sat up and braced his arms on the desk in front of him. "Tell me, is your hunt for the killer just a ruse to return to the circus, or is it a mission you intend to carry out?"

For some reason, I felt as though I was being interrogated, but I answered honestly, "Both. It just so happened that the killer was my way to persuade Mr. Young to let me come back." I explained Mr. Young's new role as investigator in The Axminster Guard. "But I won't give up on finding the killer. For my own peace of mind and for Cassius's. For every tightrope walker to come. We need to find him."

Mr. Monte looked at me for a while longer with a deep scowl on his face before he stood from his seat. "I want you to tell me everything Mr. Young found. Every clue, every detail. Don't leave anything out."

I nodded, fishing out the newspaper article I brought with Katriane

Beringer's name scrawled on the front page. I informed him of what the killer told me many months ago—that we deserved to feel Katriane's pain.

"Beringer," Mr. Monte whispered to himself in disbelief.

"Monroe," I confirmed. "Where is he?"

As of now, Monroe was my only lead, my only clue to figuring out who the killer was.

Mr. Monte shook his head, discouraged. "His mother fell ill just a week after you left. He's been gone for months."

I gripped my hands on the edge of his desk, my knuckles turning white. "Then get him back. Following my performance at the masquerade ball, the killer will come, and quickly. I need to speak with Monroe." The thought of being in the presence of the killer once again made my entire body shake. The fear he instilled was unlike anything I'd ever known, mostly because his name and his face were a mystery. As of now, he was just a dark entity and nothing more, and the anonymity made me feel as though there was no way to escape him.

Mr. Monte frowned with a lack of hope. "I'll contact him and tell him you've returned with a lead, but I can't promise he'll reply. For right now, we must work on this without him. In the time you have, find any clues that point to the killer—anything that could help us determine his identity, and maybe, if God is on our side, Monroe will return to us."

I nodded quickly, thinking about my next move. There was so much empty space, so much unknown, so many cracks in the story of the circus that I had to fill in. Where would I even begin?

At the start of it all, something whispered to me.

Penelope.

Suddenly I leapt from my seat. "Are all the performers in the field?"

"Yes, I sent them out an hour ago," Mr. Monte replied casually, returning to his work.

"Good." With that I walked out the door.

I tore open Penelope's door and snuck inside. Closing the door behind me, I leaned on the hard wood and took a deep breath. Any performer could have seen me walking down the long stretch of hallway, and I would have had nowhere to hide. Thankfully, I hadn't been seen.

After my heart calmed, I gazed around the room as memories resurfaced. The famous tightrope walker once resided here, and despite her absence, her clothes still hung on the rack and her scent still clung to the fabric. Her presence still lingered.

I shivered slightly, wondering what it would have been like to know her—to perform with her if she were still alive. But she wasn't, all because of that vile man.

I decided to pick my way through her room in search of any clues that pointed to the killer and why he would have hurt her. I started in her closet, the portion of her chamber I was most familiar with, since Mr. Monte allowed me to wear some of her old costumes last year. I leafed through boxes of shoes, cabinets with shimmering tights and leotards, and searched along every wall for hidden pockets.

Nothing.

I turned to the nightstand beside her empty bed, the white sheets ghostly empty. When I pulled open the drawer, a plume of dust rose, and I coughed on the thick cloud. I rifled through miscellaneous papers, finding a powder puff, a small bonnet, and scrap quills with broken ends. In the next drawer down, I found a single grey notebook laying idly inside, the front of it scraped and weathered. I sat on the floor with my knees pulled to my chest and carefully peeled open the notebook, which caused the binding to creak. Inside were her personal testimonies:

Aug. 2

Cassius was quite rude today. He was short with me, which was unusual. He's always been such a gentle soul. I think he's jealous that I'm gaining everyone's attention. Sure, he thinks he's prettier than every female in the circus, but the crowd knows the truth. They can't get enough of me. But despite having my share of fans, the biggest performance of the year is coming, and I can feel the nerves building every single day. Abelard Chevis will be there after all.

I laughed lightly. Cassius, a gentle soul? That didn't sound right. I'm sure I wouldn't have recognized him before Penelope passed away. He seemed to have changed greatly after her death. I flipped to the next page and continued to read.

Aug. 6

I don't know what happened. One moment I was walking back to the train and the next I was on my back. His eyes. His eyes were like empty cauldrons. Like pits of darkness staring back at me. And all I could think was, how did I get here? Before I knew it, my dress was off, and it was all over. My innocence was gone. And it hurt. Every inch of my body ached. I'm too embarrassed to tell the others. Charlotte suspects something, I'm sure of it, but I can't bring myself to tell her what really happened when I can't even fathom it. Was it my fault? Did I do something to provoke him? Why would anyone do something so terrible? And why did it happen to me?

I dropped the notebook on the ground and covered my mouth with a hand. What she saw, what she experienced…those were the same images engrained in my mind every time I closed my eyes. The four walls surrounding me slowly caved in, pressing closer and closer until I couldn't breathe. I clenched my eyes closed and remembered where I was. I was back where I belonged, and my friends were just beyond the train.

You're safe.

I slowly let out the breath I was holding and reached for the notebook, searching for the next entry.

Aug. 18

I was so excited that Abelard Chevis would be sitting in the front row tonight, but now I don't care. I don't want to walk the rope and put on a fake smile. I don't want to put on a dazzling costume when I feel so disgusting. So violated and ashamed. Too much has changed for me to love the things I used to love. It's all too much. I can't take it anymore—the fear of him lingering here somewhere and how easily he could hurt me is tearing me apart. I don't want to think about it anymore. I just want it all to go away.

The next page was blank. August 18. She *had* killed herself that night because of him. My hands were shaking so badly I could barely hold the diary. There was nothing in here that would lead me to the killer, only the lamentations of a beautiful, aspiring young woman who had been raped—her future stolen from her.

"Come on," I whispered.

I turned a few pages, until I found a small section of her words, scrawled in a hurry, almost illegibly. Almost as an afterthought—something she had to admit before taking her own life.

Cassius, I'm scared.

And those words alone broke me. The thought of her having to leave her brother behind was a sorrow I couldn't even imagine. And tears streamed down my cheeks as I began to think of the grief Cassius experienced—how traumatizing it must have been to see her body fall from that rope. I choked on a sob before I managed to continue reading, her lines blurred behind a wall of tears.

I can't get him out of my head. I'm sorry I never told you what he did to me. And I'm sorry I have to leave you. But I am in so much pain and I don't know what else to do. It has been an honor being your older sister. You've protected me in so many ways and I love you for it, Cas. I couldn't have asked for a better brother. You are my best friend and you always will be. It's your turn to shine in the spotlight. Go make me proud out on that stage. I'll be watching from up above.
Penelope

Clipped to the same page was a small photograph of a young girl and boy standing in front of the train, the word *circus* painted in bold red behind them. The little boy had dark hair curling around his ears and his hands folded nervously in front of his waist, while the little girl had bright red hair curling wildly like a lion's mane.

Her arms were thrown around the little boy's shoulders, a big smile playing on her face. Her teeth weren't perfect, but her smile was contagious. I flipped the photograph over to see a message from Penelope that read:

To the life that saved us both. I love you, always and forever.

I buried my head in my hands, not caring about the sobs that wrenched free. I wanted to scream until I had no voice left. I wanted to tear this room to pieces for what the killer had done to Penelope. Because of his demented, violent attack on this beautiful young woman, Cassius lost the only family he ever had.

My hands were numb and buzzing all at once. I wanted to itch off my own skin and wear someone else's. Maybe then I could forget the evil in this world. It was *his* fault she was gone. It was *his* fault Cassius was alone. And it was *his* fault that I couldn't bear to close my eyes at night. I wanted to do something, anything. Yet all I could do was cry.

I mourned for Penelope first—a girl who was tormented by so much pain and terror. More so, a girl who was alone in her terror. I selfishly wished she had fought harder and that she was here today. I wish I could have met her and witnessed what Cassius was really like with her in his life. Then I mourned for Cassius. Had he read this sweet letter yet? Had he heard her words, meant only for him?

I stood and brushed the tears off my cheeks. There was nothing here that would lead me to the killer. There were only memories of a girl who had been destroyed by him. It was time I left this room to Cassius, the one who would cherish her forever. I took one last look at the notebook before tucking it under my arm and closing the door behind me.

It seemed that rifling through memories of Penelope Plume had invited the killer to torment my dreams. I childishly thought that being surrounded by people who loved me would protect me from the nightmares, but no one could stop them from coming.

When I closed my eyes that evening, I was in Penelope's room once again, surrounded by all her things draped in white sheets. Everything looked plastic, fake, covered in a silver sheen. It was all hazy, like smoke had filled the room. I knew it wasn't real, but it felt real all the same.

And then a sound came from the corner of the room, and I saw him.

He was rifling through Penelope's closet, his thick black leather gloves running over the bedazzled costumes. He seemed in a hurry, as though he was searching for something. And then he stopped, having found his prize.

I stepped closer, trying to get a glimpse at what he held in his hands. It appeared he couldn't see me, for some strange reason. I was the narrator of the story, not present but watching, creating.

And it was then that he turned to me. No longer hidden, I felt his eyes staring into my soul. Once again, I couldn't detect their color, only the thick black mask that covered every inch of his face and tightened on his neck. And then he took one step, two steps forward until he stood just on the threshold of the door leading into her closet. Slowly, he raised his gloved hand and invited me to gaze at what was laying in his palm.

A human heart.

Penelope's heart.

And it was beating, thumping louder and louder until it drowned out every other noise in the room. I watched the flesh of the heart slowly expand and sink as it pumped up and down. Blood oozed out of its valves, pooling in the killer's hands. I looked down to the wooden floor, but all I found was red. Thick, hot blood filling every inch of the room, faster and faster.

It was bubbling at my ankles, rising ever slowly.

I started to scream. I didn't know if anyone could hear because the entire room seemed to be enveloped in a film, as if we were in an alternate universe where no one could see or hear me.

Then it was at my knees, crawling up my thighs and growing cold to the touch. I began shivering and shaking, begging for someone to make it stop.

And then it was at my throat. I was choking on blood, the metallic taste filling my mouth until I couldn't breathe anymore. My throat began to burn as I choked, but it just kept rising until I was drowning in it. As soon as my head sunk under the red pool, my body shook awake, and I was vomiting.

It took Charlotte a few moments to come to, but as soon as she heard me shuffling to reach the bathroom, she was up, gathering a cold towel and holding my hair back. I coughed and sputtered, spitting out the slow drawl of mucus that hung on my lip. The taste was foul and acrid. My head was pounding, and I was soaked with sweat.

After I drained the contents of my stomach, she led me back to bed and laid the cold towel on my forehead. She gently brushed my hair back and dabbed the towel against my skin. It was the most comforting thing I'd felt in a long time. I remembered having a loving mother once, but that was a long time ago. After my father left, she was completely absent. She was cold and hateful. When I was sick, she let Colette take care of me, and as the years passed, I couldn't remember if my mother was ever soft and loving, or if she had always been cruel.

"You're good at this," I whispered to Charlotte in the dark, my breathing finally starting to slow.

"I've had practice," she spoke in a hushed tone, which made my eyes close drowsily.

I hadn't slept well in almost three months. Most nights in the circus, I slept peacefully next to Cassius. After the killer attempted to rape me, Cassius was aware of the night terrors that plagued me, and to stop them from coming, I asked him to ground me. Whether it was his tight grip on my wrist, or his arms around my chest, knowing I was safe made the nightmares go away.

Charlotte continued, snapping me out of my vision. "It's uncanny the similarity between you and Penelope. She lost a lot of weight too after…it happened." She chose her words carefully.

"Really?" I still didn't know everything about what happened to Penelope. I didn't know if I ever would, or even wanted to, but at least I could relate to her. At least there was someone else who experienced the same pain I had.

"Yes." Charlotte stopped dabbing at my forehead and just stared at her hands, lost in memory. "She used to be a curvy woman. Still too skinny but she had good hips," Charlotte laughed at that. "But after it happened, she barely picked at her food. I was the only one to really notice. And then I heard her throwing up, night after night, like clockwork. It was killing her…*he* was killing her." She paused momentarily before moving on with her story, "And the times I went to check on her, she was too ashamed to mention what happened."

I grabbed her hand and held it in my own. There were tears welling in her eyes. While mourning the loss of her friend, I sensed she might fear losing me too, without having the chance to say goodbye. So, I reassured her by saying, "I've made my peace with what happened. I'm not going anywhere."

Charlotte was afraid as much as I was. She didn't want to lose another friend. "I may think about that night for the rest of my life, but Cassius—" I swallowed the lump in my throat. "Cassius was there that night when it happened. It could have been much worse." A small smile tugged at my lips. "That son of a bitch is still going to pay for what he did, I'll make sure of it."

"And I'll be right there with you to carry it out." Charlotte squeezed my hand. "I've seen what he did to two beautiful women now—what he took from them. And we won't let him do it ever again."

I nodded in agreement. As the tension in the room was sated, we sat there in silence for a few minutes. When she came to lie down next to me, she asked so quietly I almost didn't hear her, "Did you miss him?"

I knew exactly who she was referring to, but I wasn't sure why she was asking.

My silence prompted her to rephrase her question. "Cassius, I mean."

I turned my head slowly in her direction. Of course, I did. But none of the performers knew what it was like to be missed. They'd been abandoned, thrown out, convinced they were worthless. And they deserved to know how valuable they were. I looked deeply into her eyes and whispered, "Every single day. I missed every single one of you."

She nodded her head, convinced. "I know that. I trusted you the entire time, as I'm sure everyone else did. I think it's just a little harder for Cassius. You know how he is. When something goes wrong, he twists the scenario until it makes sense in his head. He knows deep down what you did saved us all, but I think he's too scared to show it."

I nodded along with her. He wasn't the only one at fault. In my time away, I created scenarios in my head—lies I told to convince myself Cassius wasn't as adoring as I believed him to be. It was just a method I used to protect my heart, and I couldn't blame Cassius for doing the same.

He has always been guarded. I knew that was going to be an element in this equation. But he'd see soon enough that I was trying my hardest to show him—show all of them—that they were worth fighting for.

Chapter Twelve

I practiced into the wee hours of the night with Mr. Monte for the past two weeks. The circus had three days left before they ventured into Hewe to tour the estate. Gisèle offered to teach the circus how to better blend into the wealthy crowd. I just wouldn't be there for it.

Truthfully, I was nervous to make my appearance. Not necessarily to the crowd; that would be the fun part. But what would my friends think? I conjured an image in my head of how the night might transpire. Once we finished the performance, I imagined little Olive running up and latching her body around my leg.

Then Hugh and Gus would come wrap me in a hug and strangle me with their strength. And then all of the dancers would crowd around me and start squealing and jumping in a circle. And Cassius…for some strange reason, I couldn't possibly imagine what his reaction would be. Would he wrap his arms around me? Would he kiss me?

I had yearned to feel his warmth for so many months, aching and empty with the distance between us. I wanted to feel his heart beating underneath his skin, the tickle of his hair on my neck, and the warmth of his cheek pressed against mine. I wanted so badly it hurt, to taste him again, and for him to hold me tight and never let go. I wanted to hear the low timbre and gruffness of his voice, the intensity when he spoke passionately, and the gentle words that fell from his lips so freely.

I smiled, remembering a time he slept peacefully next to me. It was eleven o'clock and I couldn't muster the courage to wake him, even though everyone was already outside practicing. The dark circles under his eyes had grown more prominent, and I wanted to give him just a few more minutes of rest. When he awoke and pulled me to his chest drowsily, his voice was laced with sleepiness as he spoke.

But I couldn't keep daydreaming. I had a job to do. In a week's time, I would see him, and I would feel him. I just had to remain patient. Otherwise, I'd risk being caught.

Sadly, it wasn't impatience that would lead to me being caught, but my utter foolishness. One night around one o'clock, I was in the tent practicing, per Mr. Monte's instructions. I was becoming familiar with the tricks on the rope once again, but I couldn't seem to perfect my high kick.

I attempted the move at least twenty times, becoming more frustrated with every failure, and when I began to feel burned out, I made the stupid decision of pushing myself even harder. I was irritated by the tedious repetition, but I had to get this one move before I could rest.

I gently walked to the center of the tightrope and pliéd, carefully bending at the knees. While maintaining my balance, I lifted and pirouetted in small turns. I kicked my leg above my head and held it for a few seconds, but I erred by turning my foot parallel with the rope.

Suddenly it buckled, and I was falling.

I crashed into the landing net, not on my back as instructed, but on my side. This caused the landing net to bounce with more force than expected. I heard something creak and when I looked up, the lights strung across the platform, used to illuminate the structure, came loose and fell to the ground. The little bulbs crashed and filled the tent with the sound of shattering glass.

The loud crash aroused whispers in the night. I heard a few male voices in the distance which were too close to escape, and before I knew it, three men crashed through the tent in response to the disruption. I rolled off the net and searched for cover to hide behind, but it was too late.

Gus, Hugh, and Flint stared back at me with wide eyes, as though they'd seen a ghost.

"Juniper Rose…" Flint drew out my name like I was a myth.

"I can explain," I whispered, putting my hands out in front of me.

"Lord above!" Gus yelled into the night, his voice bouncing off the thin fabric of the tent.

I attempted to hush the boys, but they all rushed toward me and lifted me off the ground. And while I was worried other people might be on their way, I hugged them back. This is what I needed. Night after night, imagining the killer standing before me, and only having Charlotte by my side was driving me crazy. I needed my friends. I needed to be reminded that I wasn't as alone as I felt. I smiled contentedly and allowed them to squeeze me between them.

"How the hell are you here?" Hugh, the man with a shiny bald head and tattoos snaking over every inch of his body, shook me.

"I came back!" I exclaimed with a wave of my hands. I didn't even notice there were tears falling down my cheeks until Gus swiped his thumb across my skin. "I'm here to find the killer and end him, once and for all. And I'm here to see all of you." Saying those words made it real. I was back with my friends, and this was a glimpse of what it would feel like in a week's time.

Flint looked me up and down. "Have you been eating? You look small."

"Yes, I have, *Dad*." I snickered at his fatherly questioning, but admitted, "It's been a rough couple of months."

Gus chuckled before lowering his voice, a tender, gentle look overtaking his wide eyes. "You can say that again. It's been different without you here."

So, they did miss me as much as I missed them.

"Wait. Cassius…" Hugh turned to fetch Cassius before I gripped his arm and pulled him back.

Although the idea of seeing Cassius made my heart leap, I wanted to stick to the plan. "Please. You can't tell him." I shook my head nervously. "You can't tell anyone! This must remain a secret."

Flint shook his head, almost angrily. "Everyone will want to know! The circus has been going through hell without you here."

"I know. And I want to see everyone so badly, but please, don't tell anyone. I plan to surprise the crowd as well as the other performers at the masquerade ball. Can I trust you to keep this between us?" I looked at the three of them, watching their heads dip synchronously. "Thank you."

"I still can't believe you've kept this a secret! You're sneakier than I thought!" Hugh exclaimed.

"I've learned from the best." I wiggled my eyebrows and rubbed Hugh's head as though he were my older brother.

"We missed you, J." Flint smiled and his eyes warmed kindly.

I remembered a time when I sought comfort with Flint. He'd given me the passion to pursue what I loved and to work hard for what mattered. He showed me that my past didn't define me, and although things did not work out between us, I didn't feel awkward. He was family now and that's all he was ever meant to be.

"I missed you too. All of you." I wrapped them in a hug and slung my arms across their broad shoulders. Then, batting at them, I said, "Now get out of here. And keep those big mouths of yours shut."

"Yes ma'am," Gus said with a slight pep in his step.

The three of them saluted me on their way out, and I giggled. A weight had been lifted from my shoulders. I knew that everything would resume as it once had. Now, all I had to do was ensure that this performance, and my return, remained the biggest surprise of the year.

Chapter Thirteen

Before the circus departed for the city tomorrow, I continued my routine of practicing into the wee hours of the night. And in the moments I wasn't running through every scenario of what could go wrong, I was becoming familiar with the secret route in the train until I had it memorized—until I could get to any spot without being seen. This newfound knowledge led me to one specific place tonight—Gus's chambers.

Gus was one of two of the circus's magicians. Last year he gave me a reading of my future, and I was curious to see if he could do it again.

Later that evening, I wound my way through the secret walls behind the main passage of the train. When I came to his door, I peeked my head out of the boards concealing me to scour the halls, ensuring no one was lurking about. After crawling out of the tight space, I knocked three times on his door, and he invited me in with a devilish smile.

"I didn't expect to see you so soon, given your secret." He poured two cups of ale and took a seat on a plush red cushion that was surrounded by rugs of varying colors, one royal blue, another turmeric orange.

Sitting across from him, I eagerly took the brown mug full of ale. I sipped it slowly, becoming reacquainted with the bitter taste after months of abstaining from it.

"What can I do for you, Miss Rose?" he inquired, his features twisting in the candlelight that illuminated his room.

I took another heady gulp before setting my drink on the floor. "Last year I asked you what my outcome in the circus would be, and your reading held true to fate. I'd like you to do it again."

He immediately garnered his crystal ball and began circling his hands over the foggy glass in a rhythmic motion. "Ask away, love."

I didn't have to think long, due to the many restless nights I'd spent in Axminster, reflecting over my worries. Before meeting with Gus, I was prepared to ask about the killer, but he was the farthest thing from my mind. "The performance in Hewe…does everything go to plan?"

"Yes," he answered quickly, after a yellow fog enveloped the interior of the glass.

"All of my intentions," I paused at the curious glance Gus sent my way before continuing, "will they come to pass?"

His shoulders moved forward as though he had to plod through mud for the answer. "Yes, but not in the way you expect."

I leaned forward, intrigued. "What do you mean by that?"

Gus took his eyes off the orb briefly. "There will be obstacles is what I mean, Miss. Very big obstacles. Ones which may cause the circus to falter."

"How so?" I asked, worry etched into the crease between my brows.

"The road to success is one of mystery. It will be a hard endeavor, with many hinderances along the way. Some will encourage us, but some may try to knock us off the stage of fame."

I nodded along with him. His revelations were something I partly expected. Because of Mr. Young's power and position, my determination to stay in the circus would be anything but easy.

Regardless, I prodded even further. "But will I succeed?"

I didn't want to reveal my plan involving the killer until after the masquerade ball. Our performance held the sole purpose of drawing him out, and if anyone was aware of it beforehand, something may go awry.

"All I see is fog. That means it's up to you and whether you play your cards right. It's in your hands now."

Perfect. That was a lot of help.

It was in my hands now? What if I made the wrong move? Then would it be my fault if everything went to hell? There was so much pressure on my shoulders to bring the killer to an end, to right the wrongs he had inflicted upon the circus, and to extract myself from Axminster once and for all.

Gus seemed to sense my worry when he said, "Trust yourself and everything that is meant to be, will be."

I nodded my head in confirmation. "Thank you, Gus."

"Of course. I look forward to seeing your *intentions* come to fruition." He drew the word out, trying to convince me to spill my secrets.

But my secrets had to remain my own until the time was right.

"Sleep well, Juniper." He covered the crystal ball in a black fabric and tucked it away.

Taking one last swig of ale, I exited Gus's chamber. I didn't know if my visit to the magician made me any less uncertain, but I believed that if I thought through every possibility and planned accordingly, there was no way I could fail. But of course, there would always be inevitabilities I couldn't prepare for. As of now, I was looking to God to decide the fate of the circus.

Whether it was from Gus's magic or the looming days ahead of me, my dreams stirred me so shakingly that I awoke screaming, the sound echoing throughout the train.

Charlotte woke with a start beside me, her breathing hurried and frightened. Just as she reached out a hand to comfort me, a serious fear took root in her eyes, and before I knew what was happening, she was pulling me out of the sheets and dragging me into her closet. I wanted to push back—refuse to be shoved into yet another dark corner, but before I could do so, I heard footsteps resounding down the hall, coming closer and closer.

I placed a hand over my mouth to quiet my breathing when suddenly someone burst through the door.

"What's going on? Are you okay?" Cassius's low voice was laced with the roughness of sleep, leaving me to melt into the door that was separating me from him. If I could just touch him, just feel his warmth for one second, maybe he could ward off the demons warring in my mind for a little while.

"Yes, sorry." Charlotte stumbled through her words. "I just had a bad dream, is all. It's okay Cassius, go back to bed," she warned him, her voice shaking.

"I've never heard you scream like that before. What were you dreaming of?" His worry caused the pitch in his voice to rise.

The concern in his voice and the comfort in his words made me start to cry, but I muffled the sobs with my hands, hoping he wouldn't hear.

I knew the card Charlotte was going to play before she even spoke the words. She delayed for a moment, wondering how to convince Cassius that she was alright—that she wasn't hiding something from him. The answer was to open a wound common to them both.

"I was dreaming of the night Penelope passed. I haven't dreamt of her in over a year. I don't know what brought it back."

And that was enough to quiet Cassius.

I leaned in, pressing my ear to the door, eager to hear him speak again. And finally, he did.

"I dream of her too," he said, so quietly, so painfully.

I couldn't hear the words that followed between the two friends, but before I knew it, the door clicked shut and his footsteps receded. I let loose a sob, allowing the tears to flow freely down my cheeks. I cradled my knees into my chest and cried into them, grieving so many things— the pain and the trauma in Cassius's voice, the fact that I couldn't reach out for him when I needed him most, and possibly the fact that I was keeping my being here a secret. He sounded so different moments ago…so lonely, and I couldn't help but think that he would want to reach out to me, if he knew I was here. I was a liar. And I was a ghost.

The door creaked quietly as Charlotte opened it. "You can come out now," she said softly, and her voice broke with tiredness.

I stepped out of the confines of the closet and crawled onto her bed as Charlotte slid in next to me. I couldn't imagine what lying to Cassius must have done to Charlotte. They must have dreamt often about the night Penelope died, but it felt wrong to use that against him to hide me.

My voice was hoarse when I said, "I'm sorry you had to do that."

"It's okay, Juniper. Let's get some sleep," she said, sounding ashamed.

And that was that.

It felt as though I'd gotten a blink of rest before Charlotte woke me with her scurrying, and I remembered that the performers were going into Hewe today. I'd been there only weeks ago, visiting Gisèle, but it felt like yesterday that she'd given me the clue about the circus performing at her masquerade ball.

I was ready all the same—ready to show the crowd that I had returned, ready to show my friends that I had come back for them, and ready to show the killer that I wasn't so easy to get rid of. It would be one hell of a night.

In the days that followed, while the circus busied themselves at the Janvier Estate, I practiced my routine, which I was sickeningly nervous about. My face would be surprise enough, so I was going to perform something easy, since I'd only been walking the rope for a few weeks.

Despite becoming comfortable with my routine in the past few days, I was fraught with worry that the circus would return from the city and discover my presence.

Just one more day and I could come clean.

The night of the performance...

The walls of the estate were a luxurious cream, spotted with sparkling onyx. The floor was smooth marble with a textile formation, and the ornate furniture was lavish beyond compare. Plush velvet sofas with adjacent ottomans, the most expensive pottery imported from across the sea, and dark oak tables set with expensive silk place settings.

The estate was rich and vibrant—one that fit the station I was born into, but one I no longer identified with. The decorations, the clothing, the money—none of it attracted me. Because beyond the walls of the estate, there was a lonesome train with creaky floorboards and thin wooden walls, but one that gave me purpose. *That* was home.

But we had a job to do, so tonight we would play the part. We'd dress in the finest gowns and tuxedos and put on a show, hoping people would see us for something more. That was our intention, after all—to peak the attention of others and raise questions. Who were we? What did we offer? What did we represent? And what could we and the rest of humanity, for that matter, become? That was our purpose—to encourage people to open their minds and strive to be something greater—to be a *part* of something greater.

A section of the estate had been transformed into a dressing room of sorts.

Women pulled on layer after layer, stretching tight stockings up their legs before fastening expensive heels—the first things to be donned simply because it was impossible to get anything else on after fastening the corset. Next came the decency skirt, which was essentially a slim petticoat, and following that a chemise for the upper body. After the basic pieces were positioned, the women moved onto creating their silhouette. A corset was used to slim the waist, a crinoline to round out the skirt in the form of a hoop, and finally the bustle to emphasize the rear of the dress.

Of course, the men's job was always easier. They pulled on their undergarments before the designated trousers, shirt, and collar, over which would be a vest and a coat with pressed lapels. Following that was the waistcoat and shiny black patent leather shoes. The last items for the wealthy were a bow tie and a top hat.

And finally, the mask.

The performers dressed in common masquerade ball fashion, categorized by a vast array of colors like rich turquoise, magenta, wildflower yellow, and sunset orange.

True to form, Juniper Rose altered this agenda by wearing the most extravagant piece of the night, fitted in gold petals, a plated bodice, diamond studded gloves, and glittering jewelry around her neck and arms.

But they all had one thing in common. Valetta, the circus's fashion designer, made it possible for the women to tear the front of their gowns open without ripping the seams, leaving them to perform in corsets and light hoop skirts, while the men only had to strip themselves of their overcoats to perform comfortably.

As the wealthy guests arrived, the performers slowly filed their way into the back of the ball room, none the wiser of which class they belonged to.

Mr. Monte knocked softly on my door at a quarter to nine. Shutting it behind him quickly, I made sure no one saw him enter. I was all dressed, ready from head to toe. I may have gotten ready two hours earlier than I should have out of nervousness. My ensemble had not lost its luster, especially with the diamond gloves snaking just past my wrists and the sparkling jewelry on my neck.

"My, my, Juniper. I can practically read the headlines in tomorrow's paper. 'The Flower of the Circus Reborn.'" Mr. Monte splayed his hands in front of him, as though he was reading from the very pages.

I giggled at his word choice. Mr. Monte always had a flare for the dramatic. But I did have to agree with him this time. "Thank you, Sir," was all I answered with.

"What did I say about calling me sir?" Mr. Monte pointed an accusatory finger at me.

I lifted my hands in surrender. "My apologies."

"I see your extensive word choice has returned. You've spent too much time away, my girl." He nicked me on the chin.

Really? Had I returned to speaking like a proper woman so soon? I hadn't realized the effects wealthy life had on me—the diction and the vocabulary one could so easily pick up.

"No worries, we'll whip you into shape soon enough," he said, with a deep-throated laugh, before turning to me seriously. "Are you ready?"

Was I? Was I prepared to reenter the world of the circus with everyone questioning which social class I belonged to? Was I ready to battle the storm that was Cassius? Was I ready to find the killer and put him to an end?

Despite my fears, I answered without a second thought, "Yes."

"Good. You know the plan. Enter at ten o'clock. That'll be right in the middle of tonight's events." It seemed he was about to continue his rant before he paused. "I've told you a thousand times before, but you know what to do." He kissed me on the cheek before exiting the room.

I stood there in awe while my hands shook at my side. I had one hour to prepare myself, to calm the nerves making my stomach turn over and over. One hour.

And before I knew it, the time had passed. I positioned the golden mask over my eyes and took a deep breath before pulling open the door of my dressing room. Everyone was already in the ballroom, so, I had a clean exit. I ventured down the hall and up the flight of stairs to my right, heaving my dress up so as not to trip on it.

First door on the left, my subconscious whispered to me. When I pulled open the door, I witnessed Gisèle seated next to her husband, yet I remained near the wall so as not to be seen by the crowd too soon.

When I poked her shoulder, she looked up at me calmy, trying to remain composed in front of her guests, but then she rose from her seat and took my hand in her own. We stepped toward the front of the balcony, in plain sight now. She cleared her throat and raised her hand to silence her guests, as if she were a queen. She might as well have been. She looked gorgeous in her white gown embedded with pearls. The crowd went immediately silent, showing just how much power she had.

"Dear friends, thank you all for coming tonight!" she began, her voice echoing throughout the colosseum-like room.

The audience began to whisper in hushed voices, no doubt about the mystery woman at Gisèle's side.

"I want to welcome a dear friend of mine, someone who has taken part in many activities around the kingdoms that most would call..." she paused, smiling at the crowd below, before exclaiming, "revolutionary. Since the theme of our evening tonight is secrecy, I won't bore you with her name, but she has come a long way, so I want all of you to welcome her warmly."

All at once, people began to clap modestly, unlike the rowdy cheering I was used to. Nonetheless, I waved politely and picked up my dress to descend the stairs connecting the balcony to the floor below. A man wearing silk white gloves stood at the bottom, waiting for me with an outstretched hand. I gently trailed my hand down the railing, hoping that I wouldn't embarrass myself by tripping, and after what seemed like an eternity with hundreds of eyes on me, I made it to the dance floor.

The man with the white gloves took my hand and led me toward the center of the room. I searched the crowd, trying not to appear too eager as I searched for anyone I might recognize. Where were Josephine's drooping earlobes? Where was little Olive? Where was Hugh's bald head? There were too many people, and I couldn't seem to find any of my friends, not like they would recognize me anyway.

I was handed off to another man wearing a black mask that covered the right side of his face. Suddenly, he swept me into a rather brisk dance. It took me a moment to recognize the steps, but soon enough, I remembered the rhythm. I danced with countless people, suddenly forgetting my nerves and the surprise performance to come. I swung round and round, and before I knew it, the man in front of me disappeared and was replaced by another, his bald head glowing under the gargantuan chandelier above.

Hugh.

"Everything going alright, Miss?" he asked, taking my hand and spinning me out lavishly. His dance moves were impeccable. If I didn't know him, I would have guessed he was a noble, taught to dance at a very young age. Mr. Monte had done well in teaching them the ways of the wealthy.

"Yes, Hugh. Everything is just fine," I answered in a whisper, surveying the area around me to ensure everyone was preoccupied.

His breathing was labored, and his head glistened with sweat as his toes jumped lightly to the music. "Good. I don't know what Mr. Monte is planning, but I know you're a part of it. It's almost time." He quickly spun me out once more before gently yelling, "Charlotte!"

And then I was in Charlotte's arms, and we were kicking our legs to the tedious repetition of high-pitched violins.

"Hello there." She smiled under a white bedazzled mask.

It felt as though I was being traded off between members of the circus. "What's going on here?" I quietly asked.

"Mr. Monte wanted to make sure you were ready. Think of us as his messengers." She hiccupped and giggled, no doubt because of the champagne in her system.

"Then you can tell him I'm more than ready. Let's get this show on the road."

"Right away." She saluted me with her petite hand before signaling for someone behind me.

As the song ended and a slower tune began, Flint had his arms around my waist. It felt strange, our bodies pressed so closely together. There were no words exchanged this time, just silence. Amidst the chaos of the night, this time to relax and reset was exactly what I needed.

Flint softly whispered in my ear, "The boys and I spoke about what your intentions might be after we found you in the tent, but we can't seem to figure it out. No matter, I trust you."

After the soft words fell off his tongue, the lights went out. Every single candle was whisked away, as if by Gus's magic, and the room went dark.

The crowd screamed.

I began to panic, thinking this could be some trick of the killer, although, that was illogical. He had no idea I was here. No one did. Before I could lose my head too quickly, one light flickered in the center of the room. It glowed like a pulsing orb around the face of a boy with charcoal locks and honey eyes. He wore a bloodred mask, golden irises glowing behind it. The mask only covered the left side of his face, leaving a strong jaw, light stubble, and unruly hair in plain view.

Cassius.

"I want to take you to a time when all was lost." His voice echoed smoothly through the room like silk.

He passed right in front of me without taking a second glance. I wanted to scream, *I'm right here*, but I was too entranced in his words and the sound of his voice.

He took slow steps forward until the crowd circled around him. "Young children were scorned for turning to the circus when they were cold, hungry, and helpless. It was a ludicrous idea in the eyes of many, to seek help from *a freak show*," he spit out the words nastily, just as the wealthy had. "But that train riding through the night, blaring its horn, saved their lives—our lives. And in the years to come, despite the disagreements and the profanity thrown our way, we came to realize that *you* saved us. No matter your opinion on our establishment, it's clear you enjoy watching us." Cassius's voice dipped even lower, the flame catching the color of his clothes.

He wore a black waist coat, and underneath was a scarlet red vest, its pocket filled with a cream handkerchief. Around his neck laid a similar cream cravat that was tucked delicately into his shirt. He looked absolutely charming.

While the room was covered in darkness, Gisèle's staff began to quietly usher in our equipment, the most important things being the tightrope and the net that would catch me. It was a rushed moment, in which the staff only had a few minutes to tie it up without anyone noticing.

Cassius had almost made it to the back of the room, but the crowd hadn't noticed because they were so intrigued by his speech. His tan skin glistened in the candlelight and his eyes gleamed as he looked at every guest, one by one. "So, tonight is a celebration of growth and the death of those dark days. Here is to the future. Here is to a new world." He dipped his head to reveal his dark, dangerous eyes from underneath his top hat. "Welcome to the show…"

Without notice, blaring lights turned on and people shielded their eyes.

The women took the front of their dresses and ripped them open, sending them into heaps on the floor, while the men threw off their coats. It was as if they were stripping off the opinions of the wealthy— disregarding the shame and becoming alight with confidence.

The music began and Cassius threw off his top hat and backed through the crowd with a smile. Running to join his fellow performers in the center of the room, all of them, no matter their specialty, performed a dance—one I'm sure they'd practiced a million times. It was a jig filled with popping shoulders, kicks, and a moment where half the performers would sink to the ground while the other half raised up. It was not lyrical or contemporary, but broken and harsh. It was technical, edgy, like nothing they'd ever done before.

I watched Cassius bend and rise with the other performers, feeling whole as I saw the concentration spread across his face.

Mr. Monte was smart. This was the first performance of the year, but it was also the first time the circus was ever seen dancing as one unit.

It was unifying.

I watched for a while as they danced together before breaking off into sections, the dancers continuing to dance, the cyclists flying between guests, and the flamethrowers grabbing their torches and throwing balls of fire into their mouths. And finally, when everyone had been in the spotlight and the show was reaching its end, I had an idea. Mr. Monte and I had practiced one routine, but in this moment, I knew I had to do something different. He would surely kill me later, but what was the circus without a bit of surprise? That's what this whole night was about, after all.

I curved my way along the back of the room before I found a man leaning against the wall where he controlled the lights.

"Turn off the lights." I must have sounded crazy, running up to him at random and shouting orders at him.

"I have special instructions. Now get lost." He waved me off disturbingly.

I didn't have time for this. The circus was finishing up their last routine, and the surprise would be ruined.

That spurred me to quickly lift my mask. The man's jaw fell to the floor, his eyes bugging out of his head.

"You recognize me?"

His jaw remained opened, so, I took that as a yes.

"Now turn off the lights."

He did so without being asked again.

The room was bathed in darkness, the crowd gasping in surprise once again, including the members of the circus. Not even the performers had prepared for this. The man managing the lights seemed to know what I was thinking, because he handed me a candlestick and lit it instantly.

I turned around and slowly stalked into the room, my face illuminated in a yellow glow. The metal pieces of my dress clicked on the tile, creating a mysterious beat as Gisèle's special guest had come to say hello.

"I want to tell a similar story," I whispered to the crowd. "A story of a girl who was betrayed by her own family. A girl who was forced to leave behind a life she loved simply because society thought it appropriate." I took step after step, coming closer and closer to my family in the center of the room. "Tonight, as you join us in the festivities, I want you to reconsider what is right. Is it leaving those who are in need of help to fend for themselves? Or is it putting the needs of others before your own?" My voice broke and my breathing hitched. This was all coming off the top of my head, but it needed to be said. "I welcome you to join the freak show, but I warn you…if you've come to destroy the life we've created, then you are greatly mistaken because I'm a prime example of what happens when you try to destroy something that has a strong foundation. It doesn't break." I paused, allowing the audience to mull it over. "In fact, it only gets stronger."

The man in the corner of the room turned on the lights once again, as I had instructed. Slowly, I pulled on the bow that held my mask in place and let it fall to the floor, my hair unraveling and falling over my shoulders.

The crowd gasped, some whispering curiously about what this could mean, and others erupting in cheers. I smiled as the crowd hushed.

"You didn't think I'd be that easy to get rid of now, did you?" I smirked.

Looking up to the balcony, I found Gisèle smiling in approval and chatting with her husband.

"What was the word I used again?" Gisèle quietly asked her husband.

"I believe you used the word 'revolutionary,'" her husband answered with a smile.

I grabbed onto my dress and ripped it down the middle, leaving me in a bedazzled golden two-piece leotard. I kicked off my shoes but left the glittering lace gloves. Above my head, a ring slowly descended from the ceiling. When it reached the ground, I grabbed the rope it was tethered to and used the weight of my body to spin the ring around me. As I pulled it tight, the ring circled faster and faster until it gained enough speed and began to ascend. I kept my hold tight on the rope and my body straight as I climbed toward the ceiling, the ring still spinning in circles around me.

Using the strength in my arms to lift my legs over my head, I performed a few quick spins and curled an ankle around the rope to secure myself. With my head angled to the floor and my feet in the air, I hooked my opposite, free leg across my knee, and was able to take my arms off the rope and open them wide toward the audience below, earning a few audible gasps. I gently sank into a seated position in the ring before twisting my hips quickly and bending my torso over it. Looking down at the audience as the ring began to lower once again, I moved my arms in a rhythmic motion, inviting them in. And just as the audience became entranced with my invitation, I dropped off the ring and onto the tightrope.

Unaware the tightrope was there until I landed on it in perfect balance, the audience erupted in applause. I performed my usual pirouettes and kicks, curling my toes around the rope and keeping my core tight as I'd been taught. Once I reached the other end, I extended my hands above my head and bowed to the crowd. And as I did this, the rope jerked, and I flipped right off it. The crowd gasped in worry, though this was purposeful, of course. I landed on the netting below, the crowd sighing in relief once they realized I was safe.

Rolling off the net, I flicked my head toward Gus. I don't know if it was due to his intellectual powers, but he knew exactly what I meant.

He nudged the other performers, and they began the dance again, their shoulders pressed against one another. As the music picked up its speed, they became jerkier with their movements. I made my way to the middle of the group, and they dropped to their knees and bowed their heads as the music started to fade. I rested an elbow on one of their backs so that my face was the only one to be seen among the group of kneeling performers. Finally, the entire group paused as the last chord was struck.

The room drowned in the sound of applause.

There it was.

The overwhelming feeling of gratification and praise that I missed—that raucous cheering that replaced their normal composure. I smiled, my chest pumping up and down with fatigue.

Gisèle stood on the balcony, everyone's attention drifting to her. "The circus...we welcome you. Congratulations on your return, Juniper Rose."

Once again, the crowd was bellowing their approval, and all we could do was smile and wave. Once we let go of our last position, time seemed to stop. The performers threw their arms around me—Flint, Hugh, Gus, Charlotte, Josephine, Evelyn, the weird twins, and even little Olive and Piper. Tears streamed from my eyes. It was such a relief to see my family again—to be welcomed with open arms. I'd missed them so much.

This was where I belonged.

But as the performers drifted by to welcome me, I knew there was someone missing. Where was Cassius? After all this time missing him, where was he now? I'd hoped he would run to me, pick me up, and kiss me as though no time had passed—as though nothing had changed.

But as I scanned the performers, I couldn't find his face among the crowd. I would have to find him later. We would have time to catch up then, but for right now we had to make our exit. We picked up our dresses and coats, leaving the wealthy to enjoy the remainder of their night. News would be breaking in the morning with pictures and stories of the night's events.

The killer would return in no time.

We all raced out of the estate, the shadow of the train looming in the distance. In the heat of summer, we ran in our little underthings, warmth rushing over our skin. We took the back route, avoiding the city and instead snaking through the forest. The air smelled sweet, no doubt from the restaurants and bakeries in the city, the ground felt sturdy beneath me for the first time, and there was a rush of electricity running through my veins.

I hooped and hollered with my friends, racing through the darkness toward home.

Chapter Fourteen

Cassius...

Icouldn't describe the feeling that coursed through me when the lights turned on and I saw her face. I recognized her voice the moment she spoke, but she couldn't be here, standing just feet away from me.

But there she was, as beautiful as ever. I watched her walk the rope in utter disbelief, and when her routine ended and we danced the finale, I couldn't even register what I was doing. Why was she here? She had a deal with Mr. Young to keep the circus safe by marrying his son. And surely, she wouldn't jeopardize our survival just because she missed us.

No, she was here for a *reason*.

But that still didn't shake the flutter in my stomach—how my heart dropped. Her eyes were the purest green behind the golden mask, and her coarse black hair was curled tightly at the nape of her neck. Her face was glowing, and when she smiled, a small dimple formed in her cheeks. I wanted to wrap my arms around her body and keep her safe like I used to and kiss her until every thought was wiped away.

I'd laid awake most nights while she was gone, wondering so many things. Was she taken care of? Was she loved? Or worse, was she *in* love? I'd convinced myself she was, but maybe this was her coming back for me.

But part of me didn't want a single thing to do with her. A terrified, unforgiving part of me wanted to never speak to her again. Because even though she was back, I couldn't trust her. She left once and she would do it again. And the least she could do was warn us, but of course, she had to come in here and make a statement.

She looked damn good doing it, my subconscious whispered to me.

I physically shook my head to rid myself of the thought. Yes, I missed her, but it was more than that. I breathed for her. And in the months she was gone, I suffocated.

I wanted her to fight for us. We could have made it through, despite the weight of Mr. Young's threat. But she had to leave and escape to the only life she knew.

Still the question remained. How could I separate my desire to be close to her and my need to safeguard my heart? I'd been abandoned too many times, and I wouldn't put myself in that position again. In the months she was gone, I vowed to do one thing: to forget. To shut it off. It was easier that way.

The walls of the train were just as I remembered them. Sneaking about and hiding in Charlotte's room had helped me adapt somewhat, but there was something different about walking through the halls. Listening to the floorboards creak and watching the light cast shadows upon the walls made it real. The compactness of the halls made me feel safe and comforted, and the dimness gave room for privacy.

But I wasn't granted enough time to reminisce because the performers pushed me straight to the dining car where mugs of ale were filled to the brink.

Wilman handed me a cup with ale sloshing over the sides, making my hands sticky. "Good ta see ya plan worked out, Miss Rose." He spoke with a clipped accent—one I'd never stop missing.

I bowed my head at him and downed a hefty gulp, the ale sliding down my throat smoothly. Finally, the members of the circus pulled me to sit in the middle of the room as they surrounded me.

"Juniper! How are you here?" Evelyn asked, astounded.

They hadn't given me a chance to breathe, but I answered easily, grateful to let all my secrets out. I told them everything, starting at my terrible journey home. "After moping around for a few months, I mustered the courage to find my way back. But it didn't come without a cost," I paused regretfully. "I can't stay forever."

Many of them gasped.

Charlotte spoke up, not having been told this news, "I've been harboring you in my room in secret and you forgot to mention this little detail?"

Shrinking into my seat to avoid her lethal stare, I said, "With the performance coming up and everything going on, I didn't want to worry you."

Her irritation seemed to settle slightly, and I continued my story, "I made a deal with Mr. Young. He recently became an investigator in The Axminster Guard and, in keeping with his promise of protecting the circus's future, I asked him to hunt down the killer."

As debate began over this, I couldn't help my mind wandering. I looked beyond my friends, searching for the one person I couldn't stop thinking about. Where was Cassius?

I turned around and there he was, sitting on a bar stool in the back, his eyes already glazed over. My heart began to race when his eyes met mine, but there was no emotion on his face. Nothing.

I averted my eyes and tried not to think about it as I continued with my story. "I found some evidence, but not enough, so he allowed me to come back," I paused, preparing for everyone's reaction, "to draw out the killer. Newspapers will publish my return to the circus tomorrow, which will prompt the killer to resurface."

The room became angry then with people flying out of their chairs.

"Are you crazy? He'll kill you!" Flint yelled, throwing his hands in the air, his previous elation gone in the blink of an eye.

"Flint, please." I held up my hand to calm him before the others began to agree.

"No, he's right! You can't put yourself in danger just to find this menace!" Olive shouted, her small voice ringing throughout the room.

"I can and I will!" I rose from my seat abruptly, silencing the room. Everyone looked at me pleadingly, desperate to understand why I would do such a thing. "Listen to me." I eyed all of them closely. "I've been plagued by that man for the past year, and you've been plagued by him for the past *six*. We cannot sit around and *hope* he is gone." I pointed outside the train, as if I could reach all the way to Axminster. "Mr. Young is not our enemy. The killer is. And if we don't stop him, he'll inflict far more damage than Mr. Young ever could."

The room was silent.

I nodded my head in finality, calming my voice. "That's why I've returned. And after we capture the killer and bring him to justice, I must return to Axminster…unless I can figure out a way to stay permanently."

The room took a breath all at once.

Gus rose out of his seat, extending his glass into the air. "Then we find a way."

I smiled, waiting for Cassius to agree, but he remained in the back, shifting awkwardly in his seat with a brooding look on his face. But this wasn't just about being reunited with Cassius. It was about being reunited with family.

So, I lifted my glass with Gus and agreed, "We find a way."

The circus pulled no stops in celebrating my return. Three cases of ale were drained while the lot of us danced around the room, the merry band in the corner never growing tired. I couldn't say the same for myself. My feet were aching, and my stomach grumbled. I went to the bar in search of something and found Wilman serving cheese, fruit, and peanuts. I sat down and began filling my mouth, sighing with pleasure.

"Hungry much?" Wilman eyed me with a smile, continuing to fill mugs of ale.

I think I spotted Hugh refilling his drink four times while I was speaking to Wilman.

"You have no idea," I sighed. "I haven't danced that hard in months."

"Betta' get used to it. Nobody'll stop dancing now that you've returned." He nodded seriously at me, which made me giggle.

I tried to count the number of drinks I had. I think it was three. Maybe four. I couldn't remember at this point. I found it hard to focus my eyes on the blurry, spinning room. While watching the many bodies twirl around and around, I spotted Flint holding on to Charlotte, his arms draped down her spine and her hands linked across his neck. By the way he leaned into her, and she let her head fall back to laugh with him, it looked as though something deeper than friendship had sprouted while I was gone. That made my smile dwindle. Not because I was angry with them. I liked the idea of them together. They were perfect for each other, both playful and charismatic. But it disheartened me because here I was, sitting alone, when I should be with Cassius. I needed to speak with him.

Noticing me gaze around the room, Olive jumped onto the stool next to me. It reminded me of one of my first nights on the train, when she pointed out every performer and their skill. It was when I was first introduced to the heart of the circus.

And here she was again, my little savior.

"I saw Cassius sneak out back," she whispered, tucking her mouth behind her hand.

I pecked her on her soft cheek before sidling out of my seat. "Thank you."

I pushed through the crowd of sweaty bodies before emerging in an empty train car, finally able to take a breath without the scent of alcohol or sweat clogging my senses. It also gave me time to think. What would I say to Cassius? What would *he* say to me? I wasn't Gus. I had no way to forecast the future, but I knew one thing. I missed Cassius…so much that my heart ached without him close to me. And I knew he missed me too.

With that, I pushed the lever on the train car to lower the ramp. Running down it, I strained my eyes against the night while looking for Cassius, but I couldn't find any sign of him. Walking down the side of the train, I came up empty handed. I thought harder. On a stressful night, Cassius wouldn't be taking a measly stroll. He'd go to the animals, where he always found comfort. Why hadn't I thought of that before?

I turned away from the train and found the largest tent in the sea of red and white fabric. The lights were on inside, the soft yellow flickering from underneath the tent, but someone was yelling inside, deep grunts echoing on the wind. Before I had time to think, I pushed open the flaps and walked inside, but what stood before me was not what I expected.

Cassius. Shirtless.

There was a white bag of grain hanging from the wall that he was punching, over and over. For a moment I was speechless as I watched him. It was terrifying, how hard his fists connected with the bag, and I thought the fabric might split. But it was also beautiful…he was beautiful. His jaw was clenched, his cheeks puffed with anger, his torso twisted to accent his rigid abdomen, his biceps toned and strong as he struck the bag with precision, and his hair was wet with sweat, dripping on his forehead. When I managed to tear my eyes away from his striking body, I was baffled. What on earth was he doing?

"Cassius!" I yelled, hoping he would hear me over the sound of his own grunting.

His head flipped toward me immediately. With his chest heaving up and down, I could see every muscle in his planed chest. That's what attracted me to Cassius in the beginning. He wasn't put together in a fine waistcoat and gloves, working in an office. He was a man, kissed by the sun, with hard muscles as proof of his labor.

Peeling my gaze from his torso and the strong lines dipping below his breeches, I looked up to meet his eyes, which flicked between mine in surprise.

I had a silly thought of him running to me and scooping me in his arms, but his feet were planted in the sand, and I realized how stupid that fantasy was.

"What are you doing?" I asked, avoiding what was really on my mind.

Cassius took a deep breath and grabbed the swinging bag to steady it. "What does it look like I'm doing?" he asked with a hint of annoyance.

"It looks like you're punching a bag. I want to know why," I demanded. I'd learned not to tolerate his demeaning tone after months of letting him push me around.

He sighed and turned away to push the hair out of his face. "Mr. Monte heard of fighting clubs in the cities where men warm up with punching bags. It helps relieve my anger." He didn't look at me once as he said this, and he continued to punch the bag as though I wasn't even there.

"And what's got you so angry?" I stepped closer, wanting him to turn around and look me in the eyes.

Instead, he steadied the bag once again and stalked to the back of the tent where the many cages of animals were located. "It's none of your concern."

I couldn't help the irritation pulsing through me as I exclaimed, "It has always been my concern!" What was the purpose of being together if it wasn't?

"If it had been your concern, you wouldn't have left." He didn't say this angrily, but with such laconic disinterest. And that collected tone worried me more than him screaming at me. I could handle his anger and ferocity because it meant he cared. But this cool, unfaltering persona scared me more than anything.

I continued to walk to him, becoming angrier with each step. "You *know* why I left."

"Do I?" Finally, he turned around, his eyes piercing. "How do I know you didn't agree to return to Axminster because you missed your pampered life? Or that you didn't leave to marry Joseph Young, the *richest* bachelor on the list, huh? How do I know what's true?" He pointed an accusatory finger at me.

"Because you know *me*!" I shouted, tears forming in my eyes.

I realized then that Cassius hadn't changed one bit, and I had killed myself for months imagining he'd be different. I thought maybe he'd learned from his mistakes, that he trusted me and understood me. But he was the same boy I met the first night I arrived here—careless, judgmental, and cruel.

"I don't think I do." He shook his head.

Those five words broke something inside me—something that may have already been broken long before I came to the circus. I had spent years trying to fix this suffocating fear of not ever being good enough, and here it was again. I drew in a quick breath, trying to stop the burning in the back of my throat.

"So, you think, after finally finding myself in the circus, after finding *you*, I left because I missed my money? Because I loved Joseph?"

The words sounded preposterous coming out of my mouth.

"Yes, I do," he said, so cold and uncaring. "I told you when we first met. You're from Axminster. Nothing's going to change that."

Despite the nausea roiling in my gut, I laughed. I actually laughed. This would never end, him condemning me. I thought he'd moved past this. I thought he'd accepted me for who I was and who I wanted to be. But I was wrong.

And then I thought of the countless nights we'd spent together. How tightly we held onto one another in the darkness and how we trusted one another. Despite the tender moments we shared, I couldn't move backwards.

"I will not allow you to continuously make me feel worthless," I finally had the courage to say.

Cassius just stood there, like he didn't truly see me. I didn't know where his resistance was coming from, but I wouldn't be caught in the crossfire while he figured it out.

I stormed out of the tent, feeling like a child for expecting anything grand from him. The real world could never match the designs in my head—of him running to me, his smile the moment he saw me, and the passion in his kiss. That wasn't real. Cassius wasn't romantic or even kind, and I was a fool for expecting him to be.

"Juniper!" Mr. Monte shouted, his head poking out from the train. "You've had enough time to dilly dally. We need to talk business!" He waved me over emphatically.

I agreed while my heart broke into a million pieces. I tried not to cry as I walked toward Mr. Monte. I needed Cassius's warmth and his reassurance because without it, I felt hopeless. I didn't feel like a star. I just felt empty.

But I convinced myself that speaking with Mr. Monte would be a good distraction. We found our way into his cabin and taking a seat at the dark oak desk, I snatched the ale out of his hand, tilted my head back, and took a gulp. My sadness had quickly turned to anger, so fierce that I needed something to wash it down before I erupted.

Cassius was a selfish bastard, only keen on protecting himself.

Mr. Monte watched my throat bob with his eyebrows raised. "I'm guessing you had a chat with the lion tamer."

I scrunched my nose at the thought of him. "That I did."

"Would you like my advice?" he inquired.

I loved this about Mr. Monte. He was like the father I never had, but even more, he was like a friend. He offered to give advice when I needed it, simply listen, or rather distract me. Whatever I needed, it was my choice. "Thank you for the offer, but I think I want to hate him for a little while longer."

"Alright then." He chuckled and braced his hands on his desk, taking up a tone of seriousness. "I want to talk about the killer."

Mr. Monte jumped right into the conversation, but there was no point in avoiding it. This was why I had returned to the circus after all. Not to have fun, but to stop the menace that was plaguing our establishment. I had nothing more important to set my sights on, especially if Cassius wouldn't be vulnerable with me.

"Tomorrow, newspapers in every city will publish the story of your return, which is likely to prompt the killer to come back. Knowing he's someone within the circus, we must be on high alert for any new additions to our team."

I mulled over his words. Cassius assumed the killer was a performer in the circus last year because he was able to deliver messages right to my door, but what if we had jumped to conclusions?

"What if we were wrong? What if the killer isn't a performer in the circus, but has a man working for him, delivering his messages?"

Mr. Monte rubbed at the deep chocolate stubble growing on his chin. "It could be a possibility. Maybe he was too afraid of being discovered so he hired someone to work on the inside, while he prepared to strike during our performances."

He looked up at me worriedly and the bags under his eyes were the shade of plum and turquoise, something I could only attribute to stress. I was not the only one kept awake at night with thoughts of the future.

"It's smart to keep both options in our arsenal."

I nodded fervently along with him.

"Mr. Young discovered that Katriane is a Beringer, which means she could be related to Monroe. I've already contacted him but haven't gotten a reply."

I nodded, half expecting this, however, I continued to walk through the information. "Katriane Beringer allegedly *mis-stepped* on October 24, roughly twenty years ago. The articles didn't provide much detail as to her demise, but I'm assuming there's more to the story than we know. I don't know if Katriane was directly related to Monroe, but it couldn't hurt to ask."

"I wouldn't know either. Monroe and I are like brothers, but he's never been comfortable talking about his past, especially not his family. He may know something, but he'll be reluctant to tell us," Mr. Monte said.

"Well, I hate to say it, but I don't care if he's uncomfortable sharing this information. It's critical we know what truly happened, and if he can help us solve this damned mystery, then by God, I will force it out of him."

My anger was getting the best of me, but what was I to do? Continue to ask nicely while the killer threatened me?

Mr. Monte laughed at my eagerness before standing to pace around the room. "I applaud you, Miss Rose, for being so vigilant, but your determination may work against you."

"How so?" I questioned.

Mr. Monte wrung his hands together. "Monroe has been gone for months, tending to his ill mother. She's suffering from smallpox."

I looked to the floor, embarrassed suddenly by my outburst. I had no idea what Monroe was going through. Smallpox was not a light sickness. It was deadly, especially with so few medical advancements. "How long?" I asked.

"About a week after you left, he received news. Disheartening to lose not one, but two untouchables in a month." Mr. Monte rubbed his temple. "He said she wasn't recovering well and that he may return soon, but I haven't heard from him in weeks."

I looked to my hands, trying to figure out what to do. I wanted to grant Monroe the time to mourn, but if our plan to attract the killer worked, there wouldn't be time to grieve. The killer had to be stopped before fire was set to the circus, and the fact saddened me, but I knew what had to be done. "This will be a difficult loss for him, but one that'll be made worse if the destruction of the circus is added to it. He needs to come back. Now."

"I couldn't agree more," Mr. Monte explained. "But how do we convince him? He's miles away, sickened by the impending loss of his mother. We can't take that away from him."

"We can and we will. It's selfish, but it's a move we must make to save what we've built. We'll write to him again and explain our discoveries. He might be more inclined to hasten his return if he understands his involvement in the situation."

Mr. Monte thought long and hard, trying to make the best decision for his friend and for the circus. He took a deep breath and a swig of his ale before saying, "I'll send a letter to him tonight. With the revenue we received from the masquerade ball, I'll have more than enough to expedite the delivery. It should reach him tomorrow, which hopefully grants us enough time for him to return before the killer does."

My blood pumped at the thought of the killer striking again. Last year, I had been paranoid by the thought of performing, knowing the killer would act with a crowd watching, and the same stress was now heightened tenfold since we planned to stop him. That led me to question, "How exactly do we plan to catch the killer?"

Mr. Monte smiled gently, sadly. "I don't know."

Chapter Fifteen

In the week following our first performance, many things ensued, the first being my thankfulness to Gisèle and her husband for hosting the event and continuously supporting the circus. I sent her a letter expressing my gratitude as well as my promise to keep her updated on the movements of the killer.

The second was my long overdue plan of becoming readjusted. I moved myself back into my old cabin, finding comfort in the soft sheets covering my twin sized bed. Moving to the clothes in my dresser, I found myself running my hands over the looseness of their fabrics, freer than the constrained corset, gloves, and heels I would normally wear. Every day since I came back to the circus, I questioned how I managed to survive those months in Axminster, feeling foreign to it all.

The third was a heightened anticipation of the killer. On cue, a day after my appearance at the masquerade ball, my return was announced in the papers. Taking no risks, we published a list of all our performances for this year, just in case the killer came from outside the circus and was unaware of our schedule. Things were progressing exactly as planned.

And the fourth was the prospect of becoming a true performer once again. I'd run through my routines on the tightrope, familiarizing myself with difficult turns and tricks, and the simplicity of regulating my breathing. After many tiresome days and sleepless nights, I regained the skill I'd lost in my time away. And I quickly became a true woman of the circus—wearing the thin, loose shifts many of the women wore in their time off. Oh, how I'd missed such lacy things.

After long hours of baking under the sun, helping other performers with menial tasks like feeding the animals, securing our equipment, and practicing routines, we crested the wee hours of the night to frolic with one another. Many nights were spent outside the train, enjoying the heat while it lasted, before the harsh months of winter came, although the approaching season didn't seem so daunting now. We made more money at the masquerade ball than we did in all of last year's performances, so this winter we wouldn't have to worry about having enough to eat or about staying warm. The difference between last year and this year was vast. The cold nights spent shivering under my thin sheets were not ideal, but they'd made the experience more memorable. The circus was a rugged place, only made for the strongest of people who were willing to get a little dirty and uncomfortable. For those reasons, it was raw and untouchable.

But I hadn't been cold in those winter months. Many nights Cassius and I had kept each other warm, and I remember nestling into him, forgetting I needed anything else.

Now, he was so close yet so far away, and I couldn't even remember how his warm hands felt around me, holding me to him. He was practically a ghost.

I shook my head, ridding myself of the thought. I had time—well, not much if our plan was to work, but I needed to allow Cassius the time to heal. I didn't understand why he was personally afflicted by my leaving, but it was up to him to come to terms with it. I wouldn't help him this time.

"Juniper, can you help me with this?" Charlotte yelled, making me jump.

I turned around, spotting her golden hair shining in the sunlight and her forehead soaked with sweat. She held a piece of the tent that had torn, while Evelyn attempted to mend it back together. The wind was brutal and unforgiving on the outskirts of Hewe, making it difficult for her to hold it in place long enough for Evelyn to sew it together.

I jogged over to Charlotte, helping her hold the two ends together while Evelyn sewed diligently. Evelyn was of a different generation, her hair greying and her voice impeccably soft. She was old to say the least. I didn't know how she was still walking if I was being completely honest, but the circus couldn't live without her. She was like my grandmother, from what I remembered of her. Soft, gentle, a bit bossy, and somewhat abusive to the men when they slipped up or said something foul, but for heaven's sake, the woman knew how to sew. Most might have thought, how does this woman fit in with the crazed, wild circus? But the reason was simple—she drank like a sailor.

"Thank you, dear," Evelyn said, out of breath.

"Anytime." I grazed her shoulder before turning toward my tent, wiping the sweat off my forehead.

Charlotte fell into step beside me, her hair blowing in the wind.

I glanced sidelong at her, finding a small smile pulling back her cheeks. "What's on your mind Charlotte?" I asked in a sing-song manner.

She whipped her head to me, appalled. "What do you mean?"

I stopped in my tracks and placed my hands on my hips. "You have that devilish smile. Tell me."

She sighed before another smile formed. "I saw you leave the train last night. Just wondering if you and Cassius hit it off." She practically squealed.

I hushed her quickly, unaware of who might be lurking about. It would be embarrassing if Cassius overheard me gossiping like a schoolgirl, still obsessed with him after how he treated me last week. I was saddened to let her down, but she had the wrong idea. "No, we did not. Quite the opposite actually." It irked me more than anything that I couldn't fix it. So, until I *could* do something, I just had to keep myself busy.

"Details! I need details!" Charlotte shouted.

Despite how sad the situation made me; I knew it would help to talk about it. Gossip wasn't as fun when our relationship was hanging on a thin line, but maybe Charlotte could offer some advice.

I huffed, pulling open the entrance to my tent. "Cassius believes I fled to Axminster with my family of my own free will, either because I missed my old life or because I truly loved Joseph."

She scoffed, "What a buffoon. I swear he doesn't know a good thing when he sees it."

I took my time dressing in my leotard as I explained everything. "He said nothing would change because of where I come from. I'm just another wealthy woman to him."

Charlotte grabbed my arm and turned me to look at her, despite my half-nakedness. Her eyes were bright and fierce as she said, "You know that's not true. After everything you did last year to become a part of our family, he knows it too. You are talented and you belong. You proved that to all of us and to him when you became the star tightrope walker."

Charlotte always knew how to make me feel better.

She continued, "Cassius is troubled. He has a hard time trusting people for fear of being abandoned, just like the rest of us. We've experienced it more than most. But you know that, and you stuck with him last year, even when he treated you like nothing more than the coin in your pocket." Charlotte frowned. "Just try and stick with him for a little while longer and allow me to do the rest. He'll come back."

I tried to smile, but it didn't reach my eyes. Cassius was stuck in his ways, and I didn't know if even Charlotte could change his mind, despite their closeness.

"Thank you, Charlotte." I squeezed her hand.

"Anytime, Doll." She winked.

Exiting the tent, she disappeared to perform her duties, which left me to perform mine. I glanced up at the tightrope, unsure of where to start. My mind was boggled with thoughts of my fate with Cassius, so much that I couldn't focus. And if I couldn't focus, my work would be for nothing. But my time in the circus had given me a sure solution to help sort out my thoughts—drinking.

The sun was already beginning to fall after a laborious day, and I was hungry. Walking the rope could wait until tomorrow. I changed into a turquoise silk dress and found a seat at the bar in the dining car.

"What can I get for ya?" Wilman inquired, his curly mustache lifting with the movement of his mouth.

"Do you have something stronger than ale?"

Wilman smiled, deep lines forming in his cheeks. "I saved just the thing for you." He reached under the bar and pulled out an expensive bottle of whiskey.

"You're a blessing." I quickly pecked him on the cheek before taking a sip of the fine alcohol, grimacing as it burned on the way down. I coughed, not used to the strength. "Oh, for Christ's sake!"

Wilman just laughed. "You'll get used to it."

Before I could respond, a group of flamethrowers came barging through the door, demanding a glass of ale. And after them came the dancers, followed by the magicians, the animal specialists, and finally Cassius. When he walked into the room with that cool swagger and confidence, he took up all the energy.

The dining car was filled to the brim with jolly laughter and haughty conversation.

Hugh waited at the bar, and when his patience ran out, he rushed up behind me and snatched the bottle from my hand. He went on and on about how Wilman was old and slow. Wilman, overhearing Hugh's accusation, proceeded to pour his drink even slower.

Hugh took a heady gulp before turning to me. "Wow, J, I didn't expect this from you." He laughed, downing the rest of the drink. I didn't mind. I wasn't going to drink it anyway. "Your little body would fall dead if you drank this." He poked my side, making me jump.

"Maybe that was the intention," I remarked, and hopped off the stool.

But as soon as I stood, Hugh began prodding at my ribs more and more. At first, I was throwing my head back laughing, begging him to stop, but then I grew angry. His large fingers were digging into my ribs so much that it hurt after a while, so I slapped the back of his bald head and pushed him off me, pointing an accusatory finger at him. "That is quite enough."

He held up his hands in defense, laughing with the men flanking his side.

I rolled my eyes and ignored them, finding a safe place to hide next to little Olive while she sipped on a Shirley Temple.

She turned her head to me with a fiery pout in her eyes. "Wilman tried to trick me into thinking this was a cocktail, but I'm smarter than that." She wrapped her arms around her waist in defeat, abandoning her drink completely.

I grabbed it and took a small sip. Feigning shock, I set it down quickly. "Whoo! That's strong!" I coughed a little, trying to be convincing.

"What do you mean?" She snatched it back, taking a large gulp and flicking her tongue around to identify the flavor.

"Olive, I think you've become so accustomed to alcohol that you can't define the taste anymore. It's definitely in there."

Her eyes widened to the size of golf balls. "You think?"

"Yes, I do." I nodded fervently. "You must be careful how much you drink, otherwise you'll be passed out like Evelyn over there." I flicked my chin to the woman across the room, snoring with her head in her arms. "But what a pleasure to know Wilman trusts you and has all this time. You're growing up, kid," I remarked, ruffling her hair.

"I'm already grown up, Juniper," she argued, shaking my hand off her head.

I just giggled before grabbing the girl and lifting her onto my hip, her eyes reaching mine. "As soon as you're too big to fit on my hip, then you're grown up." I bopped her on the nose before whisking her away toward the crowd in the center of the room. "Let's go dance, shall we?"

I was in the middle of dancing with Flint and Charlotte when Mr. Monte burst into the room with an excited smile on his face.

"Juniper!" he shouted.

Everyone paused their dancing to look at him, eager to know the reason for his enthusiasm.

"It's Monroe! He responded!" Mr. Monte shook the envelope between his fingers.

I rushed through the crowd while the performers began to throw out questions, but I didn't stop once to answer them. They would know soon enough.

Taking Mr. Monte's arm, I followed him into the hallway just outside the dining car. "What did he say?"

"Take a look."

Mr. Monte handed me the letter and I scanned through it quickly, my eyes roving over the lines. "He's returning?"

Mr. Monte nodded emphatically, in the way only a friend could. His excitement was almost tangible. "He'll be here tomorrow."

I let out a chuckle. "That's wonderful! With his help, we might figure out who the killer is."

"Precisely!" he exclaimed.

Suddenly, Josephine peeked her head out the door, with the other performers' heads stacked above hers. "Do you mind explaining what the hell is going on?"

Mr. Monte laughed. "Everyone, take a seat."

He finished explaining our plan for the killer, but after a moment of silence, a throng of questions ensued, which we answered to the best of our ability. Mr. Young's fellow officers would be arriving a week before the next performance, at which point we would explain their positions and how they would help us detain the killer. The rest of it would be left to the performers, who were instructed to act normal, or as normal as they could, so as not to give the killer any indication that we expected his presence.

It seemed many of the performers were following along with our plan—all except one.

"So, you just expect to wrangle the killer and let him threaten us until Young's officers find him?" Cassius asked, unconvinced, with a drawl in his voice and a glaze over his eyes. "How many will he hurt before Young's men can act? What if Young's men can't find him? The killer has been known to disappear without so much as a trace."

"We are trusting in the abilities of Mr. Young and his team," Mr. Monte responded dryly, obviously annoyed at Cassius's flippant drunkenness.

"Since when did we trust this guy, the same man that threatened our existence?" Cassius shouted, pushing out of his seat.

Mr. Young remained our enemy, but he had the power to help us, and if we were too angry at him to accept that help, then we were more stubborn than I thought. And, quite frankly, Cassius's constant belligerence and retaliation was getting on my nerves.

I pushed out of my seat and turned to face him. "Since he offered to help us stop this menace!"

Cassius shook his head and threw a pointed finger at me from across the room. "Don't even start with me. You're on his side. Do you have any actual knowledge of how trained his men are? Do you know if they're even capable of stopping the killer?" he asked in a condescending tone.

"They belong to The Axminster Guard, the most esteemed guard in our region; of course they have the ability to stop him!"

He tilted his head back as if he was about to start laughing. "Right. The Axminster Guard. How could I have forgotten? I expect nothing less than perfection from your hometown."

Every one of his words seemed to punch right through me.

"Cassius," Mr. Monte warned, like an angry father. "That's enough. Juniper has the most knowledge on this subject, and we need to listen to her. Not only did she help keep us afloat with regular donations, but she was the one who approached Mr. Young to investigate the killer's whereabouts!"

But Cassius went dead still. His pupils widened in surprise or fury, and by the way he clenched his fists at his side and shook his head, I knew it to be both. He asked, terrifyingly calm, "Do tell. What do you mean by regular donations?"

Mr. Monte surveyed the crowd nervously, then me, as if asking me to tell the story.

I looked at Charlotte and Flint for reassurance—anything to avoid Cassius's impending stare. "As all of you know, it was arranged that I would marry Joseph Young, and as is proper, a lady's family is expected to offer the groom's family a dowry for assuming the burden of the bride. Because I had returned to Axminster and left the ways of the circus behind, people began sending me money to help my family pay for the dowry."

Speaking about the traditions and proper life of Axminster embarrassed me. The concept was foreign, and most likely ridiculous to my friends. And it was ridiculous to me too, to be sold to a man of *my family's* choosing, not mine, and with a payment not of well wishes, but one meant to assuage the hindrance of taking on a bride. And a bride should never be a hindrance, or a burden, but a gift.

I swallowed the lump in my throat and finally met eyes with Cassius. "I never wanted to marry Joseph." My voice cracked, and I hated how weak I sounded. I hated even more the disdain that was still on Cassius's face. "And at the time I did what I could to avoid it, which was to send the money that was intended for my dowry to the circus instead. To help you."

I inhaled sharply, preparing for the onslaught that was sure to come from Cassius. And for the first time ever, I wanted to be anywhere else but here—somewhere I could crawl under the sheets and hide from the shame, the anger, and always being trapped by something that was out of my control. I didn't want my friends looking at me as they were now, so confused by the traditions I was expected to uphold. And the disgust on Cassius's face was more than I could bear.

Across the room, Cassius clicked his tongue, and without an ounce of kindness in his voice, he said, "What a pity."

Standing alone in front of everyone, I felt completely misunderstood—completely lost.

"It's shameful that your people throw away their money to secure a couple's position in society, but it's more than that. This is about a social dilemma, one that you have encouraged. It's a fight between classes—between the wealthy and the poor. Dowries have existed for centuries, and you want to know the difference in this instance?" He watched only me, as all the heads in the room turned to him.

"The difference is that the wealthy aren't only intent on seeing you married, they're intent on making a point. They want to prove to us, and to everyone else, that you belong to them—that the wealthy will never mix with the poor. The money for your dowry is just a bribe to keep you where you belong. Why can none of you see that?" he proclaimed with his hands, looking at the other performers around him.

The room was utterly silent while people began to ponder his statement. But what he said wasn't entirely true.

So, I planted my feet in the ground, trying to feel its firmness beneath me as I said, "There has been a separation between classes for a very long time, but not everyone is against the circus, Cassius. We saw that the night of the masquerade ball, and every time more wealthy men and women join the audience. We are slowly changing their minds, but it's a process that takes time."

I paused, trying to contain my frustration, but it didn't seem to work. If Cassius could lash out, then so could I. "Some people, even the wealthy, enjoy the show and enjoy the result of our hard work, which must be hard for you to understand." I hated fighting with him, but it was so easy.

The performers glanced between the two of us as though they were watching a film.

But Cassius stood his ground, looking only at me. "It is. It is hard for me to understand!"

Finally, he agreed with me for once.

"I wish you could have heard the things people said about us before you came prancing in here, looking to change everything!" Cassius looked around at his friends. "I think all of you remember! All the insults. What they called us. They don't accept us, and they never will."

And amid the anger that had erupted, a little voice spoke up. "Then what are we doing this for?" Olive asked.

My heart melted for her, and I tried to ease her mind as much as I could. "I'd like to think we're not doing this for the rest of the world, but for ourselves." I nodded to convince myself and the others around me. "This is something we love. And we're performing, not for the approval of others, but because we believe in something greater."

"No matter what we're fighting for, we are not a charity, Juniper!" Cassius declared, his hands itching at his sides.

It was the first time he'd said my name, but it didn't roll off his lips in the lovely way it used to. It was angry and irritated, making me feel small and insignificant.

"We don't need donations from those who feel *sorry* for us. We can survive just fine on our own." He paced closer to me, threateningly.

"How long are we going to just survive? When are we going to start living?" I reprimanded.

Cassius opened his mouth as if he was about to retaliate before Charlotte responded with, "She's right!" She grabbed Cassius's arm, urging him to take a breath and listen.

And he did.

I couldn't understand the connection they'd made while I was gone, or why he seemed to trust her more than me. It made me jealous that he fought against me every chance he got but would listen to her.

"We can survive on our own because that's what we've always done. We've been scraping by since the creation of the circus. It's time we had enough money to do more than survive. Don't you want that?" Charlotte asked him, a deep line of worry forming between her brows.

"If it's at the cost of trusting those who have demeaned us at every opportunity, then, no. I don't." Cassius tucked his hands into his pockets defiantly and buffed his chin up.

"That is when you let your pride get in the way of your happiness," Charlotte whispered and walked back to her table.

I stood there, my chest heaving up and down. I was sad, but I was even more angry—at Cassius, at the killer, at society for even forcing the circus to survive in the first place. Why did it have to be like this? Why couldn't we live in harmony, no disagreements to be had?

And when I managed to pick my head up from the floor, I found Cassius watching me.

"All I'm saying is that you should've kept the money for yourself." He flicked his head at me as though he couldn't look at me any longer. "We'd be better off with you in Axminster."

I couldn't help but fall apart, then and there. I looked at my hands folded in front of me, sniffing back tears, but they came anyway, sliding down my cheeks and making my jaw tremble. There it was, the one thing I'd been terrified to hear. He didn't want me here.

I swiped at my tears before rushing past the pity in my friends' eyes and out of the room. I didn't know what to do anymore. I didn't even know what I wanted. Coming back here, the one thing I wanted was to be reunited with my friends, but mostly with Cassius. And he hated me more than anything.

I needed space to sort through my thoughts before I did something rash. I tried to think about what that might be. Maybe I would go into town and petition for equal opportunities between classes. Maybe I'd demand that supporters of the circus continue donating money. Maybe I'd ask them to stop since Cassius was so distrusting.

As I made my way through the train to my room, I began to think. Cassius was wrong, but not entirely. What price were we willing to pay in order to keep the circus afloat? Were we willing to barter with the wealthy, who had always put us down? Were we going to lose our sense of pride by taking handouts from them? On the other hand, would we risk cutting off our only supporters out of spite?

"Juniper!"

I turned to find Cassius following briskly behind me.

I needed peace and quiet, not his constant badgering. "I don't want to fight with you," I responded tiredly.

"I don't care what you want." His voice rose, making my blood run cold.

He didn't care. He didn't care about what I wanted or what I needed, and it made me sick. I hated this Cassius, the one who was angry, loud, ambivalent, and uncaring. His words struck me like a knife, over and over, my blood pouring out before his feet. That was what Cassius did to me. He hurt me time and time again, and I let him. I let him drain me. And sometimes I was okay with that because it meant having him around, but it was too painful to let him treat me this way.

How had it come to this? How, after months of waiting to see him again, could he shut me out so easily?

"Listen to me!" Cassius screamed.

"You listen to me!" I turned around, unable to take the noise any longer. I stepped toward him and pointed at his chest. "I came here for you! I came here to avenge your sister's death and end the killer—to free you from his sickness!"

Cassius just laughed and shook his head. "What do you want, a trophy?"

I bit the inside of my cheek to keep from slapping him. "I want you to understand. And I want you to hug me and tell me that everything will be okay, because I didn't only do this for you. For months, I was alone, plagued by *him*. I can't get him out of my head. That's why I'm doing this. For Penelope, for you, and for me." I was standing in front of him, our bodies only inches away from touching.

Please. Please reach out and hold me. I need you. That's what I wanted to say, but I couldn't, not until he felt the same way.

But then his anger dissolved, and his eyes softened. "You left."

His voice broke, and I so badly wanted to hold him, but I couldn't, not after what he said to me. Did he want me or not? One moment he was hurt by my leaving, and the next he was wishing I'd stayed in Axminster. Which one was it? And why was he holding back?

He continued, "You left, and you thought sending money would fix everything. We're not a charity case, Juniper. We didn't need your money. We needed you." He looked deep into my eyes, those caramel irises thick with a sheen of tears. And then he turned over his shoulder and walked away.

Chapter Sixteen

Monroe's return was anything but mundane. The entire circus stood outside the train waiting for him, and when he strode out of the tree line, we erupted with cheers and *hoots and hollers*. I hadn't realized the impact Monroe had made while he was here. He was a quiet man, keeping to himself most of the time, but he'd kept us afloat. And I hadn't realized how much I missed him.

All at once, the performers ran toward him. In varying cloths and colors, the performers looked like a sea of animals, all dressed in different coats. The crowd surged around him and wrapped him in a giant hug, each one shouting and shoving their way through to cling to him.

Monroe laughed all the while, garnering hug after hug. And when it was my turn, I stepped up to him and said, "Welcome back."

"I could say the same for you." He smiled warmly and hugged me, his fingers barely touching my skin. He'd always been reserved in his affection for others.

His long black hair had grown past his shoulders, and his former stubble was growing into a full beard now, looking rugged and disheveled. I couldn't imagine what he was going through back home.

"I'm sorry for what happened to your mother, my friend." Mr. Monte stepped forward and wrapped him in a tight hug, their embrace lasting.

"It's quite alright, Edward." Monroe looked down to the ground, surprisingly with no tears in his eyes. He was better at holding it in than I expected. "It's the circle of life, I'm afraid."

"You're absolutely right," Mr. Monte said while the performers nodded in agreement. He cleared his throat, "I hate to make your welcome short, but we've got to talk about a few things." Mr. Monte showed Monroe to the train, helping him with his other duffel bag. "But don't fret, there'll be quite the party tonight. We're taking you to the city!" Mr. Monte exclaimed, and all the performers jumped up and down like little children.

"Oh, you know me! I'm one to party!" Monroe proclaimed sarcastically, making all of us laugh.

After the warm welcome, Mr. Monte and I took a seat in Monroe's office, as he situated his things in perfect order, as he always had. His pens were arranged in perfect lines and the papers on his desk in a neat pile.

"Must you be such a perfectionist? We have business to attend to." Mr. Monte shook his head.

Monroe seemed irked at the idea, his hands fiddling to fix things that were strewn. "Go on, then."

"What do you know about Katriane Beringer?" I blurted out.

There was no use in wasting time. We needed to figure this out, and fast. The next performance was only a few weeks away. That, and, after my argument with Cassius last night, the only thing I had hope for was catching the killer.

Monroe began coughing on his own spit, holding his stomach while he caught his breath. His eyes darted around the room, pointed anywhere but mine. Finally, he sat up straighter in his chair and cleared his throat. "I know a lot about Katriane."

"Do you mind telling?" I inquired, pushing him. I didn't want to make him uncomfortable, but we needed answers.

He sighed heavily before explaining, "Katriane was my sister."

"Your sister?" I exclaimed.

"Yes, my sister." He looked up at me reluctantly. "And she passed away a long time ago, so I'd be grateful if we could stop talking about the many people I've lost." He got up, preparing to work on matters of business he'd left unattended in his time away.

I grabbed his hand and looked into his eyes pleadingly, "Please, Monroe. I'm sorry for pushing you, and I know this is difficult to talk about, but this is pertinent to finding the killer. Katriane fell on the rope, correct?" I didn't wait for him to answer. I only asked so he wouldn't have to tell me himself. I kept my voice gentle to avoid interrogating him. "It was the first time anyone was hurt in the circus, and the first incident that someone, a tightrope walker, died."

"And why do you think that's important?" He leaned closer. His long hair fell over his shoulders and swayed.

"Because we believe the killer has a personal vendetta against tightrope walkers and that he might have started by killing Katriane, your sister. Do you know of anyone who might have had any ill will toward her?" I asked.

"Katriane's death was an accident due to the lack of safety in the old circus days, not because she was killed. Sure, there were people who were jealous of her, but no one would have murdered her." His face was wrought in utter confusion.

I looked to Mr. Monte, hoping for some guidance. I didn't know what this meant. If Katriane fell accidentally, then why had the tightrope walkers that followed been threatened?

Monroe shook his head and his hands fidgeted as the memories of his sister's death resurfaced.

"I think that's enough for today," Mr. Monte said, glancing warily at his friend.

"But Mr. Monte—" I tried to convince him to let me continue.

"Juniper," Mr. Monte warned me.

I sat quietly with my hands folded on my lap like a little girl scolded by her father.

Mr. Monte turned to Monroe then and clapped him on the black. "We'll leave you to get better situated. I apologize for pressing you." Mr. Monte glared at me before continuing. "But we've got an exciting night ahead of us. Welcome back, my friend."

"Thank you, Edward. I'm glad to be back." Monroe nodded and hung his head back on his chair, losing a great sigh.

Seeing him sitting there with his knees pressed tightly together and his hands balled in his lap made me regret my actions. Monroe had just arrived after months of tending to his sick mother and I'd thrown the death of his sister in his face, asking questions he might not even know the answer to. What was wrong with me?

I rose to leave, turning back to say, "I'm sorry."

"It's alright." He forced a smile, but his cloudy eyes were sad.

I left him in peace, exiting with Mr. Monte. While we walked down the corridor, I felt a reprimand coming my way.

"We have to be careful in the way we go about things," he said kindly, much to my surprise. "Monroe is hurting, and if we push him too far, he might flee. He came back because we needed him, but there's nothing stopping him from leaving again."

I could see in Mr. Monte's eyes that he didn't want Monroe to leave. He'd been running the circus alone for months, without the help of his financial advisor and friend, which was surely stressful. "I know. I'm sorry. I'm just antsy."

Mr. Monte stopped me in the hall and grabbed my hands within his own. "I know, me too. But if we're not patient, the circus might be torn apart, not because of the killer but because of our own hastiness."

I nodded, knowing he was right, but how could I sit idly by with the killer on the loose? We weren't going to stop this menace if we didn't search with every minute we had. I excused myself, knowing it was unwise to argue with Mr. Monte any longer.

I retreated to my room, searching for some quiet, only to be flogged by the dancers.

"What are you wearing tonight?" Charlotte asked in a rush, picking dresses out of my closet and discarding the ones she didn't like, as if she didn't have enough dresses in her own room. Her closet was chock-full of them.

"I haven't thought about it yet," I sighed groggily, laying across my bed.

"Well you'd better start. This is our first day in the city where we're allowed to enjoy some free time. We need to look our best, especially since we'll be surrounded by the wealthy," Raelynn exclaimed, her twin sister nodding emphatically by her side.

"I thought none of you cared about the wealthy." Maybe I *had* changed them by taking them to the Janvier Estate last year. Regardless, I was too tired to take my eyes from the ceiling. With Monroe's return and the stress of finding the killer, I couldn't think straight. And in the time I wasn't thinking about the killer, I was thinking of Cassius—of his hateful words, of his distaste for me, and of the unlikely possibility of us ever fixing things.

"We don't, but they are watching. We might as well give them a show!" Piper added, forcing Olive to zip up the back of her little dress. It hung down to the floor, but it was as thin and transparent as tulle.

"Piper, you can't wear that. I've got something much fancier for you." I tried to avoid the real explanation as to why she shouldn't wear something so immodest. Every man would be peering through her dress, even despite how young she was. Men are vile creatures who believe the law doesn't apply to them—who believe they should get whatever they want, without facing any repercussions.

I led her over to the closet, handing her a rather short dress, one that had layers upon layers of tulle pouring out at the waist.

"You look like a princess." I lifted her onto my hip so she could glance at her reflection in the mirror. Her mouth fell open and she squealed before kissing me on the cheek.

"Has anyone ever told you that you'd make a great mother?" Evelyn pranced over to me with a faint smile pulling back her thin lips.

I laughed a little too loud. "I don't even have a husband; how can I begin to think about children?"

"Well, then we need to find you a husband, don't we, ladies?" Evelyn exclaimed to the group and the girls all clapped along, laughing haughtily.

"One you actually like." Charlotte flicked my chin.

She knew me too well. Sure, I had a bachelor waiting for me in Axminster, but I hadn't thought of him once since returning to the circus. I'm sure he was dumbfounded, as was my mother, to find that I'd fled. I would pay any price to have seen their reactions.

But then my mind turned to the man that did remain in my heart. Cassius. It was silly, but I couldn't escape the thought of having children with Cassius. I thought about little boys with dark curly hair running around in the fields of grain, the sun shining on their tanned skin. Their pure little laughs would ring throughout the train, and as they grew older, they'd take after Olive and continuously try to sneak ale into their cups. But they would have a family to watch over them, take care of them, and love them.

I shook my head and the smile off my face. Why the hell was I thinking about the children I might have with Cassius when he couldn't even look at me without glowering?

"That brawl between you and Cassius the other day was quite entertaining if I'm allowed to admit it." Scarlett giggled with wide eyes.

"Well, you've already done it," I commented, which made the girls laugh. "But I'd rather forget it." I began picking out a dress to keep my eyes averted from their stares.

"Oh, you will. We'll drink so much that you'll forget a lot more than that!" Charlotte exclaimed, linking arms with Finley and Autumn.

And as I followed the girls out, I was prepared to do just that.

As the moon crested in the sky, the circus made their way into the city. Our shouting and laughing filtered into every home. We swarmed the city as though we owned it. We might not have belonged here, but we were fortunate enough to own the minds of all the residents by offering them a touch of magic.

We entered the Burrowing Hedge, a famous pub in the center of the city, right next to Granby's Headquarters, the most famous ballet studio in the kingdom. Inside, many of the tables had been cleared, leaving us room to frolic. We ordered a pint of ale for everyone, keeping the tab open per Monroe's request. The man drank to appease Mr. Monte, becoming loose and free like the rest of us.

I drank to my heart's content, allowing my mind to wander, and thoughts of Cassius to seep away. Before I knew it, Flint grabbed my waist and pulled me out onto the floor. I laughed and swayed my hips alongside Charlotte, being traded between the performers until I couldn't match their faces to their names. My head was spinning, and my body felt as light as a feather, but after a few hours my stomach was full, and I excused myself to find the restroom. Down a dim hallway, I joined the strangers standing outside the door waiting for an opening.

After relieving myself, I intended to return to my friends and dance some more, before I was stopped by an older man.

"Juniper Rose, right?" he inquired, taking his top hat off to reveal a receding head of wiry yellow hair. "I watched you at the masquerade ball. Your performance was the best I've seen in all my years."

"Thank you, Sir, I appreciate that," I said honestly before I tried to brush past him.

He held out his arm, blocking my path, and panic began to course through me. If he was a kind gentleman, he would let me return to my friends.

"I thought you might be interested in helping the circus. I know a few men who'd pay a handsome price for a darling like you." He winked, lowering the arm that was blocking me and placing it on my waist instead.

I searched for help but found my friends too enveloped in their dance and drink to even notice me. I gently pushed the man's chest to stop his advancement while his hot breath snaked down my neck, reeking of alcohol. But the man pressed his hips into my own, the bulge in his pants making my stomach tighten up. I felt sick.

I tried to remain calm as I said, "I'm sorry, Sir. I'm here on business tonight, to celebrate the return of a friend."

He grabbed me harder this time, his hands meaty and sticky. "Then invite your friend to tag along," he drawled in my ear.

The man proceeded to pull me into him, and I turned my head to the side, his lips meeting my jaw. I tried to push him away, but I was a little too drunk to use all my strength, and the man was too strong. Suddenly, I froze, my body not feeling my own. My arms were stuck to my sides, my feet planted in the earth. My chest heaved up and down and I choked on the loss of air. I couldn't form any words, so instead, I closed my eyes and tried to imagine Cassius's lips on mine instead—anything other than this man's chapped lips, dry and sucking for any friction he could get.

When he pushed me into the wall, images of the killer wove into the darkness behind my closed eyelids. I remembered the hot feeling of his large hands traveling up my thighs, pulling the dress around my hips. The grass I'd laid on was achingly soft, as though it might pull me under, but itchy all the same. I remembered the killer looking into my eyes even though I couldn't meet his. All I saw was darkness and all I felt was the harshness of his hand when he struck me.

I ripped my eyes open when the man's finger ran along my ribs and up toward my breasts. "Get your hands off me!" I screamed and shoved my forearm into his body.

His lazy strokes turned violent when he slammed me against the wall. "You're a selfish little girl, you know that?" He squared his jaw and pressed his teeth together, spit flying onto my cheek at the force of his words. "You get everything you want. You should be ashamed of throwing dirt on the wealthy name." He pulled at my curls to force my head back and kissed my neck fervently, the kisses wet and sloppy.

"Stop!" I yelled, squirming while trying to push him off me. But two other men had joined him, each of them holding one of my arms down. Their hands were hard, pushing into my skin painfully.

As soon as I realized what they were going to do to me, I screamed at the top of my lungs. "Cassius!"

I closed my eyes so as not to watch their hands travel over my body. I wrestled as much as I could, but three men against one woman was impossible. I'd never been angrier to be a woman, to be helpless against men like this, to be so easily defeated. And I was angry at the men who thought they could take whatever they wanted, not caring whose life they destroyed.

But I didn't have time to be angry as he lifted my dress and began tearing at my undergarments.

"Cassius!" I screamed again, pleading for someone, anyone to come help me.

And then suddenly everything stopped.

Their hands stopped groping and I heard a loud grunt. I ripped my eyes open to find Cassius behind the man in front of me. He grabbed the back of his neck and pulled him off me before slamming his head into the adjacent wall. The man fell to the floor, immediately unconscious. Cassius then moved to the next, his knee flying into his groin, causing him to fall to the floor. He kicked the back of his head, and it snapped forward before his eyes closed. The last man slowly backed away while holding his hands out in front of him, begging for mercy. Cassius slowly stalked toward him until the man was trapped between bodies in the crowd of drunken people. And before I knew it, his arm snapped and connected with the man's jaw.

The performers leapt up from their seats due to the commotion, prepared to help Cassius fight.

"For heaven's sake! Again?" Mr. Monte yelled from his seat across the room at the fight that had begun. He kept hold of his drink, which sloshed over the rim as he ran to us.

I remained pressed against the wall, unable to move. I rubbed my fingers along the tough grains of wood behind me and closed my eyes, finding momentary relief. I couldn't shake the feeling of his hands digging into my ribs, or how his fingers had hurriedly slipped into my undergarments, while the other two held me down. It all reminded me of that night with the killer. Flashes of images entered my mind—the killer holding my throat to the ground, his black gloves raising my dress over my hips, and his violent attempt to undo his pants.

Peeling open my eyes, I tried to remind myself of where I was. I wasn't with the killer. I was in a bar with my friends. They were coming to help. I was safe. But erasing the killer from my mind wouldn't erase what those three men attempted to do to me. Tears began to stream down my face as I let out a quiet sob. My heart was pounding, and I was so afraid to close my eyes, but even more afraid to keep them open, so I let my head fall, surveying the floor as a wall of tears covered my vision.

"Charlotte!" Cassius yelled across the room, and she came rushing. "Get her out of here." He disappeared out of sight to find Mr. Monte.

Come back. Come back and hold me, was my quiet plea to him.

I sank to the floor, my jaw quivering.

Charlotte grabbed my face and looked me in the eyes before I could fall to the ground. "You're okay. You're okay," she repeated. "Come with me." She grabbed my hand, far gentler than the harsh hands that had just stained me.

She wove through the crowd quickly, pulling me with her and out into the night. Our way back to the train was a blur, the city and the lights passing by in a haze. I didn't remember a second of it. And when we finally made it back to the train, I was in my room in the blink of an eye. I began to convince myself that none of it had even happened.

Charlotte tucked me into bed, sitting next to me to lull me to sleep. Her soft strokes made my eyes close, and the alcohol in my system made me drowsy. Within minutes, I blacked out.

That night, headlines proclaiming Katriane Beringer's death returned to haunt me. I saw her on the ground, her neck twisted oddly to the side, her eyes wide open in fear. I pictured a man in a black trench coat pulling her body away from the crowd and dumping her in an open grave. While he poured dirt over her pale white skin, her mouth started moving as she tried to call out for help. He was burying her alive. I watched as an outsider, trying to yell for help, but I was unable to help the girl swallowing dirt right in front of me.

Then the killer, standing over the grave, slowly turned to me. Lifting up his black mask, he was revealed as the man from the party this evening. He smiled disgustingly, his yellow, crooked teeth twisting. And when I blinked, he was standing in front of me, his hands around my throat. My lips parted in surprise, and I slapped at his hands, but it was useless. There was no one there to help me this time.

I couldn't breathe. I was dying.

I lurched forward and awoke to complete darkness, screaming for help. I couldn't move, stuck in a pool of sweat once again. My lungs were dry and scratchy from screaming, and suddenly someone ripped open my bedroom door.

"Is everything okay?" Flint asked in a panic.

"Turn on the lights!" I screamed, covering my eyes.

He lit the candle on my bedside table, his face washed in light. But despite the darkness being gone, I continued to rock back and forth.

Flint gently sat down next to me on my small bed, close enough to be comforting but far enough away to give me space. "You're okay, J. You're back in the train," he reassured me. And as my body started to relax, and my breathing slowed, he asked, "What's going on with you? You're different."

"Was I supposed to be the same?" I huffed out a laugh, wiping the beads of sweat from my forehead.

"Not after what happened to you, no. It just seems like it's getting worse." He looked me up and down, noting the bags under my eyes.

My nose burned with the approaching tears. "I'm scared, Flint."

"I know." His voice was so gentle I wanted to cry.

After all the noise in my head, I needed quiet.

"But it's not always going to be like this," he continued. "Trust me. Years ago, Cassius was the same, waking up soaked, bags under his eyes so dark it looked like he'd been punched, and screaming with such terror it sounded like he was dying. He scared the shit out of all of us. But he got better. Eventually, the nightmares went away, and he was able to rest. He's okay now, and you will be too."

It was comforting to know that Cassius had been through the same terrors and that he'd survived, but it still didn't ease the ache in my heart. "Then why isn't he here?" I asked, hot tears sliding down my cheeks.

Flint shook his head, a frown forming on his lips. "I don't know. I think he's more scared than he lets on."

"So, six years down the road, Cassius is still terrified out of his mind?" I frowned, not wanting to lie in bed every night, afraid of the dark—not wanting to live my life in constant fear.

"I said it would get better, not that it would go away completely. It's going to be hard, and some nights you might not be able to sleep, but you'll be alright in time." He squeezed my hand as his lips pressed into a thin line.

I remembered the softness of his lips, and how delicately he used to kiss me. I squeezed his hand in return, thankful to have him by my side. "I should have picked you," I whispered, not realizing the weight of my comment.

If I had chosen Flint, I wouldn't be plagued by Cassius's drama. I could have him by my side, helping me through my nightmares. He would be kind and show his affection easily, and I wouldn't have to fight so hard to feel appreciated.

"Yes, you should have," he laughed. "I was crazy about you, J, but we all know Cassius is right for you."

"How do you know? He barely speaks to me. I can't figure out how to help him with the past, and he can't seem to help me with the present."

Flint shuffled next to me, trying to find the right words. "That may be so, but last year, he was the happiest I've ever seen him. You might not see it, but you just being here is helping him sort through all the shit he's been through," Flint explained. "And I think he can help you too. It'll just take time."

"What if I don't have time?" I asked, tears continuing to fall as the realization hit.

"What do you mean?"

I sat up then to look Flint directly in the eyes. "My being here isn't permanent. I have to leave after we find the killer. I'm not allowed to stay."

Flint leaned closer, the candlelight making his eyes flicker. "So, the wedding is still on?"

"Yes, unless I find a way to call it off. Something Mr. Young can't argue with."

Flint let go of my hand to rub his temple. "Even if you do find a way to stay, he'll take us down like he promised months ago. He'll destroy us."

I looked at the lit candle on my bedside table, thinking hard. "Not if I challenge his image. He wouldn't dare threaten us if it meant tainting his own name in the process."

He nodded in understanding. "His image is everything to him, so we have to find something that will damage it." Flint looked across the room, trying to figure something out.

I grabbed his hand again. "It's okay. I'm sure we'll come up with something."

Without realizing, I'd already stopped shaking and my breathing had calmed.

"Do you want me to stay, or to fetch Charlotte?" he asked.

The fact that Flint was willing to stay with me after I rejected him last year proved how kindhearted he really was. But I answered with, "I think I'll be alright."

He nodded once before rising to leave.

Before he could go too far, I grabbed his wrist. He turned around, his eyes glazed over.

"Thank you," I whispered. He would never understand how much he meant to me—how much I needed someone in that moment.

"Anytime you need me, Rose. I'll be here," he whispered.

The last thing I heard before eternal darkness swept over the room was the soft click of the door, the last sliver of light fading away.

Cassius...

I heard everything that night. Her screaming, her crying.

And I cried with her. I laid with the sheets over my head and fists against my ears, trying to block out her screams. I almost leapt up and ran to her. I'd cried out many nights too, hoping someone would save me from the terrors in my mind. I knew what it felt like to be hopeless, yearning for someone to hold onto.

But my heart was battling with my mind. I needed to keep my distance from Juniper to protect my heart because if I held her in my arms, even just once, then my promise to forget her would be for nothing. I'd find comfort holding her and forget ever being angry. When I was around her, all sane thoughts vanished, and I was left at her complete disposal. And that was why I had to stay as far away as possible, even if it killed me.

The next performance was in Turnstead in one week. Performers bustled around, gathering their equipment and placing it in the back of the train. It was tough work, packing up our lives in just one day and taking off to a new city.

When the train departed, as everyone prepared for a night of dancing and drinking, I found Mr. Monte securing more equipment in the last train car with harnesses and buckles.

"Mr. Monte, I have a question," I began, sneaking up behind him.

He didn't even flinch, and asked without looking at me, "What is it, my dear?"

"Well, I've got something heavy on my heart." I wrung my hands together nervously.

He stopped immediately and his eyes moved to mine, offering me his full attention.

"I don't know if you've spoken to Cassius recently, but things aren't going well between us."

Mr. Monte's raised his brows so high they nearly touched his hairline. "From the way he ran to you last night at the bar, I'd say things are going just fine."

I shrugged my shoulders in defeat. "He protected me, but he didn't comfort me like he used to. I miss that. And I want him to know that I still need him."

After the events at the bar yesterday and the night terrors that followed, I needed him more than I'd needed anything in my life. I wanted Cassius to know how I felt about him, but more than that, I wanted him to come back to me. Truthfully, I didn't know if I could do any of this without him.

"Alright, what are you thinking?" Mr. Monte inquired, seemingly on board.

I told him my idea and he nodded along. "I want it to be the first act of our performance in Turnstead, but Cassius can't know."

He grabbed my hand and linked it through his arm, pulling me down the corridor. "Leave that to me. I'll see to it that he has no idea what's coming."

"Thank you, Mr. Monte." I kissed him on the cheek, feeling a weight lift from my shoulders. If this didn't convince Cassius of my feelings for him, then I don't think anything could.

Chapter Seventeen

Mr. Monte...

The stadium seats were filled to the brim in The Mirage Assembly Hall, located in the town square, and created so that the stage was in the center of the auditorium, with seats surrounding it in a colosseum style. There was a small bridge connecting the stage to a backstage area, cutting through the audience. We were invited to perform at the lavish hall due to the peaked interest of the wealthy that saw our show at the masquerade ball. It seemed being connected with Juniper's people had its perks.

I peeled open the curtains to peek out into the auditorium. This would be an odd adjustment for the circus, seeing as though we typically performed in a tent on a pile of sand. But the performers would have more than enough room on the stage where a mat had been placed to protect the finish. I wondered what the problem was with a few scratches, but I guess that was the difference between the wealthy and the less fortunate. We didn't have nice things to protect.

I stepped away from the wall and weaved through the crowd of performers backstage, where I found the dancers stretching their limbs above their heads or falling into the splits—a feat that sent shivers down my spine. Meanwhile, the flamethrowers prepared their gear and oiled their skin. And there was Cassius, pacing back and forth, brushing lint off his crimson vest.

He was in for quite a surprise.

One week ago...

"Cassius, I have an idea," I presented, as he was preparing to feed the twin onyx panthers.

He didn't blink an eye or shudder at their ferocity when they snapped at the pail of bloodied meat he was holding. "Don't ask me to strip in front of the crowd this year. You know what happened the last time I did that. Practically every parent protested and claimed the circus was, 'exposing young children to profanity and pornography.'"

I rolled my eyes at his exaggeration. "That is not what happened." Cassius opened his mouth to protest, but I pointed a finger to stop him from continuing. "I wanted to ask you if you would be interested in opening our show in Turnstead. I think it could be a good change of pace."

Cassius huffed out a laugh. "You sure you don't want Juniper to be the star of the show?"

I snickered along with him, trying my best to hide Juniper's little secret. "She can't be the center of attention all the time, can she?"

"You know I'm not a religious man, but I could say amen to that," Cassius looked at me with a flicker of excitement. "What would you like me to do?"

Cassius...

It'd been a while since I'd opened a show. When I first became the lion tamer, I opened every show, but that spotlight faded quickly, and now my hands were shaking, and my heart was pounding. But the people were expecting a show, and that's what I'd give them.

I pushed through the crimson velvet curtain and began to walk down the small bridge toward the stage. I was immediately praised with polite claps from the pompous audience. I was expecting more of a hollering, rowdy crowd, but this would do.

I walked deliberately toward the cage in the center, which was covered in gold silk. Turning to the audience, I ripped off the fabric to reveal beautiful Abbas. The crowd gasped when the lion's roar echoed throughout the cavernous room. I slowly approached the door to the cage, the members of the audience leaning forward in their seats, intrigued. I'd come to trust Abbas many years ago, but the audience hadn't. My goal tonight was to convince them that he was worth trusting.

I unlocked the cage and led Abbas out and around the perimeter of the stage, watching as the people in the front row shied away. If only they knew he was a sweetheart, as I did. Many people were unlikely to discover this about him because of their fear, but I learned a long time ago that fear was the greatest enemy of potential.

After we'd made our round, I stopped Abbas in the center of the stage and ordered him to lay down with the simple cue of raising my hand into a balled fist. Following my command, Abbas laid down until his chin hit the floor, and I rewarded him with a slice of red meat. This routine of cuing and then rewarding took Abbas about a month or two to master. He was stubborn, but the movements and commands had become second nature to him.

"Up!" I shouted in a clipped tone and clicked my tongue, snapping my fingers at a raised platform in the center of the stage.

Abbas leapt up and then off the platform gracefully, making the audience *ooh* and *ahh* in amazement.

There we go. We were gaining their trust.

As I picked up the chair sitting on the edge of the stage, preparing to complete my signature move, my attention was caught by a little boy with brown curly hair, almost as dark as mine. His eyes were like emeralds, shining through the dark audience like a candle flickering in a void. His mouth hung open in awe and his eyes were filled with longing. In that moment, I saw a younger version of myself, yearning to be more than what I was.

I cleared my throat, "Young man, what's your name?" I was startled as my voice echoed throughout the room.

The audience turned all at once to gaze at the boy I'd set my sights on. He looked at me nervously before answering in a frail voice, "Timothee."

I smiled at the boy, trying to assuage his nerves. "It's nice to meet you, Timothee. My name is Cassius."

He nodded his head respectfully and straightened the waistcoat over his small chest. He was finely dressed—a little nobleman—but I saw in his eyes that he didn't belong there. It was clear he wanted more than an ordinary desk job—one that would satisfy so many others. He wanted to face a beast, even if he failed, then pick himself back up and do it all over again.

"Would you like to come up here and tame the lion?" I inquired, stepping forward so my toes hung off the stage.

A small smile grew on Timothee's lips, although his mother spoke up before he could. "Are you sure it's safe?" she exclaimed, placing a hand over her heart.

Must she be so dramatic?

"I assure you, Ma'am, it's quite safe. I wouldn't ask if that wasn't the case."

"Come on!" someone in the crowd shouted.

"You got it!" another eager onlooker yelled, encouraging young Timothee.

The little boy spoke with his mother briefly before standing up and walking down the aisle. He was young, probably as old as I was the first time I confronted a lion. He trembled as he walked up the stairs, and when I offered my hand, he gripped it firmly with a sweaty palm.

I leaned down next to him and whispered in his ear, "Everything's going to be alright. This is Abbas." I pointed to the lion, which I'd locked back in his cage before inviting Timothee on stage. "All you have to do is trust me. Do as I say, and we'll have some fun."

The boy nodded and I clapped him on the back. The audience watched in complete silence as I brought out a chair and instructed him on what to do. Despite our mysterious whispering, you could hear a pin drop in the hall it was so quiet. I came to stand behind the little boy, facing the crowd. "I want you all to give a warm welcome to Timothee, the lion tamer!"

The crowd cheered and I spotted Timothee's mother clapping aggressively, with worry lines marking her face.

"I'm scared." The little boy turned around and looked up at me, his eyes welling.

I smiled and knelt beside him, asking, "Do you trust me?" Those words reminded me of the time I'd said them to Juniper—and all that I hadn't said.

Timothee looked at me so hopefully with his big, round eyes, bringing me back to the present. And if I was right, this little boy was different. He wasn't like the pompous men and women out in the crowd. He was willing to take a risk.

"Yes," he whispered before turning to face Abbas. He picked up the chair as soon as I unlocked the cage.

Abbas stalked toward Timothee, as though the little boy were his dinner. And, as I'd instructed, Timothee held strong and lifted the chair to block his body. When the lion drew closer, he whipped the chair from right to left, up and down, distracting the lion by forcing it to focus on the legs of the chair. This technique took the focus off the tamer, which was the lion's main target.

It shocked me how swiftly he moved—the boy seemed to have a natural talent for this.

The little boy's face had turned red, his hair sticking to his forehead after a few minutes of diverting the lion's attention. And finally, I came to Timothee's side and instructed him to drop the chair. The audience gasped when he did, thinking the boy might be in danger.

The lion focused his gaze on the boy, growling low while stalking closer. I grabbed Timothee's hand in my own, just as his chest began to heave up and down.

As I raised his hand into the air, I spoke softly to Abbas, keeping my eyes locked on his. "Arrête." The r's rolled off my tongue, and suddenly, the lion stopped and looked us both in the eyes.

"Bow your head," I whispered to the boy, which was unheard by the audience. "Let Abbas come to us."

At once, we both bowed our heads, and I saw Timothee close his eyes in absolute terror. A second later, he felt the soft fur of Abbas's head in his outstretched palm. Timothee looked up in excitement, finding Abbas laying beneath us, rubbing his palm lovingly.

The audience erupted in cheers while the animal purred beneath us. Timothee's smile was the goofiest thing I'd ever seen, and my cheeks pulled back at having given him such an incredible experience.

I turned us both to the audience and lifted Timothee's arm into the air, watching the crowd rise to their feet and shout for joy. The animals were not to be feared, but loved and befriended.

I patted the little boy on the back and instructed him to return to his mother. Lord knows how terrified she must have been. And sure enough, when he returned to his seat, she wrapped him in a bone crushing hug.

"Thank you, all!" I turned my back on the crowd and snapped my fingers, leading Abbas back into his cage. I covered the metal bars with the golden fabric and prepared to wheel it out of the room just as the lights dimmed. The next act was about to occur, meaning the dancers would make their way out onto the stage.

But while I made my departure, I heard something strange, almost like a melody in the silence of the cavernous room. I stopped in my tracks and listened closer. This didn't fit with Mr. Monte's plan. Something was amiss. I didn't want to delay the performance in any way, but I figured I should get rid of whatever the distraction was before the dancers came on.

That is until I heard a voice.

"Stay with me. Boy just hold my hand, and I'll see you till the end," a woman sang, the lyrics rolling off her tongue beautifully.

Her voice was soft and melodic, floating through the air on a whisper. It wasn't too high or too low, but perfectly warm and resounding with such clarity.

A slow beat filled the room, matching with her every note. "Lay next to me. Take a deep breath, and I'll help you through the rest."

Where was she? Who was she?

Suddenly the curtain at the edge of the stage pulled open and a spotlight shown down on a small figure in a white gown. Nothing fancy, just a plain slip dress reaching her pale ankles. Her onyx hair was frizzed about her shoulders, making her face appear round and jovial. A small quartet sat behind her, picking different stringed instruments while she gripped the pole of a microphone in her dainty palms.

Juniper…

Juniper was singing, but why? In a dazed stupor, I stood there and listened to every word that poured out of her mouth, as though she were speaking to me directly. Maybe she was.

"I worry about times you fall from me. And I think through every possibility." She raised her pitch, and I watched as the muscles in her neck strained.

Right then she looked at me, her eyes turned down in a frown. She looked sad but hopeful at the same time. How could that be?

"Are we at the edge? Or could you fall with me?" She held a hand over her heart while separating each word beautifully. "Close your eyes and take a leap."

I'd never heard this melody before, nor did I understand its meaning. I was too struck by the fact that Juniper was singing and how beautiful she sounded. I'd only heard her sing once last year during a performance, but this was different. Her lyrics weren't overpowered by the instruments. This time I could hear her as clear as day, and her voice was so full and sincere.

But then she started walking toward me. "Walk with me. Let me guide you out of the darkness you're seeing now."

And that's when I realized this wasn't some act for the audience to enjoy. This was for me.

She came to stand in front of me and circled around my body, forcing me turn with her. It was as though I was hooked on her every word. She'd mesmerized me.

"Dance with me. Have a bit of fun. Let me loosen you up." She playfully tugged at the bowtie around my neck and smiled the most beautiful smile I'd ever seen. Just the brush of her fingertips on my chest made my heart flutter, but when her voice dipped lower in the next chorus, I quivered at its seductiveness.

"I am so afraid I'm losing you."

Her lip quivered. Losing me? She'd fled to Axminster and *chose* to leave me.

"Don't lose sight of what you know."

What did I know? Everything that once made sense, didn't anymore.

"I am here and there's nothing to fear." Suddenly she grabbed my hand, her eyes wide and honest.

Tears formed at the edges of my eyes, about to spill over. I needed to hear her say those words—needed to know that she was here for me, not because she was on some mission for Mr. Young.

Her words shook as she struggled to sing the last line of her song. "My friend, you are the one."

Her chest heaved up and down with emotion while the crowd leapt out of their seats and applauded wildly.

And I stood there like an idiot, not knowing what to do or what to even think.

She dropped the microphone to her side, and someone quickly came to take it from her. And then she looked at me and held out her hand. "Will you dance with me as you once did?" Her voice was undetectable to anyone else, but I heard her as though she were the only one in the room.

I looked around nervously at the crowd. I was torn in my heart. I wanted to stay away from her because she'd left me. I couldn't trust her. And I was afraid that if I let myself hold her for even a moment, I wouldn't be able to let go.

But the words she'd just sang…they had to mean something. I didn't understand it all completely, with the pressure of the audience as they watched us. All I knew was that instead of walking away, I wanted to touch her. I wanted to hold her.

I grabbed her waist and pulled her body to mine, allowing my fingers to dig into the small of her back. The curve of her spine sent a lick of electricity into my fingers. On stage I usually felt the expectation to give the audience something they'd remember, but in that moment, I couldn't have cared less about what they wanted. Everything faded out of view and all I could see was her—the way her chest pressed against mine, the way her breath brushed across my cheek, and that nervous gleam in her eyes.

As we began a slow waltz across the room, I didn't feel sorry for watching her body move—the way her hips swiveled to the music, or the way her breasts peaked under her thin dress. She was intoxicating, her closeness like a poison. And I didn't want to be soft or gentle with her. I wanted to feel her pressed against me and kiss her roughly, our tongues interlocked. I wanted more.

I stepped back, and she followed. Every step, she moved in synch with me, like our bodies were one. Back, left, forward, right. Over and over, we repeated this pattern, circling around the stage. Her eyes never left mine, and mine never left hers. I felt attached to her in a way I hadn't before. It was like I knew everything about her, but at the same time nothing at all. And for the first time in my life, I wanted to know someone—know every little thing about them.

How had I arrived at this moment? How had a woman from high society woven herself into my life?

When I heard whispers in the audience, I remembered there was a crowd watching and that it wasn't just Juniper and me alone in this room, despite how much I wished that was the case. Mr. Monte would want us to make a spectacle—two lovers joined once again. But I didn't want our relationship, whatever it was, to be a public experience. While performing for others and debuting our love brought us closer last year, it still felt like an act. I didn't want to make the same mistake again. This was our story and no one else's.

Juniper gripped my hand harder and pushed me forward, silently telling me that we needed to bring this to a close. So, I spun her gallantly, watching as the hair flying around her face made her giggle. I smiled with her while we waltzed across the stage, quicker this time. We picked up our steps as the music grew in rhythm and volume, until it stopped all at once. Halting our bodies with the music, we stood with our faces only inches apart. She looked up at me with her red painted lips popped open, and I couldn't take my eyes off them. I was itching to grab her face and separate her lips with my own, but something was holding me back.

She seemed to sense this, so she turned her back so that it was pressed against mine, feigning shyness. As the lights dimmed, the audience waited in silence, anxiously anticipating more. But my head fell to her shoulder just as the room was cast in darkness and the crowd erupted in cheers.

Chapter Eighteen

I found my way across the stage and behind the curtain with Cassius following closely behind, but before I could even gauge his reaction, the other performers were gathering around me.

"That was beautiful." Charlotte squeezed my arm, calming the nerves I hadn't noticed were there.

Olive ran up to me, jumping up and down. "I didn't know you could sing!"

"Dancers, on stage in two!" Mr. Monte called to the women.

The ladies jogged toward the curtain, straightening their hair and pushing out their breasts. Before I knew it, they were racing out, beckoned with applause.

I searched through the crowd of bustling performers to discover that Cassius had disappeared. I needed to speak to him but perhaps it should wait until we were alone. So, for the next hour, I listened to the audience's reactions to every act until it was time for the final bow. The performers joined hands and bowed, the wealthy standing to their feet with resonating applause. I spotted Cassius far down the line and the joy on his face was tangible. I loved seeing him in these moments, surrounded by people he loved and being honored for the hard work he put in. In these moments, he looked unbreakable.

The circus had worked extremely hard for this performance, and to know that the wealthy enjoyed it was a job well done. I clapped Emmet, one of the flamethrowers, on the back as we waved goodbye and exited the stage.

Once the curtains had closed and the audience shuffled quickly out of the assembly hall, a different feeling washed over me—one of worry. I'd almost forgotten him entirely, too consumed with my surprise for Cassius, but the killer…he hadn't struck during the performance. Had he returned at all? Or was he just waiting for the right moment?

My thoughts were interrupted when Mr. Monte cleared his throat. "I wanted to say thank you to everyone," he exclaimed while stripping off his top hat. "I know the past few months have been difficult with the loss of our rose, but we are so honored and excited to have you back, Juniper."

My heart swelled at his words and at the performers who smiled back at me.

"I could not be prouder of each of you for the time and energy you put into this show. This—what I saw today—is the dream I envisioned for the circus. Thank you for making it come true." He placed a hand over his heart and bowed his head.

Evelyn stepped forward and kissed Mr. Monte passionately on the cheek, eliciting a few rowdy hollers. Her sudden gesture made Mr. Monte fumble with his hat in surprise, but Evelyn spoke for all of us when she said, "You gave us a home, Monte, and that's something we'll never be able to repay you for."

The performers nodded along with her every word.

"It's been an honor." Mr. Monte tucked a strand of hair behind his ear.

Before things could get too emotional, Monroe hollered from the back, "Let's celebrate with a drink!"

The performers erupted in cheers and Hugh, the perpetual drunk of the circus, practically ran to Monroe and said, "I can't say no to that!"

Grabbing the many drinks on the table in the back, we began mingling, and I spotted Cassius talking passionately with Gus in the corner. He laughed heartily, his head falling back and his hand coming to rest on his vest. When he turned, he caught me staring, which forced me to avert my gaze quickly.

I had to speak to him, but I knew the night held much celebration and I wouldn't get the opportunity for a long while. After an hour of dallying, the performers gathered their things and we exited the hall, causing a raucous throughout the city. I was sure every household could hear our cheers as we made our way back to the train.

We spent hours drinking and dancing in the dining car to celebrate. It gave us a chance to be ourselves, and we'd earned it.

But I didn't have the same energy as the others because of the tension between me and Cassius. I sat back in a chair, sipping slowly on a mug of ale, thinking through every moment tonight—when Cassius's hand gripped my waist, our skin touching for the first time in months, the way he looked into my eyes, unyielding yet uncertain. I gazed across the room, finding him in the same position he was an hour ago, seated solemnly at a table in the back, a dim candle making his eyes flicker wickedly. A little piece of hair curled along his eyebrow, making him look exactly as he had the night I first met him. Dangerous and unapproachable.

Suddenly he rose from his seat and tipped back his head to drain the contents of his glass. I watched out of the corner of my eye as his throat bobbed and he wiped a thumb across his full lip. He stalked forward with a sheen in his eyes, and I looked down at the table in front of me as though it was the most interesting piece of furniture I'd ever laid eyes on. He was walking right toward me, but he didn't stop. No, he just kept walking.

I couldn't hide anymore. I needed answers, so I pushed out of my seat and followed him. His steps were long, almost hurried, as though he was trying to escape me. I walked behind him for a good while before he exited the dining car into an empty hallway.

He had to have known I was following him, but he just kept walking, and with all the anticipation, I couldn't stop myself from shouting his name. "Cassius!"

He didn't turn around but pressed on more quickly than before.

"Cassius!" I said again, this time more demanding.

Still, he didn't turn around.

I quickened my steps until I was only a few feet away from him. I was getting tired of him ignoring me, so I reached out to grab his arm and said, "I'm talking to you!"

He spun abruptly, looking me up and down in annoyance. "I can hear you. I'm not deaf." He squinted condescendingly and shrugged out of my grasp to continue toward his chamber.

"Well you sure are acting like it." I jumped to catch up to him.

He remained silent, finally reaching his chamber, and pushing open the door.

Instead of allowing him to lock me out of his life again, I pushed through, demanding his attention.

"I don't know what you want from me," he admitted, turning his back.

I took a deep breath, preparing myself for the battle that was sure to come. There was always a war to fight when it came to Cassius. I clenched my fists at my side and tried to remain confident. "I want you to look at me."

He stood motionless, the muscles in his back straining against his shirt.

I lost the breath I'd been holding, my voice defeated when I asked, "Why can't you look at me anymore?" And when he didn't turn or even flinch, I stepped closer and placed my hand on his shoulder. His skin warmed mine briefly before he shrugged me off again. "Why won't you let me touch you?"

I'd finally evoked a reaction in him because he turned quickly to look at me with desperate eyes. "Because I can't!" he exclaimed, as if he couldn't hold it in any longer.

"Why not?" I didn't mean to shout, but I'd spent months alone in Axminster, engaged to a man I didn't love and didn't want to love. And I'd made the risk of coming back here to be welcomed with this?

"Because I'm angry with you!" He clenched his jaw and stepped forward, his frame standing tall over mine. "I'm angry that you abandoned us all. We could have figured something out."

"You know that's not true. Mr. Young is a powerful man with too many connections that we can't fight on our own," I attempted to reason with him. I loved the fact that Cassius wanted me to stay and wanted to push through any trial that came our way, but he was being naïve.

He ran a hand through his hair. "And I'm angry at that too! Everyone is against us, Juniper. There's not a single moment we can be happy. We're in a never-ending battle against the rest of the world," he paused to catch his breath before continuing, "we'll never be enough!"

I sighed, finally understanding. Cassius was someone who wanted to be seen and appreciated, but he already was by the people that mattered. "We don't have to be enough for them. We just have to be enough for one another." I motioned between the two of us.

Cassius threw his head back and turned away from me, scoffing. "That's not enough! I want the world to adore us. I want to finally be treated with some damn respect."

The room echoed with the silence that followed, allowing me the time to think over my words. I had to be careful about what I said. Cassius was easily angered, and I didn't know how to get through to him. So, I responded calmly, "Then you have another problem on your hands it seems. You need to stop seeking the world's approval because you're never going to get it."

"Well, that's easy for you to say." He laughed. "You've never had to deal with people hating you. With people being *disgusted* by you, Miss Prune."

Before I knew it, my hand was in the air, colliding with his cheek. My palm stung with the impact, but I didn't feel sorry in the slightest for it. "Don't you dare call me that. I will not go through this again with you. It's time you realize I'm not the woman you perceive me to be."

His face shook, his cheek burning red after I struck him.

But I didn't allow him the time to argue before I continued. "I don't understand what it's like to be treated so horribly, but I do know how it feels to want to belong somewhere. And for the past year, you have never once made me feel like I belonged here. You have degraded and disapproved of me in every aspect, and I won't tolerate it anymore." I was fuming, finally able to say the things I needed to say to him for so long.

"Then you better run home to Axminster. They'll welcome you with open arms." He tipped his head at the door, motioning for me to leave.

Even though his words punched me straight in the gut, I couldn't let him push me away again. I knew that behind his anger, he still cared about me. "Did you not hear anything I just said out there to you tonight?" My chest heaved up and down and I couldn't help my voice from shaking. "I'm right here." I shook my head back and forth, trying to push away the tears that threatened to spill out. It was such a lonely feeling to be waiting for someone who didn't seem to want you. "I'm right here and you won't have me."

Cassius stood there like a wounded animal. "I *can't* have you, Juniper. Everyone knows it." He shuffled back and forth between his feet. "You don't belong with someone like me, and I sure as hell don't belong with someone like you."

"Why? Because you're a low life and I'm a rich girl from Axminster?" I was so tired of this age-old argument. "I would give every coin away if it meant that I got to stay here—if it meant that I could be with you. I don't give a damn about what other people think or expect of me, and neither should you."

Cassius retreated to the other side of the room, as far away from me as he could manage. He allotted himself some time to think before responding, "I came to the circus when I was six. I've spent years and years learning how not to care about other people's opinions, but I don't think I'll ever shake the feeling of hopelessness—of turning to others for help as a child for heaven's sake, just to be pushed out on the streets. Do you know how worthless that made me feel?"

I listened intently to him, his soft tone of voice leading me to think that he was beginning to open up.

"I was lost, Juniper. My family left me and then my sister left me." He drew in a shaky breath, one that was riddled with pain, and the way his jaw trembled made me want to kneel in front of him and hold him. "And for the first time in five years, when you showed up on our moving train, I thought things were getting better. I thought I could be happy." Cassius ran a hand through his hair—one of his nervous habits—and shrugged his shoulders in defeat. "And then you *left*."

I broke down then, tears rolling down my cheeks.

Cassius turned away and gazed out the small window in the wall, the moonlight casting a bright hue on his large frame. His skin was tanned and glistening, his hair a brilliant black, like the darkness of quill ink. He turned around on his own accord this time and looked at me with heavy eyes. "Why did you really come back?"

I wasn't nervous to admit my reasons for being here. I'd run through this conversation hundreds of times in my head. "I came back to avenge Penelope's death and put that horrible man in prison for what he did to me. I came back because I care about you Cassius, and I worry about you. And you're right. The world doesn't respect you. But I'm here, asking that you let me show you that you mean something to someone."

A small tear rolled down his cheek, making him close his eyes gently. "No matter how much I may mean to you, there's nothing stopping you from leaving. When this is over…when we find the killer, you're going back to Axminster, and you're going to marry Joseph Young. I can't go through that pain again. I won't."

I'd wondered for months how Cassius was coping with my departure. And there it was. He'd missed me. So much that he couldn't let his guard down because he knew he might lose me again.

"I know." I took a step toward him, and his face fell out of surprise that I was agreeing with him. "It's your decision to make." I took step after step, his body drawing me in like a tether. "Tonight, I asked you one simple question. Would you fall with me?"

He didn't take his eyes off me as I came to stand in front of him.

"It's not going to be easy, and I don't know what'll happen in the future, but this thing between you and me?" I pointed between us. "It's not meant to be easy." I reached up and gripped his face, his warmth igniting a fire in my fingertips. "But I won't let them take me away again. I'm not going anywhere," I whispered.

And then he broke right before me.

Chapter Nineteen

It was the first time I'd seen a man cry. A sob broke loose from his lungs and when he fell to his knees, I fell right with him. I cradled his head into my shoulder as he cried into my neck. He held tightly to my waist, almost suffocatingly, as if he feared that if he let go, I'd disappear completely.

I stroked his hair softly until he quieted, and all I could hear was his soft breathing and feel his warm breath on my neck. Something about this grown man kneeling in front of me, finding comfort in my arms, broke my heart. All I ever wanted was to find safety in another person, and by the way Cassius was holding me, it was clear he'd been searching for the same thing.

"I'm sorry," he whispered, his voice breaking.

I kissed his temple and held him to my chest. It had been a long night, filled with many decisions, but it brought us back together, and I couldn't be angry with him for the things he said. "I'm sorry too," I whispered as I pulled away and forced him to look me in the eyes. "Let's go to bed." We hadn't discussed everything, but we didn't need to yet. Tonight, we just needed to hold each other.

Cassius nodded and wiped the tears from his face, his eyes glazed over.

I stood up from the floor and grabbed his hand, leading him to the bed. His chamber was nicer than most, and consumed by a large bed with plush duvet covers and fur throws. It was warm and welcoming. And it was my favorite place on earth.

Cassius didn't even bother stripping off his clothes before climbing under the covers, and he sighed as his sadness evaporated slowly.

I laid down beside him but kept a healthy distance away, hoping not to invade his space. We laid there for a moment, side by side, not touching. Then he grabbed my hand and intertwined his fingers in my own, and I couldn't help but smile. This moment wasn't awkward or tense. It was simple. And that was what we needed after the strain of the law few months. I didn't need to shower him with kisses, and I didn't need his hands trailing over my body. All we needed was a moment of silence to lay with one another hand in hand.

Despite the ease we both felt, a lot had changed in those months. Cassius seemed like a different person now—someone I didn't know very well.

It seemed he knew exactly what I was thinking—that we'd have to get to know each other again. So, Cassius asked me what it had been like back home, and I asked about how the last performance went.

"It was chaotic to say the least." Cassius huffed out a laugh while staring up at the ceiling. "Without you, the circus felt different. We fell apart and argued and struggled to work together as we once had."

I listened intently and before I knew it, hours had passed. We were turned on our sides to face each other, recounting the moments we'd lost. We shared some laughs and some memories, and I was grateful for this time alone to become comfortable with each other again. By the end of the night, it felt as though I'd never left. Cassius knew everything about me, and I knew everything about him. There would be no secrets between us.

A moment of silence fell over us, and Cassius's eyes were beginning to droop. I wanted to let him sleep, but there was something I couldn't stop thinking about—something I wanted to share with him.

My voice came out hoarse when I said, "I had a dream."

He offered me his full attention and by the concern in his eyes, it seemed he'd heard my night terrors over the last couple of weeks, but the dream I was talking about was different.

"I was in the chapel." My voice turned to a whisper. "It was my wedding day. My mother was leading me down the aisle, but I wanted my father to be by my side on what was supposed to be the biggest day of my life. And he wasn't there." My eyes began to sting with tears. "Instead, my mother pulled me along, holding my arm so tight it hurt. She forced me onto the stage where Joseph was waiting, and Mr. Young held me there, like his prisoner." I couldn't take my eyes off the ceiling, not even to gage Cassius's reaction. "I was terrified by this image of my future. It wasn't the life I wanted." When I turned my head, I found Cassius staring at me so tenderly, as though he understood even the things I couldn't say. "I decided then and there to return to the circus." I shook my head, and the images of my dream only left me when Cassius's warm fingertips grazed my cheek. "I can't go back."

"We'll figure something out," he said it to convince himself, I was sure of it. The future was uncertain, and I had no idea how to get Mr. Young to let me stay, but I nodded along with him.

"If it helps any, I was drunk eighty percent of the time you were away." Cassius raised his eyebrows, and a smile pulled his cheeks apart.

"Really?" I exclaimed, memories of my life in Axminster slowly dissipating.

He huffed out a laugh, and it felt good to laugh along with him. "Yes. Gus had to scoop me off the floor and force me to eat most days."

My face sank at that news, regretting the pain I caused him. All I thought about was my own suffering, but it seemed we both had been miserable the last few months.

Cassius thought a moment longer before asking, "Was it Mr. Monte's plan to have you sing to rekindle the story of our love?"

I shook my head. "It was my plan, but it wasn't for the audience. It was for you."

He smiled faintly. "I didn't mean to erupt on you tonight. I really did enjoy the song."

"Thank you," I said shyly.

His eyebrows furrowed together, and he took my hand in his. "I think I was too awed to really grasp the meaning of it. Will you sing it again?"

I raised my eyebrows, surprised by his request, but I cleared my throat and began the song I'd written for him.

He listened carefully to every lyric while his eyes started to close. His eyelashes fluttered and I watched his breathing slow, and before my song was even over, he'd drifted off to sleep, his head drooping on my shoulder.

I kissed his forehead and pulled the covers up over him, finally deciding I would name the song Cassius's Lullaby.

The birds were chirping a sweet little melody, singing me awake to the sun glittering through the window, casting warm rays of light onto the ruffled sheets. Little specks of dust floated through their golden rays while the sound of voices yelling in the distance drifted through the crack under the door.

The circus was awake and alive, waiting for us to join them. A soft breath tickled my cheek and I found Cassius to my right with his arm draped over my stomach. I took a moment to gaze at his features—the space between his mouth where his lips popped open, the soft breaths he took, and the shadow his eyelashes cast on his cheekbones.

But when I tried to shake him awake, he groaned and buried his head under the covers to hide from the light.

"Come on lazy bones, we've got work to do." I pushed him once again and he finally emerged from the covers with his hair tussled. Sleepy Cassius was my favorite Cassius.

"What if I don't want to work?" He laid his head down and closed his eyes once again.

"Then you shouldn't have joined the circus."

I got out of bed, the brisk morning air hitting my skin and making me shiver. It was almost August, and that meant the cool air of autumn was approaching. I wasn't prepared for the cold months of winter that followed. "I have to meet with Mr. Monte to discuss our plans for the killer."

Cassius rose at that and moved to the dresser. "Plans? I thought we were waiting for him to make his appearance."

While he stripped off his shirt and changed it out for a clean one, I watched intently, unable to take my eyes off his defined torso. There were two strong lines on either side of his abdomen that disappeared beneath his trousers, and the muscles in his back contorted as he lifted the shirt over his head. I wondered what it might feel like to touch his stomach and feel the rippling muscles underneath his skin. But I turned my head away before he noticed me staring and said, "How kind of you to wait for the killer to make his move and allow my life to be put in jeopardy."

Cassius giggled, which had come to be my favorite sound. It was light and airy and made him sound like a little boy as opposed to the gruff persona he had perfected for everyone else. He peered over his shoulder with a quirk in his smile. "I know. I've turned a new leaf."

I just rolled my eyes. "I'll see you later, won't I?"

I had a lingering doubt that last night had been a dream—that none of it was real.

"I'll be here." He nodded with a gentle smile.

He wasn't going anywhere.

I exited the room in search of Mr. Monte. Returning to the circus, *check*. Making my appearance known for the killer, *check*. Securing my relationship with Cassius, *check*. Now I just had to find that damn killer and see him behind bars.

"He wasn't at the show last night," Mr. Monte began, locking his fingers together.

I paced around the room anxiously. "I thought my return to the circus would push him to seek me out, but it hasn't. What if he's disappeared for good? Maybe he got tired of hunting me down and trying to kill me."

The thought was too good to be true and we both knew it.

Mr. Monte shook his head and pushed out of his seat emphatically. "If we're right, the killer has made it his life's goal to hunt down tightrope walkers and bring them to an end. He wouldn't stop out of the blue because it got too hard. No, the difficulty of it would make it even more enticing. This is a game for him. He threatened you for months and toyed with you for sport. He won't rest until the job is done."

"Until I'm dead," I said, because Mr. Monte couldn't. The killer wanted me dead and that thought alone terrified me. "We need to do something about this," I urged.

Mr. Monte held out his hands to stop me from proceeding any further. "I understand your eagerness, but if the killer senses it, he'll use it against us. We have to be careful."

"So, what do you expect me to do? Sit around and wait for him to make his move?" I asked in anger, waving my hands around.

Mr. Monte sat back down in his chair. "That's exactly what I want you to do."

I raised my eyebrows and opened my mouth to argue with him, but he stopped me.

"I will not let the killer get close to hurting you. We'll make sure you're protected, but the plan stands. We have to let him come to us."

I took a deep breath, trying to calm the blood boiling in my veins. I couldn't wait—couldn't continue performing with the fear of him watching and waiting to make his move. "But how will you keep me safe if we don't even know if he's among us, or how he'll attack, or when? You can't!"

"I spoke with Mr. Young and he's sending a barrage of guards as we speak. We will do everything in our power to keep you safe." Mr. Monte retrieved a batch of paperwork from his desk just as Monroe walked into the room.

"Just the man I was looking for!" Mr. Monte exclaimed. "I need to run into town to pay off the Mirage Assembly Hall. Would you mind overseeing the circus tonight? You know how much trouble they can get into."

When Mr. Monte winked at me, I had to stop myself from giving him a rude gesture.

"Babysitting a bunch of ruffians is not exactly how I wanted to spend my evening, but of course I will." Monroe turned to me. "Juniper, are you staying to learn more about finances, or leaving it up to the old men? Edward gets cranky when asked to do paperwork, so I might need your assistance." Monroe laughed lightheartedly and took a seat next to Mr. Monte, patting his friend on the shoulder.

I understood then that the conversation between me and Mr. Monte was over. "No, I will not be staying." I stormed away, slamming the door on my way out. Possibly a bit dramatic, but I was done playing the killer's game and allowing Mr. Monte to make the calls.

"What's her problem?" Monroe asked.

"Women." Mr. Monte rolled his eyes.

I quickly changed into a leotard and loose breeches before making my way to the dancer's tent. I spoke to Charlotte about my anger while stretching my limbs. Mr. Monte had instructed me to join the dancers that afternoon to help me loosen up, claiming that I was too rigid, whatever the hell that meant.

But I was glad for their company and their insight on the issue at hand. Thankfully, they took my side, agreeing it wasn't right that Mr. Monte was allowing me to be a sitting duck. Despite their encouragement, I was still on edge, and I needed a release.

I searched for something that would take my mind off it, finding myself in Cassius's tent before I knew it.

"Couldn't stay away, huh?" he asked, shoveling a pile of manure into a bin.

"God, you reek." I pinched my fingers over my nose when I came to stand next to him.

"Not used to seeing real men do hard labor, are you? I bet all the men in Axminster smell like fresh flowers."

"They do, and at the moment I'd prefer it to this." I tried to get used to the smell. "Where is that punching bag you were using a few weeks ago?"

Cassius stopped mid-scoop, looking at me out of the corner of his eye. "Why, might I ask?"

"Well, I'm frustrated, and I want to punch something," I claimed nonchalantly with a shrug of my shoulders. If my mother knew that I was doing this right now, she would have a heart attack and die.

Cassius stared at me for a moment before laughing wildly. It was the first time I'd heard him laugh that hard. "Miss Rose, I don't think your little arms would do much to that punching bag no matter how hard you tried." He felt my arms for muscle, raising an eyebrow as if to say, 'I told you so,' when all he felt was soft, pliable skin.

I ripped my arm away from him. "I'll have you know I'm stronger than you might think."

He rolled his eyes before setting down his shovel and going into the back to retrieve the bag. That's one thing I appreciated about Cassius. He didn't ask questions. Finally, he rolled it out and set it in front of me. Grabbing my hands, he began to wrap white tape around my knuckles.

"Okay," Cassius began, clearing his throat. "Feet shoulder width apart, hands up and elbows in, and bend your knees a little." He walked around me to determine if I'd followed his instructions. When he was pleased, he moved up to the bag, assuming his own fighting stance. "You're just going to jab at the bag. It might hurt your hands at first, but you'll get used to it." He showed me exactly how, keeping his head straight and punching the bag with his left arm, making it swing back and forth.

Cassius was much stronger than me and suddenly I felt embarrassed. I was weak. And in the past, I hadn't been able to protect myself and still couldn't. I was angry that we, as women, couldn't fight back—that we were never taught how to. Why had God made women to be such weak creatures? Such easy prey?

He seemed to sense my nerves. "Just hit it once."

I took a deep breath before putting my hands up to my face and remembering to tuck in my elbows. Then I struck the bag, my fist connecting with the grain inside. The impact stung, but overall, it felt good to hit something without consequence.

"Keep going." Cassius nodded his head when I stopped.

That was a good sign at least. He watched from every angle, circling my body as I continued to punch. Suddenly he stepped behind me and placed his hands on both of my hips.

My breath hitched at the feeling of his warm, strong hands on my waist, permeating the fabric of my leotard. "Keep your core tight, like when you walk on the tightrope, and use your hips to propel your motions. Your arms can't do the job alone. If you swivel your hips when you jab, the punch will be that much stronger." He pushed my right hip forward, his fingertips digging into my skin.

When his breath brushed down my neck, I couldn't seem to move. I just stared at the bag in front of me. He had no idea the effect he had on me.

"Okay," I finally whispered. I did as he instructed, pushing my hips forward when I hit the punching bag, and this time, the impact seemed much stronger.

"There you go," he said in approval, watching until sweat gleamed on my temple.

There was something so appealing about a man being pleased with a woman. It was strange, but it was enticing the way Cassius was teaching me, and I think I'd do anything he asked.

My fists were burning and sore, and my clothes were beginning to stick to my body with sweat. Finally, when I couldn't seem to catch my breath, I grabbed the bag to stop it from swinging, and took a moment to rest. I could have kept going for hours but for now, I was able to breathe without thoughts of the killer pressing on my chest like a ton of bricks.

Cassius stood with a proud smile before unwrapping the tape from my fists. "Do you mind telling me what's got you so frustrated?"

After such an exhausting day, I just wanted to lay down. "Let's get out of here and I'll tell you," I said, brushing the sweat from my forehead.

Without another word, he grabbed his things and we returned to the train. He walked straight to his room and I followed him inside, crashing into his inviting bed. It was funny, that only after one day of being reunited, his room had become ours. I remembered Charlotte telling me long ago that Cassius never let anyone lay with him through the night. That gave me hope, even though the thought of him being with other women made me jealous. Cassius was mine and I was his. And he didn't have to ask me to spend the night, I just knew. This was our place to come together at the end of a long day and speak freely without everyone else watching.

Cassius stripped out of his shirt and sat down on the edge of the bed to unlace his boots. The muscles in his back shifted and I watched his slow movements until he finally laid next to me, resting his palms on top of his bare stomach.

I wanted to get Cassius's opinion on Mr. Monte's instruction to see if he thought Mr. Monte was as crazy as I did. So, to pull us out of the silence I said, "The killer didn't make a move at the last performance, and Mr. Monte doesn't want to take action to provoke him, so he told me to stay put and let the killer to come to us."

Cassius turned on his side to face me. "He said that?" he asked in disbelief.

I just nodded, which prompted him to continue.

"Why would he ask you to just wait around? The killer's intention is to hurt you and you should be prepared."

"Exactly!" I exclaimed, encouraged that he was agreeing with me. "I can't just sit around anymore. I've been haunted by that man for over a year. And now, we're on *his* schedule, waiting for him to make an appearance? That's ridiculous. And it puts me in an extremely vulnerable position."

He agreed with a shake of his head. "That's not fair to you. But, if we were to pursue the killer, what would we even do? We can't force him to come out of hiding. We tried that when we announced your arrival at the circus."

"That's what I'm stuck on," I groaned, rubbing my temple as a headache formed. I covered my eyes with my hands and allowed myself to think. "Part of what Mr. Monte is saying is valid. We can't push the killer or he'll know we're trying to stop him. And Mr. Monte said Mr. Young is sending some guards to protect me in the instance that the killer does strike. Maybe that's enough."

"Since when are Mr. Monte and Mr. Young pen pals?" he scoffed and sat up to cross his legs in front of him.

I knew that would upset him. He didn't like the idea of the circus being connected with the wealthy in any form, even with the Janvier family.

"Since I got Mr. Young involved in this to begin with. He's holding up his end of the bargain so long as I agree to marry his son when it's over."

There was a painful silence that followed, and his eyes were cast down in defeat. "How about we put Mr. Young behind bars?" he joked, but I knew he was serious.

"I wish we could." Although the killer was our main concern, Mr. Young would be yet another enemy by the end of this. If we managed to even catch the killer, I'd be stripped from the circus again, because of the deal I made with him. There was no way out of this—no way for me to win.

Cassius seemed to sense the conflict in me, so he braced his arm on the bed and leaned closer. "Don't worry, we'll figure it all out."

I nodded along with him, but I didn't see a way out of the deal with Mr. Young.

"I think you just need to distract yourself in the meantime." He leaned even closer, slowly trailing his fingertips up my arm.

"And how do you suppose I do that?" I asked, leaning up on my forearm.

"Well, I have a few ideas." He chuckled as his teeth caught his bottom lip.

I watched, delirious, as his teeth slowly let go of his lip, his pink tongue darting out to lick the hurt. Was he implying what I thought he was? I'd been given the chance to reconnect with Cassius, we'd shared every detail of the last few months and come to trust one another again, but I yearned for him in a way that went beyond all that. I wanted to feel him, touch him, kiss him. And I think he wanted the same thing. I told myself that we couldn't move too quickly and lose sight of the friendship we'd built, but in that moment, I wanted to lose myself.

I found myself looking at his lips—the soft pink color and the fullness of them. I remember what it was like to kiss him, how complete it felt when our lips met, yet how I always yearned for more. It'd been too long.

Before I could overthink it, I grabbed his arm and pulled him to me.

He didn't hesitate before pressing his lips against mine. I weaved my fingers through his hair and pressed my chest against his for some sort of friction or heat, or whatever it was that I needed to feel closer to him. I ran my hands down his bare abdomen and held onto his waist as his lips roved over mine hastily.

Separating my lips, I allowed his tongue to slip into my mouth, and the softness of it made me clench my knees together. Swinging my leg over his waist, I crawled on top of him. As I ran my hands down his strong chest, his fingertips grazed my spine until he was grabbing my hips tightly, holding me in place. His mouth moved to my neck suddenly, placing wet kisses down my throat until he reached my collarbone. He paused to breathe for a moment, and his warm breath tickled my chest before he sat against the headboard. I leaned my head back to allow him more access as he moved toward my neck, but instead, he nipped lightly on my ear. A gasp escaped me at the feeling, and I grabbed his jaw and forced his mouth onto mine once more, eager to taste him.

He tasted like home—like cool mint and a summer's breeze—like the feeling of the sun warming my skin. I wrapped my arms around his neck just as his hands slid under my shirt. Arching my back, I gasped as his lips moved to the middle of my chest. His tongue licked at the soft skin on the outside of my breasts, but he pulled away too quickly and pushed me onto my back.

It was difficult with Cassius. I wanted to touch him, and I wanted him to touch every inch of me, but I had this troubling feeling that I was expected to control myself. I was taught my whole life to marry a man before ever laying with him. But more than that, I was nervous. This was all new to me, but not to him. And it held me back, the fact that he'd slept with other women.

Despite my worry, he slowly sucked on my bottom lip, sending a tingling sensation into my stomach and down into my toes. That was by far the best feeling I'd ever experienced. He continued to kiss my jaw all the way down to my navel, but just as I closed my eyes in pleasure, someone burst through the door.

"My apologies!" Gus covered his eyes like a little boy and turned away from us quickly.

My eyes widened out of embarrassment. Me sprawled across the bed below Cassius was not an image I wanted anyone to see. And I didn't want the other performers to think of me as another one of his playthings, especially because that was how Cassius had treated women in the past. And maybe I was wrong to think it was in the past. Maybe Cassius hadn't changed. Maybe he wanted to sleep with me more than know me, and maybe he was growing tired of waiting for me to be ready.

But Gus's interruption hadn't affected Cassius in the slightest. He just gazed across the room at Gus with a smirk, still hovering above me. "How can we help you?"

I laid unmoving beneath Cassius, absolutely mortified, and his easy response to Gus made me spiral into a sea of questions. How many times had Cassius done this? With how many girls? And how many times had he been interrupted, just like we were?

"Uh," Gus stuttered, still covering his eyes. "Mr. Monte's asking for you."

Cassius raised his brows and pushed himself into a seated position. "Could he wait? I'm a little busy at the moment."

Gus tried to hide the little snicker that leapt out, but I heard it well enough. "I was actually speaking to the lady."

I picked my head up in surprise before crawling out from under Cassius. I was grateful for the space between us—for any distraction that would take me away from that destructively tempting mouth of his. Despite how easily I was pulled to him, I was worrying again about things I thought I'd gotten over—about his character and his past. I didn't know why this was bothering me so much, but I needed to sort out my thoughts for a moment, so, I brushed out the wrinkles in my clothes and straightened my hair.

Cassius just sighed and threw his head back on a pillow, the tension of our heady actions putting him on edge. "Gus, do me a favor and tell Mr. Monte that if he takes Miss Rose from me again, we'll have a problem."

Gus just laughed and saluted Cassius.

Putting the worry I had about Cassius aside, I bit back a smile. Hearing Cassius claim me as his made me want to rip off his clothes. But I needed to be careful and listen to my doubts because there may be truth in them. So, I stopped myself from reminiscing in how Cassius's lips felt on mine, or about what we were about to do, as I followed Gus down the corridor and entered Mr. Monte's office.

"Ah, Juniper, take a seat!" he exclaimed, rifling through page after page of reports.

What kind of reports, I didn't have a clue, so I took a seat to get a closer look and found them to be newspaper articles with different headlines proclaiming the circus's successes.

Suddenly he set the newspapers down and folded his hands atop them, looking at me sincerely. "First, I wanted to apologize for my actions this morning. I know how tedious this process must be for you, and I'm sorry."

I nodded my head, thankful for his apology.

"I don't know where the killer is, and therefore, I don't have a plan to stop him."

"Then how do we draw him in or know with certainty that he's already in our midst? I don't want to be unprepared." I was glad Mr. Monte had the courage to apologize, but an apology meant nothing if it was not met with action. We needed to make a plan because I couldn't sit around any longer and *wait*.

"We can't. There is no—" Suddenly Mr. Monte stopped, caught on something. His eyes widened and he looked at the door behind me. "I think I might have just the solution."

I sat there waiting, but he said nothing. I braced my arms on the desk, before I asked in anticipation, "Would you like to explain?"

Mr. Monte finally looked at me, a smile tugging on his lips. "We're going to need Flint."

Chapter Twenty

I didn't ask questions. I had no idea how Flint fit into the situation, but I trusted Mr. Monte, and since this was the first sign of a solution, I didn't really care who took part in it.

When I gathered Flint and brought him back to Mr. Monte's office, he was just as confused as I was.

Mr. Monte pulled out a chair for him. "Take a seat, my boy. This might take a while."

And it did. It took hours to work out all the details, but soon enough Mr. Monte had a well-devised plan with little room for failure.

Flint tapped his fingers lightly on the arm of his chair. "I just want to make sense of this…you're asking me to disguise myself as an ally of the killer?"

Mr. Monte smiled proudly. "To put it lightly, yes. Our next performance is in Eanverness, one of the wealthiest kingdoms on our side of the sea. We'll be given a stage to perform on, similar to the one in Turnstead. You'll be disguised, so no one will recognize you, and I want you to leap onto the stage and accuse her of being an imposter— someone who doesn't belong in the circus. We'll work out the details of that later." He paused to gauge our reactions. Mine was contemplative and Flint looked utterly shocked. "Once you give this speech, we'll detain you as just another naysayer, but if this goes according to our plan, the killer will be watching. The crowd will see you as a lunatic outsider, but the killer will know who you are. He'll believe he has a companion, one I assume he'll seek out, and if he does, all you have to do is lead him to the perfect position come the next show and we'll be there waiting for him."

Flint interrupted Mr. Monte immediately, "How will the killer know it's me under the disguise? How is he going to contact me?"

Mr. Monte stood from his chair to pace the room, racking his brain.

"Well, you're a rider. And riders always wear a small rope dangling from the waist of their pants to signify their ranking—sort of like an officer, it's an article of pride. And fortunately for you, the captain of the riding team wears gold."

"But won't the audience recognize him as the captain? We can't have them knowing he's one of us," I said.

Mr. Monte shook his head. "No, no, the rope is something so small, so insignificant, the audience won't even notice it. They'll have no idea what it means. But the killer surely will if he's a part of the circus, as we believe he is."

"Wait, wait." Flint flung out his hands to stop Mr. Monte from continuing. The technicality of this plan was rather confusing, and he took a moment to think through it before listing his questions. "What happens if the killer isn't a part of the circus as we anticipated?"

"He is," I insisted. I was certain of it. There was no way the killer could have threatened me with those letters last year if he didn't live among us. And he couldn't have threatened me during a performance if he didn't know the order of the performance.

"He's going to recognize the rope hanging from your belt and understand who's really under that mask," Mr. Monte assured him.

"Okay," Flint nodded repeatedly, considering it. "If the killer does know it's me under the mask, what will my excuse be for wanting Juniper dead? That's a serious accusation—one that I'll need to back up with a really good reason."

Mr. Monte thought, although I already had the answer. I turned to Flint then, a wariness in my eyes as to what he might think of my proposal. "I chose Cassius over you."

Flint's face fell slightly. Whether he was stunned, or sad, I couldn't tell. Was there still a part of him that was hurt by that fact? I knew we both meant something to each other, but I figured he'd gotten over it.

Regardless of what he felt, I continued, "You're angry that I left you for him. And after I left, you resented my good fortune in Axminster. Play into the fact that I'm wealthy—that's a good enough reason to be angry. And play into your past—how you were degraded and cast aside while high society was wasteful and frivolous."

Flint nodded once again and dropped his head into his hands. "I don't want to make a mistake and risk him finding out that I'm lying."

"You won't. We'll go over every detail and write a script to prepare you. You just have to put on a good act. Convince him." I grabbed Flint's arm and nodded reassuringly.

This could work. This would give us a man on the inside to inform us of what the killer was planning, ahead of time. It was perfect.

Flint gazed at Mr. Monte's desk for a while and the room grew quiet. His eyes darted back and forth while he thought through every aspect of our plan. It was a lot to take in, and a lot to risk. The killer may be targeting tightrope walkers, but if he were to learn that Flint was coming away with information to feed to us, he wouldn't hesitate to kill him.

I watched Flint warily. He had every reason to say no. It would be dangerous, and it was out of his arsenal. He was kind, caring, and loving, and even if I did break his heart last year, he didn't have a bad thing to say about me. It just wasn't like him to hold a grudge. So, if he went through with this, Flint would have to summon true hatred for me— enough to convince the killer. And he would have to be very, very careful.

But despite how dangerous it would be, Flint picked up his head and said, "I'm in."

I leapt up at that moment and strung my arms around his neck. The next few weeks setting this plan into motion was going to be chaotic, but it was better than sitting around waiting. Finally, we were taking steps to end the killer once and for all. It was in our hands now, and I couldn't thank Flint enough for taking this risk.

"Thank you." I cried into his shoulder.

He gently patted me on the back. "What's the worst that could happen?"

Tell him, my subconscious warned me. *Tell him how this could really end.*

I shook my head. It'd be fine. Everything would be fine. The killer would be put behind bars soon and everyone would be safe.

The room turned quiet and the echo of our plan drifted away into the night. We would only speak of this among the three of us, to prevent word from reaching the wrong person, perhaps the killer. So, sealing it as our secret, we bid each other goodnight. Mr. Monte began drafting the speech Flint would practice for the next performance, while Flint and I retired as the sun fell in the west, behind the fields of corn and green rolling hills.

I walked alongside him in the dim hall before saying, "Thank you, truly, for agreeing to do this. It means more to me than you'll ever know."

Flint smiled down at me. "I'm terrified if I'm being completely honest, but I know it'll work. In a mere month, we could end the killer. And I know how big a victory that would be for you. That's why I agreed—to ensure you don't have to live in fear any longer."

Tears welled in my eyes at the realization of how fortunate I was. Despite my fear, I had friends that were willing to risk their lives to protect me. Especially Flint, who I'd hurt so carelessly last year.

While considering the other performers, I thought of Cassius. What would he think about us willingly leading the killer to me, or about Mr. Monte and Flint being involved? I knew the answer without even having to ask him.

He'd be livid.

So, before Flint could retreat to his chamber for the night, I grabbed his wrist to stop him. "Cassius can't know about this."

Flint nodded. "My lips are sealed." He pressed his lips together to show his promise, which made me giggle.

"Thank you," I whispered. "Goodnight, Flint."

"Goodnight, Juniper." He turned over his shoulder and vanished into his bedroom.

I couldn't help but feel guilty and ashamed as I meandered down the corridor to Cassius's room. Cassius and I promised to be honest with each other. No secrets—that's what we agreed on. And here I was, keeping this from him. But he would be worried sick if he found out, and deep down I knew he'd try to stop it from happening.

I couldn't let him do that. This was our best chance to find the killer and I wouldn't let him ruin it. But despite Cassius's incessant need to control every situation, I had a different reason for not telling him. Before Gus interrupted me and Cassius earlier, I was growing sick with doubt. Yes, I was jealous that Cassius had slept with other women, and yes, I had my own insecurities, but it was more than that. And maybe it was because we'd spent months apart and were only just beginning to reconnect, but I didn't fully trust Cassius yet. When I returned to the circus, we started back on square one, and Cassius was still showing traits that I couldn't reconcile. And his tendency to revert to his old ways really worried me.

I knew it was unfair to hold his past against him, and I didn't want to argue over an issue that may be coming from my insecurities, so I decided it would be wiser to think about it.

When I clicked open the door, Cassius was in the same position I'd left him in. He was sitting on his bed with his ankles crossed in front of him, reading through a small book. His eyes flicked between the lines, and he bit at the side of his cheek in curiosity, making me wonder what must have been so interesting within those pages. Without taking his eyes off the book, he said, "That took longer than expected. What's Mr. Monte up to now?"

I cleared my throat, guilt pressing on my chest like a ton of bricks. "You know Mr. Monte. Rambling on about the next show and finances and such." I rolled my eyes, hoping my annoyance would convince him of my story.

"That I do," he remarked, still not averting his eyes from the page.

Before he could say anything else, or lure me into bed with him, I began to grab the few things I'd left in his room. "I think I'm going to spend the night in my room, if that's all right."

Cassius's eyes flicked up to mine and he set the book down promptly. "Why?"

Sensing a note of confusion in his voice, I tried my best to come up with a reasonable excuse. "I'm just stressed. Mr. Monte and I were arguing about the killer again, and I think I just need some time to sort through it all. I don't think I'd be very good company."

He frowned then, sitting up straighter. "You're always good company."

I took a deep breath, hating myself for the worry in his voice. Cassius was willing to work with me, comfort me, and be with me, and now I was losing precious time with him because I was jealous and mistrusting. I shook my head and moved to the door. "I just don't want to worry you. I promise I'm okay. I just need a little time."

He nodded, but it was clear he was confused, if not saddened. Every time I was angry, worried, or scared, I found comfort with him, and out of nowhere I'd opted for the opposite.

"I'll see you in the morning then," he said in defeat.

I tried to smile to offer him some semblance that it would be alright. The truth was, I didn't know if it would be.

Chapter Twenty-One

He was standing on the stage, shrouded in darkness. He was alone, empty stadium seats surrounding him. Rose petals were strewn across the stage, the sign of a performance well done. He looked out across the expanse of an empty crowd before slowly pacing around the stage, his black boots thudding and creating a hollow beat.

He tilted his head back and forth, possibly imagining what it would have been like to perform for a crowd of his own. And when he took the next step, his foot caught on something. He slowly looked down to find a golden rope hooked under his foot. Bending down, he picked it up to examine it, spotting the initials F.R. stamped on the back.

"Flint Rye," the killer whispered, turning his head to the curtain at the back of the stage.

I felt as though I was watching the future play out right before my eyes.

"You can't fool me, Juniper." The killer completely disregarded the evidence of Flint being there and spoke to me instead. "I know where you are." He turned his head around the room, trying to find me, as if I were actually there with him.

I thought I might vomit. The killer was always ten steps ahead. He knew. He knew it was a trap. Our plan didn't work. And he was going to kill Flint and me both because of it.

"And I'm coming." His voice faded into silence, echoing across the high colosseum-style walls at the same time his figure melted to ash and floated away in the wind, never to be seen again.

I tore my eyes open and drew in a sharp breath of air, but I couldn't move. My legs were stuck to the bed, my arms planted at my side, as though I was frozen in time. Unable to move my head, only my eyes shifted around the dark room—one I barely recognized. I had to remind myself that I wasn't with Cassius—that I was in my own room. And with that, the overwhelming reality of being completely alone washed over me.

Then I saw something move out of the corner of my eye.

It was a small movement, and then it was gone, but I focused on that corner of the room, where a small desk cast a shadow on the wall. I watched it for a few minutes, not daring to blink, and when I confirmed nothing was there, I directed my attention toward the other side of the room. And there he was, standing beside my closet, his frame a hulking shadow in the dark. The killer was inside my room, right in front of me. This was it. This was when I would lose the circus and everyone I loved.

"Help," I whispered, my vocal cords scraping together painfully.

The killer moved toward me. Step after step, he came closer and closer until he was standing right over me.

"Help," I said again, a little louder this time. I wanted to close my eyes, but I was completely frozen.

Suddenly the killer crawled across the bed, his arms snaking toward me. The mask he wore gave his face no form; it was like an empty abyss. I felt as though if I touched his face, my hand would just melt through a sticky pot of black ink. And then it was mere inches away from mine and I felt his serpentine breath whispering across my cheek.

I began to shake then, gasping for air or for some form of movement. Why couldn't I move? Why couldn't I shake away this fear and *move*? I felt the bed shift as the killer crawled on top of me.

No. No, no, no. I had to stop this. Now.

I opened my mouth, forcing out one single name. "Cassius," I spoke too softly.

The killer straddled my hips as his face inched closer.

"Get off," I cried and suddenly felt my fingers twitch and my toes wiggle.

There we go. Then, I could move my hands and my ankles.

"Get off," I said louder, my voice coming back to me. "Get off!" I screamed. Moving my arms felt like carrying bricks. But in the next few moments I was able to move fully. I pushed at him, connecting with a solid, warm body. "Get off of me!" I screamed.

And suddenly the killer took a knife out of the sheath at his side and aimed it over my heart.

This was it. And there was nothing I could do. I was going to die. My eyes widened and I took one last breath before closing my eyes.

"Juniper!" someone screamed, but their voice felt far off in the distance, almost undetectable.

I didn't dare open my eyes, for fear of what I would see. I cried and gasped for breath, grappling with his body while trying to push him off me.

Then, warm hands gripped my cheek and I screamed as if it was the last thing I would ever do.

"Juniper!" My name was called again, clearer this time.

But all I could feel was the killer on top of me, his hands touching my body, his fingers cold, like ice. He was going to take my life right here and now. I'd never see my friends again. I'd never be able to walk on the tightrope, dance with Charlotte, drink with Gus and Hugh, laugh with Flint, or kiss Cassius ever again. I'd never be able to thank Mr. Monte for giving me a home. And I'd never be able to see my sister married or my mother finally happy.

"Juniper, open your eyes!"

I knew that voice. I ripped open my eyes to find Cassius sitting on top of me, gripping my face in his hands. The whites of his eyes were wide and apparent in the darkness.

"Get off!" I screamed, pleading for him not to touch me. "Get off, get off," I cried, covering my face. My hands were shaking—every inch of my body was shaking.

Cassius leapt off me and came to stand by my side. "Open your eyes, Juniper. Open your eyes for me," he instructed softly.

I did as he said. When I saw that the killer was nowhere to be seen, and it was only Cassius standing by my side, my breathing slowed, and my chest stopped heaving up and down. The killer hadn't been there. I'd seen him and felt him, but he hadn't been there. I imagined the whole thing.

I turned over on my side and cried into my hands, trying to forget everything I'd just seen. It felt so real. Every time I opened my eyes, I imagined him standing across the room, covered in darkness, the walls pressing in as he inched closer. And if I stayed in this room, I would suffocate to death.

"Get me out of here. Please," I begged Cassius.

He lifted me up and pulled my legs around his waist, carrying me like a child. When he tenderly secured me to his chest, his hand pressed firmly to my spine, my muscles suddenly relaxed. I understood then that he was real—that I was safe.

"Shhh," he cooed, hurrying out of the room. "Keep your eyes open, okay? Everything is alright. You're safe," he whispered.

I followed his instruction and peeled my eyes open, watching as we wound through the corridor, the hallways receding behind me. I counted every door as we retreated from my room, trying to keep myself from closing my eyes, and by the time Cassius stopped moving, I had the entire train memorized. Every crack in every floorboard, every panel in the wall that was loose, every name on every door.

Suddenly I heard the train door drop down onto the grass below and felt a cool breeze wash over the back of my neck. Cassius slowly walked down the ramp before sitting on the edge. He kept me on his lap while lightly stroking my hair.

"Look at the sky," he whispered.

I leaned back from his chest and tilted my head up to the night sky, met with hundreds of glittering stars.

"Beautiful, isn't it?" He looked up too, his eyes shining as silver stars danced through his golden irises.

A small smile formed on his lips, but when he turned to me, his face fell. He spoke quietly, so as not to startle me. "The killer has made you afraid of the dark, and I told you not to close your eyes because I knew what you'd see. I've seen it hundreds of times myself. But it isn't possible to keep your eyes open every moment of every day." He laughed lightly. "So, instead, I want you to think of darkness as something beautiful, like this." He pointed up to the sky once again.

His encouragement meant more to me than he'd ever know. But regardless, I had doubts. "What if it doesn't work?"

What if the killer remained in my thoughts for years and years to come? What if, even after he was caught and detained, he haunted me for the rest of my life?

"It will, I promise." He nodded his head to reassure me.

"Tell me how." I looked deep into his eyes, curious as to how he'd survived the months after his sister's death.

"Well, after my sister died, I blamed myself. I was so ashamed that I couldn't save her. Most nights that followed, I saw her fall in my dreams. Over and over, I watched it happen. I would wake up, absolutely terrified, and all I could think to do was escape the confines of my room. So, I went to look at the stars."

Cassius paused and looked out toward the sea of trees that bordered our train. "I found comfort in them, and they took my mind off my sister. The dreams still came—they'll always come—but somehow the stars were a reprieve."

When I pulled back to look at Cassius, I knew I wasn't alone.

He tucked a stray piece of hair behind my ear. "So, if you can help it, don't close your eyes when you're afraid because the killer will be right there waiting for you. And when it comes time to rest, maybe you can use the stars like I do." Cassius let his head fall back so he could witness the sky above him.

I followed suit, flicking my eyes back and forth, trying to see how many stars I could count. Before I knew it, images of the killer vanished completely and all I could feel was Cassius holding me steadily in his arms. I gently tucked my head into his shoulder, grateful for the protector in him.

"Thank you," I whispered into his neck.

"There's nothing to thank me for." Cassius grasped my shoulders and pulled me away so he could look at me. "When I came to the circus, I needed hope. That was Mr. Monte. And after my sister's death, I needed a savior. That was you." Cassius smiled lightly. "And right now, I think you need a savior too."

Tears welled in my eyes, but they were good tears—the kind that reminded me I was loved. The kind that meant I was still breathing. That I'd survived another day.

"I already have one," I said. I leaned forward and wrapped my arms around him, curling my nose into his neck so I could breathe him in.

And when I grew tired once again, he cradled me into his chest and carried me back to bed. This time, when I closed my eyes, all I could see was stars.

Chapter Twenty-Two

That morning, I awoke in the familiar confines of Cassius's room. Light peeled through the window, revealing small flecks of dust in the air. I took a gulp of that warm, autumn breeze and, rolling over groggily, came within inches of Cassius's face. His full, pink lips were parted beautifully, and the shadow of his eyelashes rested on his cheeks.

Memories of last night suddenly came back to me. He was there for me even after I tried to push him away, and despite what my sleeping alone might have meant, he still helped me. He was *good*.

So why was I so nervous? So uncomfortable in my own skin? So afraid to say anything at all? Reconnecting with Cassius meant making up for lost time. It meant being closer to him than I'd ever been before. But how could I be close to him in that way if I was constantly competing with the reputation of half the other women in the circus?

I held my breath as Cassius's eyes flickered and took that as my cue to silently creep out of his room, trying my best not to wake him.

I felt terrible, leaving after he rescued me last night, but I needed some space to sort out my thoughts about Cassius's prior relationships before I could move forward with him. So, I hurried to my own room and dressed quickly, finding my way to the field beyond the train, per Mr. Monte's instructions last night.

The next show was in two weeks, and with so little time to fashion a theme, we'd have to work quickly. I arrived early to the main tent, but soon enough the rest of the performers gathered around me.

I couldn't bear to search the crowd to find where Cassius stood or gauge his reaction to my disappearing act.

"I need the riders in the center!" Mr. Monte shouted, and the men ran obediently into the center of the ring.

"Dancers line up in front of a rider of your choosing."

The dancers obeyed Mr. Monte's command while the rest of the performers sat in the stands to watch.

The girls skipped quickly to their places and stood quietly, waiting for further instruction. But what came next, surely, they were not expecting.

"Now, I want you to dance," Mr. Monte said with a wicked gleam in his eyes.

"We did our part at the masquerade ball, and I will not perform another waltz in my lifetime," Walter exclaimed, and the men agreed with emphatic nods and low grumbles of disapproval.

"I did not ask you to waltz, did I, Mr. Keen?" Mr. Monte smiled. "Indeed, we dazzled the wealthy at the masquerade ball, and I don't doubt they'll be returning to our next show. So there's no mistaking who we *really* are, I want us to dance in the way only we know how…" he paused and his eyes flicked around the room. "Wildly."

At that, the band struck a chord, and the group of riders and dancers joined hands. The performers were jumping and kicking, throwing dust into the air as though a sandstorm had washed over the circus.

I stood with the other performers in the stands and clapped my hands along with the music. There was no problem in playing dress up for a night, but the wealthy needed to understand that we would always be ourselves, no matter our audience.

We erupted into cheers when they finished dancing, and Mr. Monte instructed everyone to disperse to practice their own acts. I was about to powder my feet, preparing to walk the rope when Mr. Monte called me and Cassius aside.

My heart began to thunder, and I looked across the stand to find Cassius being his usual self, clapping the backs of the men at his side and jogging to join Mr. Monte on the floor. Maybe he hadn't taken my leaving this morning personally. So, I wiped my sweaty palms on my breeches and moved to join them.

When I reached the floor, Mr. Monte had his hands folded in front of himself in excitement. "I have a different idea for the two of you," he began. "And prove me wrong, but I think you can anticipate what I'm going to ask of you."

Cassius turned to me with a gentle smile and said, "I'm in," stopping Mr. Monte from saying anything further.

Cassius, the boy who had detested me and my past, not interested in proving us as lovers to the crowd, was now agreeing without question. Who was this man at my side? Where had Cassius gone? Rather than being secretive about his feelings toward me, he was now ready to share it with the world.

But something in me had changed. I was guilty of hiding our plan for the killer from Cassius, and I was vulnerable being in the same room with him. It was so easy to love him. But I worried that if I let myself fall into that, I would be heartbroken by the end of it.

That was what led to me to say, "Are you sure that's a good idea? Us working together?"

I noticed Cassius's smile falter, despite how well he tried to hide it.

But Mr. Monte's bundled eyebrows and his concerned frown were what hit me in the chest.

"It's a great idea! The audience fell in love with you two all over again when you sang him that song, Juniper. And now we need to give them what they want. Plus, with the killer possibly lurking around, performing with Cassius will give you more protection." Mr. Monte quirked a brow to remind me of our plan.

My heart clenched at what I was hiding, but he was right. With the killer's whereabouts unknown, I needed someone by my side. It was a good idea.

I nodded my head in finality and offered them both a smile. "Alright. What were you thinking?"

Mr. Monte straightened his top hat and went to tend to the other performers. Turning over a shoulder he said, "Go warm up and I'll meet you in an hour to go over the specifics."

I stood there uncomfortably, not knowing what to do with myself, and even more so when Cassius spread a hand across the small of my back, his warmth crashing into me.

"Is everything alright?" he asked quietly, despite the shouting in the tent.

I finally looked to him with a bright, unconvincing smile. "Everything's fine."

I agreed to meet him in my tent after I changed. If Cassius was at odds with me or the situation, he didn't show it.

But walking into the tent twenty minutes later proved me wrong. He was most certainly at odds, at this would not blow over as I had hoped.

Cassius promptly turned to me with his hands on his hips and conflict in his eyes. "You wanted there to be no secrets between us, so I'm going to be honest with you." He paused and ran a hand through his curls, possibly wondering how to phrase what he was going to say next, before he came out with, "What the hell is going on with you?"

I chuckled faintly at his brazenness and shook my head. "Nothing's going on."

"Now you're the one lying."

I was. I was lying. And I wanted to talk to him about it, but I didn't know how.

But before I could offer a reply—a half-hearted, lacking reply—he continued, "You mean to tell me that *you* opting to sleep in your own room to 'sort through some things,' and being wary of performing together—something you've been pushing for, I might add—is normal? Come on, J. That doesn't sound like you."

I didn't want him to be angry, but I needed him to understand. "I just need time," I answered quietly.

And when he stepped forward to meet me, I wanted to cry at the kindness in his eyes—the kindness I was taking for granted.

"Time for what?" he asked, not angry.

I took a step back and rubbed at my temple, my brain running too quickly for me to catch up. But I couldn't look him in the eyes, so I opted to tilt my head back. "Everything. There's no time for anything anymore. If I'm sad, I have to get over it, otherwise I'll be wasting precious time here. Time that I may not have. And if I'm scared, well, I'm just stuck being scared."

There was half of it—the half that I could explain. And there was this looming pressure that I needed to resolve it all quickly, because I didn't have much time left. But that pressure didn't allow me to feel what I needed to feel.

He reached out to grab my hand and whispered, "I get it. You're going through a lot right now. With the killer, and with Mr. Young and your deal. But you don't *have* to do anything. You can be sad, or angry, or scared. Hell, I would be if I were you."

I slipped my hand out of his and stepped back. He didn't get it. "I can't be any of those things. If I could, we wouldn't be having this conversation right now." I looked into his eyes, trying not to get angry. "I asked you to give me time, and you couldn't. So can I really be sad, or angry, or scared if you're always asking me to be better?"

He looked at me in defeat then. "That's not what I meant, Juniper. I just want to know what's going on in your head." He paused to contemplate what he really wanted to say, but it seemed he was holding back. "I'm not asking you to get over anything, just to let me in."

I pressed my lips into a thin line. I couldn't let him in. I couldn't tell him about the killer and how we planned to draw him out. And I couldn't tell him why I was so nervous to be around him all the time, because as soon as I did, it would cause a rift between us, and he would know how frightened I really was. And maybe he'd be tired of the fighting and the back and forth. Maybe he'd want to go back to what was easy.

"I can't," was all I said. My head felt like it might explode. I had no idea what to do.

I turned away from him and eagerly grabbed my things, wanting to be anywhere but here, looking into Cassius's disappointed eyes. "And I can't do this right now. I'll come back when Mr. Monte's ready."

By that point, hopefully I could hold it together. So, I rushed out of the tent, leaving Cassius on his own. I couldn't do what Mr. Monte wanted me to do. I couldn't put on an act and play lovers. That was Cassius's specialty.

I spent an hour in my room, curled up, counting every scratch on the wall, to take my mind off of what was at stake.

And then, a little knock sounded on the door and Olive entered the room. "Mr. Monte requests you on the lawn."

I sat up slowly with a yawn. "What for?"

She shrugged. "Not sure, but it seems important. You should come quickly."

Perfect. Another thing to worry about. Could there be just one moment where I could be by myself and not have to worry about a single thing? Regardless, I trailed behind Olive.

We called the empty field outside "the lawn." It was the closest thing we had to a front yard, and when I stepped outside, I was dumbfounded.

Twenty guards had arrived, standing in a uniform line with their chests puffed out and their fists glued to their sides. They wore black breeches and matching waistcoats with ironed lapels. Golden braids decorated their chests and the sides of their pant legs. And black bowlers, similar to a top hat but shrunken in size and rounded at the top, covered their heads. They stood so still it looked as though they weren't even breathing.

The other performers surrounded them but kept a safe distance.

"What is this?" I questioned, coming to stand next to Mr. Monte.

He motioned toward the guards. "These men are at your mercy, Miss Rose. Mr. Young sent them this morning. They'll be safeguarding you until we contain the killer. They'll be posted outside your bedroom, your tent, and at every door during our performances."

I tried to think logically instead of erupting in annoyance. Sure, having someone trail behind me and watch my every move would be irritating, but my safety was important, as was the rest of the performers'. And these men could help catch the killer. I'd learned well enough from my mistakes last year that I needed to let go of my pride and allow others to help me.

Although the frustration remained. Being a woman, I couldn't defend myself well enough, and I detested that. But I couldn't change it, so I'd accept their protection, even if it drove me out of my mind. Maintaining the little liberty I was allowed, I said, "I have terms."

"Is that so?" Mr. Monte sighed. But, knowing how stubborn I was, he allowed me to continue. "Spill it."

I looked to the guards before me. "First, if I'm with any of the performers, you must stay at a distance. I don't want our time together to be interrupted. Second, you must protect *every* member of the circus. I don't hold more importance than anyone else here. Third, if you spot something amiss, don't hesitate to stop it. Don't ask for permission. Act, because there are no second chances. And most importantly, don't ever report to Mr. Young. The information we gather about the killer cannot spread. Otherwise, we'll risk our plan being undermined by the killer himself. The information stays within the circus and the circus alone. Can I trust you to do that?"

I couldn't have then blabbing to Mr. Young about their movements. Not only was it dangerous to have information filtering about, but it would ruin my chance to stay at the circus after catching the killer. More than anything, I needed more time. And keeping Mr. Young in the dark would give me that.

I looked to each of the guards, watching their heads nod. "Good." I dismissed the guards and turned to Mr. Monte. "Cassius and I are ready for you."

He followed me back to my tent with the company of guards following us at a safe distance. When we entered the tent, a few guards remained outside to watch the door, while the others dispersed to watch the performers as I'd asked.

Mr. Monte positioned himself between Cassius and me, and I was grateful for the separation.

"At the next performance I want the two of you to dance. I want it to be sexy, close, and quick. So, I brought in some help!" Mr. Monte motioned to the entrance of the tent exactly as Charlotte walked in. "Charlotte is going to teach you some moves today. You can play around a bit with the style before we draft a routine. Tomorrow, you'll begin practicing choreography."

With that, Charlotte skipped into the tent and Mr. Monte bid us farewell.

"This should be fun!" She clapped her hands, and I couldn't help but smile along with her. "Mr. Monte wants this dance to be sexy, which means your movements must be precise and quick, but closely knit. I'll show you a few things before you try it together. Cassius, you're up first."

Cassius stepped up uncomfortably while I positioned myself in the back to watch them. He placed a hand on her waist and intertwined their other hands together, in typical waltz fashion.

"In this dance, I want your form to be tight and technical. This is not a romantic or slow dance. This is sharp. So, elbows at ninety degrees, chins up, and chests out." Charlotte made quick work of fixing Cassius's posture before moving on. "I want you to bend your knees, which will allow you more strength to move across wide spaces in a short amount of time."

I watched closely as they moved synchronously, and with Charlotte leading, Cassius followed wherever she went. If she stepped back, so would he. And if she propelled them forward, he would follow. It was fast and articulate, even without any spins or dips.

After finishing her lesson with Cassius, Charlotte grabbed him by the arm proudly and remarked quietly, as if I couldn't hear, "The only time I could get you to dance like that was when I promised you a night of amazing sex."

She flashed her eyes and Cassius chuckled along with her, the two reminiscing about times past. It felt like I wasn't even there, as I stood in the back, ignored, waiting for Cassius to stop laughing with her and looking at her like that.

"Alright, Juniper, your turn!" Charlotte exclaimed with a saccharine smile.

And I knew she hadn't intended to make me jealous, but why would she mention their past when Cassius and I were now in a relationship? But were we even in a relationship or were we just…something? Suddenly I felt like I'd made things worse—that by my lack of communication and my distance, I'd pushed him further away—far enough away to assume that we weren't anything, which is why he was so blatantly flirting with Charlotte.

I watched as she brushed Cassius's arm, trying to think nothing of it as we swapped places.

I did my best to smile and learn from her. It wasn't her fault she was naturally beautiful, gifted with confidence, and probably out of this world in the bedroom. So, I tried to match her steps and her rhythm for the next hour until I was sweating and ready to take a nap.

"Great job today. I'm going to draft a routine tonight with Mr. Monte that you can practice. Remember to keep a strong frame and bend your knees. I would suggest practicing together before tomorrow!" she said excitedly before leaving us to our own devices.

I couldn't help but scoff as the flaps to the tent closed.

"What?" Cassius asked, harsher than usual.

"Nothing." I shook my head in surprise. "I just didn't think one day of my quietness would convince you to jump back into bed with Charlotte."

He took a step back and squinted at me in utter confusion. "What are you talking about?"

"Oh, come on. Don't act stupid," I said, fed up with his feigned confusion.

This was common for Cassius. He lived for compliments and was proud of his conquests in the bedroom. It made him feel special…wanted even.

"I'm not playing dumb. I never said I wanted to jump into bed with Charlotte!" he exclaimed.

"Sure looked like it." I couldn't even muster any tears. I wasn't sad. I was exhausted. I had so many things on my plate, and this was the last thing I wanted to deal with. "Look, forget about it. I'm exhausted. I'll see you tomorrow."

"Charlotte said we should practice!" he said with desperation in his voice as I began walking away.

"We can practice tomorrow morning before Mr. Monte arrives." I didn't even try to sound enthused as I walked out.

Deep down, I knew Cassius didn't want to sleep with Charlotte, but he didn't make it any easier to trust him when he was giving her that charming smile. I knew we'd have to talk about it before we'd be able to perform together, but that didn't mean it had to be today.

I was hoping to grab a drink and relax for the night, but when I passed Monroe's office, I noticed the door slightly ajar. That was odd. Monroe's door was always locked. Memories of our interaction passed through my mind—the brief story of his sister and the lack of information regarding what really happened all those years ago. We had a solid plan of drawing out the killer once again, and we had guards to protect me, but we didn't know who the killer was or his motives.

I rapped on Monroe's door, waiting a few moments, but no one answered. The door was open, and I didn't feel like I was intruding, so

I slunk into the room, finding it empty. While I waited, I scanned the room diligently. His desk was pristine, as always, the books on the shelf organized by color, and the pictures on the wall positioned symmetrically. Finally, the door creaked open, and a befuddled Monroe walked in.

"Oh! Juniper, nice to see you!" Monroe looked taken aback, his face a bit paler than usual.

"Sorry. I didn't mean to intrude." It looked like I meant to do just that by the way I was snooping around.

"No worries. What can I help you with?" He moved to take a seat behind his desk to sort through a mound of paperwork.

"Well, I know we had a conversation a few weeks ago about your sister, and I wanted to apologize again for being so forthright, but I have a few questions." I gaged his reaction carefully, hoping he wouldn't completely shut me down.

His hands immediately paused their fiddling, and he looked up at me before losing a big sigh. "After you questioned my sister's death, it made me think. I'll never come to terms with what happened to her, but if it'll help us find the killer, then I'll do whatever I can."

That surely wasn't what I was expecting, but I wouldn't complain. "Can you tell me about her? How was your relationship with her?"

Monroe cleared his throat. "We were close, like anyone would expect a brother and sister to be. I made sure she was safe…I was the protective older brother. Meanwhile, she made sure that I had fun. She was a wild card, but I was a complete deck of cards with rules to follow. We worked well together despite our differences."

"Worked well together?" I inquired, tilting my head at his choice of words.

Monroe wrung his hands together and looked down at the desk, lost in memory. "We walked the tightrope together. We worked side by side for years."

"*You* walked the tightrope? You, Monroe Beringer, our financial advisor?" I exclaimed in wonder. How had I never known this? It seemed Monroe had more secrets than I knew. Monroe…a tightrope walker just like me. It was impossible to imagine.

"Yes, I did." He forced a chuckle. "She and I were adored by the crowd. They were enthralled by the idea of a duo on the rope." His eyes were lost in wonder while he explained.

"And did you adore it? Did she?" I leaned closer with every detail he offered, drawn in by the picture he was painting in such vibrant colors.

"It was her passion. And it used to be mine." His face fell. "It was the love of my life before she passed. Then, everything changed."

I let him breathe for a moment without berating him with more questions. Obviously, this was difficult for him. "How did it happen, if you don't mind me asking?"

I understood that Penelope had fallen on purpose, but made it appear as an accident, but how had Katriane managed to fall so violently that it killed her? I hated to ask him this, but I had to understand the past in order to protect the future. My future.

Monroe shuddered and closed his eyes. "The old circus wasn't what it is today. It was woefully underfunded, and we were scraping by with barely enough to eat and less than fifteen performers shacking up in the train."

Fifteen? How had they even performed with so few people?

Monroe continued, "We couldn't even afford to buy new equipment, and it was torn and tarnished from years of use. It was *dangerous*." Monroe looked into my eyes then, vigilance apparent. "Something was bound to happen. And on the night of our last performance of the year, the buckle snapped. Something went amiss with the lever holding the rope in place, and before I knew it, she was falling. In a matter of seconds, she hit the ground." Monroe paused, tears building on the rims of his eyes. "I'd already made it to the platform. I survived but I watched her die right in front of me."

"I'm so sorry," I whispered in disbelief.

We sat in silence, which prompted me to gaze around the room curiously to pass the time. On the other side of the room, I spotted a large photograph hanging on the wall. I'd never noticed it before, but now it loomed over me, illustrating a woman walking a tightrope. Looking closer, I found her to have black hair, like mine, but it was more contained, falling down her back in soft waves. She had a bright smile on her face and her arms were poised above her head in her finishing stance. Even in the picture, I could pinpoint her flawless form. She was perfect.

"That's her, isn't it?" I touched the glass frame as though I could reach her.

Monroe's head was turned down, his lip quivering. "Yes," he whispered.

As I inspected every detail, I spotted a man standing on the other side of the rope, bowing his head. A young Monroe with trimmed hair, an awkward smile, and wide eyes filled with wonder. The boy in the photo looked so different from the saddened, tired man with me now.

I glanced back at Monroe. His sunken shoulders and teary eyes moved me to place my hand on his. He looked up at me with a silent thanks. I couldn't prod at Monroe anymore. He was hurting and I sure as hell wouldn't appreciate anyone meddling in my business if I were in his position. We'd find the killer, one day. It wasn't worth making him suffer any longer.

Chapter Twenty-Three

The next morning, I met Cassius to practice the steps we'd learned from Charlotte before Mr. Monte arrived with our choreography, despite my fear of doing so. It felt so strange standing so close to Cassius but feeling so far away. I was too upset to speak to him, so for the next hour we practiced in silence, working on the basics.

And it seemed luck was on my side when Mr. Monte didn't arrive with the choreography, which meant I wouldn't have to practice with Cassius for the rest of the afternoon. By his hasty exit, it was clear he was still angry about yesterday. I couldn't blame him. Although my reasons were valid, I was unkind. But if he needed space, as I did, I would give it to him.

So, that afternoon I practiced with Charlotte for a couple of hours for help with my technique. Before I knew it, it was dinnertime, and I was heading into the dining car to grab a bowl of stew. With the mess I'd gotten myself into, I needed a drink, and what better way to distract myself than with the circus's renowned drunks—the riders.

I found myself sitting between Flint and Hugh, who had already downed two mugs of ale and were starting on their third.

"Sorry, Henry, but you're off the list," Flint explained to the youngest rider on their team.

Henry, a full fourteen years old, whined like a little girl when he said, "Why? That's not fair!"

"It's fair because you haven't even kissed a girl yet." Flint shoved him playfully and Henry looked as though he was ready to blow steam from his nostrils.

"What am I missing?" I asked with a laugh.

The men around the table turned to look at me as Hugh explained. "We've composed a list, or a ranking of the best man in bed. Henry here thinks he belongs on it." Hugh just rolled his eyes and took a long swig from his cup.

"And who's number one?" I inquired curiously, taking a couple long pulls from my own drink.

"Why don't you try and guess," Flint leaned in and whispered, with a glossiness to his eyes.

He was leaning dangerously close, but I blamed it on the drink. Looking to the other men and to Gus who had come to join them, I winked and said, "I'm guessing it's Gus."

The table erupted and the men proceeded to jostle Gus from side to side. Then they began to poke fun at me for such a laughable answer.

I was quick to defend myself. "He's a magician. I'm sure he knows what he's doing with his hands."

And as their mouths dropped open, I felt a sense of accomplishment wash over me. Flint looked at me with a nod of approval before Henry spoke up, eager to join the argument.

"I hate to disappoint you, Miss Rose, but Flint has taken first place for the past three years. I figured you would know that much."

And the proud, haughty smile he offered me sent the men jumping out of their seats to clap him on the back.

"That's my boy!" Hugh ruffled Henry's hair. "You may be a virgin, but you'll be breaking girls' hearts before you know it."

And as their roaring settled, Gus turned to me pointedly. "What do you think, Juniper? Would you agree?" he asked gently, which was uncharacteristic among the wild riders.

I looked at Flint awkwardly, not knowing how to answer, but before I could, a deep voice spoke up from behind me. "You better answer that question carefully."

Shit.

I turned, and there was Cassius with his hands tucked into his pockets. How much of that conversation had he heard?

"Oh, come on man, let the girl answer," Hugh exclaimed.

Cassius looked at me, terrifyingly calm, before motioning for me to continue. "Go ahead. Let's hear it."

No. I wouldn't make Cassius jealous by agreeing with the riders' ranking. It was an impossibility anyway. Flint and I had never slept together. But just earlier, Cassius didn't stop Charlotte from speaking so openly about their past. So why should I be concerned about his feelings?

I looked to Flint then with a smile. "I think I would agree."

"Oh, damn," Hugh remarked, chuckling behind a balled fist. "Looks like you've got to up your game, Cas."

I threw Hugh a withering glare, which made him hide behind his mug of ale.

Flint stood then as the awkwardness became palpable. "It was just a joke, man. We were just having a little bit of fun."

Cassius unfurled his hands from his pockets to face Flint. "Oh really? Just a bit of fun?" He swiped a hand across his mouth. "Here's my definition of fun."

And before we knew it, Cassius's fist was flying into Flint's jaw. Flint rocked back, unprepared, holding his jaw in pain.

"Cassius!" I yelled and sprung out of my chair. "What the hell is wrong with you?"

The other riders jumped up to steady Flint.

"With me? No, what the hell is wrong with you?" he yelled, unashamed of his temper.

And his eruption forced the rest of the room into uncomfortable silence as they watched us. As embarrassment set in, I knew we needed to take this conversation elsewhere, if only for Flint's safety. If we remained here, Cassius might pummel him to death. So, I grabbed Cassius's forearm and tugged him out of the room. To my relief, he kept his mouth shut as we wound down the hall.

But when we entered the confines of his bedroom, he let me have it. "What the hell was that?"

"It was a bit of fun, just like they said," I answered in irritation, despite how stupid it sounded coming out of my mouth. If Cassius ever said that about another woman, I would be livid.

"Well if you're just interested in having a bit of fun, you can go back to sleeping with Flint. I don't want anything to do with you if you're just like all the other girls," he said.

And with the hurt in his eyes, I suddenly felt terrible. I shouldn't have said that to make him jealous. And maybe I needed him to say something like that to wake me up—to show me that if I kept up this attitude, he wouldn't stick around. So, despite how small it made me feel, I needed to be honest. "I didn't sleep with Flint. I was only joking when I agreed with them."

"Why did you agree with them in the first place? To make me jealous?" Cassius paced around the room and ran his hand through his hair.

"Isn't that what you were doing this morning with Charlotte?" I asked, still angry over the fact that Charlotte, my closest friend here, said something like that in front of me, and that Cassius had the nerve to entertain it.

"That's childish, even for you, Juniper." Cassius rolled his eyes.

"It's the same situation, Cas. Charlotte made a joke about your past, just as I did tonight with Flint. And if it made you that angry to hear it, I think you can understand why I'm frustrated."

Cassius was prepared to speak up before he let loose a sigh. "Okay, yes. I can understand why you're angry, but that doesn't mean you should retaliate and make me feel the same way!"

"Why not?" I screamed.

This is what I needed. I needed to yell at him and let out my anger, otherwise it would eat me alive. So, I laid it all out for him.

"You've slept with almost every woman here, and I can't get it out of my head!"

"That was in the past," he interrupted me, stepping closer so that he could gain some ground.

But I wasn't finished. "Is it though? Is it in the past? Because by the looks of it, you miss the attention. You miss the easy sex, don't you?" I yelled, coming closer with every word, until I was standing directly in front of him.

He looked me in the eyes, unflinching. After a moment of silence, he just shook his head. "I'm sorry the past bothers you, I really am. But it's the past." He moved to open the door for me. "I'm done arguing. Come talk to me when you're done making me feel like a piece of shit."

I just looked at him, trying to figure out what was going on in his head. Then I realized he'd been doing the same for the past few days—trying to understand. And I had given him nothing.

Hating myself, I slid out of his room. What was wrong with me? This was all my fault. I should have communicated my feelings instead of making him feel ashamed. I was stressed about the killer and our upcoming performance, and I didn't want yet another problem on my shoulders, but by giving myself space to think through it, I'd lost Cassius's trust. And I didn't know how to earn it back.

Before I knew it, I found myself knocking on Charlotte's door.

When she saw my tears, she wrapped me in a hug. "What's wrong, J?" she asked quietly, making me sob even harder into her shoulder.

"I don't know what I'm doing," was all I could say.

"What do you mean?" she asked gently, holding my hand the whole time.

I took a deep breath and wiped the tears from my cheeks before explaining everything. And when I finished, she smiled, so understanding and so kind.

"Juniper." Charlotte's voice broke, and she swallowed deeply. "You're not alone. Every single woman here has felt the same way. I'll tell you a story." She nodded and sat up straighter to prepare herself. "Before I came to the circus I worked as a prostitute."

My heart dropped at imagining such a beautiful, kind woman having to do something so terrible—something that likely tore her apart.

"It was what I had to do at the time, but it made me feel ashamed of myself. It was sickening, pleasing those men, and I felt gross for doing it. I didn't feel beautiful, or sexy. I felt dirty. Every night, after my last customer left, I would watch the street below me. I would watch husbands or admirers taking beautiful women on dates and treating them to what they deserved. And I was jealous because they looked so gorgeous, so clean, and so pure."

She looked down at her hands in embarrassment, lost in memory. But she continued, even as tears welled in her eyes. "And I'd wanted a man to love me that way for so long, but I didn't think I deserved it. I was tainted because of what I had to do to provide for myself. To escape all of it, I left to join the circus. And I swore off men for a long time. I threw myself into dancing and I tried my hardest to forget about my old life. And then I met Cassius."

"And you know how he is." She chuckled, and I laughed with her, nodding my head. "He's charming and he's sweet when he wants to be, and when you finally break through that wall of his, you feel important—like you've made a difference in his life. Like you're special." She shook her head, frustrated at the memories. "But at the time, he just wanted sex. And I hadn't told anyone about my past, but to be asked only for sex, after yearning for something more…well, it broke my heart."

She paused again and I wiped the tears that fell onto her cheeks, encouraging her to take her time.

"What I'm trying to say is don't feel ashamed for being nervous or insecure. I was for so many years…I still am. Even though I don't ever have to go back to working as a prostitute, and even though I get to dance with my friends every day, I still feel dirty. I feel marked in a way that I can't explain. And some days, I don't feel beautiful or sexy. Just know that you're not alone—you have all of us girls to support you."

Charlotte pinched her lips as she weighed her next words. "And on the flipside, yes, Cassius slept with many women, but that doesn't mean that's what he wants to do anymore. And it doesn't mean he's not in love with you. So, you have to trust him and voice your concerns, and you have to do your best to be confident in his feelings for you. There will be hard days, but you can't push him away. If anything, you need to draw closer to him on those days."

I nodded my head and wrapped my arms around her neck. "Thank you." I held her tightly. "And I'm sorry you ever had to do those things." I pulled back to face her. "You are not dirty, and you are not stained. You are beautiful, and if you ever forget that, Charlotte, then I'll be here to remind you."

I was beyond grateful to have her by my side—to have all these women supporting me. And I was so fortunate to have Cassius. I didn't want to make him feel ashamed as Charlotte had been ashamed, because he was everything to me. And it was time I told him that.

"I know what I need to do, but it can wait until tomorrow. How about we have a girl's night? You don't think Wilman would notice that nice bottle of whiskey missing from under the bar, do you?"

"We can put it back in the morning before he even notices it's gone," she said, and yanked me from the bed, both of us squealing as we raced through the halls.

Chapter Twenty-Four

Waking up next to a disheveled and dangerously hungover Charlotte had me feeling back to my old self. Last night was filled with laughter and it brought me and Charlotte closer than ever. On this crisp autumn day with fire brazen leaves falling upon the ground, I felt rejuvenated, hopeful, and ready to work through things with Cassius.

I threw on a thin silk shift and left Charlotte and her heap of golden knots to rest. I found myself wandering to my tent, where Cassius and I intended to practice our dance routine every morning. If things weren't as dreadful as I anticipated, he'd be waiting for me, ready to practice despite the awkwardness.

And as I sauntered into the tent with a pep in my step, I found him sitting on one of the benches surrounding the circle of sand, wringing his hands together. Spotting me across the room, he stood to his feet and wiped his hands on his legs.

"If you don't want to do this, I can tell Mr. Monte the routine is off. I'm sure he can figure something else out before the—"

"I'm sorry," I interrupted him.

The room echoed with my last words and silence filled the space between us. Cassius just watched me in that nervous way—his eyes growing bigger, hopeful even.

"I'm sorry," I repeated. I stepped closer, feeling so far away from his warmth. "I haven't been honest with you these past few days. There's been a lot on my mind, but it's no excuse for how I treated you. I didn't mean to push you away or make you feel ashamed of your past. I guess I was just…" I paused, trying to figure out the right words to say. My heart was thumping against my chest, telling me to retreat into silence where it was safe. I didn't want Cassius to know how scared I really was.

Charlotte's words came back to me then, encouraging me to continue. *Draw closer to him on those days.*

I nodded to myself and took another step forward. "I was just scared. Scared to be a burden, or insecure, or weak."

"You are not any of those things, Juniper." Cassius shook his head, making his curls waver back and forth. "Tell me what changed a few days ago. I want to understand."

And in that moment, I felt such relief. He *did* want to understand me.

So, I started at the beginning. "I'm jealous. A few days ago, when we were in your bed, things were getting...more intimate, and all I could think about was that you've been with other women." I raked my hands through my hair, hoping I didn't sound like a complete idiot. "I can't help but think you're tired of taking it slow with me. And I don't know if I can give you what they gave you."

Cassius listened intently, allowing me to speak freely without interrupting.

"I think it's just hard for me to trust that you won't go back to your old ways. But I also think it's my fault because I don't feel pretty enough or good enough to be with someone like you. And I have no idea what I'm doing half the time."

The tears came suddenly, without warning, and my head fell into my hands. But the burning in my eyes and the ache in my chest disappeared when I felt Cassius remove my hands from my eyes. He curled his fingers around mine and placed my hands on his chest.

And he looked at me with those gentle, loving, brown eyes and said, "You are more than enough. You are gorgeous and talented, and you are loving, above anything else. And if you need me to remind you of that every single day, I will. That's my job, Juniper. And as for sex..."

I choked out a laugh at the uncomfortable expression on his face.

He smiled a goofy smile and squeezed my hands in his own. "I don't expect anything from you. I want those things, but I don't *need* them." He tucked a strand of hair behind my ear before curling me into his chest.

I wiped away my tears and tucked my nose into the warmth of his neck. Closing my eyes and breathing him in, all my insecurities vanished. I had him and that was all I needed. Pulling away, I looked up into his eyes. "Please know that I'm sorry for judging you for your past. I never meant to make you feel ashamed of yourself. I just have a habit of wanting to be perfect for you."

Cassius nodded and wiped at the stray tear on my cheek. "You already are."

Entwining my fingers in his curls, I pressed my body tightly against his. "Thank you. For being so understanding."

"I'm here for you, J. Anytime you need any reassurance, all you have to do is ask," he whispered in my ear and kissed my temple.

I wanted to stay like this forever, in his arms, so safe and protected from every other worry. I didn't want to think about the killer or Mr. Young, and right now, I didn't have to. I stopped those debilitating thoughts from eddying in my mind, and instead just focused on the here and now.

Suddenly, the flaps of the tent burst open, and Mr. Monte stepped through, breaking Cassius and me apart.

"Sorry lovebirds, but it's time to get to work. Charlotte told me you'd be busy practicing, not caressing one another. I'll go over the choreography quickly so you can start practicing some of the moves before tomorrow."

And so, for the next hour, Mr. Monte discussed every step of our routine, showing us what flips, turns, and dips we'd be performing.

But before we knew it, it was time for Mr. Monte to leave. "Get to work. I'll be back in a couple of hours to check in on you!" he proclaimed and rushed out of the tent.

Cassius and I chuckled before stripping off our shoes and finding ourselves on the white mat in the center of the tent.

"I guess we should do as he says. He might beat us later if we haven't made any progress," he quipped.

"I guess so," I agreed and took his hand in my own. An electrical current pulsed through my veins as his fingers touched mine. And it only burned stronger in my gut when he placed his hand on my waist, squeezing gently on the pliable skin.

"Do you remember?" I looked at him under my brow while softly stroking his hand. I wasn't sure what I was implying. I just wondered, after all this time, if we were ready to show ourselves to the crowd as one?

Cassius began to sway and spoke under his breath, the low timbre of his voice tickling my neck. "Do I remember how to touch you? How to hold you?" He spun me around quickly, so my back was pressed to his chest, then snaked his hand around my waist, and splayed it across my ribs, the veins in his hands popping a bright blue. "How to show the crowd what's mine?"

I laid my head back on his shoulder and closed my eyes while listening to him speak so assuredly. Suddenly he whipped me around again and I grabbed onto his shoulders so as not to stumble.

There was a wicked gleam in his eyes when he declared, "Yes, Juniper. I remember."

My chest heaved up and down and I slowly trailed my hand down his chest. "Let's get to it then."

We started with simple moves, trying to maintain the strong frame Charlotte taught us until our movements became quicker. Cassius spun me out, and when I spun back in, I lifted my leg and hooked my knee around his arm, my head dropping to the floor as he lifted my legs into the air. I bounced back up and landed, continuing the sequence of steps until we could barely breathe.

And after another hour of practicing our choreography, Cassius grabbed my waist tightly and stopped me in my tracks. "I'm sure you could go all day, little sprite, but I can't feel my legs anymore." His chest was heaving, and sweat was beading down his temples.

I was flattered, but I was about to fall over too. Although, I still liked to play with him. "You can't handle it?" I clicked my tongue. "It seems you've gotten lazy, Mr. Plume." I circled around him, trailing my fingers across his broad shoulders while he craned his head to follow my movements.

"I never said I couldn't handle it." He spun around to face me and grabbed my waist to pull me into his body. His hands roamed over my lower back, rubbing gently at the sore spots.

I gave into his touch and tucked my head into the crook of his neck. His heartbeat was pulsing vibrantly there, and I savored every moment in his arms. Cassius had been so understanding the last few days and something had changed between us. After days of feeling so far apart, I'd never wanted him more in my life.

I pulled back and found that same look of yearning and desperation in his eyes. And his full, rosy lips were already parted, begging me to separate them even further.

So, I obliged.

I crashed my lips into his and didn't waste a moment as I speared my tongue into his mouth.

He grabbed my hips and pulled them into his body, his fingertips biting at my skin. And I wanted him to touch me harder until there were bruises marking my body. I was so desperate to feel every inch of Cassius that I pushed him back and slammed him against one of the posts in the tent.

When his back hit the strong wood, his lips parted from mine, and he looked at me with a gloss in his eyes—something so demanding and wicked that I found myself grappling at his shirt. Finding my hands underneath the seams, I pressed my palms against his hard abdomen, groaning at the warmth there. Cassius's stomach clenched then, either from the cold bite of my fingers or the moan that had escaped me.

This time, I wouldn't let my jealousy, my fears, or my insecurities get the best of me. This felt good and I wanted more of it. So, I focused on the pounding of my heart, the tight grip on my stomach, and the insatiable need for Cassius. I closed my eyes and pressed my lips against his, the moving of our mouths something I could only describe as a perfectly choreographed dance.

And as our kiss quickened, I moved up his shirt and threw it over his head. Finding one hand on his bare chest, I tightened my grip until my fingernails were close to puncturing his skin. Pulling at his curls, I forced his head back to allow myself more access to his neck, and when I suctioned my lips to the tight skin, he groaned—such a guttural noise that made me want to do vile things to him.

I kept kissing down his neck, sucking until there were little red marks dotting his skin. He was panting, his chest heaving up and down, until he forced my lips back onto his. Gripping my cheeks, he held me there while our kiss deepened. His soft tongue rolled over mine and when I captured his top lip, he bit ever so softly, making me press my thighs together to stop the ache in my center.

I tucked my head into his neck and nipped at his earlobe, which made him grab at my silk dress in a rush and lift the bottom over my hips. He grabbed my bum in his large hands and kneaded the skin, making me gasp. But when he let go, the absence of his hands, and the imprint they'd left on my skin had me whining for more.

But he pulled away and moved my chin up so he could fully look at me. He looked drunk, sick with desire by the red, glossy sheen in his eyes. And when he spoke, his voice was low and gruff, as though he'd just awoken. "What do you want?" he asked.

This was in my control. I had the power to do what I wished—what I was comfortable with. So, I looked into his golden eyes and said, "More. I want more."

He hoisted me onto his hips, turned us around, and pushed my back against the wood column. My spine groaned and I crossed my ankles behind him to secure our bodies together.

He pushed his hips into mine, and I gasped at the sensation in my core—the feeling of being completely full and alive. The apex of my thighs tightened uncomfortably, yearning for release.

I pulled him closer with my legs, sank down slightly, and moved my hips in a circular motion against him. When he grabbed at my hips and pulled me harder into him, I gasped in surprise and moaned his name.

"There you go," he slowly drawled, only looking at where our bodies met.

The knot in my center grew so tight I felt as though it might burst. He was unrelenting and I was so close to coming undone before him, but before I could sense that high, voices sounded from outside the tent.

Cassius quickly stopped, set me down and rearranged my dress so that I was covered, before moving to shove on his shirt. Just then, Charlotte walked through the door with a look of confusion.

"What the hell happened to you two? Looks like you just ran a marathon," she said suspiciously.

Cassius nodded vigorously. "We did. Took a lap around the field. Just a little exercise to get us warmed up." He turned to me and winked.

I almost burst out laughing but managed to hold it together. By the look in Charlotte's eyes, she knew what we'd been up to, but I was grateful Cassius tried to keep it quiet either way. He understood this was all new for me and that the whole world didn't need to know it.

So, he brought his hands together and clapped, ready to get to work. "You wanted to see our progress?" he asked, motioning for me to come to his side so we could begin our routine.

Charlotte just smiled at me and shook her head. "I think I've seen it already."

Chapter Twenty-Five

Mr. Monte had just finished the speech Flint would give at our next performance to lure the killer in and had called Flint and me to his office to go over it.

After mending things with Cassius, I knew I needed to tell him the truth about our plan. I'd been hiding so many things from him, thinking I could solve it all on my own. But the truth was, I couldn't. I needed help.

That evening, I took Cassius's hand and asked him to follow me to Mr. Monte's office, which he did trustingly, unaware of what was going on. But when we reached Mr. Monte's office, I paused outside the door.

"There's something else I haven't told you."

I expected surprise, anger, or confusion, but all I got was unfaltering trust. In the aftermath of our heated moment in the tent earlier that morning, we both understood that openness was our best shot at loving one another.

"I don't want to hide things from you. So, tonight..." I motioned to the door beside us, watching Cassius's eyes flicker before continuing, "Can you promise me that you won't be angry with me? That you'll try and understand?"

Cassius stood there for a moment, kneading my palm between his fingers while he thought. And when a couple performers slid past us, pushing Cassius to lean against me to give them room, he looked at me closely, so understanding.

With our breaths mingling, he said, "I'll try," and pressed a kiss to my cheek before opening the door.

Mr. Monte's eyes were pinned to the paperwork before him as the door opened, and he didn't dare take his eyes away as he said, "Juniper, take a seat, we've got lots to discuss."

Flint, sitting awkwardly in front of the desk, cleared his throat, prompting Mr. Monte to pick up his head.

Worry flickered in Mr. Monte's eyes before he masked it with a smile. "Cassius!" he exclaimed, too excited to be normal.

Before Mr. Monte could make the situation any more awkward, I spoke up. "I think Cassius deserves to know what we're planning. I thought he might be of use." I couldn't help the guilt that settled over me. I shouldn't have kept this a secret. I shouldn't have kept Cassius in the dark.

"What's going on?" Cassius asked authoritatively. I could tell it wasn't anger he was feeling, but rather betrayal. I'd been meeting in secret with Mr. Monte and Flint, the latter being someone Cassius detested.

Mr. Monte stood to pace around the room with his hands folded behind his back and sighed before stating plainly, "We have a plan to catch the killer."

"And you kept it from me?" Cassius balled his fists at his side before tucking them into his pockets, trying to remain calm.

The defeat in his voice was so much worse than his anger. "Cassius—" I began, eager to stop him from twisting this situation in his mind. He often convinced himself that everyone was against him. "I was worried you would try and stop us…to keep me safe."

He chuckled to himself before rubbing at his chin. "You're damn right I would have." He then flicked his hand to Flint. "My question is, how is Mr. Pretty Pants here involved?"

Flint just rolled his eyes. "I'm involved because Juniper wants *me* to be the one to draw out the killer."

"Oh, she wants *you* to be the one?" Cassius stepped closer to Flint with a dangerous quiet to his voice. "Well, she didn't want you to be the one in her bed last year, so it seems she just feels sorry for you."

Flint quickly stood up to defend himself, his face coming within inches of Cassius's.

"Will you two please stop?" I stepped between them to stop the situation from escalating. "You're acting like children!"

They looked at each other with deadly glares before Flint deemed their argument unworthy and sat back down.

I turned to Cassius then and rested my hand on his wildly beating heart, his eyes slowly tearing away from Flint's to meet mine.

I quieted my voice to try and calm him. "This is not about me trusting Flint over you or desiring his company more than yours. He's here because he can help us. Sit down and let me explain."

Thankfully, Cassius listened and took a seat across from Mr. Monte's desk.

Mr. Monte proceeded to inform Cassius of our plan. He listened intently the whole time, nodding his head along, but when Mr. Monte finished, he was silent.

So, I took over and said, "I chose Flint because he has a reason to hate me. We can make the killer easily believe that Flint has turned against me. But we could use your help, Cas."

And when I said his name, he turned his head to me, his eyes gentle and fierce all at once.

"After Flint gives his speech in front of the crowd—in front of the killer—you can force him off the stage to prove to everyone that Flint is a real danger to me."

His eyes flicked back and forth, and it was clear there was a battle being fought in his head.

"What do you think, my boy? Will you help us?" Mr. Monte urged him.

Shaking his head back and forth, Cassius said calmly, having already made up his mind, "I won't purposely put Juniper's life in danger. My answer is no." He sat there defiantly, unable to look at me.

I grabbed at his arm again, my fingertips glowing white. "Please, Cassius. This is our only chance. This is going to work," I pleaded with him. Cassius understood the situation I was in—how torturous it was to wait for the killer knowing my life was in danger. I'd told him as much, and beyond that, he'd watched my terrors unfold right before his eyes. And yet he was still refusing to help?

When his eyes met mine, there was a sincerity in them. "How can we know that you'll be safe when he violated you in the open? When he threatened your life with a crowd of people watching? We don't even know where he is!" He shook his head. "None of us are safe."

I calmed my voice to a whisper, "That's why we have to take this risk...to stop him before he hurts anyone else." I laid my hands out before him earnestly.

Cassius searched my eyes as he battled between two decisions. Either he could bring the killer to justice, avenging all those who had been hurt by his hand, or he could insist on keeping me safe while the killer roamed freely. The fate of the circus was in his hands.

"Please," I begged him.

"Even if we did manage to draw the killer out of hiding, Flint may not be able to deceive him. And if he *is* sly enough to do so, no matter how prepared we are, the killer could still hurt you," Cassius explained.

I nodded in agreement. "You're right. He could. But what happens if we do nothing? The chances of me ending up dead are even higher." It was time to be realistic about the situation. "There's no good ending to this, Cassius. But if we're prepared and lure him toward us, we'll have the upper hand."

He shook his head and looked between Mr. Monte and Flint, wishing we were alone to speak about this. Ignoring the company in our midst, he looked at me with absolute fear in his eyes. "I just got you back. I won't lose you again. It's an unnecessary risk we don't need to take. And I won't let either of you help her do this." Cassius looked at Mr. Monte, then Flint. "I'll inform the guards of your plan, and even Mr. Young if I have to. This isn't happening."

Mr. Monte turned his head dangerously at Cassius. "This is my circus, and I will decide what to do with my performers. You'll do no such thing."

Cassius leapt up and slammed his hand upon the desk, startling me. "So, you're willing to risk Juniper's life just to catch him?" he exclaimed.

"Her life is already at risk!" Mr. Monte yelled.

At that moment, I saw the subterfuge in the killer's plan. I watched as Cassius, Flint, and Mr. Monte screamed back and forth at one another. He was tearing the circus apart from the inside out in his deliberate hiding.

"Stop it! All of you!" I stood out of my seat, silencing everyone. "I will talk to Cassius in private while you get ahold of yourselves." I grabbed Cassius by the arm, ignoring his protests, and dragged him all the way to his room.

"There's no point in trying to convince me." He slammed the door behind him.

I pointed a finger at his chest. "You will listen, whether you like it or not. Sit down." I pushed him onto the ottoman in front of his bed. "You are stubborn. And I've put up with it, but I won't any longer." I took a deep breath, trying not to let my emotions get the better of me. "I am in pain, Cassius. I'm terrified to close my eyes at night, and I can't help but creep around corners everywhere I go. You've seen what he's done to me—what he's done to *you*. I need you to help me, no matter the cost."

"No matter the cost? Since when were you willing to risk your life for this?" Cassius squinted and stood up to face me.

"Since I found this." I retrieved the Penelope's diary and laid it in front of him.

He flipped it open in anger before discovering his sister's words on the page. He froze in place, and his eyes filled with tears as he read through it carefully. "Where did you find this?"

"In her room." I hadn't noticed I was crying until everything grew blurry behind a wall of tears. Those were the last words Cassius would ever hear from her. My intention wasn't to hurt him, but to show him the gravity of this situation, so I knelt before him and rested my hands on his knees. "This is what he does to people. He terrorizes them until they can't handle it anymore. And if we don't do something soon, I might go crazy, Cas. So, please. Help me."

Cassius looked at the notebook for a second longer before grabbing my shoulders, lifting me to stand, and wrapping me in his arms. He laced his fingers into my hair and curled my head into his chest. And his breath shook when he said, "I let Penelope die. I wasn't there for her," he paused before whispering into my ear, "but this time I *can* help. I'll do whatever you need me to do."

I cried into his chest, the relief of having him on my side washing over me like a wave. Suddenly something dawned on me—something Cassius needed to see. I gently took the notebook from him and flipped to the last entry, where a small photo of Penelope and Cassius was clipped to the page. I handed it to him, watching him study it while memories of her rushed back.

But he surprised me by smiling. "We had a lot of fun back then."

"I can see that. Look at your smiles." I smiled with him while pointing at the picture.

He chuckled, his tone reminiscent when he said, "She forced me to take this picture—grabbed me by the neck and led me in front of the train like a dog, preaching about the importance of holding onto memories."

My heart sank that I hadn't met her. "She seems strongheaded."

He eyed me and gently stroked my cheek. "She would have liked you."

I wrapped my arms around his torso. "I wish I could have met her."

"We'll see her again one day." Cassius looked up to the ceiling as though he could peer into heaven itself.

"Yes. One day," I whispered.

Chapter Twenty-Six

That afternoon, the circus set up at Celeste's Opera House for our performance later that evening. The venue was named for Celeste, the world's most famous opera singer. With flowing golden locks and blooming green eyes, her beauty was unmatched, and her money even more so. She was known for wearing the most fabulous diamonds and gowns of the most lavish fabrics.

After her tour two decades ago, they created Celeste's Opera House in honor of her esteemed work around the country. The interior was furnished in scarlet red, with plush sofas at the entrance to the theater, covered in velvet and golden tassels. Chandeliers of amber light flickered in the high ceilings, casting a warm golden hue on the black marble floor.

I found Flint among the bustling chaos, scanning the lines of his speech. Tonight was the night he would speak out against me in hopes that the killer was listening.

He nodded to himself, forcing his lips into a thin line. "I can do this."

It seemed he was trying to convince himself more than me.

I smiled lightly, trying not to show him how nervous I was. "You have to make this believable—you have to convince him. Summon all the hate you have for this world and direct it at me."

Flint nodded again and winked. "I've got lots of pent-up anger. I can manage."

Standing before a team of guards, Mr. Monte began giving orders. "You three will be positioned at the entrances to Celeste's Opera House, one at the front door, one at the back door, and one at the side entrance for the performers. Don't you dare leave your posts and watch with a keen eye for who comes and goes." Mr. Monte then looked to the two guards who had the most important job of the night. "You two will guard Juniper at all times. Don't let her out of your sight." He turned his attention to six other guards who nodded in sync. "The six of you will be backstage, monitoring the other performers, while the rest of you," he finished as he gazed across the last of the guards, "will be seated among the other guests. Try to blend in as best you can but watch for any movement—the killer might very well be seated in the audience."

"Tonight, we don't plan to capture the killer. We're luring him out so that we're more prepared in our next performance to bring him to an end." Mr. Monte clarified and dismissed the guards.

I knew Flint's speech would be convincing, but what if the killer attacked before he could deliver it? But the theater was designed in such a way that it would be difficult for the killer to strike without being noticed. There would be too many people watching and with the protection of the guards, even if the killer struck, there would be no way for him to escape.

But I had no time to dwell on the reliability of our plan or the killer's unforeseeable actions, so instead, I took to practicing my routine. Cassius and I decided to save our performance as lovers until after the killer was captured. It wasn't the right time to perform such a meaningful act. So, tonight, we settled for something more playful. Many years ago, the circus had attempted impalement arts—a type of performance in which a human acted as a target, strapped to a spinning wheel, while a skilled performer demonstrated their accuracy in knife throwing.

All I had to do was stand there and look pretty and hope to not get stabbed to death. *Easy enough.*

Meanwhile, Gus had the difficult job of throwing the knives, but he'd been practicing for years. It was Monroe's idea, having seen it when he was a performer in the old circus, and because he took it upon himself to prepare Gus with practice sessions, I was confident I wouldn't be impaled by the end of the night…for the most part.

The circus dispersed to get ready, and I joined the company of the dancers in the women's dressing room in the east wing of the theater. I pulled the small duffel bag from my shoulder and retrieved the silver bedazzled mess I was to step into.

"Charlotte, can you help me dress?" I asked.

She came running and laid the leotard open at my feet to help me step into it. "When Cassius sees you in this, he'll melt right before you." Charlotte snickered while admiring the embroidery.

I rolled my eyes. "We're worrying about impressing the crowd and trying to avoid a killer on the loose, and you're commenting on how Cassius might drool over my costume?"

She just laughed harder. "There might be a lot on our plates, but that doesn't mean you can't have fun." She wiggled her eyebrows playfully.

I ran my hands down the bodice, laced with silver diamonds and pearls, trying to imagine Cassius's thick hands on the fabric. "I don't know if even this fancy costume would seduce him."

"And why's that, darlin'?"

I shook my head. "I don't know. Things have just been different recently. I think we're too stressed to even focus on getting handsy with one another."

Charlotte tilted her head with a chuckle. "He's got something dangling from his groin. Trust me, he's thinking about that."

I burst out laughing at that comment. "Yes, indeed he does. And I want him in that way, believe me. We just can't seem to find a moment alone."

Charlotte pulled the leotard up my waist and helped me pull my arms through it. "You will. When the time is right, it'll happen."

I nodded with her, trying to be hopeful. I straightened the costume over my torso and focused on its details as I gauged my reflection in the mirror. The leotard was tough and covered in silver diamonds. It was long sleeved with a single hook looping around my middle finger, and it rose high over my hips, making my oiled legs appear luscious and long.

Someone knocked on the girls' dressing room, walking in without an answer as to whether anyone was indecent. Then, Cassius's dark curly hair came into view.

"Next time you might want to wait. We could have been naked!" Charlotte exclaimed, waving her hands at the other women around her.

"It's nothing I haven't seen before." He shook his head annoyingly before turning to face me. Extending a hand, his body towering over mine, he said, "Mr. Monte's waiting."

I gently took his hand and looked up at him, his eyes curving wickedly as he looked me up and down.

"Good luck, ladies." I tipped my head at them before exiting with Cassius. He held my hand the entire time as we weaved through the theater, to the stage, where Mr. Monte was waiting with Flint.

Tonight, we would make a move against the killer. And whether or not it went as planned, I could be hurt. I grabbed Cassius's arm and pulled him to a stop before we could reach the others.

Standing in an alcove before the entrance to the theater with the lighting dimmed, Cassius asked, "What's the matter?"

I took a deep breath. "I don't know how tonight will go, but if something should go wrong—"

Cassius stopped me by cradling my cheek in his warm palm. "You're going to be fine. The killer didn't strike at the last performance, and I have a feeling he won't this time either. Our plan is going to work." His eyes blazed with a fire of confidence.

I nodded, trying to reassure myself. Our plan was good, and I didn't doubt that it would work, but there was always room for mistakes. Before I could say anything further, he pulled me in and tucked my head into his neck. I closed my eyes, breathing in his scent and taking in his warmth.

"You trust me, right?" he whispered into my ear.

"Yes," I whispered back. And I did. Cassius wouldn't let anything happen to me.

"Then there is nothing to worry about." He gently caressed my spine before pulling away. "I, on the other hand, might have something to worry about."

"And what's that?" I pulled my eyebrows together while running my hand along the midnight vest he wore. It fit nicely across his strapping chest.

Cassius let go of my hand and moved to delicately finger the fabric of my costume, his hand brushing along my ribs. "I might not be able to keep my head on straight. Must you always look so ravishing?" His voice was deeply concerned.

I giggled. "I only followed Mr. Monte's request."

"I'll have to speak with him about this." He clicked his tongue and rested his hand complacently on my waist. His warmth seeped through the fabric of my leotard, but when he looked up once more, his face was serious instead of playful. "I'll see you after the performance."

And that reassurance made every doubt within me vanish. I would see him soon.

Pushing into the theater, I found Mr. Monte and Flint on stage patiently waiting for me.

"There she is!" Mr. Monte exclaimed. "You ready to get to work?"

"Always am," I answered.

Chapter Twenty-Seven

The world was spinning. I couldn't make out the difference between up and down or right and left. I was dizzy, trying to hold onto the contents of my dinner. My arms and legs were spread in the formation of an X and strapped down to a circular wooden wheel that was spinning around and around.

I clenched my core and pressed my back to the wheel while the audience clapped in excitement. Gus stood at the edge of the stage, his back to the audience, about twenty-five feet away from me. He was dressed in a brown vest with red tassels hanging off his shoulders and a mesh bag over his head. To the audience it was apparent that Gus was completing this act blindfolded. What they didn't know was that he had some ability to see through the fabric.

Gus took his stance, opening his legs shoulder width apart. He raised the first of five knives up to his ear, holding it by the blade, and took a step before launching the knife.

It was a blur to me. I saw a flash of silver before it connected with the wooden wheel between my ankles.

The audience applauded, shouting, "You can do better than that!"

That was the trick. Gus was luring in the audience. Every time he threw the knife, it would get closer and closer to my body, provoking the audience to the edge of their seats.

He flipped the knife in his hand before securing the sharp end in his palm. I didn't even see him step this time. He just threw his arm forward and I heard the wood split to my right, where the knife had lodged itself next to my forearm.

I heaved a sigh of relief. Three more and this would be over.

Gus waited longer this time to add suspense, transferring the weight of his body back and forth. He threw, and this time the knife landed within an inch of my armpit.

Two more. I tried to focus on Gus, but his figure was contorting into a brown blur somewhere in the distance. Choosing to look at the audience instead, I saw a mass of people I couldn't define. The wheel groaned beneath my weight and I heard the whoosh of the knife close to my head. I strained my eyes to the right to find the handle of a knife too close to my skull. My heart was pounding. This was far more terrifying than walking the tightrope, but I had no reason to worry. Gus had been doing this a long time.

I didn't have time to prepare for the next knife. I blinked and it was flying toward me.

Blinding pain sliced through my thigh. I screamed and the audience leapt up in panic, but I couldn't hear anything except the beating of my own heart and the ringing in my ears. Looking down to my leg, I found crimson blood bubbling out of the wound, the knife secured in my thigh. Somehow not being able to move made the pain so much worse, and I pulled at the shackles on my wrists, trying to get free. As my vision blurred, I closed my eyes and clenched my teeth together to let out a wheezing breath.

I coughed out a cry of pain at the burning sensation in my leg. I felt my skin being torn apart ever so slowly, the knife searing a fire in my tissue. Blood continued to pour from the wound, pulsing out of my leg to soak the wood.

The crowd frantically whispered amongst themselves, but at least they remained seated. This surely wasn't supposed to happen. Gus was supposed to throw a knife close enough to hit me, but not actually puncture me. And as soon as he threw the knife, he disappeared. But Gus wouldn't do that. He would rush to my side and help me.

No…Gus wasn't the one throwing the knives. It must have been the killer standing on stage with me. And I was stuck to this damn wheel like a sitting duck. I had to get down. I turned frantically, searching for someone to help me as I thrust my arms out, ripping against the shackles. But as I strained my neck to the side, my eyes began to gloss over, and it was a struggle to breathe without feeling nauseous.

Suddenly, I felt hands on my arms and legs, unstrapping me from the wheel.

"Hold her up!" a male voice whispered, in a rush to get me out of sight.

I briefly opened my eyes to find a dull image of Cassius and Mr. Monte. Cassius pushed himself against me, and I let my torso sag over his shoulder. When he turned to Mr. Monte and instructed him to remove the knife from my leg, immediate panic set in.

"This is going to hurt, but we have to get you off stage. Take a deep breath," Cassius said into my ear, pressing my body tightly to his.

But before I could, Mr. Monte ripped the knife out of my leg. I screamed again, and I couldn't have cared less what the audience was thinking, or if they ever came back to watch a performance again because I'd never felt such pain in my life.

A dark tunnel started to slowly creep into my vision, and every blink that kept me awake became slower and slower.

"Keep your eyes open, Juniper. Remember what I taught you," Cassius encouraged me while pulling me into his arms.

I molded my body to his for warmth, aware of the constant *panging* in my leg. But before I knew it, I was off the stage and the voices from the audience had faded.

Cassius laid me out on the ground gently while Mr. Monte returned to the stage to reassure the audience. As far as I could tell, no one was running out of the theater. That was a good sign.

"Cas," I began, trying to warn him about the killer, but my throat was so dry from screaming that I couldn't form the words.

"You're okay, J. You're going to be okay." Cassius quickly unbuckled his belt and stripped it from his waist to loop it around my thigh.

"Hugh!" he ordered, and the firebreather came running. "Pull this as tight as you can and hold it!" Cassius then grabbed the torch Hugh had been carrying and gently pushed it in between my teeth. "Bite on this."

When Hugh yanked the belt taught against my flesh, my eyes slammed shut and the stick of wood muffled my scream. But soon enough, the tightness around my thigh vanished and my leg was numb.

Cassius's hair shook wildly in his face as he began stripping off his vest, pulling harshly at the buttons until it fell on the ground. He pulled his shirt over his head and pressed it onto my leg to stop the bleeding. I groaned again as agonizing pain rushed through my entire body.

Cassius turned around in a flash to scream at one of the guards patrolling backstage. "You! Find Gus, the man in the brown vest! The one who just performed!"

As the guard rushed to find him through the mess of performers, I grabbed at Cassius's arm, squeezing hard until he looked at me. And it took all my strength to take the wood from my mouth and mutter the words, "Not Gus."

But Cassius brushed it off as he yelled out for Charlotte, who had just arrived, horrified by what she saw. "Find Valetta and retrieve a needle and thread!"

"Juniper, can you hear me?" a distance voice asked, sounding far away.

Cassius appeared on top of me, but his features were all starting to blend. His caramel eyes turned into black globs, his nose into an unnoticeable line on his face, and his mouth almost impossible to find.

But before I could study his face any longer, Charlotte was back, pulling thread through a thick needle.

Fear coursed through me, and I began to breathe faster, my chest heaving.

"Hold her down." Cassius looked dangerously at Hugh, who was still pulling the tourniquet tight.

As soon as Cassius pushed the needle through the wound in my thigh, I began screaming in agony. The needle pushed through my tough skin repeatedly, and the feeling of the thread pulling and stretching my skin was unbearable. Before I knew it, my eyes were closing, and everything went dark.

Cassius...

"He disappeared, Sir," one of the guards addressed me.

My nostrils flared and I bit my lip to keep myself from saying anything I'd regret. Instead, I grabbed his shirt and pulled him to me. "There's nowhere for Gus to go. It shouldn't be that hard to find him!"

But as the words left my mouth, they didn't quite make sense. Gus wouldn't run. He would do whatever he could to help her. Something wasn't adding up.

The guard leaned as far back as he could. "I'm sorry. He's just another one of the performers. I didn't think there was a problem!"

"Stop talking." I spit in his face, trying to sort through the mess in my head. And as I stood there, racking my brain, it came to me.

Not Gus, Juniper had said.

"Shit," I mumbled, tearing my hands through my hair. Gus hadn't been the one on stage with her...

The killer had been standing in plain sight. And he might still be. I turned to the guard quickly. "It wasn't Gus on that stage. The killer is here. You round up everyone you can and find him!" I ordered.

The guard nodded promptly before disappearing, and I hurried over to the curtain to explain to Mr. Monte. "The killer...he was the one on stage. And after what he just did, he won't stick around to get caught. Flint has to give his speech at the next performance."

"No, we can't wait!" Mr. Monte shook his head. "Juniper will go mad."

"I don't care what Juniper thinks!" I erupted. "This is about keeping her safe. And if we go ahead with the speech now that the killer has left, it will be for nothing."

Mr. Monte nodded, knowing I was right.

One of the guards rushed forward, his face flushed from running. "A man was found exiting backstage after Juniper was struck."

Mr. Monte stepped forward. "Where did he go?"

"We last saw him joining the audience."

I whipped toward Mr. Monte. "He knows there are guards at the front door. He wouldn't risk fleeing the theater and being caught. He's waiting until it's safe."

Mr. Monte looked at the ground, puzzled.

"What do you want me to do, Sir?" the guard with wide eyes asked.

"I want you posted at the doors to the auditorium. Inform the other guards in the audience to watch for him." Mr. Monte dismissed the guard before turning to me. "Tell Flint to get ready."

I ran in search of Flint to inform him that our plan was still on, looking backstage and even in the dressing rooms, but I couldn't find him anywhere. Where the hell was he?

Suddenly, I heard a faint groaning close by. Either Hugh was drunk again, or something was wrong. But my gut was twisting, telling me it was the latter. I followed the constant grunting to a small closet nestled in the corner. The noise was replaced by a loud *bang,* and the door of the closet shuddered from the force.

I pulled it open quickly, thinking it may have been another dressing room.

"Gus?" I exclaimed, my eyes widening at the sight of him lying on the floor with his hands tied behind his back and a gag in his mouth, his clothes missing.

I kneeled and ripped the saliva-drenched gag from his mouth.

"The killer. It was him!" Gus stumbled on his words, his eyes filled with fear.

I moved to his hands, trying to remain calm as I untied the binds around his wrists. "What happened?" I asked, struggling with the tight knots. "Did you see him? Who was it?"

"No, I didn't see him. He wore a mask." Gus looked mortified while he relayed what had happened. "I was getting ready in the dressing room with the other men. It was almost time for me to go on, so I made my way backstage. Everyone was bustling about getting ready for their own act, and suddenly, a man came from behind and put a cloth over my mouth. I was knocked out cold and woke up in the fucking dark, naked."

The killer had taken Gus in the open. He was walking among us, and nobody noticed. Who the hell was this man? "You didn't perform then?" I clarified.

"No, I was stuck in here until you found me!"

It was confirmed then—the killer was a member of the circus because he knew Gus would be hidden under a mask for his performance. No one else would have known that.

Seeing my worried expression, Gus asked, "What's wrong?"

"The killer knocked you out so he could perform your act."

"With Juniper," Gus concluded. "What happened? Is she alright?"

"She's going to be okay." I rubbed at my temples to alleviate the pounding in my head. "She's got a pretty deep cut in her thigh, but we stitched her up."

Gus's head fell into his hands. "I'm sorry. I should have been there."

I looked up from the ground and patted him on the shoulder before helping him to his feet. "It's not your fault." I cleared my throat and straightened the vest over my chest. "The final bow is coming up. Let's get on stage."

Gus and the other performers might not know what we had planned, but it would all make sense to them in time. It was better no one knew. If the killer was to be convinced, then the performers needed to be as well. The killer might be skilled at playing games, but so were we.

The dancers finished their performance, scheduled to be the last act of the night, and the crowd clapped and cheered, despite the violence demonstrated only an hour ago.

The performers moved to the middle of the stage in a straight line, and linking hands, they bowed their heads, while roses and coins were thrown onto the stage in praise.

But suddenly someone from the crowd stood up, with what might have been mistaken for enthusiasm, were it not for his surge up the stairs. And when he leapt onto the stage, the crowd began to murmur in confused whispers.

"Ladies and gentlemen, may I have your attention?" Flint exclaimed. With the help of Valetta, Flint had changed into a fine waistcoat, a pair of glasses, and a top hat which disguised his features in shadow. However, he wore a golden rope dangling from his waist to signify him as the captain of the riding team—something the audience wouldn't notice but the killer surely would.

"In the past year, there have been many changes to the circus…and not for the better. We all know Juniper Rose, but we know nothing about her intentions."

The audience leaned forward, intrigued. Many people questioned Juniper's motives. Did she come to the circus to escape Axminster and wealthy life? Or did she come to usher in a new era—one in which the classes could support one another?

"Juniper Rose is from Axminster's high society. She is beloved by all and has an esteemed man waiting for her hand when she returns. So, why is she wasting her time in the outskirts with the likes of these freaks?" Flint waved his arms to show the line of performers behind him. "I don't know her intentions, but I do know one thing—she is a danger to our way of life!"

The wealthy members in the audience began to whisper amongst themselves, contemplating the strange man's words. With the voice of a single man, they were beginning to rethink what their reputation truly meant to them. Juniper brought an enigmatic energy to the circus, and it was with great enthusiasm that the audience watched her, but how much would they pay to see her at the risk of their image being tarnished?

He continued with more anguish, "Even if you're not concerned with the way society is undoubtedly changing, think of your children! When they saw a woman break her arm, fall from the sky, or get stabbed through the leg, did you fear for their emotional stability or their safety?" Flint pointed at the audience as if to accuse them of negligence. "There is only one answer tonight—Juniper is a danger. How long are we going to follow the circus and allow them to teach our children that risking your life for a bit of adrenaline is okay?"

An old woman in the crowd stood up and shouted, "The man's right!"

Then a man with a cane stood from his seat. "The circus is not a danger. It's a form of entertainment!"

There was much opposition, but Flint's final statement would surely convince the killer.

Flint pointed toward the back of the audience, to those who were cast in shadow, speaking to him directly. "Here me now. Juniper must be brought to an end. We cannot allow her to alter our ways. Before we know it, we'll allow these lowlifes to live among us. She must be killed!"

Cassius burst forth from the row of performers, grabbed Flint, and kicked his legs out from under him. He fell onto the stage and wrestled to escape, but Cassius banged his head into the floor. Flint continued to push at his chest, to no avail, while Cassius threw a few punches.

The people in the crowd leapt up in fear, wondering if this man would escape or be brought to justice. After the stranger called for Juniper's death, the audience now thought of him as a crazed man. His warnings about the changes in society would surely be ignored because of his insanity.

Flint's face was now bruised around his eye and cheekbone, and he spit out a mouthful of blood before kneeing Cassius in the groin.

Cassius groaned and fell over on his side, rolling off Flint.

Flint leapt up and quickly dodged three of the guards that raced toward him. When he reached the door, he threw his arm at the guard posted there, knocking him out cold. Then he ran out the door to disappear in the back where no one would find him.

Cassius rolled onto his side, gripping his crotch in pain while still trying to crawl toward the man escaping. To the crowd and the rest of the performers, this was a bizarre spectacle from a man who was determined to end the circus, but only few knew that this was yet another act put on by the circus.

The Killer...

The crowd had cleared out and the circus had packed up and left, but I remained in the dark shadows of Celeste's Opera House. What a show the circus put on tonight. And it proved one thing to be true—I had an ally. I'd worked alone for years, but Juniper Rose was harder to kill than Penelope Plume. I would need help if I was to bring her down.

I'd remained hidden for months, but now it was time to bring her and the circus to an end, once and for all. And finally, someone seemed to agree with me.

I walked through the aisles, trailing my hand across the plush velvet seats in the auditorium. The lights had been turned out, all except the single row of footlights on the edge of the stage, illuminating something that had fallen on the marble floor among the many roses. I slowly stalked up the stairs before bending down to retrieve a small golden rope which had fallen during the brawl, it seemed. I turned it over in my fingers while examining it. On one end, there was a golden tassel, and on the other, the insignia of the riding team, illustrated by a galloping horse.

Well, well, well. It was time I paid a visit to Flint Rye.

Chapter Twenty-Eight

I'd been awake for hours, but I couldn't move. All I could do was stare at the white bandage fastened around my thigh. I would be immobilized for the foreseeable future. Our next performance was in three weeks, but I'd be lucky if I could walk the rope by then. How many times would I be threatened and maimed, stripped from doing what I loved? Walking the rope gave me a sense of passion I'd never known before. And he'd taken that away from me…again.

Someone rapped softly on the door, and a small head of curly black hair peeked through.

Cassius slid into the room and sat gently on the bed next to me. "How are you doing?"

For some reason, I didn't want him to see me cry. It seemed like I'd been crying ever since I returned to the circus, and I didn't want him to think of me as some wounded animal, always in need of protecting. And for that reason, I couldn't meet his eyes. I shrugged, not knowing what to say.

To avoid his question, I posed a different one, gently fingering the bruise around his eye. "How are *you*?"

He chuckled, but I saw him stiffen at my touch. "Still sore," he winced. "Flint got a couple jabs, but only because I let him."

"Of course." I nodded along and snickered. God forbid Flint ever get the upper hand.

He gently stroked his hand up and down my calf, his smile fading. "We found Gus tied up in a broom closet last night after the killer struck you."

When the knife found its mark, I knew it couldn't have been Gus under the mask, especially after he vanished.

"I have good news though," Cassius continued, hoping to raise my spirits. "With so many guards patrolling the theater last night, the killer wasn't able to escape. He was spotted returning to the audience, and

Flint did a fine job delivering his speech, if I do say so myself. The killer heard every word."

I turned to him and smiled faintly. At least the chaos last night hadn't been for nothing.

"And…" Cassius drawled. "Flint received a letter this morning. He thought to open it with you, if you're ready for it."

I tried to sit up, but a sharp pain sliced through my leg and up into my spine. I winced, before Cassius gently grabbed my lower back and helped me to sit up. Because of what happened last night, I was more than ready to bring down the killer. So, I looked to Cassius and said, "I'm ready."

When his cheeks pulled back, his eyes crinkled under the shadow of his hair. But then his demeanor seemed to shift. "You sang to me in the performance before last, asking me to walk with you—to fall with you. Doesn't that mean I'll lay with you, cry with you, and mourn with you too?"

I looked up from the bed into his earnest eyes and nodded.

Taking my cold hands in his own, he said, "These are hard times, Juniper. But I'll do all that with you if you ask me to."

I pulled him into my chest, crying softly into his shoulder. "I'll want you by my side for the rest of my days, Cas."

We sat there for a moment, memorizing the safety in each other's arms before Cassius pulled away and cleared his throat. "Alright Miss Rose, you're looking at your escort." He waved at himself handsomely. "Mr. Monte spoke to the doctor. They advised you shouldn't walk for a week, so you're stuck with me until then."

"Only a week?" I inquired. That's not as bad as I was expecting.

"Yes. But for the next week you're on bedrest if your leg is to heal correctly," he explained, matter-of-factly, and scooped me into his arms.

I winced from the movement, but after a few seconds, the pain numbed. I pecked him on the cheek and gently tapped his shoulder. "Hop to it, Mr. Plume."

He scoffed at his last name, which I'd taken a liking to using. It sounded rather posh.

When we reached Mr. Monte's office, Flint was already seated on the other side of the desk, deep in conversation, but it halted when Cassius not so subtly kicked the door open with his foot.

"My Rose, how are you holding up?" Mr. Monte pulled out a chair.

"Better than when I broke my arm last year, that's for sure." I attempted to appear enthusiastic, but I couldn't help but groan when Cassius sat me down.

"That's good to hear!" Mr. Monte exclaimed.

I glanced sidelong at Flint, giving him a small smile. "Good job last night. I heard it worked."

"Indeed, it did. I woke this morning and found this sitting under my door." Flint handed me a letter, embossed with a scarlet wax seal. "I think you should do us the honor."

I eyed it for a moment, recognizing the cream-colored parchment. I took a deep breath, my hands shaking. It had been months since I'd received a letter from the killer.

Cassius laid his hand on my arm. "Take your time."

I didn't need any more time. I needed revenge. The killer had haunted me for long enough, and it was time we brought him to justice. I flipped open the letter and scanned over the lines scrawled in fanciful lettering.

Flint Rye,

I applaud you for delivering such an exquisite speech last night. I was impressed by your diligence. It appears we share something in common—our resentment of Juniper Rose. But I have more information to offer you. Meet me at Bayard's Tavern at eight o'clock.

Yours Truly

This was really happening.

The killer was falling right into our trap.

"Bayard's Tavern," Mr. Monte whispered, recalling the place from times past. "It sits right on the edge of the city, well-hidden and not crowded. He chose it for that very reason."

Suddenly the reality of the situation set in. Flint could be killed if it was ever discovered that we were behind this. I closed my eyes, not able to stop my hands from shaking, but I felt Cassius's grip tighten to reassure me.

There were no words exchanged, but I knew what he was thinking. This needed to be done, no matter the risk.

But I turned to Flint and approached the conversation with a warning, "We must be careful. The killer is already suspicious about who he can trust, so you have to be convincing. This is your chance to draw him out. Any ideas?" I looked to the three men surrounding me.

Mr. Monte spoke first. "He's hurt you again. We can't wait any longer. If we're to capture him at the next performance, we need to figure out *how*."

Cassius sat up then. "We've got a battalion of guards from Axminster. We could have them set up just as they were last night. As soon as the killer strikes—"

Flint cut Cassius off then. "We don't know when he's going to strike or how. Last night he was in plain sight, but in every other instance, he was nowhere to be seen. We can't guarantee he'll reveal himself like he did last night, and we can't give him that opportunity. If we do, he might just kill her."

Mr. Monte mumbled his agreement while weighing our options.

He opened his mouth to speak but I stopped him. "Let him catch me." My voice was nothing more than a whisper, but every head turned to me. And when I looked up, three pairs of eyes were watching me. "Let him catch me," I repeated, the plan unfolding in my head. "If Flint sets up an opportunity for him to kill me, he'll walk right into it." I turned to Flint, who's eyes were wide and confused. "Tonight, you hatch a plan with the killer to lead him right to me when the next performance comes. He'll be even more convinced that you're on his side."

"No!" Cassius raised his voice and stood out of his seat. "That's not going to happen."

"Listen." I urged him to sit back down, and he did so begrudgingly, with suspicion written on his face. "We're taking risks sending Flint out to meet the killer. We need to send me into the fire as well." I glanced between the three of them before explaining my idea. "The next performance is in Wimborne at the Moonlight Hall, a small theater in the city. I did some research, and it just so happens that the Moonlight Hall is used for local plays."

"And why is this important?" Mr. Monte inquired, curious as to where I was going with this.

"Because, Edward." I smiled deviously. "The Moonlight Hall is the newest theater in the country, renovated only four years ago. And in recent productions, an orchestra plays as background music in the pit below the stage. Clear it out and we've got the perfect trap for the killer." I laid back in my seat and crossed my hands over my lap.

Turning to Cassius, I said, "Pick your jaw up off the floor, Mr. Plume. We've got a lot more to discuss."

And I giggled, thinking this might just work.

Chapter Twenty-Nine

We'd spent the better part of the afternoon hatching a plan for Flint's meeting with the killer, and before the sun could set completely, it was time for him to venture into the city.

"Go get 'em soldier." I straightened Flint's jacket, permitted to stand just this once with Cassius's help. I was scared for Flint. If he didn't deliver his message with enough conviction, he might not come home.

Having similar worries, he brought me into a tight embrace.

Cassius looked at him warily with a raised brow.

"I'm going to be fine, J," Flint said, tucking his head into the crook of my neck. Despite his attempt to sound confident, I heard his voice waver. He was scared.

Mr. Monte clapped him on the shoulder. "You've got this, my boy."

Putting his trepidation aside, Flint nodded and turned toward the tree line in the distance. He sauntered away and we watched his figure disappear into the night. Flint would be okay. He was strong. And on the small chance the killer discovered Flint was undercover, he would fight back. He'd make it back to us.

"Come on, now. It's growing cold. Let's get you inside." Cassius picked me up and carried me back into the train.

Cassius was right. It was getting colder. Autumn had fallen upon us, turning the leaves to a whiskey-colored orange. Brisk air swept through the atmosphere, lifting the leaves in a whirling tornado throughout the sky. I didn't enjoy this time of year because the harsh temperatures made practicing outside almost unbearable. My limbs were stiff in the cold, rather than loose and relaxed, like in the warm months of summer.

We ducked inside and found warmth in Cassius's room. After he laid me down, I stared at the ceiling in silence, wondering what we were supposed to do for the next few hours while Flint was coercing the killer.

"We need to take our minds off this." I sighed, turning to where Cassius was currently stripping off his shirt. "Do you have any ideas?"

He turned to me with a saccharine grin. "I have plenty of ideas, but seeing as though your paralyzed, I don't think most of them would work."

My mouth fell open in offense. "Paralyzed?"

He just giggled before coming to rest beside me. When the bed sank under his weight, all I could do was watch him. His skin was golden and smooth, toned and mature, but soft all at once. I couldn't help but reach out to touch him. Tracing my fingers up his forearm, I placed my hand on the muscled planes of his torso, where a fire spread through my palm.

"Your hands are freezing," he commented, grabbing my hands and tucking them within his own. As he gently blew warm air into the pocket he'd created, my fingers began to relax. "How are you?" he asked.

He'd asked that question a hundred times today. "I'm fine, Cas. You don't have to keep checking on me." I rolled my eyes.

"Then you need to stop getting into so much trouble," he spoke softly, his tone dripping with sweetness.

"Oh, it's my fault now?" I inquired, leaning closer to him.

"Mm-hmm," he hummed, leaning forward to kiss me, his tongue slowly caressing mine.

I sighed into his warmth, attempting to move closer to him, which sent a sharp pain through my thigh. Pulling away quickly, I found Cassius's lips still parted, his eyes glossy, and his hair tousled.

Charlotte's voice suddenly replayed in my mind. *When the time is right it will happen.* I blinked rapidly, trying to get her voice out of my head, and slid into a sitting position.

"What's goin' on up there?" Cassius gently poked my temple.

"I don't have time, Cassius. I keep thinking about the circus, and you most of all. When we catch the killer, I'll have to leave. We've barely gotten enough time together with all this fuss over the killer, and I'm angry because now I *am* practically paralyzed," I used his words from earlier which made him giggle. I closed my eyes in fear, unable to stand the thought of sitting across from my mother at the dinner table, sipping tea with Colette and her soon-to-be husband William, or pretending to love Joseph Young and appeal to his father as though he were my own. I couldn't do it. "I'm terrified to go back there."

"You won't have to go back." Cassius tucked a piece of my hair behind my ear, his caress making me close my eyes. "Not as long as I have something to say about it."

I turned to him then, wishing I could share his optimism. "But what can you do? What can any of us do? It's Mr. Young we're talking about." I laid my head back against the headboard, suddenly at a loss for what to say.

"And what about what I want?" Cassius asked, grabbing my chin to turn my head toward him. His eyes were blazing with anger, jealousy, and desire. "What about what I want?" he repeated in a whisper. The line between his eyebrows creased as his mouth fell open. "I want you and I can't have you. How's that fair?"

"Life isn't meant to be fair." I let my head fall. But if I did have to return to Axminster, I needed to spend my last moments with Cassius without regret. With a click of my tongue, I picked my head up. "I may not have very long, but I'm *right* here Cassius."

"But you're not!" he raised his voice, suddenly backing away. And within the blink of an eye, the atmosphere in the room changed. "Not until Joseph Young refuses your hand." He moved to the edge of the bed with his back turned to me.

And as much as I wanted to reassure him, I couldn't think of anything to say. I didn't have an answer.

"This isn't going to work, is it? You and me? You said it yourself. What can *I* do?" He squinted at me, before pulling a shirt back over his head.

It looked like he was about to storm out and leave me there alone, but I wouldn't let him run away this time.

"Cassius Plume, you look at me." I moved to the edge of the bed, the muscles in my leg straining. "We are going to make this work. But to do that, we must put Joseph behind us and focus on the future. You can't beat yourself up for things that are out of your control."

He stepped toward me, infuriated. "It seems everything is out of my control, Juniper. You're meant to be married to another man, and I can't do a single thing about it. Look at me!" He pointed to himself in the most derogatory way, and it killed me.

Cassius was more special than he'd ever know.

"Look at you." He lowered his voice and flicked his eyebrows. "You've been injured more than you've been healthy. You're not safe here. And you're meant to be with someone like Joseph. Not me."

"That is not for you to decide!" I tried to push off the bed, but my leg suddenly buckled, and Cassius pushed me back. I continued, my chest heaving. "Joseph represents everything I detest. He is wealthy and yes, he's kind, but he doesn't work hard, and his only passion is pleasing his father. So please, don't tell me that I belong with someone like him." I reached out to grab his waist and bury my head in his stomach. "But you...you are everything. And I *am* meant to be with you."

Cassius sank to his knees in front of me. "But he could give you more than I ever could. Don't you want that, Juniper? Don't you want to be spoiled and not have to worry about jumping from one town to the next, never having a place to call home?" Cassius picked my head up and held my cheeks in his palms.

I tilted my head curiously. "Don't you? Doesn't everyone here? No one wants to live in the cold, banished from the rest of society, and looked upon as *freaks*! But we're in this together. And I don't want a string of pearls, or a new dress, or box seats at the opera. I don't need a lavish life, Cas." I sniffed away the tears, hoping he would just stay with me. "I need you."

He blinked rapidly before tucking his head into my lap.

I took a deep breath as I twisted his soft, dark curls between my fingers. "Look at me," I raised his jaw. "You have to find contentment within yourself, Cassius. If you don't, it will destroy us. You aren't perfect, and I can't even begin to understand what you've been through, but I love you."

Saying those words made me seize up. It was the first time I had ever truly loved someone, and telling him made it so much more real.

By the looks of it, Cassius was just as surprised.

"You have to get past the betrayal and loss and pain. You have to find the real Cassius."

He looked down for a moment, weighing what I'd just said. "So, the Cassius who drank and fucked and had fun…that's not what you want?"

I winced at his vile language. "If that's who you are then that's what I want." I smiled softly, shaking my head back and forth. "But I think there's more to you than you're willing to show. I know there is."

Tears welled in his eyes, making it obvious that not enough people had told him these things. And that made me sad.

Cassius nodded, his head bobbing up and down. "You're right. I'll try."

And that was enough.

Chapter Thirty

Flint...

The sign for Bayard's Tavern swung in the cool breeze over an old red brick building, with dull glass windows covered in dust, so that you could only depict shadows on the interior. I took a deep breath as a drunk man with a wet beard stumbled out of the tavern, mumbling nonsensically. I shuffled past him quickly despite being nervous about who was waiting on the other side, and pushed into the tavern. I peered around momentarily, and finding no sign of the killer, I took a seat at the bar and ordered an ale.

"What are you here for?" the bartender inquired. The man wore a stylish top hat, a brown suede vest, and a monocle over his left eye, looking rather sophisticated to be working in a run-down tavern. "Business?" he pushed me further.

I eyed him briefly, before answering, "You could say that."

"Whatever it is, you look rather stressed," the man commented.

I'm meeting with an infamous killer who has threatened my friends and is set on killing Juniper. You're damn right I'm stressed.

"No matter." The bartender shrugged. "This one's on me, lad."

The bartender pushed forward another pint of ale, and I nodded my thanks just as the bell over the door rung and heavy footfalls filled the room. Turning over my shoulder, my heart dropped as a man dressed in a long black trench coat walked through the door. His shoulders were broad, and he was taller than most men. And of course, he refused to show his face. He wore a black mask, and his head was adorned with a matching black top hat. He was the picture of ease and restraint, but of unyielding force.

I set down two gold coins and stood from the table while the bartender shook his head at the sight of the new guest. It seemed he knew I was in trouble. Flicking him an extra coin for his generosity, I grabbed the extra pint of ale, and strode to the table the killer had settled into. All I had to do was remain composed and confident, so I pushed my shoulders back and walked leisurely toward him. Calming my breathing, I slid the pint of ale across the table to the man cast in shadow and took a seat across from him.

"Good evening, Flint," he began.

I was surprised to hear such a low voice. Not a rough kind of sound, but smooth and refined. He sounded almost like a nobleman. Could he have come from outside the circus, contrary to what we thought?

The killer gently tossed a golden rope across the table.

It bounced once, twice, and landed before me with a hollow *thud*. I spotted the emblem of the riders at the end of the rope.

Prod him. Search for his name without appearing too desperate. Juniper's voice sung in my head as I recalled our meeting earlier that afternoon.

"Good evening—" I paused, considering his name. "What should I call you?"

The killer looked straight at me before changing the subject as though he hadn't heard me. "I meant what I said, Flint. Your performance was impeccable."

Keep going. Keep the conversation flowing as though you're speaking with a friend. Convince him that you're against Juniper Rose. Mr. Monte had encouraged me.

The killer knew me, that much was evident. No one knew my name except those in the circus, so he had to be one of us. "Thank you. I meant every word I said."

"If I'm correct, you and Juniper were close. You may have even loved her?" the killer began.

I pondered his question. Had I loved her? I'd only known her closely for a few months. Was it possible to love someone in such a short time? I loved her passion and commitment, and her hope for the future and a new society—one where the poor and the rich wouldn't be separated—one where we could live together in harmony. And I knew the answer then. "Yes. Yes, I did love her."

Good. Now tell him how much you hate me. It was as if Juniper was sitting next to me, guiding my responses.

"But she broke my heart." I looked down to the table, trying to muster some resentment. This wasn't a lie, by any means, but it was far less serious than I was making it out to be. Yes, Juniper hurt me when she chose Cassius over me. She refused my protection and my kindness when she opted for that brute of a boy, but I've had many hardships in my life, and her refusing me paled by comparison. Nonetheless, I put on my best act. "She chose another man over me. She changed the circus by connecting us with wealthy patrons, like Gisèle Perrault. Instead of performing in red and white tents, we perform on stages." I slammed my fist into the table. "The circus used to be a place for those who were lost, and our audience was just as flawed as we were. It used to be about giving them hope and doing what we love. Now it has nothing to do with us. The morning's paper is all about the latest magnate to attend the performance, not the magic of the performance itself."

"I couldn't agree more. Juniper comes from a wealthy family, and her affiliation with the wealthy is undermining everything we stand for."

We. So, he was a part of the circus.

The killer continued, "We cannot avoid the fact that she's dangerous. She has more power than any of us—more connections. And she's careless." The man gently sat forward and folded his hands on the table in a business-like manner. "If we don't stop her, the circus will be changed forever."

You can't only speak of how much you detest Juniper. You must prove your willingness to kill her. Cassius had told me.

"I want to hurt her for what she did to me and for what she continues to do to all of us. She doesn't belong here," I declared.

I swore he smiled under his mask. "You're in luck. I want the very same thing, Mr. Rye. But how do I know you're willing to go to any length to stop her?" he inquired.

Surely, killing a woman was not palatable for most people. He had to know I was willing to go to extremes.

Shit, shit, shit. I hadn't prepared for this question. How could I convince him that I was capable of killing someone? I thought for a moment on the question he asked, and answered with, "I'm just like you, aren't I?" More than anything, the killer wouldn't want to feel isolated or crazy. He needed a partner who would validate him. "I'm a poor man with little hope outside the circus. And I don't want Juniper destroying my only hope."

The killer nodded over and over, seeming pleased.

"How do you propose we finish this?" he whispered.

Now, tell him the plan.

I leaned closer to discuss it quietly, my chest hunched over the table. "The next performance is at the Moonlight Hall. There's an orchestra pit below the stage. Since we don't use an orchestra, the pit will be empty." I paused so the killer could take in this information. "You're skilled at little tricks. From cutting the silks, to tampering with the lion's cage, you know how to hurt her. But Juniper is stronger than you anticipated, and we can't let her get away unscathed this time."

The killer looked up from the table to meet my eyes, although I hadn't a clue as to who I was looking at.

I cleared my throat. "A trap door is what I propose. Mess with the floorboards and loosen the hinges in the intermission that we schedule right before Juniper's act, and when she comes out on stage, she'll fall right into the pit where you'll be waiting for her."

The killer was unmoving and silent as he gazed at me. He then clapped his hands in midair. "My boy, I am rather impressed. I didn't think you had it in you."

Don't let him doubt you.

"We all have our motives." I shrugged carelessly, with ease, as though I'd been thinking about this for quite a while. Mr. Monte, Juniper, and Cassius had specifically instructed me not to interfere with their plan by asking the man his backstory. He would become suspicious if I asked too many questions. But I couldn't resist. I had to know. "I'm guessing there's a bigger reason you want Juniper Rose dead. Would you mind telling?"

To my surprise, the killer revealed his reasoning without hesitation. Maybe he took comfort in finally being able to convey his anger. Maybe he took comfort in having a friend. For a moment I felt sorry for him because he was alone, feared by all, without anyone to rely on. But he didn't deserve my sympathy.

He began his story then. "I knew someone in the circus who died a painful death, and I've resented the circus ever since. It's a dangerous activity with not enough revenue to safely protect its members. It's a futile venture. And Juniper Rose isn't powerful enough to raise revenues and convince people that it's safe. It's *hell*. The performers can barely afford to eat, they're constantly getting hurt, and they have no life to speak of. It has to stop. Juniper Rose is just the beginning."

My heart stopped then. Juniper Rose was just the beginning? What did he mean? We assumed that he had a vendetta against tightrope walkers, but by the sound of it, it was bigger than that. "And what do you plan to do after that?"

No. Stop. Juniper's voice urged me in terror. *He'll know what you're doing.*

I shook her out of my head and added quickly, "I resent the circus because I'm stuck living like a bum instead of pursuing my dream. I had the chance of going to university, and because my parents squandered our money, I couldn't. I was forced to join the circus because I had no other option. And now I feel nothing but disdain for it."

In reality, the circus had saved me. I didn't resent it one bit. I didn't need or want to go back to the real world. I was just making up any lie at this point to get answers.

"I understand the feeling, Mr. Rye." He said nothing more on the subject.

My heart pounded in my chest. Did he know that I was fishing for information or that there were people waiting for me back at the train, intent on hearing every detail? But he wouldn't have told me anything if he doubted me, so, I pushed my shoulders back and relaxed in my chair. "At least allow me the pleasure of telling me how you're going to kill her," I drawled slowly.

The killer chuckled, amused, as if this was a game—as if this wasn't a life he was planning to take in cold blood. "Based on what you told me, she'll be easily trapped under the stage. All I need is for you to ensure that she doesn't escape, and I'll do the rest. It'll be quite the show." He giggled faintly, and I felt bile rise in my throat.

I had to get out of here. My body was shaking, and if I stayed any longer, I'd heave all over the table.

The killer stood and brushed invisible lint from his coat before sauntering up to me. "I'm confident you won't mention this to anyone," he whispered, standing by my side. "If you do, you know what will happen." He rested his hand on my shoulder and softly stroked my arm, almost in a loving way. His warm touch made my skin crawl and the back of my throat itch, and it took everything in me not to shrug away. "You can wear this, unless you want Juniper to know what she made you do." The killer handed me a black cloth. "I'll see you at the Moonlight Hall."

I nodded briefly, my shoulders tense, and listened for the small jingle of the bell that signaled his departure. When it rung softly, I buried my head in my hands and let loose the breath I'd been holding. The man who raped Penelope Plume and assaulted Juniper had been warming the seat across from me only seconds ago. He was a sick and twisted man that I was just beginning to make sense of, and he was willing to do whatever it took to kill Juniper. And what's more, he had a plan for the circus that we were unaware of.

Do not linger. Their last piece of advice rang through my head like an alarm, warning me to get out.

I rose out of my seat quickly, almost tipping over the chair, and I had to remind myself that this wasn't the place to lose my composure. I threw my head back and let the remnants of ale slide down my throat in hopes that it would calm me, before snatching the black cloth off the table.

Hanging my head low to avoid the curious gazes of the customers around me, I exited the tavern and meandered through alleyways toward the tree line bordering the city. I walked slowly in case the killer was following behind, watching. I didn't want to look like I was in a rush, so I tried to relax, but when I reached the outer city and saw the looming fields of wheat in the distance, the train not far beyond, I ran. I leapt through tall fields of corn, grains of wheat nicking my cheek as I pumped my arms as fast as I could.

I had survived. That's all that mattered. But despite that I'd fooled the killer, I couldn't get his voice out of my head—how the pitch rose when he spoke of Juniper's death…as though he was excited. And with no distinct feature to pinpoint on his face, all I could remember was a dark shadow.

Cresting over a small hill, the train came into view. My breathing was ragged but I couldn't stop. The danger of what I'd just done came crashing over me, and if I didn't keep moving, I'd collapse. But soon enough, I reached the train and ripped open the door, pushing my way into the main hall.

I looked around frantically for someone, anyone who could bring me to Mr. Monte, but no one was in sight. Suddenly, Raegan and Raelynn rounded the corner, hand in hand, with jubilant smiles on their faces. "Flint!" the pair exclaimed, but worry fell over their faces when they noticed the sweat dripping down my temple and the terror written on my face.

"Take me to Mr. Monte." I tried to remain calm, but I couldn't stop my voice from shaking.

They stood there, unflinching, curious as to what was going on.

"Did you not hear me?" I screamed, my face shaking.

Suddenly the two girls leapt into action. Raelynn grabbed my arm and tugged me toward the animal cages, while Raegan followed closely behind. Grunts, tweets, and the moaning of animals filled the cramped hall, beckoning me closer to our leader.

"Mr. Monte!" Raelynn shouted, pulling me toward him.

He turned over his shoulder, appalled when he saw my distress. "Flint! What happened? Are you hurt?" He raced to me, looking me over for wounds.

"I'm fine," I whispered, unable to even look Mr. Monte in the eyes. The circus used to be such a lovely place, but it had changed into something dark and dangerous, filled with secrets.

Mr. Monte looked to the twins on either side of me. "Take Flint to my office immediately." And before they could move an inch, he sauntered out of the train car.

Chapter Thirty-One

Cassius and I laid next to each other, talking through ways to keep me in the circus, but so far, we'd come up with nothing.

Before we could get very far, Mr. Monte came crashing through the door. He looked haggard, as though he'd just run from the shores of Isleburry and back. He tried to calm his heaving chest, but said in alarm, "Flint's back."

I gasped, and before I knew it, Cassius was pulling me into his arms, and we were following Mr. Monte down the hall.

But when we entered Mr. Monte's office and I spotted Flint, I knew the situation was worse than we thought. He looked stricken, appalled, traumatized. Those were the first words that came to mind in a list of a hundred—the same hundred I felt when I saw the killer.

"What happened?" I inquired as Cassius sat me down next to Flint and took the chair on the other side for himself.

"It worked," Flint said quietly, rubbing his hands together tediously. "It worked," he repeated, as if that's all he could manage to say.

I looked to Cassius and Mr. Monte with a big smile. I didn't ever think I'd be happy about getting caught by the killer, in danger of being hurt or even killed, but if we were successful, we'd be rid of this nuisance in a matter of weeks.

I reached over and grabbed Flint's arm with tears in my eyes. "Thank you, Flint. This means the world to me."

He nodded with a faint smile and then looked to the floor, contemplating his conversation with the killer. I couldn't keep myself from diving into our plan, but I faltered at Flint's quietness. Clearly, there was something on his mind.

"What's wrong?" I asked, silencing the others.

"There's something else," he stated blankly.

Everyone turned to Flint at once.

"The killer explained that you were just the beginning. He's planning something bigger—much bigger. And we need to figure out what."

"Why? We're going to catch him at the next show. He can't do any damage from behind bars," Cassius insisted.

"I doubt that's true. The killer is far more clever than we give him credit for. He must have connections, so even from prison, he could destroy us."

"You think he has accomplices outside the circus?" Mr. Monte asked him nervously.

Flint nodded. "I do. To accomplish whatever he's planning, he'll have to have help." Flint stood to his feet and placed his hands behind his head, racking his brain for answers.

Luckily, I already had a guess. "Last year, on the same day the silks were cut, someone threatened to sue the circus for its dangerous activities. We discovered that instigator to be my mother," I proclaimed.

"Are you insinuating that your mother could still be in cahoots with the killer?" Mr. Monte laid his hands on his desk, as if he couldn't believe it.

I looked to Cassius, my anchor. His face was twisted in confusion and what looked to be fear. Was my mother capable of conspiring with a killer just to return me to my rightful place? I didn't think she would go that far…unless she didn't know he was a killer. Cassius nodded lightly, urging me to speak my mind.

I took a deep breath. "Yes, I am. She'll do anything to get her family back. It would make sense that the killer sought her out. She's my mother, after all, and if he told her he could bring down the circus, she would jump to help him." I paused, shaking my head. "She wouldn't know I'm in danger."

Mr. Monte swallowed hard and Flint looked at me as though I was wounded. If this was true and my mother was helping the killer, she could be put in jail for aiding and abetting a murderer.

"You could contact her," Flint spoke for the first time in ten minutes, the color returning to his face. "You could confront her."

I shook away the idea as soon as the words left his mouth. "That won't work. My mother's too stubborn. She wouldn't give up this information easily."

"Unless you make her believe you're considering returning to Axminster. Maybe then she'd tell you," Cassius said softly, his arms strapped across his chest.

"Yes, that could work. Convince her that you may agree to come back if she tells you the truth." Mr. Monte nodded along.

Flint, risking his life to catch the killer? My mother, friends with the killer? Returning to Axminster? This was all too much. I tried to stand out of my chair but the pain in my leg tore through my thigh. I needed to get out of this claustrophobic room and think.

I looked up at Cassius for help. "I need some fresh air."

Cassius nodded, and without thinking twice, he pulled me into his arms. Before he shut the door to Mr. Monte's office, he reassured him that we'd get this sorted out. As we wound through the train and made our way outside, he didn't say a word.

I took a deep breath, the thick scent of autumn cooling me. At night, the businesses were closed, and less pollution filled the air. The night smelled pure and clean. I closed my eyes while trying to comprehend all that had happened in the past few months. My mother was not a terrible person. She was vengeful and selfish, but she wasn't dangerous. If she was working with the killer, she must not know how dangerous he is.

I agreed with Cassius. The killer would be behind bars soon enough, and no matter what he had in store for the circus, he wouldn't be able to accomplish it.

Cassius sat me on the ledge of the open train car, and after giving me time to think, he said, "You could contact your mother and ask about her affiliation with the killer, but if you feel uncomfortable speaking to her, you don't have to. I know there's a lot going on right now, and no matter what the killer said to Flint, our focus should be on catching him. Don't worry about anything else right now."

That's exactly what I needed to hear. I just needed him to make a plan and reassure me that we were doing *something* right. When it came to the killer, it felt like we were always one step behind. And he was here because of me. My mother was threatening to sue the circus because of me. And Mr. Young was threatening to burn it to the ground *because of me*.

"It's my fault. All of this." I shook my head, unable to take my eyes off the dark tree line in the distance. "I brought all of this here. And none of you deserve to go through any of it."

Cassius turned my chin so that our eyes met. "You think none of this would have happened if you hadn't come? The killer would have resurfaced as soon as Mr. Monte found another tightrope walker to fill Penelope's shoes. And your mother and Mr. Young aren't the only ones who detest the circus. If they hadn't interfered, someone else would have. You coming here has been difficult, but it's given us the chance to fight for what we love and prove to everyone else that its worth fighting for."

"You really think this would have happened with or without me?" I inquired.

He pulled me in tighter by my waist. "Yes, I do. And I think it's a good thing that it's happening now, so we can put an end to it." Cassius nodded encouragingly. "This is not your fault."

I searched his eyes, trying so hard to believe him.

He gripped my arm tightly. "You are not a nuisance or a burden. Truth is, we couldn't have survived without you."

"You sure as hell wouldn't have had to survive if it weren't for me," I pleaded with him.

Cassius sighed deeply and closed his eyes. "Juniper, we've been surviving every single day of our lives. But when we joined the circus, that survival was worth it. And you made it even more worth it by convincing us that the rest of the world could come to respect us. You showed us that not everything is black and white—that people from all walks of life can come together and love something greater than themselves."

My nose burned and I tried not to cry at the realization that I'd helped in some small way amidst all the chaos.

"Look at me if you need further proof that you belong here. Before you arrived, I was a drunk with no intention of living any longer than absolutely necessary. I was unable to see the meaning of life after my sister died, until you showed it to me. And I've become a better man because of it. Because of *you*." The corner of his mouth curled into a smirk.

I leaned closer to him and wrapped my body around his, melting into his warmth. "Thank you," I whispered. "For always encouraging me." I nuzzled my head into his shoulder and looked to the sky above us. The moon glistened like a crystal over the milky grey sky, and the city lights in the distance lit up the clouds like a beacon. I looked down the row of train cars, the word "circus" shining just a little brighter under the light of the moon. I was blessed to have come to such a beautiful place, filled with the likes of dancers, flamethrowers, and most importantly, the lion tamer. I gripped his hand in mine.

"I think we're going to be just fine," I whispered softly, my voice seeming too loud for the gentle breeze that fluttered past us.

Cassius laid his head on top of mine. "Oh, we'll be more than fine. We're the circus after all.

Chapter Thirty-Two

After a long night dissecting the future of the circus, we took comfort in the dining car where the music wafted through the train and our jumping feet shook the floorboards. Cassius was vehement that distraction was the best remedy for stress, so he took my hand and led me onto the dancefloor.

My leg had since healed, giving me the freedom to dance carelessly. Charlotte, accompanied by the other dancers, sidled up next to me, and Olive and Piper, the youngest of the crew, grabbed my hands and jumped up and down with me.

Suddenly, Olive turned to Cassius and grabbed his arms. He smiled gently, somewhat uncomfortable, but he didn't push her away. He shuffled her back and forth and before I knew it, he was teaching her how to swing dance. It was a funny spectacle, watching her try to reach him at such a small height, but he laughed heartily, wearing the warmest smile. Quickly bored by the activity, he stopped, and she jumped up and threw her whole body around him. He *hmphed* out a breath before scooping her up to settle her on his hip, and swaying back and forth, he dipped her down to the ground, making her scream.

I stood there like an idiot in a sea of dancing people with my feet planted in the ground, watching him. He smiled and laughed with this little girl hooked around his waist. It was silly to even think of it, but I couldn't help but wonder what a great father he'd make. I could envision it so perfectly. If he was ever blessed with a little girl, he would dance with her in the train car before sending her to bed with a full stomach of stew, and he would show her the animals in the morning and teach her how to take care of them. And maybe, just maybe, she would learn to fly on the trapeze as he had. There's no doubt he would love and protect her always.

An image of the circus years down the road ran through my mind.

When we survived this mess, we'd spend our nights like this, drinking and hollering so loud that the city beyond would hear. We'd wake up early in the morning to the sound of the clock tower ringing in the distance, but we wouldn't work like everyone else. No, we would be busy perfecting our acts while the sun tanned our skin. And when it came time to perform in front of a crowd that was yearning for a bit of magic, we'd offer them a dream—our dream.

I was *whooshed* out of my vision by a pair of golden eyes, like warm hazelnut orbs, or the aureate leaves falling off the trees. Cassius grabbed my waist, and I laid my hands on his chest, swaying back and forth to the rhythm of the music. When he pressed my hips into his, our bodies had never felt closer, and with his forehead against mine, the tickle of his breath snaked across my cheek. But when our soft touching grew tedious, he grabbed my jaw and pulled my mouth to his, with his fingers lost in my hair.

I kissed him deeply, not caring who was watching. While the others danced around us, we stood in the middle of the room, surrounded by noise and motion. And I was reminded that I was allowed to enjoy myself—to live in the moment. Because in a week's time, the killer and I would come face to face, and we would end it all.

The week passed faster than any before, and performance night had come.

Early that morning all the equipment had been transported to the Moonlight Hall, but as the sun began to fall, the circus gathered their costumes and ventured into the center of the city.

A harsh wind blew through the streets, mixing the smell of baked goods and gasoline fumes. Wimborne was a comfortable city, home to many accomplished businessmen, but it was rather small and confined. The theater here wasn't as grand as Celeste's Opera House, but it was beautiful, with old antique decorations. It was modest but expensive.

I sauntered through the streets with Charlotte and the dancers on my left, and Flint and Cassius on my right. We were a team—a family. And no matter what happened tonight, that would never change.

Cassius gripped my hand in his and glanced over with a devilish smirk. Given the circumstances, he seemed rather lively. Tonight would be a great feat for him. The killer, who led his sister to take her own life, would be gone for good.

Thoughts of the killer momentarily vanished when we entered the Moonlight Hall. Mr. Monte disappeared to talk to the owner and set up with the theater crew, while the performers split off to the dressing rooms to primp. I covered my eyes in a dark shadow and spread blush across my cheeks and glitter along my cheekbones, before teasing my hair wildly.

Women bustled around me in a flurry, naked bodies shuffling in every direction.

But Charlotte stopped the commotion when she sprang over to me and yelled, "Ladies, on deck! I'll need every hand if we're going to get Juniper in this dress!" She clapped, as if commanding the theater herself.

The dancers sprang to her side, and I was pushed to the corner of the room where a billowing gown was hanging. As they gathered it and lifted it above their heads, I shuffled underneath and raised my arms, allowing the dress to spill over my body. The black tule fell around my waist in heaping layers, and the embroidered silver flowers sparkled in the candlelight. The corset was tight, the neckline high across my collarbones, and the sheer sleeves ended with a little loop hooked around my middle fingers.

Suddenly Valetta stormed into the room, and when the dancers retreated, she gasped at her work. The little woman, whose glasses continually slid down her nose, scurried over to me and began patting down the fabric and checking the seams. She smiled, obviously proud of herself. "The skirt detaches. Pull this string on your hip and it'll fall right off." She led my fingers to the little bow on my right hip.

I nodded to show her I understood. "Thank you for designing such a beautiful piece."

The corners of her mouth curved into a smile, creating deep laugh lines along her cheeks. "Of course, my dear." She turned around and grabbed a matte black hat, accessorized by a silk bow and a large brim that cast my face in shadow. The mirror reflected someone I didn't recognize—someone posh and refined, but dangerous, elusive, and…sexy.

Valetta nodded promptly. "Mr. Monte instructed me to grab you. He means to talk business."

I quickly turned to the ladies around me. "Thank you for your help. And thank you for welcoming me into this family." I swallowed to keep from crying. Despite how hopeful I was for the night, I was scared. If things went wrong, I'd never see them again.

Charlotte stepped forward and grabbed both my hands in hers. "It's going to work. You have to believe that."

Mr. Monte met with the rest of the performers a few days ago, informing them of our plan, and they were instructed to do what they did best—put on a show and pretend nothing's out of the ordinary.

"Thank you, all of you, for your support." I nodded my thanks. "I'll see you later." I would make it out of this alive. We all would.

I followed Valetta down the twisting halls of the theater until I found Mr. Monte, Flint, and Cassius standing outside the entrance to the auditorium.

I watched Cassius's jaw drop to the floor as he eyed the extravagant gown, looking me up and down. Valetta snickered and flicked his chin, making him aware of his ogling, and he cleared his throat to compose himself.

"My Rose, you've done it once again." Mr. Monte wrapped me in a hug and whispered in my ear, "You look flawless."

I held on tightly, trying to remember the joy of the circus instead of the darkness that had overcome it.

"I'm going to meet with the killer." Flint stepped forward and crossed his arms around my neck, receiving an eye roll from Cassius. Pulling away, he tried his best to smile. "The plan is set. All you have to do is look pretty and play the part. You'll have no trouble with that." He winked.

"I wanted to thank—"

Flint cut me off before I could finish. "Thank me later."

It was a promise that we'd see each other again, and I nodded in agreement before Flint sauntered out of sight.

Since the audience already mistrusted us after our last performance, we agreed the killer's capture would be kept a secret. And after Mr. Monte droned on about the events of the night out of nervousness, he left me to Cassius.

He opened his mouth, as if to say something, but then closed it again. What was there to say? I'd always needed his honesty, but tonight was a mystery, and it could go very differently than we hoped. I didn't blame him in the slightest for not knowing what to say.

So, to set him at ease, I stepped forward and pulled him in by his waist, curling my head into the warmth of his chest. Right now, I needed to be in his arms. Thinking of it, Cassius had often been the one to comfort me. Maybe it was my turn. "After tonight, we'll be living in a different world, and I can't wait for it."

He drew away to look at me for a moment before retrieving something from the table behind him. "This is for you." And then he was kneeling before me, gathering the fabric of my skirt into his hands. He pushed it up onto my hips to fasten a small dagger around my thigh. "If the killer tries anything, don't hesitate to use this."

He tightened the strap around my thigh, pausing to spread his hands across my leg. As his fingertips grazed the back of my knee, my core tightened. He looked up from under his brows and said, "I'm going to get the time to touch you after this. Really touch you." Something darkened in his eyes. "I'll have you in the way I've always wanted."

I lost my breath listening to the low rasp of his voice.

He pressed his lips to my leg, gently kissing the soft skin on my thigh, but before I could savor the moment, he'd already stood up.

Yearning for more, I pulled him to me, separating his soft lips with my own. But he didn't have the same fire as I did. His lips just brushed mine, as though he knew this wasn't our last moment together.

Finally, he opened his eyes and pressed a tender kiss to my forehead, his lips lingering. He looked down at me and smile before turning to leave. His shoulders moved expertly, visible even through the black silk vest he wore. Instead of the common white poet's shirt underneath, he dawned a much frillier grey one. He looked sophisticated, but dark and brooding.

I took a moment to memorize the way his hair curled at the bottom of his neck, sticking out at odd angles around his head, making him look like a little boy who'd just finished playing with the wind. I tried to remember the dimples in his cheeks when he smiled, his slightly crooked teeth, his dark eyebrows, and his golden eyes, so piercing and full of life. I smiled to myself, remembering the boy I once detested but had come to understand and adore. And then I turned my back on him, wishing I'd kissed him one more time.

Flint...

The dressing room was now empty and dark except for the single candle burning weakly on the vanity. The flames illuminated the mirror in strange ways, light flicking across my cheekbones and distorting my face. And in front of me laid a black mask. It seemed to absorb any light the candle offered, devouring it into its chasm. My fingers trembled as I touched its seam, and I took a steadying breath, trying to remember my face in the mirror as I stretched the mask over my hair, my cheekbones, and finally my jaw.

Pulling the mask taut, I closed my eyes as my breathing became strained. I was clenching my hands so hard to keep them from shaking that my nails etched crescent-shaped patterns into my palms. When I peeled open my eyes, I could see a dim version of the world through the mask. And, looking in the mirror, I didn't know who was gazing back at me. I stared at a man with no features, no depth, just…emptiness. My face twisted in demented shapes, growing terrifyingly oblong, and as it grew darker and darker, I clawed at the mask to get it off.

I threw it to the ground, finding my hair a tousled mess, my eyes wide and afraid. A tear slipped down my cheek at the thought of what I was expected to do tonight—who I was expected to become, and I'd never felt so afraid. I tore my eyes away from the mirror, unable to see its reflection anymore, and buried my head in my hands.

Chapter Thirty-Three

Fire erupted and warmth gushed throughout the room, orange embers reflecting in the eyes of the audience. The fire breathers' gilded skin was wet with a sheen of oil as they placed pillars of flames at their mouths and spewed fuel toward the crowd. With shirts stripped off revealing tattoos emblazoned upon their muscles, they opened their arms to welcome the crowd to the show.

The crowd gasped, amazed by the blinding light filling the room. Then, all at once, the fire breathers brought down their pillars of fire and extinguished them in buckets of water, drowning the room in darkness.

The curtain was pulled back and a spotlight glowed on the middle of the stage, welcoming a man in shadow. He wore a black suit with a waistcoat hanging below his hips and golden buttons trailing down his chest, a cane in hand and a crimson top hat on his bowed head. The golden buckles on his boots shone in the limelight as he took a step that resounded throughout the room. The spotlight followed him as he slowly raised his head, coming to meet the eyes of the audience.

"You all live in a distinct reality that moves forward without change. How dull it must be to continue performing the same routine, day in and day out. To break the tedium, I invite you to a night at the circus, where we live in a world of make believe." Mr. Monte smiled faintly, his white teeth the only thing gleaming under the shadow of his hat. "Anything is possible here. I encourage you to let your minds be free and experience the wonders of our world…allow it to be yours too. Welcome, my friends, to the circus."

Mr. Monte turned on his heel and strode for the back of the stage. Once he reached the curtain, he turned once more to face the crowd and clicked his cane on the ground, turning off the spotlight and casting the room in darkness once again.

The curtain closed and suddenly the audience hushed as the slow beating of a drum began. And then the curtain's red fabric curled back and revealed the performers. The dancers leapt onto the stage, kicking their legs into the air. Creating a V-formation, they welcomed the main attraction—an Asian elephant, some 6,000 pounds and nine feet tall. She stepped out softly, trained to tread on her heels to avoid crushing the stage, wearing a ruby headpiece over dark grey skin that was dotted with patches of light pink. Cassius named her Onyx because of her black eyes.

And sitting atop this magnificent creature was Juniper Rose, decorated in her midnight gown and a large-brimmed hat covering her face from view.

The dancers welcomed the tightrope walker by performing a series of spins and flips, spreading their arms and inviting the audience to join their lulling spectacle.

Meanwhile, I waved softly, sitting with my legs thrown off the side of Onyx, instead of being strewn on either side of the animal like some wild gypsy. I was the image of wealth, after all.

The audience was surprised when the elephant halted in the middle of the stage and I rose onto my hands and knees.

Carefully avoiding stepping on my dress, I balanced on Onyx's spine while she remained as still as a stone. Looking down on them from this height should have been terrifying, but I was used to heights by now. Speaking of…

I reached my arms up, motioning to the tightrope that was hooked near the top of the curtain, and the audience gasped at how they'd missed it completely. Before pulling myself up, I grasped the bow on my dress and pulled at the strings, the gown cascading down my hips.

The crowd applauded at the dress that had magically transformed into a leotard. I'd forgotten about the knife strapped around my thigh, but it added a dangerous element to my act, and I knew exactly how I'd put it to use.

I raised my head into the light and gripped the edge of my hat, removing it slowly to reveal my appearance to the audience who clapped in anticipation of the famous tightrope walker, Juniper Rose.

A light jig filled the room, making the dancers spin quickly with precision, and I did a small dance of my own on top of Onyx by dipping my shoulders up and down and swiveling my hips. I gently tossed my hat down to Charlotte, and the audience giggled in their seats at my playfulness, which I took as my cue to bend my knees and kip my ankles up to the rope. Once standing on the rope, I let my torso fall forward and pushed my legs into the air to perform a handstand, pointing my toes to keep my balance.

I let my legs fall over my head and straightened my back, coming out of a front walk over. The room became dizzy as I pirouetted, so I focused on one point—a man in the distance wearing a bright blue suit and a matching top hat. That's what my dance teacher taught me back home. *'Find one point in the room to dial in on, otherwise you won't know which way is right or left, up or down, and you'll lose your balance.'*

I took a deep breath before I pointed my toes and bent my knees to complete a front handspring and then a roundoff. The crowd erupted in cheers at my nimble body flipping atop the rope.

Suddenly, the dancers retreated backstage to grab more equipment and the audience brought their full attention to me. This was my chance. The music shifted to a light jazzy scat, and I bounced my hips to the rhythm. Slyly retrieving the knife from my thigh, I tossed it between my hands and twirled it in my fingers.

The audience marveled at what I would do next, leaning forward in their seats with every move I made. It was exciting, thrilling even, to know that I possessed that much control.

Every move I made occurred in slow motion. I walked carefully across the rope, pretending to lose my balance, and faltered off the side. Before I could fall too far, I grasped the rope with one hand and sliced it with the knife in my other, making it look like an accident. The rope tore with a small *ticking,* unwinding ever so slowly, but I'd need more force to cut it completely.

Just then, the dancers emerged from backstage carrying a net to catch me if I fell. I stood with a foot on either side of the fray in the rope to separate the divide, and to put the audience on the edge of their seats, I flipped backwards off the rope, barely catching myself once again. With a forceful tug, I heard the bindings of the rope split. Just a little bit more force and it would snap in two.

I dangled from the rope and swung back and forth to gain some momentum while the dancers took their positions below me, pulling the net tight. My attention snagged on the rope when it ripped again, with only one string tethering it together.

"Be careful!" a woman in the crowd stood up and shouted.

I giggled to myself. If only she knew I'd planned all of this.

Using my upper body strength to pull myself up, I rested my hips on the tough bindings and wrapped my left knee around the rope to lay back leisurely, my weight making the rope bob up and down.

Looking down at the audience, I blew them a kiss, raised my right arm, and cut the rope in half.

Shlink.

It tore in two pieces and fell out from under me. Gravity wrenched me to the ground and my stomach caught in my throat as I fell toward the floor. The dancers prepared for my landing by stretching the net as tight as they could, and I straightened my legs and placed my hands over my heart right before colliding with the net.

The audience stood to their feet and applauded my landing.

The dancers bent their legs and launched me into the air so I could dazzle the audience with some aerial stunts. With my body in a straight line, I crossed my ankles and tucked my arms into my chest, spinning faster than I ever had before. Catching me again, the dancers bent their knees to slow my momentum, and finally, after throwing me up once more, they removed the net completely.

I registered three things as I plummeted toward the ground:

1.　Someone in the crowd screamed.

2.　The trap door in the middle of the stage burst open as my body crashed through.

3.　Everything went dark.

Chapter Thirty-Four

My shoulder collided into the hardwood floor of the orchestra pit underneath the stage. Rolling onto my back, I watched the singular light shining in the opening of the trap door, groaning in pain as I clutched my arm. A figure appeared over the opening and closed the door, looking one last time at my wrangled body. Now the room was truly dark, the consuming kind, and my body was crawling with invisible shadows.

I was alone, but not alone in the slightest. I shook my head to rid myself of the images, but I only grew dizzier. I just needed my eyes to adjust to the dark and then I would be okay. Then I would make it out of here alive.

Something shuffled behind me, and I jumped to my feet to squint into the darkness. The faint sound of a match being struck echoed in the chamber, where a small flame bloomed, casting a halo of light around the man I dreaded more than anything. He was here. After months of imagining him, he was right here, standing in front of me.

He held the match gently in his thick fingers, staring at it as if it was the most interesting thing he'd ever seen. His head tipped to the left curiously as he watched the flame dance back and forth. He was wearing the same black mask he always had, and his eye sockets were pits of darkness, but this time I was allowed a glance at the outline of his twisted smile behind the fabric.

My stomach dropped and I considered laying down right there and letting him kill me. I couldn't do this. What was I thinking? I couldn't put on an act and draw this out. I needed to get out of here.

Play an honest victim and we'll be there to help you, Mr. Monte's voice drifted to me in the silence of the cavernous room.

I could do this. I could convince the killer that he'd caught me.

The ceiling was low, although there was plenty of space to move around. If I had to run, I could. But I promised Cassius a new world, and I would give us that.

The killer looked up at me then, and the emptiness of his eyes made me swallow in fear.

Play the victim.

"How did I get here?" My voice shook honestly.

The killer snickered softly, as though this was a childish prank he was playing. "Your friend and I thought it would be quite the showstopper." He laughed again.

He was right. The crowd was cheering above at what they assumed was all part of the act. Little did they know this was a trap.

"My friend?" I asked, dumbfounded, taking a step back from him.

He chuckled, "It seems there are plenty of people who loathe your presence in the circus, Juniper Rose."

Of course, there were. I was wealthy. I didn't belong here.

"You're right." I extended my hands to warn him not to get any closer. "But all I want to do is unite us. I don't want us to be separated anymore because of our status. We're worth more than that."

"I applaud you for trying, but that will never work." He shook his head in judgement.

"Is that why you want to kill me?" I asked honestly, my voice far more composed than I expected it to be. There must be something more to his hatred for me.

The flame slowly burned down the wooden wick, reaching his fingers before extinguishing completely. The light vanished, casting the room in darkness, and I gasped as I tried to blink away the orb of white still in my vision. Terror struck me as I realized I had no idea where he was.

I remembered Cassius urging me once to think of darkness as something beautiful. So, I tried to summon an image of the night sky with stars glittering above me. Looking up, I spotted slivers of light through the floorboards above, which looked strangely like shooting stars.

Then, I heard the match strike again, the killer standing only a few feet away. He'd grown closer in the darkness. He was playing a game, intent on picking at his food before eating it. Finally, he answered my question, "I want to kill you because you're encouraging everything that is wrong in this world. Because you don't understand the danger of what you're doing."

My eyebrows pulled together as I contemplated his words. "What do you mean?"

He scoffed. "You're teaching children that it's okay to risk their safety for this kind of life. You're continuing the reign of the tightrope walkers when they should have gone extinct long ago."

"When Katriane fell?" I questioned with more authority.

The killer shuffled back and forth, making something of a grunt. "Yes." His voice was eerily quiet, as though he'd descended into his memories. "When Katriane fell. And it's because of this institution that she died. So, as compensation, you will meet the same demise."

I backed up when the killer took a step toward me. I could only stall for so long. Where were the others? With no sign of help, I tried to continue the conversation as long as I could. "You took vengeance on Penelope Plume and me because you think walking a tightrope is dangerous?" I shook my head. "Every act in the circus is dangerous. That's why people come to see our show. Because they want to be amazed—scared even. They want to be brought to the edge of their seats. We're giving them a show, not a bedtime story. *None* of this is supposed to be safe, but we signed up for this knowing the dangers." I attempted to reason with him.

"You performers are daft, small-minded people. You take risks without understanding the consequences. I have seen the dark side of the circus, and you will see it too if you continue on this path," he shouted emphatically, raising his arms as though he were preaching. "You will never have to experience what Katriane experienced. I'm saving you!"

This man was crazy. Mentally insane. What had he seen or experienced to make him believe that killing me would ultimately save me?

"What happened to you?" The words came out as a whisper.

The killer just shook his head and laughed louder and louder until he was doubling over and holding his stomach in pain. "Oh, Miss Rose. I've seen such terrible things. I've seen blood pool before my feet, and I've heard a heart stop beating. And you've never been subjected to that kind of pain." He shook his head angrily, his tone rough and clipped. "But I've also seen such lovely things." He then looked up at the ceiling with a smile. "Such lovely things," he mused. "For when crimson blood stains the sand and a body finally stops twitching…well, it's only natural. I've learned to welcome death—love it, even."

"You'll understand soon that I'm right. You'll thank me." The killer began walking toward me, his heavy boots thudding on the wooden floor.

"Please! We can work together." I put my hands out in front of me. "We can fix the circus. We can make it safe!" But trying to reason with him was hopeless, and I began to cry. I couldn't die here, in the darkness, alone. I didn't know the reason for his pain, but I attempted to soothe it to delay him. "Katriane died a horrific death, and I am so sorry, but killing others is not what she would have wanted. She would have wanted you to make the circus a safe place again for others to enjoy."

His steps grew closer and closer, and his voice was decisive when he said, "I will do right by her. I made that vow long ago. That's why I'm putting an end to the circus once and for all, not just you, Miss Rose."

My heart dropped then. Flint warned me that the killer's scheme went beyond me. "What are you going to do to us?" I asked, while hot tears dripped from my chin. I was scared—more scared than I'd ever been. This time, he wasn't letting me get away.

But then he stopped for just a moment. "Oh my, Juniper, so many questions. But I sympathize, since you won't be around to help your friends soon enough. I'll give you one hint." The killer paused, holding up a finger as though he had to think about it. Then, the match dangling between his fingers burned out, a small fizzle of orange flame being the last thing I saw. "Run," he whispered from what must have been only inches away.

I shot to the right, my hair lashing the front of my face, but it didn't make a difference. I was consumed in darkness, unable to see even my hand in front of me. Before I could even take a second step, his cold leather gloves grasped my arm. When he spun me and secured my back to his chest, I couldn't feel any warmth emanating from his body.

He was like a corpse, ready to drag me down into the earth with him. He locked the crook of his arm around my neck, cutting off my air supply, and I gasped as blazing pain seared through my lungs. The headache that formed was unbearable, and I could feel the veins in my forehead close to bursting, but I kicked and beat at his arm to no avail.

I pinched my eyes together as tears filled my vision. And in that moment, I thought of my home in Axminster. I saw the sunflowers gently waving back and forth in the summer breeze. I smelled the faint aroma of cinnamon drifting from the bakeries in town, where fresh bread and delicious treats were made every morning. I could hear the ringing of the church bell, signaling the noon hour.

I pictured Colette and my mother sitting on a love seat in the living room, reading a book and chatting nonsensically about the news of the week. And when the images of my old life blurred and began to fade, my eyes shot open. I lifted my arm and cranked my elbow back as hard as I could.

The man instantly released me and grunted in pain.

Lurching forward, I grasped my neck and wheezed, trying to get air back into my lungs. "Help!" I screamed as loud as I could, but my vocal cords only scraped together weakly. I was going to die here. "Help!" I screamed again.

"Now, now, do you think that's the way to kill a lady?" A delicate voice drifted into the room, like the sound of a silk day dress brushing along the floor.

The killer halted his efforts and turned to the man in the corner who stood pliantly with a lantern hanging over his head. The dull light cast a warm glow on his features—a long, thin nose, accented cheekbones, a round chin, and his brown hair hanging loosely in his face. And lastly, his bright blue eyes. Flint.

I heaved a sigh of relief, shrinking back to the wall to gain as much distance from the killer. "Flint?" I asked quietly. "You have to help me!" For this to work, I had to play my part.

"I told you to stand guard!" the killer erupted.

"And I told you I wanted a piece of the action. I deserve it." Flint squared his shoulders and clenched his jaw, making the muscles in his cheeks pulse up and down.

That's when I saw the black mask clutched in his palm, identical to the killer's. "Flint? What are you doing?" My voice was small and wounded as I retreated, my back hitting the wall.

"Juniper Rose, the darling of the circus," he mused, shaking his head back and forth. "You've gotten everything you wanted."

"Flint—" I warned him.

"Shut up!" he yelled, his voice bounding off the orchestra pit walls and his face shaking violently.

Flint was quite the actor. And if I didn't trust him with my life, I might believe he was actually angry enough to hurt me.

He pointed and said, "Listen to me when I say this. You never should have boarded our train. Mr. Monte never should have welcomed you. You've done irreparable damage to the circus. You take what you want and manipulate others, as though playing chess, moving your pawns across the board until you own them." The lantern swayed, revealing the clench of his teeth. "But you don't own any of us. And it's time this little game of yours ended."

He took a quick step toward me before the killer held out his arm. "I told you how this would go, and you're not going to mess it up. Go guard the stairwell," he ordered.

Flint, baffled at his ridiculous outburst, obediently fell back and apologized for his eagerness.

Before he could leave me alone in the darkness, I screamed for his help, "Flint! Come back!" I paused a moment and watched him scurry up the stairs that led to the stage. "Don't leave me here!" I screamed again, losing the power in my voice. I began to sob as Flint disappeared, holding my hands against my chest and curling in on myself.

But if I was right, Flint was going to retrieve the battalion of guards waiting upstairs. I only had to survive this a little while longer. So, I stood up and took a fighting stance as I pulled the knife out of the sheath on my thigh. I brushed back my tears, determination taking over. I wouldn't make this any easier for the killer.

The blade quivered as I held the knife in a death grip. "I will kill you," I began, my voice wavering. "If you take one more step, I will kill you."

"Little girl, you can't kill me." He laughed, moving too quickly for me to evade. He elbowed my hands with such force that my arms shuddered, and then kicked me between the legs. I lost grip of the knife as I doubled over in pain, falling to my knees and clutching the space between my legs.

Kneeling over me, he wrapped his fingers around my neck until I couldn't breathe.

It became clear I wasn't going to make it out alive, but I had to at least know who he was, so I reached my hand toward his face, regretting it as soon as he stepped on my wrist. A blinding pain shot through my arm, and I clenched my teeth together to avoid screaming.

"This is for Katriane," he whispered, before lifting my head up and smashing it into the floor.

My ears rang and the back of my skull began to throb as the killer's grip on my throat grew tighter and tighter. I couldn't breathe.

He lifted my head and slammed it to the ground again. I heard my bones crack under his weight, and I couldn't move—couldn't even *think* to move with the pain running down my spine. My head was pounding, my hair felt sticky against my scalp as blood pooled around me, and the space behind my eyes trembled as the killer's hands crushed my esophagus. I was out of breath and out of time.

But if I didn't do something, I'd never make it back to the circus…back to Cassius. And I needed to make it back to them.

I slowly reached my hand out, searching for the knife that had been thrown to the floor. Stretching my arm as far as I could, my fingers trembling and my wrist shaking, I felt the sharp tip. Just as I'd gotten a grip on it, the killer brought his fist into the air, and I barely managed to block his blow.

His fist came down on my forearm. Hard. I screamed in pain, grasping my arm tight to my chest, just as he threw another punch at me. This time, I wasn't quick enough to block it, and his fist collided with my jaw, filling my mouth with the coppery taste of blood.

The killer raised his arm once again, and this time I thought I might black out. My head hurt, my arm hurt, and now my cheek was throbbing. I coughed out a puddle of blood on the floor, not knowing how much longer I could take this.

And just as I considered giving up, I heard the blade of a knife slide across the floor. I turned to my right to find Cassius standing next to me, the knife hanging in his palm.

"Remember me?" He flicked his eyebrows.

"Cassius Plume," the killer mused. "How could I forget? Your sister was a lovely—"

Before he could finish, Cassius kicked him in the face. The killer's jaw snapped, and he tumbled to the floor as Cassius crawled on top of him.

He threw a single punch before turning to me over his shoulder. "Get out of here!" he screamed.

I wasn't going to leave him here. No matter how determined he was, the killer was much bigger than him. He would kill Cassius. And I couldn't let that happen.

But Cassius seemed to know exactly what I was thinking. "Get out, now!" he yelled, his fist connecting with the killer's jaw. A deep gash spread across his opponent's face, and when Cassius threw his fist back again, I knew there was nothing I could do.

I had to get help. Stumbling through the darkness, I pressed my palm against the open wound on my head, trying to stop the blood. When I found the staircase at the edge of the room, I raced up the stairs, emerging into blinding light, and closed my eyes as the room began to spin.

Setting the pain aside, I yelled for the guards, and five men came racing from their posts to follow me into the darkness below.

Flint led the group by lighting the path to the orchestra pit. As we reached the bottom of the stairwell, I saw that Cassius had managed to stay on top of the killer, but he was growing tired, putting all his strength into his punches. As soon as Cassius heard us, he took a second to look back at the help that had arrived.

In that moment, the killer reached for the knife that Cassius had discarded by his side—which turned out to be the worst mistake he could have made.

Time passed in slow motion.

"Cassius!" I screamed. "Watch out!"

Cassius arched his back and flung his body away, but it was too late. The killer slashed his arm violently, and the knife connected before he could deflect the blow, his shirt ripping and a large gash spreading from his lower ribs up to his shoulder. Cassius fell back and grabbed his chest in terror as blood poured out of the wound.

I screamed, racing over to him before I knew what I was doing.

Flint threw down the lantern and ran toward us, flanked by the guards at his side. Before the killer could move, Flint was on top of him, pinning down his arms while the guards retrieved a set of swivel manacles.

"You bastard! You tricked me!" the killer screamed at Flint. His mouth moved underneath his mask and his face shook, but there was nothing to be afraid of anymore. He was caught. It was over.

"And you were foolish enough to believe it," Flint groaned in a struggle to hold him down.

Finally, the guards hauled him to his feet and prepared to take him away. Cassius stood wearily, holding his chest in pain, and stripped off his shirt, urging me to press it against my head.

He walked over to the guards dizzily and ordered them to wait.

I wrapped an arm around his waist to help him while the guards hung back, waiting for further instruction.

As we approached the killer, I'd never felt more relief, and Cassius was now towering above him, prepared to say goodbye, once and for all.

"You are a sickness. A plague," he began, his voice sturdier than I'd ever heard it before. "You raped my sister and forced her to take her own life. And she's gone because of you." Cassius's jaw trembled but he held back his tears. "You tried to kill Juniper. You scared her half to death and violated her in the worst way possible." He nodded with conviction. "But you didn't get away with it. No, you got caught." He chuckled at the deserving asshole. "Because bad people get caught. And now you'll spend your life rotting in a cell," he seethed, clenching his teeth together.

The killer squirmed under the guards, trying to worm his way out, but he wasn't escaping this time. No, he was finished. And everything he sought to do was finished.

I had one word to describe this moment. Victory.

Cassius took a step forward and reached up to the killer's face, despite the pain it brought him. "You can't hide anymore," Cassius whispered. And then he ripped the mask off.

I gasped and stepped back, horrified. The man that stood before us was someone all too familiar. The man that had once been known as the killer, was now known as Monroe Beringer.

"Monroe!" Cassius staggered back in shock.

Monroe was one of our own. He'd sung with us, danced with us, and drank with us. He'd supported us and made it possible for us to function at all. He was our rock. Our foundation. And he had fooled us all.

It was Monroe that raped Penelope Plume. It was his hands that had been all over me, intending to do the same. It was Monroe that threatened me for countless months, attempting to kill me. Monroe Beringer, the quirky accountant who pretended to love the circus, had cut the silks, tampered with the tiger's cage, oiled the rope, and thrown a knife into my leg on the spinning wheel.

Just then, Mr. Monte burst through the door and came running down the stairs. "The show's ended. Is everyone okay?" he inquired. Just then, he spotted Monroe in the black costume of the killer. "Monroe? What are you doing down here?"

Monroe just looked at Mr. Monte, his eyes dreadfully small and filled with a profound sadness. They'd shared many years and many memories together, and now Mr. Monte was about to lose his closest friend.

By the looks in our eyes, it was apparent to Mr. Monte what was going on. "No," he began, backing up and running a hand through his hair. "This can't be."

"Edward," Monroe began, as if to console his friend after he was condemned of the most heinous crime.

"Don't you say another word!" Edward screamed.

I'd never heard him raise his voice before, but it held so much power.

"I thought I knew you," he whispered, unable to keep from crying. His best friend had turned against him and his entire family. "I thought you were an honest, caring man, but you are a monster! How could you do something like this to Penelope? To Juniper?"

Monroe shook in his holds. "Because they killed her, Edward! Katriane, my own sister, was killed by the circus. And they deserve to know how that feels." Tears were now falling down his face as spit flew from his mouth.

Of course. Katriane Beringer. Monroe walked the rope with his sister and witnessed her tragic death. And he took his rage out on the tightrope walkers that followed to avenge her.

"You bastard!" Cassius flew forward and punched him, and I watched his jaw snap to the side and a spittle of blood dangle from his lips. "I know now what it feels like to lose someone because of you! You understood how painful it was to lose your closest friend, and you put that dread on *me*!"

Monroe shook his head. "You expect me to be alone in this pain? It's not fair."

Edward stepped forward and held Monroe by the fabric of his shirt, looking closely at the stranger in front of him. "I saved you. I saved all of these performers. We were in the trenches, fighting to escape the lives we were born into, but we found each other, and we made a *home*. We've all experienced death and abandonment. Every single one of us." Mr. Monte shook his head as his voice cracked. "You were never alone."

Monroe wrestled with the guards, trying to get out of their grip. "I'll spend every breath I have trying to destroy you."

No matter what sense Mr. Monte offered, Monroe would never understand it. He wasn't just angry; he was sick. And there was no fixing that.

"Take him away," Mr. Monte instructed the guards. He could barely look at the man in front of him.

The guards began to shuffle Monroe away before Cassius intruded. "No! I deserve an explanation and so do all of you. He stays here." Cassius stood confidently with his shoulders squared, despite the blood dripping down his chest. But as the men around him began to argue, he looked to me. Cassius was right. He needed this. We all did.

"He's right. We need answers. Only then can we move on from this." I came to stand in front of Monroe, barely able to fathom the fact that he had been the mystery under this mask for so long. "You're going to answer all of our questions honestly."

Monroe stood up straighter with a smile on his face. "My answers won't stop what's coming," he snickered.

Cassius punched Monroe again, making the man cough and sputter. "Stop laughing, you fool, or I'll kill you right here like you deserve."

Monroe went quiet, allowing me the chance to question him. "You sent a letter to my mother last year, offering her a sum of money when she threatened to sue the circus. You told me that paying her off would convince her to stop trying to destroy us. Was that true?"

"I didn't give her money to send her packing. I gave her money so she would help me take you down," Monroe offered easily, without any reservation.

And just like that, everything clicked into place. My mother would have done anything to return me to Axminster's high society. That's why she befriended Mr. Young, a wealthy businessman who would threaten to burn us to the ground. That's why she convinced him to marry me off to Joseph. But it was all a ploy. While my mother and Mr. Young played the part of proud parents, fussing over their children's wedding, something much bigger was happening. And Monroe was behind all of it.

Monroe encouraged my mother to sue the circus, and when that didn't work, he convinced Mr. Young to threaten its future, hence my marriage to Joseph. He wormed his way into my family to destroy me. But for what purpose? My mother wanted me returned home safely, not dead.

"You want me dead. You want me to experience the pain your sister did. So why work with my mother to force me to leave the circus, when you could have killed me instead?" The gears in my head were turning as I tried to fit the pieces together.

Monroe shook his head. "I was buying time, Juniper. You weren't as easy as Penelope Plume. You fought harder."

Cassius's nostrils flared at Monroe's indifference toward his sister. Nonetheless, he kept his hands to himself and let him continue.

"I needed time to figure out how to get to you. So, I encouraged her to take you away, so I could get into your head. It worked, didn't it?" He smiled, the gaps in his teeth making me gag.

Yes, yes it did. When I was in Axminster, I was haunted with images of the killer—Monroe. It was strange to call him by his name.

"But there was a different reason behind my approach. My inclusion of Mr. Young in this whole charade was completely worth it. He was the beginning—he was the one person to speak out publicly about his animosity toward the circus, and many more will follow. Even after you lock me away, you'll have another issue on your hands—the people of high society. They won't stand much longer to have their voices silenced."

I shook my head. I'd heard this far too many times.

"Yes, I wanted to kill you," he continued. "So, I bought myself some time to figure out how exactly I'd do that. In the meantime, Mr. Young offered me an intriguing, new idea of how to end the circus."

"But you failed," I shook my head defiantly. "Mr. Young offered to protect the circus as long as I put you behind bars and return to him," I explained.

"Or so he said," Monroe snickered with a shrug of his shoulders, but continued, "Mr. Young is not my concern anymore. After months of exchanging letters with him, I now know what I need to do."

His information was cryptic to say the least. What was coming? And how had Mr. Young helped Monroe succeed? I had no doubt that Mr. Young was scheming behind my back. Sure, he'd protect the circus for a time, but only at the price of a wedding band on my finger. Meanwhile, he'd been conspiring with Monroe to find a way to end the circus completely. And he lied to me the entire time. I thought we would be safe once we got rid of Monroe, but we were so focused on him, we didn't realize that something far greater was coming.

"Care to tell us what you have planned for our future, now that you'll be behind bars for the rest of your life?" Flint asked, holding him harder.

"You'll find out soon enough. It's almost here!" he exclaimed excitedly.

"Your mother was never sick, was she?" Mr. Monte asked, counting the lies.

Monroe chuckled, without any remorse. "My dear mother is the picture of health."

"I have all the answers I need. Take him away." Mr. Monte flicked his hand at the guards. But before he could be taken away, Mr. Monte approached his dear friend and looked deeply into his eyes. "There is nothing that you, or anyone, could ever do to stop us. I think we've proved that."

The guards pushed Monroe up the stairs, prepared to show the rest of the circus who the killer really was.

It would take time to heal. Years, maybe. And the pain would stick with us forever, but we'd be stronger because of it. We'd feel the sun on our backs, the drinks in our stomachs, and the ache in our heels as we danced. We'd live as we were always meant to live, without the terror of the killer. And maybe, just maybe, we'd have the chance at being happy.

Chapter Thirty-Five

That evening, after the magic of the performance had faded, we were left with the debilitating truth as Monroe walked shamelessly in front of the circus, the shackles around his hands and feet rattling. Every performer was utterly distraught at what Monroe had done. How had we missed it? Monroe had turned against us, and despite threatening the tightrope walkers, he was intent to end the circus as a whole. Soon enough the tears gave way to anger. He was no friend of ours and he never had been.

The audience was long gone by now. Meanwhile, Monroe was being escorted onto the cobblestone street where a prisoner carriage—a cage-like contraption with bars for walls—was waiting.

The performers followed him out on the steps of the theater in their odd costumes, watching as Monroe wrestled with the guards.

"You'll hear from me again! This isn't over!" Monroe shouted, trying to turn around to face us before being slammed into the rickety carriage head-first. Scrambling to his knees, he gripped the bars separating him from us, and smiled madly. "You can't escape what's coming!"

That was the last we heard from Monroe Beringer. As he was whisked down the road, the carriage wobbling out of sight, images of him sitting at a desk, eagerly filling out bank statements crossed my mind. And all those nights he sat at the bar, snickering at the raucous people dancing around him, made him seem so normal…so much like family. But those joyous memories of him had never been real.

The mask he wore dissolved in my mind to a pair of dull, grey eyes. Monroe Beringer. I knew his name. I knew his face. And now, I could forget him completely.

The performers stood outside, battling the cold winter that was approaching as a gust of wind drew upon us. I couldn't take my eyes off the carriage rolling away, its wheels spinning around and around, like the gears in my head. Some part of me wondered: was that it? Could it all be over in one night?

Cassius pressed into my side with his shoulders squared and his jaw tense, looking out at the city in the distance. It *was* over. Recognizing this, he grabbed my waist and pulled me into his body. I placed a hand on his mangled chest, his warmth filling my cold, numb fingers and he gathered my jaw in his hands and brought his forehead to mine. Cassius and I took the first deep breath in months, together. And when I closed my eyes, the killer wasn't there waiting for me, but instead an image of what the circus might become. And I was more excited than ever.

Readjustment took time for the circus. When we returned to the train after detaining Monroe, Cassius and I went to the infirmary. He was stitched together from his hip to his collar bone, the red gash reduced to a thin line, and the swelling on his chest covered with ointment and a white cloth. After being evaluated for a concussion, they stitched my scalp back together, and I was given an ointment to rub on the split in my cheek. It would take time for our physical wounds to heal, and even longer for the emotional ones.

A week had passed and still Monroe was weighing heavily on us. Our days were dwindling in motivation. One day, as the winter winds blew heavily outside, a brutal storm rolling in, the circus remained in the dining car, and we drank without music or dance.

Mr. Monte sat with his head in his hands, his mind blurred by the effects of his drink. Charlotte's head hung low while the rest of the dancers sat motionless around her. Even the fire-breathers—the rowdiest of them all—were uncharacteristically quiet. Something had to be done. With that in mind, I stood from my seat and walked to the small stage at the front of the room.

They eyed me warily as I began my speech. "I know this past week has been troublesome. We lost a man we once held close, but we no longer have to live in fear. I'd say that's something to celebrate. We're here to protect each other and that's exactly what we did. So, let's raise our glasses and do what we do best…get wild." I smiled, trying not to hide at the awkward silence that followed.

Before too much embarrassment could overcome me, Charlotte jumped onto the stage, holding my hand in her own. I smiled at her as the dancers hurried to clear away the tables.

Cassius stood out of his chair and tipped his head to the musicians in the corner. "You heard her. Pluck those strings!"

All at once, music filled the room and people began to dance. Arms flew into the air, dresses swished, and men and women grabbed each other as though no one was watching. Just as I was about to join in, I caught Mr. Monte sitting alone with such sadness in his eyes.

Dancing would have to wait.

I strutted over to Mr. Monte and took a seat next to the man I'd come to love as my own father.

"Edward, I want to give you something," I said, reaching into my vest pocket to retrieve a small photograph.

Mr. Monte looked up suddenly with dull, unconvinced eyes. That is, before I handed him the picture.

"You took this photo of Penelope and me a year after we joined your company. I remembered that being the happiest day of my life. I was learning the ways of the circus alongside my sister and I..." I paused, finding it difficult to say, "I finally had a home."

Mr. Monte looked up at me with tears in his eyes.

I smiled, at peace for the first time in a long time. "I want you to hold onto this for me." I patted Mr. Monte's hand. "And when you look at it, I want you to remember that you saved us." I cleared the lump in my throat before continuing, "You gave us a life we looked forward to living."

Mr. Monte set down the picture in shame. "But I wasn't able to save him," he admitted as his tears fell quickly, hitting the fraying grain of the table he was hovering over.

"He was too far gone to save, Edward," I encouraged him. "He was sick, tortured with what happened to his sister, and he didn't want to be alone in his pain. He let the grief, sadness, and anger consume him. It wasn't your fault."

Mr. Monte shook his head. "I can't stop thinking that there was more I could've done. And if I'd been there for him...maybe he wouldn't have done those terrible things to my girls."

I thought for a moment. "Mr. Monte, there's something wrong with him. There's no excuse for what he did."

"You're right," he said, nodding his head to convince himself.

I grabbed Mr. Monte's shoulders and squeezed him tightly. "I can't count the number of times you've picked me up off the floor and thrown me into the tub to sober me up. And even though I wanted to kill you for almost giving me pneumonia," I joked, watching Mr. Monte's shoulders bob as he snickered, "I realized that all anyone ever needs is a friend. And you've been more than a friend to me. It's my turn to pay you back." Standing from my seat, I offered my hand. "Like you always tell me, we're in it together. It's going to be hard, but we've never backed down from a fight, have we?"

"No. We haven't." Mr. Monte pushed back his chair and grabbed my hand, following me onto the dance floor. "I love you, my boy." He ruffled my hair before being swarmed by a throng of performers.

Mr. Monte laughed, and when he looked up at me, he tipped his head to the girl that was dancing in the middle of the room, her black curls bobbing up and down as she jumped. *Go get her*, he mouthed over the loud music.

I nodded my thanks before winding through the crowd. And just like that, the bodies around me seemed to part, and there she was, hands in the air and hips swaying to the music. Her smile was bright, and her cheeks glistened with sweat in the packed room. Her beautiful hair bounced up and down on her soft, olive-colored shoulders. She looked so happy—so relieved, and I wanted to keep her happy like that always.

Without thinking, I walked straight toward her. Sensing me, she turned around, and I reached out and grabbed her neck, crushing my lips against hers. I heard Charlotte practically scream beside me, but I didn't care. I closed my eyes and melted in her sweet mouth. She tasted of honey and smelled of flowers in the spring after a light rain.

Her tongue danced across mine and then she pulled my bottom lip between her teeth, making my heart skyrocket, and when she grabbed my arm desperately, I knew I needed her. Grabbing her waist, she jumped onto my hips, and crossed her ankles behind my back.

I tried to make a clean exit, not wanting to waste any time. It was torture enough to feel her body pressed against mine, and now I had to fight my way through a crowd. But before we could make it out, the room erupted.

"Bed her right, my man!" Hugh clapped wildly, receiving a dangerous glare from Juniper while I gave him a thumbs up.

"Better treat her right, you fool!" Charlotte yelled, making Juniper giggle in my ear.

"And don't you dare hurt her, or you'll be dead by morning!" Evelyn, the old hag croaked, making me roll me eyes and walk even faster for the door.

I liked when my friends jabbed at us because it meant our relationship was public—that our joy was shared. In the past I'd always kept my affairs secret, but it was different with Juniper. I wanted everyone to know that she was mine.

I laughed with Juniper all the way to my chamber about what the other performers must have thought of us, but I didn't really care for their opinions. It was me and her now. No one else.

I set her down gently, but she held onto my neck as though she were connected to me.

She opened her mouth, prepared to say something before I stopped her by pressing my lips to hers. She walked back to the bed, and I followed her, feeling like the happiest man in the world for having her alone. I smiled into her kiss as her hands trailed across my shoulders to the back of my neck, making my skin tingle. As she lazily leaned her head to the side to deepen the kiss, I devoured her. And when she pulled back for air and looked at me with those sparkling green eyes, a twinge of sadness crushed my heart, telling me this wouldn't last forever.

How long before she returned to Axminster? The thought of her leaving me again made me physically ill. I backed away, trying not to think about it.

She was quiet, offering me a moment to think before treading lightly to stand in front of me. Turning my jaw to her, she asked, "What are you thinking?"

Why did she have to know me so well? Why couldn't I be left to my thoughts? No. I couldn't think like that. Juniper was what I needed. She was making me the man I wanted to be. And sure, sometimes I wanted to curse at her for being so annoying and intrusive, but I needed her far more than I liked to admit.

"Cassius," she said, and my name never sounded so sweet.

I sighed and admitted everything, "I want you, Juniper. All of you. But there's a little voice in the back of my mind that sounds an awful lot like that son of a bitch, Flint, reminding me that you won't be here forever."

She sighed, understanding my hesitation. "The time we have isn't guaranteed. And on the chance that we can't figure out a way for me to stay, I want to spend every moment with you." She looked at her hands quietly, nervously. "I want you to have me," she whispered.

Her lips parted as she said this, her head hung low. I was sure she'd never uttered those words to anyone by the way she fidgeted. And that made me happy—that she wanted me more than she'd ever wanted anyone. She trusted me.

I liked Juniper so much that the thought of losing her was unbearable. And when it comes to sex, that's a whole different story. I don't want to sleep with her for the fun of it, just to ignore her the next morning like nothing ever happened. If we're going to be intimate, I want it to be deeper than that because we understand each other. We talk about everything, she encourages me, and she's not afraid to fight with me.

Of course, I wanted to sleep with her. I've wanted to touch every inch of her body since the day she stepped onto our train. But if we slept together, and I could hold her body as my own, and then she left, I'd lose myself completely.

I looked away from her. "If I have you in this way and lose you again, I won't be able to live with myself."

"Cassius Plume, I'm right here. I'm not going anywhere." She placed her palms on my chest.

I sighed, her touch lighting a fire deep in my core. I couldn't focus when she was this close to me, so I stepped away from her until my back hit the wall—like it would hold me there somehow.

"I can't do this." I shook my head and looked to the ground.

"What do you mean?" she inquired, anger clear in her voice.

"I want you so bad it hurts." I looked toward the ceiling to take my eyes off her red lips. "But I want to have you when I know I won't lose you. And I'll want you every day after that."

Juniper tilted her head to the right, looking at me with a small smile.

"Don't give me that seductive smile of yours." I pointed a finger at her chest to keep her at a distance.

"I'm not trying to seduce you, Cas," she laughed lightly. "I've spent many nights dreaming of when we'll lie together, and this moment isn't the one I imagined. So, we'll wait."

I sighed, thankful she didn't fight me on the subject. My entire life, I'd distanced myself from other people. My parents abandoned me, and Penelope left long before she was meant to, and I came to believe that no one would ever *stay*. But Juniper wanted to stay.

"Thank you," I whispered. "For…sticking around."

Juniper then spoke as if she was in my head, understanding my every thought. "You're rather difficult to like." She giggled at her own joke. "But you taught me something I'll never forget. You taught me to fight for the people you love. And your mother and father, and even Penelope, may not have been strong enough to do that, but they loved you regardless. If you can't see their love for you, then see *our* love for you," she whispered. "All of your friends are here for you until the very end. You can't get rid of us."

My eyes darted between hers, wondering how she could possibly be so understanding, so perfect. I couldn't help but say, "I'm convinced you're a witch. You've put me under a spell, and you have me at your complete and utter disposal."

She gave me a wicked smile, the corner of her lips curving, and then sat me on the edge of the bed and said, "Good. Because it's time we change your bandages."

I tilted my head back and groaned, anticipating the pain to come. Nevertheless, I allowed Juniper to gently strip me of my shirt and the white bandage around my torso. The torn pink flesh was slowly beginning to heal, the stiches not as irritating as they were a couple days ago.

Once she removed the bandages completely, she gently crawled on my lap, straddling a leg on either side of me. I laid on my back as she opened a bottle of ointment and dipped her fingers into the gooey mixture. It was working wonders, but it made my skin burn, so to take my mind off the pain, I allowed my hands to wander across Juniper's soft thighs.

She smiled, all the while remaining focused on my torso.

When she touched the sensitive area, I gasped and dug my fingers in to keep from squirming.

She squealed when I pulled her hips into my own, and she didn't think I noticed as she moved in a slow circle, hoping to get some friction, but I did. I smiled at how this innocent girl was now grinding on top of me, but I didn't want to embarrass her, so I kept quiet and allowed her to continue, feigning pain so I could pull her closer every so often. Watching her little mouth pop open while her cheeks heated red was the most attractive thing I'd ever seen.

But before I knew it, she was climbing off my lap and retrieving a fresh bandage. I clenched my stomach to sit up, and the wound across my chest burned a new kind of pain. She made quick work of looping the bandage around my torso, and when she finished, she eagerly sat on my lap again. She didn't say a word, but I knew exactly what she wanted. A feeling. A morsel. Something.

So, I grabbed her hips and pulled her forward. She gasped, her eyebrows quirked and her eyes wide in surprise at the feeling it gave her, and if I could see this reaction on her face every single day, I'd be content.

She continued to move back and forth as I tucked my head into her neck and sucked at her soft skin. She let out a small moan then, the softness of it caressing my ear. I'd never heard a sound like that before, and it made my heart gallop, my hands itching to touch more, do more.

Her hips were rocking back and forth, quicker now, making my pants strain uncomfortably. If she didn't stop, I'd have her pinned underneath me in a few seconds. And although I longed to feel her legs hooked around me and have her moaning my name, we made a promise.

So, I allowed myself a few more minutes, pulling my hands around her back to help her rock her hips as she grew tired. My chest heaved up and down and as our bodies grew slick with sweat, she relaxed in my arms with her forehead pressed to my shoulder, her breathing heavy.

I ran a hand through her hair and asked, "Are you okay?" giggling at how she was unmoving, like a brick on top of me.

"Yes," she whined, straightening her spine to look at me with glossy eyes.

I held her cheek in my palm, which she melted into. Meanwhile, I was still uncomfortably hard underneath her. "Ugh, to wait." I tilted my head to the ceiling and closed my eyes.

She grabbed the back of my neck and brought my lips to hers. I opened my mouth slowly, and her lips pulled on mine with desire and need, but they were gentle all the same.

She pulled away too soon, her eyelashes fluttering as she whispered, "To wait."

Chapter Thirty-Six

"One, two, three, four!" Mr. Monte clapped his hands to the beat.

Sweat was dripping down my forehead as I trained with the riders that afternoon, per Mr. Monte's request. Unfortunately, Cassius was assisting this lesson, having been a rider, and that meant constant criticism. And since his injury, the doctor had instructed him to take a break from taming lions to rest. But Cassius couldn't sit still for the life of him, so resting wasn't an option. I could see him giggling in the stands of the riding arena, his shoulders bobbing up and down. He was enjoying this far too much.

By this point, I'd learned how to ride a horse fairly well, but if I wanted to impress the audience, I'd have to learn some tricks. Trick riding sounded rather dangerous to me, but nothing was safe in the circus.

"Use those manners of yours and straighten your back, Juniper!" Cassius yelled, chewing on his fingernails while he watched me.

I didn't like Cassius watching over me, critiquing every move I made. I knew everything there was to know about walking the tightrope, but when it came to trick riding, I felt inexperienced. Granted, I was, but I didn't need him to remind me of that.

"Pull up your right leg. If you create more resistance, there's no chance of your leg falling out of the hold," Cassius commanded as I slipped out of the hold and almost fell face first in the sand.

Despite how irritated I was, I did as he instructed.

"Juniper, what did I say about your toes? Keep them pointed!" he yelled across the arena.

I rolled my eyes just as Mr. Monte cut in. "My God, Cassius, you don't have to bully the girl."

I just giggled as Cassius raised his arm to the riders, bringing them to a halt. "Get out of here. We'll resume tomorrow morning at 7 a.m. sharp! Great job today."

I hopped off the horse and unwound the bindings across my palms, prepared to meet the dancers for girls' night, as Charlotte liked to call it. Last year, when I participated in girls' night, I was forced into a silk nightdress and encouraged to find a man of my choosing. That's when I met Flint. I laughed, thinking of that wild night so long ago.

"Good job, J. You're getting so good you might just kick Henry off the team!" Flint slapped my back as a brother would, making me lurch forward and rub at the sting.

"Hey, I've had years of practice and you're willing to give my position to a *girl*?" he scoffed, only reaching Flint's shoulder. Henry was only fourteen years old—the youngest rider on the team.

"A woman, not a girl." Flint slapped Henry on the back of the head. "Just as you are a boy, not a man."

The other riders *oohed* with their fists over their mouths.

"If I haven't earned the title by prancing around with you buffoons, then I don't think I ever will," Henry spat.

Two of the riders shoved each other back and forth, excited for what was to come.

Flint just smiled, looking down at his shoes and back up at Henry. "Meet me in the dining car and we'll find out who can finish a pint first."

Henry's smile faltered briefly before he stormed off, throwing a begrudging, "Fine," over his shoulder.

All the riders burst into laughter as soon as he disappeared.

"The boy won't last ten seconds." Hugh chuckled, and Flint joined him, grabbing the top of his bald head.

I just raised my eyebrows. "Good luck tonight, Flint." Patting him on the back, I left the tent with a duffel bag over my shoulder, and as the sun hit my face and a cold breeze met my skin, a voice made me jump.

"It's kind of fun telling you what to do."

I turned to find Cassius leaning against a panel of wood with a toothpick between his lips. The wind rustled his hair, blowing the curls off his eyebrows, and the sun made his olive skin just a tint darker. In his thin black shirt and matching breeches, with a dark blue vest overtop, he looked rather ravishing.

"I can tell you're enjoying it." I smiled, trying to take my eyes off the sleeves rolled up to his elbows, revealing bright blue veins running up his forearms.

"You can't fool me, J. I know you like it too." Cassius pushed off the wall and moved the toothpick to the edge of his mouth where a smirk was forming. He gently tucked a curl behind my ear. "Don't have too much fun tonight."

I chuckled and patted him on the back. "I know you'll miss me but don't pout about it. You can't lock me in your room."

"I sure could try." His smile turned devilish when he removed the pick from his mouth.

"And I wouldn't mind it." I pecked him on the cheek before he could make me late, inhaling the scent of pine on his neck. "But I'll be busy gossiping with the girls tonight."

"Oh," Cassius said as his eyebrows danced up and down. "Try to refrain from talking about me the *whole* time, okay?"

"Sure thing, Mr. Plume. I know you have a bad reputation. Wouldn't want them thinking you've gone soft." I began to walk away.

He let a deep-throated laugh escape before pointing a finger at me. "Training. 7 a.m. Don't be late!"

"I promise, *Dad*. I'll be there." I rolled my eyes before prancing off to find the dancers.

We all sat in a circle in the dancers' tent as Charlotte passed around mugs of ale. Olive and Piper were offered apple juice, which they groaned incessantly about.

The women turned to me first as the gossip session began, and my stomach immediately dropped.

Scarlett spoke up before anyone else could, "Last night you and Cassius galivanted off to his bedroom. Any juicy details?"

I looked over to find Evelyn and Matilda covering Piper and Olive's ears. This felt more like an interrogation, and I couldn't help but tip my head back and finish my drink to avoid her question. Cassius was right. How did he manage to be the topic of conversation in every situation? Damn him. "There's nothing to tell. We're waiting until the time is right, since I might be returning to Axminster."

"Mr. Young hasn't sent word yet?" Charlotte piped up, worry straining her features.

I just shook my head, eyeing the sand beneath my feet. It was on my mind every waking moment, but it'd been a week since we caught the killer, and I hadn't heard anything.

"Maybe he's forgotten!" Mila exclaimed, trying to cheer me up.

I forced a smile, knowing that couldn't be the case. "Maybe." I didn't want to put a damper on the evening, so instead I turned the conversation to Charlotte. "You and Flint, huh? What's going on with that, missy?" I wiggled my eyebrows and she burst into laughter before explaining every detail of their relationship. And I mean *every* detail. At one point I had to cover my ears.

It felt good to be surrounded by my friends. Over the course of the night, my head grew fuzzy, and all I could think about was how Cassius would reprimand me tomorrow. Even being with my closest girlfriends, I couldn't get him out of my head. What was he doing right now? Was he thinking about the moment we shared last night as I was?

"Juniper, Cassius can wait." Josephine snapped me out of my vision. "It's time we dance!"

Before I knew it, I was being carried to my feet. Dear God, this was going to be a long night.

The next morning, I woke with a pounding headache and my back ached as I crawled up off the floor in Charlotte's room. But looking over to the small bed in the corner, Charlotte sprawled out amongst the sheets with her mouth wide open and her hair a frizzy mess, I knew she had it worse. I huffed out a laugh, my throat dry and scratchy. I needed to find water.

But before I could, I spotted the clock hanging on the wall. 7:05.

Shit.

Shit, shit, shit.

I raced out of the room toward the exit of the train, forgetting about my thirst. Jumping off the platform, I sprinted for the biggest tent, hearing the pounding of hooves. Cassius wasn't kidding. It was 7:00 and the riders had already begun practicing. When I burst through the opening, my lungs were on fire, my stomach was growling, and my head was still pounding. Suddenly all the riders stopped.

"Finally decided to show up?" a man with abnormally long limbs yelled from across the arena.

"I'm five minutes late, Beau, relax!" I yelled, and the echo in the arena made my head want to explode.

Cassius chatted briefly with Mr. Monte before climbing down the stands and coming to meet me. "What did I tell you?" he asked with his hands on his hips, but he didn't seem too angry, which was a good sign.

"'Don't be late,' I know, I know. I'm sorry. The girls and I drank way too much, and my head is aching," I complained, rubbing my temple.

He shook his head back and forth and smiled. "Luckily I like you, which means I won't go too hard on you."

I sighed with relief.

That is before Cassius called the men off their horses. "Seven laps! When one is late, all are punished!"

"Wait, what?" I questioned, stepping in front of Cassius.

"You're going to get hell for this you know." He just smiled. "You better start running. If you let the boys catch up, they'll kill you."

He smacked my ass, and I squealed, throwing him a glare. Catching up to the boys was more difficult than I thought it would be. Pumping my arms, I tried to ignore the pounding in my head and the tightness in my limbs, but I was too damn tired for this. I just wanted to hide in bed where it was warm.

"Come on, Juniper. Can't go any faster?" Eric prodded, just a few feet behind me.

"We're catching up," Densel taunted, coming to stand on my right.

I just scoffed and ignored him. I had completed three laps so far, and my limbs were gelatinous. I felt bad for making everyone run just because I was late, but their long legs could handle it. I, on the other hand, wanted to burn this arena to the ground. It was larger than any of the other tents, and after the fourth lap, I thought I might pass out.

Suddenly, Jasper, an extremely tall man with the darkest eyes I'd ever seen, came to run next to me. He looked at me as if he wanted to kill me. "You're going to pay for this," he said.

"It's just a run. You'll be fine," I huffed through the intervals of my breathing while my legs felt like they were going to give out on me any second. As soon as I made it around the sixth lap, I knew I was done. I didn't eat last night or this morning, and the alcohol had turned to acid. As a gag pushed up, I sprinted to the edge of the arena and expelled what little I had left in my stomach.

"Stop!" Cassius proclaimed. "You're all done. Get back on the horses." He quickly jogged down the stairs and met me at the bottom of the arena. "Are you okay?"

I gave him a thumbs-up, unable to speak. Another surge of vomit made me lurch forward, and Cassius moved behind me to rub slow, soothing circles on my back while gathering my hair into his hands. The warmth in his hands gave me a moment of reprieve, and after I stopped retching, I braced my cool hands over my face.

Cassius's hand slowly curled around my waist and rested over my stomach, which did wonders. "You okay to ride?" he inquired.

It was the last thing I wanted to do, but I knew I had to if I wanted to be prepared. That, and I was afraid the other riders would legitimately kill me if I opted out after making them run. I nodded my head, walking slowly to the white stag that bounced from foot to foot. Mounting her, I led us to the middle of the arena, straight into a series of glares.

Cassius climbed the steps once more and came to stand beside Mr. Monte.

"I want to see the opening act!" Mr. Monte demanded, wringing his hands together. "I'm looking for uniformity. Watch out of your peripherals to see that you're moving at the same pace as the others, and we'll be alright."

We started the act in a small pod, shoulder to shoulder, and as the music grew more upbeat, we slowly spread out to cover the expanse of the arena. After that, we lined up behind one another to circle the perimeter where the fun tricks began.

For most of the morning, Cassius shouted obscenities at us, making us feel utterly incapable of doing anything right. He was a tough instructor, but the men looked up to him. We performed the entire act one last time as noon dawned, while Cassius and Mr. Monte spoke quietly in the stands.

Then Cassius turned to the group and shrugged. "It didn't look completely terrible. Go get some food."

He turned to Mr. Monte, not sparing a second glance at us, and emphatically moved his arms, which prompted Mr. Monte to nod up and down. Either they were speaking about our shortcomings, or Cassius had a good idea.

Before I could determine which one it was, Wilman tore through the flaps of the tent, holding a small cream-colored envelope. "You've got mail, Juniper!"

Mr. Monte had warned Wilman to watch out for any mail, knowing that instructions for my return would arrive soon. I had silently hoped the news would never come, but the past week of silence had been too good to be true.

My stomach dropped instantly, and I thought I was going to be sick again. With my feet planted in the ground, I was unable to move. I knew what that letter was—we all did. Mr. Young had finally written, requesting my return to Axminster, and I wasn't ready. I didn't have a rebuttal to convince Mr. Young to let me stay. And if I opened that letter,

I would have to go back. If I opened that letter, all of it would become real.

Cassius and Mr. Monte descended the stairs side by side. I couldn't take my eyes off that small piece of paper waving in Wilman's grip. That is, before Cassius snatched the letter and tore it in half before everyone.

"If he wants you, he can come and take you for himself." Cassius nodded decidedly before marching out of the tent and letting the pieces of paper fall behind him.

Before I knew what I was doing, I was piecing the papers together to read the elegant handwriting:

Juniper,

I am happy to inform you that the killer has been locked away in Axminster's prison. You and the rest of the circus are safe. I have business that will occupy me until month's end, and if you have not returned by then, I will come and collect you. Please say your goodbyes.

See you soon,
Mr. Young

My heart beat so fast I thought it would explode in my chest. Mr. Young had finally come to collect on my promise. I had roughly three weeks to find a way to stay in the circus, or I was going back to Axminster…for good this time.

I couldn't imagine a life without the circus. I'd finally found a passion—something that made me feel complete. And if I left, I'd never see my friends again, I'd never hear another of Mr. Monte's crazy ideas, and I'd never again walk the tightrope wearing one of Valetta's exotic costumes. And Cassius…after everything we'd been through—the fights, the anger, the passion, the healing…I would never see him, hold him, or kiss him again.

I needed my family—my true family, not the one I'd left in Axminster—and I couldn't bear the thought of returning to such small-minded people.

Chapter Thirty-Seven

That night I dreamt of life in Axminster. I dreamt of what it'd be like to sit with my mother and sister drinking tea and planning a wedding I didn't want. I wondered what it'd be like to embrace the Young family as if they were my own. And I dreamt of falling asleep next to Joseph, my soon-to-be husband. I imagined the conversations we might have, the lies we'd tell the world about our happiness, and how much we'd detest each other in the years to come.

In the darkness of our future home, I saw Joseph lying next to me, snoring softly. He would be kind; I knew he would, and he'd offer me anything a girl could ever want. Except what I wanted was far from acceptable.

In my dream, he slowly turned toward me, and I realized it wasn't Joseph at all. The man lying next to me was Monroe Beringer with a sweet smile on his face. But his smile slowly started to widen until his jaw unlocked completely. His mouth opened unnaturally, and I heard a labored gasp from deep within him.

And then he swallowed me whole.

"No!" I screamed and my body lurched out of its dream state. I clawed at my throat, unable to swallow a breath.

Air. I needed air.

Cassius rustled beside me, turning to find me dripping with sweat. "Juniper?" He immediately moved to sit behind me, straddling his legs on either side of mine. "Breathe," he encouraged, laying me back against his chest. "Breathe."

I memorized the feeling of his fingers rubbing up, down, up, down, until my breathing finally calmed. Curling onto my side, I leaned into his warmth.

"I saw him," I whispered, almost inaudibly. Even though we'd caught him, he was still haunting me. Would I ever forget him?

"He's not going to go away," Cassius answered in a soothing voice.

I started to cry then, my entire body trembling.

"He disappeared after my sister died. There were no more threats, and everyone thought we were safe, but I saw him every single night. Every night," Cassius drawled as he fell into memory. "It never went away. Even after five years, I still see him." He smoothed my hair back, his controlled motions making me sleepy. "But as the years passed, it became easier."

"How?" I inquired, sitting up straighter to look at him.

His eyes flicked between mine, before he answered, "Well," he paused, trying to figure out the best way to explain it. "Every time I had a nightmare, I'd wake up and exert myself until I passed out. I'd train, drink, anything to get him out of my head. And over time, I began to think more of training and drinking—the two things that made me the happiest at the time," he laughed, "more than I thought of the killer. Distracting myself made him slowly fade away, and when he wormed his way back in, I recited the names of the people I loved. It gets tedious at times, but it works."

Listening to him share these stories made me realize just how hard he'd fought. "I'm proud of you," I whispered.

He just smiled. "Now you know what to do."

Somehow, instinctively, he knew to hold me tighter, and when I closed my eyes, I created a list in my head of the people I loved. And Cassius was number one.

The following morning, I met with Mr. Monte in his office to discuss Mr. Young and my approaching return to Axminster.

"What can I do?" I asked fervently.

"I don't know." He shrugged.

It surprised me because he was never without an answer.

But he continued, "Mr. Young threatened us because he believes the circus is dangerous, and he has powerful businessmen prepared to support him. What would change his mind?" Mr. Monte thought aloud.

"Surely nothing related to business. He has too many assets—too many allies. We need something that will destroy his reputation—that's what he cares about most." I nodded, like I was getting somewhere.

"He allowed you to return to the circus because you threatened to tell the Axminster Guard that he was a fraud—that he threatened to burn us to ash. Could we use that again?" Mr. Monte inquired.

"No, it won't work. I told him I wouldn't expose him if he let me return here. So, even if I went back on my promise, he'd still take down the circus because of my betrayal. We have to think of something new."

Suddenly someone rapped on the door and Cassius walked through absent-mindedly. "Juniper, what are you doing here?" he asked, confused.

"We're trying to figure out how to cut off Mr. Young once and for all. Join us. We could use your opinion." Mr. Monte motioned to the empty chair on the other side of his desk, and Cassius took a seat next to me.

"Now that Mr. Young has captured a killer under his own investigation, the guard won't care about his dirty methods. They trust him now as one of their own. We have to go deeper than that. We have to do something that will completely shame him and everything he's worked for—something that will destroy his name."

We continued for another hour, rifling through option after option with no answers.

And after we'd exhausted all possibilities, Cassius and I decided to take a walk. He was eerily quiet, so I asked, "Do you want to grab a drink?"

He kept his eyes pinned to the floor. "I think I'll spend the night alone."

With no further explanation, he turned into his chamber and left me there. I tried my best not to be hurt, thinking that Cassius needed some time to sort through things, but I could be gone in a matter of weeks. And we'd never get this time back.

Axminster was the new killer. The thought of being completely helpless and unchallenged in that suffocating city made me want to hurl. But Cassius was just as confused as I was, and he deserved some space to think about what would happen next.

I abandoned the idea of having a drink and took to walking the rope instead. I spent hours in my tent, walking on a fine line, feeling absolutely weightless. At last, I fell onto the net below and bobbed up and down until my body settled. I laid there with my arms spread out and looked up at the peak of the tent where the red and white stripes met. I closed my eyes and pictured the colors slowly swirling into oblivion. That's what the circus was like—getting lost but rediscovering yourself all at once. Diving into the current of a sea storm, unsure of whether to paddle your way out or be swept away forever. But that moment where you choose to stay—to swim instead of sink—is the moment you come alive.

I realized suddenly, looking at the rope bobbing up and down above me, that I'd never perform again. I'd never wave to the crowd or bow with my friends.

I understood then, how furious Cassius was. It wasn't fair of high society to rule over us just because we didn't have enough money or support. It was ridiculous. And it had to stop. I remembered then what I promised myself long ago. I didn't happen upon the circus by accident. I was here for a reason. Being a woman of higher class, I had every privilege in the world and still decided to walk beside vagabonds. Why? Because I believed in their commitment and their joy. More than anything, I wanted to unite the two classes so that we might live peacefully together. That was my hope for a new world.

Chapter Thirty-Eight

The past couple of days, I'd kept myself busy practicing, dancing with friends, and drinking to my heart's content. I spent as much time as I could with Cassius, but he was distant. He had been racking his brain to find a way for me to stay, as I had, but before we knew it, a week had gone by. I was beginning to realize that a decision had to be made.

We had been deluding ourselves, and I couldn't handle it any longer. Being surrounded by the magic of the circus and the people I loved, knowing it was all coming to an end, was just too hard. My time was already dwindling, and there was no use in putting it off. I was finally resolved that it was time to go home. No, not home. Just the place I was raised—a place on a map. It didn't hold the love of my friends, the passion of walking the rope, the constancy of Mr. Monte, or the tender warmth of Cassius. There was nothing for me there. Despite that, I couldn't prevent the inevitable.

As I packed my bags, I thought of the loneliness that would ensue. When I returned to Axminster for those few months, I'd never felt more lost, and this wasn't mere months. This was forever.

I suddenly thought about forever with Joseph. When I was a child, my father divorced my mother, which brought shame upon our family. Marriage was decreed by the Lord as sacred and unbreakable, and my parents broke it. The townspeople looked down on my mother for years after that, believing she wasn't a true member of the Church if she couldn't manage to stay married. Divorce was unacceptable. And my mother paid the price for it.

It was the hardest time of our lives, struggling to stay afloat without my father's income and with the wrath of society pitted against us. But my mother requested a loan from her father, which helped us make do until she begged for a job as the director of the ladies' auxiliary at the chapel to get back in their good graces. Why she stooped to their level was beyond me, but it worked. Her name was spread around town—Axminster being the hub of religious activity—and she began to accumulate her own wealth. The divorce hadn't entirely ruined her life, but it had damaged her image far more than she liked to admit.

I wondered if divorce was inevitable for Joseph and me. Would I remain under my mother's care without an income of my own? Would I be forced to get a low paying job that I had no interest in? Would I be shamed by society for the rest of my life?

I pushed aside the thought before I became too angry. I'd been born into this. And I decided to board this train almost two years ago, knowing exactly what might happen.

I grabbed the duffel bag resting idly on my bed and slung it over my shoulder, glancing around my room one last time—the small bed in the corner and the wardrobe on the opposite wall where some of my favorite costumes were hung. Walking over to it, I trailed my hands down a velvet leotard, its soft, midnight blue fabric tickling my fingers. I skipped to a bedazzled costume with hundreds of golden gems embedded into the fabric. And lastly, I found myself gripping the plain, tan leotard I used for training. It was so dull, so dirty, but it was stained with months of hard work—months of memories.

I giggled softly before closing the door behind me and sauntered through the halls, remembering the first time I walked through them. I was so afraid, spotting performers half-naked while shadows danced on the walls. It had all seemed so blasphemous to me at the time—the thought of drinking into the next morning. Even the clothes they wore were extreme, blouse undone at the naval and skirts high on their hips. But I came to understand it as freedom.

Taking a deep breath, I entered the dining car where the performers were waiting. I noticed Mr. Monte first, standing at the front of the team with a sad smile. I wrapped my arms around his neck, and he rested his head on my shoulder.

"Dear girl, you will be missed. But we'll figure out how to get you back," he vowed, stepping back to look at me.

I nodded once, sniffling back tears. "Promise me something."

Mr. Monte nodded apprehensively, his brown hair swinging across his shoulders.

"Don't waste your time trying to get me back. If I can't return, it's simply because God has a different path for me." My breath wavered as I exhaled. "There's one thing I want all of you to do." I looked across the crowd of saddened faces. "I want you to practice until you can't anymore, and when it comes time to perform, I want you to imagine that I'm right there next to you. I want you to work your asses off. This is your chance to change the world and you must take it." I pinched my eyes shut, unable to say anything more.

The dancers huddled, holding onto each other tightly. That's what I loved about them. They stuck together and relied on one another. Sisters, not by blood, but by choice. I smiled at every one of them before I met the eyes of the twins, bedecked in animal skins and furs. They smiled in unison, their hands mirroring each other's in front of their waists.

I looked to the riders next, standing near the bar. They had strapping figures, long legs, and lean arms, aside from Henry who was still growing. They were strong. I spotted Flint amongst them, the boy who had welcomed me with open arms and always kept me safe, the boy I spent countless nights with, learning the ways of mathematics. I smiled at what seemed like simpler times.

I turned my attention to the flamethrowers—the men with gangly beards, golden gauges in their ears, and tattoos covering every inch of their skin. Hugh shook his head back and forth, but I just nodded to reassure him that everything would work out as it was meant to.

The two magicians sat in the corner of the room, where Gus had his hands shoved deep in his pockets. His eyes were puffy and red, although he breathed deeply, understanding that even if he glanced through his crystal ball, my future wouldn't change.

After gazing at all my friends, I noticed there was one missing. The lion tamer. I almost burst into hysterical tears at the thought of never seeing him again, never witnessing his devilish smirk, his honey eyes, and that unruly, raven-colored hair of his. Cassius might not be here, but the memories we shared would never fade. It was better this way. Better I didn't see him.

Examining the crowd once more, I spotted the little blonde dancer looking at me with tears streaming down her face.

I looked right into her eyes when I said, "I'm so proud of all of you. I'm so grateful to have been part of your team—your family. Because of you, I finally know who I am. And that is the greatest gift I've ever been given."

The crowd rushed to me then, crushing me in a hug. I pulled Charlotte into my chest while Olive clung to my leg, and Flint wrapped an arm around my side, the others piling in behind. I laughed at the image of all of us joined together. This was family. And I'd have this forever, no matter how far away I was.

When everyone pulled away, a lighthearted laughter filled the room.

I sniffled back the rest of my tears. "All of you deserve so much more than you've been given. You deserve respect, kindness, and love." I paused, thinking over my next words carefully. "You are the future. Go out there and give it your all." My last words were a whisper as my heart broke into a million pieces.

But before I could fall apart in front of them, I turned my back. My steps were slow, my legs weighed down by what I was leaving behind.

I reached the entrance to the train and pushed the lever down, letting the wall fall into a ramp. I treaded down quickly and made my way across the clearing while a light snow fell. The sun broke through the clouds momentarily to shine on the crystals, making the air glitter around me.

Magic. That's what this place was.

I turned around one last time to witness the letters painted on the side of the train, my breath fogging in the cold air. *Circus*, it read in red paint. And the words seemed to shine a little bit brighter.

Chapter Thirty-Nine

I soaked in the fresh air as I slowly drifted through the decaying corn field. Maybe after things had settled, a couple years down the road, my mother and Mr. Young would let me visit the circus and watch their shows. Maybe I could still be a part of their lives in some small way, but that might be more painful that letting them go completely.

I thought about how the circus would change without me. While I became the wife of a prosperous businessman, the circus would continue performing. They'd travel until the end of their days, but on the off chance they decided to settle down, where would they be? And when Mr. Monte grew old, would he step down and allow someone else to lead the circus? Evelyn would pass soon, I was sure of it, although sometimes I believed she was immortal. And what about Charlotte and Flint? What would happen between the two of them? What would happen to Cassius? Would he continue lion taming? Would he find another woman to understand him as I had?

I shook my head, unable to bear the thought.

The circus would move on without me. Time would pass, and the years I was in their company would become a distant memory. I tried to reassure myself that I was doing the right thing, but it killed me to know what I would suffer because of it.

And then I heard his voice.

"Juniper!" Cassius screamed over the light wind, his voice commanding yet pleading all at once.

I whipped around to find him standing just beyond the train, his cheeks flushed from running. He slowed his pace and walked fervently to the edge of the field, his arms dropping to his sides almost in defeat.

I smiled at the way his curls flipped in the wind, how his caramel eyes glinted in the sunlight, and the small quirk of his lips that formed a dimple in his cheek. His eyes were so honest, filled with grief, and he looked at me as though I was the only person left in the world. I thought of the warmth and security I found in his arms, and suddenly, an array of images passed through my mind.

First, I saw him sitting on the floor of a train car with Charlotte in his lap. His eyes were dark, and he looked at me with indignation. It was the first time I'd seen him. Then, the scene shifted, and I remembered him in his tent, towering over me.

You will never belong here.

His voice came back to me as an echo of days far behind us. Then, I imagined him standing behind me with pride in his eyes.

You didn't need me.

It was the first time he'd spoken to me fondly—the first time he believed in me. The image blurred before colors exploded across my mind, a picture forming of Cassius and me standing side by side.

I want you to meet Mildred.

Our trust was only starting to form then.

The image faded as splatters of gold, red, and white spread like watercolors on a page—Cassius and me laying in the sand with Abbas. Our laughter was genuine as he taught me to trust his beloved lion.

Our figures were then whisked away like smoke, to when he asked me to walk the rope. I feared I would fall, but he caught me that day, and I knew then that I wasn't afraid of falling through the air and feeling my stomach drop. I was afraid of falling for him—afraid of how much control he might have over me. And then, one final image came to mind. It was the night of our performance in Eanverness at the L'Acre Du Grand Ours.

Do you trust me? He'd asked before planting his lips on mine. It was then that I realized I did. No matter what, I trusted him with everything I had because he saved me, time and time again.

The visions were erased by a cool breeze, and suddenly my eyes opened to the blinding sun and the sparkling snow drifting through the air. Cassius was closer now, only a few feet away. I tried so hard not to fall for him, but he made it impossible. He was a mystery, rude and untouchable, but as I got to know him and his past, I wanted him to know that he was worth loving— that I loved him. And he deserved to know that.

My jaw shook as he walked toward me, coming to stand right in front of me.

"I love you," I whispered. I wanted to say more—say why—say anything to express how much he meant to me, but I couldn't. My lungs were burning, and the tears wouldn't stop flowing. I hoped that proclamation convinced him that he was the most important person in my life.

His eyes widened as tears formed, threatening to spill over. He just shook his head, not taking his eyes off me once. "You can't leave," he whispered, and looked up to the sky, trying to figure out what to say. "I need you." He bit his cheek, as if saying that made him weak. Regardless, he continued, "I need you, Juniper. I was afraid to admit it, but when you left the first time, it killed me. I can't lose anyone else. Especially not you."

"It killed me too." I grappled with the string of my duffel bag for something to hold onto. "I wasn't the same without you, Cas. I was lost." A sob escaped me, and I closed my eyes. "And I don't want to be lost anymore. I just want to be with you." Tears streamed down my face. "I don't want to go."

Cassius spread his fingers across my cheek and gently brushed away my tears, but I only cried more at the thought of losing his touch.

"Don't leave me," he begged, a tear sliding down his cheek.

Seeing Cassius again made my departure only that much harder. How could I leave him while he was begging me to do the one thing no one had ever done for him—stay. But if I stayed, Mr. Young would come and take me away or burn the circus to the ground. I had to do this.

So, I stepped back, out of his touch, despite how empty it left me. I was losing my best friend. I wanted to scream in anger and fall to the floor.

"You are going to do great things." I nodded my head repeatedly as his mouth opened and tears poured out of his eyes. "Please, for my sake, keep loving the way you do. Get revenge on those rich bastards. Expect praise, respect, and kindness because you deserve it." I stepped toward him and placed my hand over his heart, feeling the drumming beneath his chest. "I'm not leaving you, Cassius Plume. I'll be right here if you let me."

Cassius's lip trembled and he opened his mouth to say something before closing it.

I stood there memorizing the features of his face. I couldn't imagine a life without him by my side.

But I had to.

I smiled before walking away from him forever. My feet were so heavy, and I felt like I was outside of my own body, watching this happen. No way in hell could it be real. No way in hell was I saying goodbye.

All I could hear was the whistling wind and the crunch of my footsteps in the snow. The months we'd spent together had been the best of my life. I almost turned back to look at him, but if I did, I would run back to him and never leave again.

I'd almost reached the tree line—the separation between the circus and the city. I could do this—I could leave this all behind.

"Marry me!" Cassius's voice resounded across the expansive field and echoed off the trees in the distance.

I stopped immediately in my tracks. My heart stopped beating in my chest, and all the air left my lungs.

I turned on my heel and watched Cassius slowly walking toward me, his strides confident.

"Marry me," he repeated. "I don't have much money, or a big estate, or a name for myself. I'm nobody." He stopped a few feet away from me and shrugged his shoulders, searching my eyes to find some sort of reaction. "But I'll give you everything I have. My heart, my body, my mind. My trust, my honesty, and my protection. It belongs to you completely."

My eyes darted between his. Heart, body, and mind—we would belong to each other wholly, and I couldn't imagine it any other way. He was the man I wanted to spend my life with.

I threw my bag down and ran into Cassius's arms, crushing his body into my own.

He giggled earnestly and held my head close to his chest, but underneath his laughter, I could hear his wavering breath. He was scared. We'd almost lost each other. I held onto him for a little while longer, just eager to know that I was safe in his arms.

I pulled away and looked into his eyes. "You really want to do this?" I asked. This was a big commitment, especially for someone like Cassius who'd never thought about the prospect of marriage before.

"I'm positive." He nodded his head once in confirmation. "I need you too much to let you go. Marriage can't be that bad, can it?"

I rolled my eyes, but a laugh escaped me.

Cassius eyed the ground with a goofy smile before looking up at me. "So, Juniper Plume," he drawled out my name, making my insides queasy.

Juniper Plume...it had a ring to it.

"Are you ready to do this?" he finished, scooping me into his arms.

I wrapped my hands around his neck and looked into his eyes. "I've never been more ready."

He swung me through the air, making me laugh like a little girl. When he looked at me, his eyes softened, as if he knew now that everything would be okay. He pressed his lips to mine, and it was a soft, gentle kiss. In that moment, I was so happy, so complete, that it made me cry. And when he drew away, I realized something. I would kiss him for the rest of my life.

This was forever.

Chapter Forty

The sun was glistening through the snowflakes, making them sparkle like crystals, as Cassius and I walked hand in hand. I looked up at the sky and drank in the sun's warmth, taking a deep breath and filling my lungs with the cool, icy air. My shoulders relaxed as I exhaled and the pressure that was there only moments ago had already dissipated.

I didn't know if my family would ever accept my marriage to Cassius and my refusal of Joseph Young and wealthy life entirely. I didn't know if my mother would ever respect me, or if I'd see Colette again. But I hoped that after everything settled, we could find a way to love each other. For now, my life in the circus was far more important, and if I never saw my family again because of that decision, then I could live with that.

As of now, everything was right in the world. The air was breathable again and everything around me seemed more real—like I was noticing it for the first time. The train looming ahead was bigger, the wood on the exterior a deeper oak. The vegetation swayed in the wind, leaves drooping to the ground, ready to rest for the winter.

The sky was a more vibrant blue, and the storm clouds approaching looked soft and cozy, like something I could melt into. And when I looked at Cassius, I saw the same thing. His hair was so dark I thought it might stain me like ink if I touched it. His skin was golden, similar to the glow of a dying sunset when orange light meets the yellow horizon. His lashes blinked delicately, as though delayed, like a branch bobbing up and down in a windstorm. And his eyes glinted in the sun, like golden wax melting over a flame.

Cassius strung his arm around my waist as we ascended the ramp in search of the others. No one was milling about the halls like they usually were. It was quiet. When we reached the closed doors of the dining car, we looked at each other and shrugged; and despite the suddenness of it all, we pushed through those doors together.

The performers hadn't moved an inch. Some were sitting quietly and others had tears in their eyes. I'd been in the circus for just short of two years, while others had been here for twenty. Surely, they didn't miss me that much.

As soon as I walked through the door, Charlotte leapt out of her seat and ran into my arms. "Juniper! What are you doing here?"

The others stood out of their seats eagerly as I nuzzled into Charlotte's thick, blonde locks, inhaling her sweet floral perfume. While I was busy being suffocated by her, I saw Cassius disappearing through the back doors. I hardly had time to wonder what he was doing before he returned, out of breath and red in the face.

I glanced at Cassius, who had a smirk playing on his lips, and he nodded his head, urging me to tell them.

There was no use beating around the bush, so, I cleared my throat, and exclaimed, "We're getting married!"

The entire room fell quiet, the enthusiasm I was hoping for nowhere to be seen.

"You and the lion tamer?" Evelyn chuckled and her entire upper body shook with laughter. "You're funny."

Everyone laughed nervously with her, thinking it was a joke.

"Where's the ring?' Charlotte ran up to me again and snatched my hand to inspect my finger.

Cassius didn't need to give me a ring. Jewelry was excessive, and it didn't show our love for one another in any way. I simply didn't need one.

"It's right here," Cassius said confidently behind me.

And when I turned around, he was kneeling in front of me, his golden eyes peeking out from underneath his curls, with a little golden ring between his fingers.

I gasped and heard Charlotte physically smack her mouth with her hand. This felt like nothing I imagined and everything I imagined all at once. I'd never been able to picture a man kneeling in front of me— never *wanted* to until Cassius. And now he was asking to walk by my side for the rest of our lives. My heart stopped beating in my chest, and it was as though time had stopped.

"No way this is happening," Flint whispered behind me, and the riders slowly walked toward us as if approaching a pack of lions.

Marriage was unheard of in the circus. No performer had done it before, not that I recall.

"Juniper Rose," Cassius began, looking up at me as though I were the only woman in the room. "Since the moment you walked in here, I haven't been able to resist you. You are stubborn and relentless, yet you're the most selfless person I've ever met. And you're beautiful, kind, honest, and accepting. You make me want to be better every single day."

He shook his head nervously. "Despite our differences, you are a breath of fresh air. For years, I've felt like I was drowning, but you helped me breathe again." Cassius cleared his throat. "I can't promise you this will be easy, but I love you, Juniper. So," he paused, his voice shaking. "Would you do me the honor of marrying me?"

I stood there like an idiot with my hands over my mouth, tears streaming out of my eyes. "Yes," I whispered, barely able to contain my excitement. "Yes!"

He smiled brighter than I'd ever seen as he slipped the ring on my finger. I couldn't help but pull him up off the floor and press my lips to his.

"Oh my god!" Charlotte screamed, accompanied by the dancers rushing over to me. They jumped up and down giddily, and when I broke away from Cassius, they almost pulled my arm off.

"Let us see the ring!" they screamed, all thirteen of them grabbing at my hand. I laughed, getting a good look at it for the first time myself. It was a golden band, with small flower petals surrounding a dainty diamond. My eyes filled with tears at the simplicity and the beauty of it.

"You're getting married!" Olive jumped up and down excitedly. "Are you sure you want it to be with Cassius though?" She smushed her face in disgust, making all of us laugh.

"Positive." I bopped her on the nose.

I briefly turned over my shoulder to find Cassius being bombarded with hugs and some aggressive slaps on the back. When Flint pointed an accusatory finger at Cassius, I thought things might get ugly, but Cassius surprised us all when he clapped him on the shoulder and drew him into a hug. Maybe Cassius and Flint could set their differences aside and be friends. We were getting married for heaven's sake! He didn't need to worry about Flint anymore.

The other men hooped and hollered, exclaiming some rather profane things about our wedding night, making Cassius smile devilishly along with them.

"Wait!" a voice rang out, silencing the cheers and the commotion.

Mr. Monte stood in the middle of the group with his mouth agape, startled by our excitement. "Isn't this a little premature? Mr. Young expects your return in two weeks. This doesn't change anything."

The concern in his eyes and the will to keep his family safe was almost tangible. No matter the happy occasion, being the leader meant he had to put the circus first.

And he was right. Despite how much I wanted to marry Cassius, it wouldn't stop Mr. Young from coming after me. Or would it?

As the performers watched me in apprehension, I thought back to my mother and how she was shamed for being divorced. It's been engrained in my mind, even to this day, that divorce was a sign of failure. My mother wanted her daughters to be respected, and that's why she and Mr. Young encouraged me to marry Joseph.

But what if I married a different man? If I married Cassius, my mother and Mr. Young would be tempted to do everything in their power to tear us apart, perhaps even force us to divorce. But if they encouraged that, their reputations would be tarnished. They would be known as the people who sabotaged a happy marriage, and they would be looked down on by everyone in society.

And my mother loved her image more than she loved me, as did Mr. Young. She would never make a move to tear me and Cassius apart because it would mean destroying her life all over again.

This could work. This was my way to stay in the circus.

So, I cleared my throat and turned to Mr. Monte. "It changes everything." Everyone seemed to lean in at that news. So, I told them of my mother's upbringing and her exile from the church…all because she was divorced…a cardinal sin in their eyes. I explained that, in my world, marriage was sacred, and divorce was impermissible. "If Cassius and I were to be married before my two weeks are up, my mother and Mr. Young wouldn't dare try to infringe."

"You really think that will work?" Charlotte asked, worry now staining her features.

I nodded. "But we must be officially married. If we're simply engaged, my mother could just as easily drag me back home to fulfill my commitment to Joseph. So, this wedding needs to happen quickly, or it's not going to happen at all." I glanced to Cassius to make sure he wasn't bothered that we were rushing this.

He just nodded and stepped forward to speak to the group. "Juniper knows her family. She knows what will make them lay down their arms. We have to trust that this will work." He paused, giving me a small smile to reassure me. "Let's make this happen."

I met Mr. Monte's eyes again for confirmation.

He looked at me a moment longer with resolve written in his features. "Alright then, Mrs. Plume. Looks like we better start planning a wedding."

With the logistics out of the way, the celebration began. Tables were cleared, drinks were poured, and the dancing had reached its pinnacle.

I was sweaty, out of breath, and I desperately needed to rest my feet, but just as I was about to find a corner table, Mr. Monte plucked me from the crowd and led me to a seat in the back.

Taking my hand, he said, "I'm sorry I interrupted the fun earlier. You know how I am." He looked around at the dancing performers, their arms entwined as they spun around the room. "I'm protective of my family. But I couldn't be happier for you and Cassius. You both deserve this, after what you've been through." He smiled then, his hand squeezing mine tighter. "I've known Cassius a long time, and believe me when I tell you that you've changed him. I just wanted to thank you for that."

I smiled in return, squeezing back. I wish I'd come to the circus sooner to see what Cassius was like before—to really understand the gravity of things. But I could imagine what Mr. Monte must have done for him—the countless nights he'd picked him up off the floor and told him to keep going, the prayers he'd said, and the dreams he'd envisioned for him.

As if reading my mind, Mr. Monte said, "I've dreamt of this day for so long. I watched him struggle to find himself, hoping that someone…someone that wasn't me," he clarified, "would encourage him and love him. And my dear, you have been that person." His whisper was such a contrast against the hollering in the room.

"Thank you, Mr. Monte. You were there for him when he needed you most. I don't think you'll ever understand how much that means to him." I shook my head. "And thank *you*, for welcoming me and keeping me. If you hadn't, I wouldn't have met him, and I'm eternally grateful for that."

"I'll always keep you," he said.

When he began looking around the room, I knew there was someone else he needed to congratulate. "Go find him." I nudged his shoulder and tipped my head toward the crowd.

He smiled in thanks and leapt up in search of Cassius. When he found him on the dancefloor, he grabbed him by the neck and pulled him into a hug. I watched as they exchanged words I couldn't hear, but Mr. Monte looked proud, like a father would be.

The celebration continued late into the night, serving as an engagement party of sorts. It was declared that the wedding would happen immediately after our next performance.

When the events of the night came to an end, everyone headed to bed before a full day of practice in the morning. I walked hand in hand with Cassius through the thin halls of the train and took in the dark, quiet atmosphere around us. I smiled in the silence until we reached his room, which would soon become *our* room. It was late and with an exhausting morning looming, I was eager to climb into bed. I moved to pull the silk night dress over my head before rethinking it. Cassius had never seen my body under the lavish costumes, and if I laid myself bare before our wedding, then what was the point of waiting at all? So, instead, I stayed in my clothes and climbed under the sheets while Cassius worked at the buttons on his pants.

"Something wrong?" he inquired about my fully clothed state.

"I'm just cold," I lied, and laid my head on the pillow as Cassius climbed in next to me. I turned on my side and curled both hands under my head, where the cold metal on my ring finger pierced my scalp. The night had been so hectic I hadn't gotten the chance to look at the ring— *really* look at it. I surveyed the details in the golden band and the intricately placed gem in the center of the rose.

Cassius laid his hands on top of his stomach and closed his eyes, taking his first deep breath of the day.

"Where did you get this?" I asked quietly.

He cracked his eyes open to peek.

"You aren't secretly a rich nobleman with a vault of money stored away, right?" I questioned and he let out a *huff* of a laugh.

"No, I'm not." His eyes fell to the bed as he fiddled with the sheets. "It was Penelope's ring. My mother gave it to her about a year before they left, and Penelope wore it every day." Cassius looked up to me with a genuine smile, not one filled with sadness as I expected. "She would have wanted you to have it."

My heart sank and I turned over my shoulder to look at him. "I love it," I whispered. It was the most beautiful ring I'd ever seen. It wasn't extravagant or haughty, but delicate and dainty. "I wish she was here today." I didn't want to dampen the excitement, but it was sad that neither of our families would be here to celebrate with us.

"Me too," he said quietly, before a smile took over the frown on his face. "But she's looking down on us." And then he turned over and blew out the candle on his nightstand.

Chapter Forty-One

After such an eventful night celebrating our engagement, it was time to focus on more pressing matters. I needed a wedding dress.

I practically skipped down the hall in excitement, finding Charlotte waiting at the entrance to the train.

When she spotted me, she squealed. "Ready to get your dress fitted?" She jumped up and down before clutching my arm in the crook of her elbow and dragging me down the ramp.

Valetta had volunteered to make my wedding gown, but she was pressed for time with only a couple weeks to finish it. And Valetta didn't work well under pressure.

Charlotte and I ran out to the small red and white tent in the distance, where Valetta's transportable boutique sat idly. She'd explained rather aggressively to Mr. Monte that a bedroom in the train didn't give her enough room to tailor costumes and demanded a larger tent, despite it being outside in the dead of winter. However, the little woman scurried so quickly to curate our costumes that she kept warm just fine.

Charlotte and I ripped open the flaps of the tent, trying to get out of the cold as fast as possible. It was as though we'd entered a brothel, the lighting low, and varying fabrics laid out like forgotten pieces of clothing. We stopped in our tracks to marvel at the mannequins covered in unique designs. Taking up the most space was a table in the middle of the room, with multiple rows of white fabric covering its surface, and small containers of pins and hooks ready to be used.

"Hi, girls!" Valetta exclaimed, her head popping out from underneath a billowing skirt of lavender she'd been working on. "I'll have you stand up here for the fitting!" She directed me to a round platform in front of a mirror, her large glasses sliding down her nose, making her eyes bug. "I'll just take your measurements today, but you have full reign in its design, Juniper. This is your wedding. You tell me what you want, and I'll make it."

I opened my mouth to say something before Charlotte spoke up, "Big and flashy. That's what the circus is, right? We need lace, rhinestones, fur, anything and everything!" she exclaimed.

I opened my mouth, prepared to stop her, but she just pressed forward.

Suddenly she shouted, "We need something seductive that will woo Cassius. A drooping neckline down to her navel, and big skirts! As big as you can make them."

I loved her excitement, but I couldn't get a word in. This would be the most important day of my life, and I wanted to feel beautiful in my wedding dress.

"Wait!" I exclaimed, holding my hands out in front of me.

Charlotte and Valetta stopped their blabbering and froze.

"You're right, the circus is flashy, but that's not me."

Charlotte smiled gently, looking almost embarrassed. "You're right. This is your wedding. What are your ideas?"

I looked at the platform I was standing on. Ever since I was a little girl, I wanted a big ball gown, but now I wasn't so sure. My mother had encouraged me to look like a princess, and now Charlotte wanted me to look like a queen, but what did I want? And without trying to, I thought of Cassius standing by my side, and an image popped into my head. "I want something simple. Elegant."

I explained exactly what I wanted to Valetta and watched her nod along with a faint smile drawing her wrinkled cheeks back, and when I finished, she answered with, "I think I can do that."

For the next hour, Valetta laid out different fabrics, soft silk, thick satin, and textured velvet. Pieces of lace, batiste, chiffon, and tule were spread out for me to choose from, while she jotted down my measurements on a small pad of paper.

"Alright!" She clapped her hands. "I've got everything I need. You can check back in a week to make sure it's meeting your expectations."

"Okay," I whispered, growing more excited by the minute. I stepped off the platform at the same time the flaps of Valetta's tent ruffled across the room. It must have been the wind growing violent. Mr. Monte predicted a storm was coming our way, which would make our departure for Isleburry more treacherous. But as I continued to gather my belongings, I heard the rustle again, followed by a pair of whispering voices.

Charlotte heard it too and stormed over to the shadow of two pairs of feet under the rim of the tent. When she ripped open the flaps, she found Hugh kneeling on the ground, his bald head covered in a wool cap, and Cassius on his left with snowflakes spotting his black hair like salt. She gripped Hugh viciously by his collar and forced him to his feet, moving to drag Cassius in with him.

"What the hell do you think you're doing?" she screamed in their faces.

"We were just tryna' get a glimpse of Juniper's dress. This is the first wedding in the circus. You can't blame us for being curious," Hugh explained with his hands raised in the air defensively.

Charlotte bit the side of her cheek before slapping him upside the head. "You imbeciles!"

Cassius cleared his throat, obviously embarrassed by his intrusion, but looked to me with his head tilted in confusion. "Aren't you supposed to be wearing a dress?" he asked.

"You're as daft as they come." Charlotte rolled her eyes. "It's not done yet. Plus, everyone knows the groom shouldn't be peeking at the bride's dress before the wedding. Now get out!" She shooed them with her hands as if they were mice.

Cassius attempted to fight Charlotte off to get one last glance at the fabrics scattered across the table.

"You better design something fitting!" Hugh yelled. "And by that, I mean *revealing*!"

Valetta sighed while Charlotte pushed his head forward.

"Ow!" Hugh complained.

Cassius smirked and glanced back at me, cupping his hands to his mouth so his voice would carry. "You'll look beautiful either way. I won't be able to take my eyes off you!"

I giggled and covered my mouth at his excitement.

Charlotte pushed the men out of the door, preaching with a pointed finger until Cassius held up his hands in surrender and ran back to the train with Hugh on his tail.

"That won't be happening again on my watch!" She stormed back into the tent wearing a proud smile.

I looked at her sheepishly and said, "There's something I've been meaning to ask you." She leaned forward in curiosity as I continued, "Seeing how you've always been there for me...I was wondering if you'd want to be my maid of honor?" I asked nervously.

She gasped and her hands flung to her mouth in surprise. "Oh my gosh!" she shrieked.

Her loud shrill enveloped the room, leading Valetta to cover her ears.

She ran up to me and clasped my hands. "I would love to! What if you ask the dancers to be your bridesmaids?"

I gasped, an image already forming in my head, and looking over her shoulder to grab Valetta's attention, I said, "Valetta, we're going to need a heap of dresses."

She sighed heavily and her shoulders caved in. "Out. I need to think!" she ordered, pushing her glasses up her petite nose.

Me and Charlotte suppressed a laugh and scurried away before Valetta beat us both. We ran across the field that had been covered in a light dusting of snow before leaping into the warm train.

After brushing ourselves free of snow, Charlotte turned to me seriously. "I have something to ask you too," she began as we meandered down the hall.

"I hope it's nothing serious. I heard there's stew tonight and I'm absolutely starving. If I wait much longer, I might become violent," I joked.

Charlotte bumped her shoulder into mine. "It's nothing to worry about. I was just wondering…" she paused, trying to figure out how to phrase it. "Are you prepared for the wedding?"

"Prepared? For what?" I feigned confusion, but I knew what Charlotte was referring to. Looking down at my boots scuffing the floorboards, I hoped she'd drop the subject.

"You're sleeping with Cassius on the night of your wedding. That *is* one of the rules of religion, isn't it? To wait until marriage to sleep with your partner? I never understood the point." She rolled her eyes.

I did.

I didn't have many opportunities to bed a man back home with my religious fanatic of a mother, but I was glad for it, because it meant that I'd waited for Cassius. And when I gave my body to him, it would belong solely to him.

But even so, I was scared. And who better to admit that to than my closest friend? "I'm nervous, Charlotte. I've never slept with a man before, and Cassius has so much experience. What if I don't do it right? What if he doesn't enjoy it?" I leaned over and whispered, but the halls were too crowded with passersby rushing to dinner for anyone to overhear us.

She giggled lovingly, not judging me in the slightest. "There is nothing to be nervous about. Sleeping with a man—your husband of all people—is something you'll never forget. It's meant to bring you together, not to mention how *good* it will feel. Cassius will be gentle with you. He understands that you may not have ever done this before." She thought for a moment, biting her lip. "That doesn't mean you can't surprise him," she giggled. "I've had lots of experience, some I'm not proud of, but I know what I'm doing. Allow me to give you some tips."

We entered the dining car and she launched into a rather lengthy, in-depth description. I lost my appetite halfway through her explanation of the different techniques I could use, and to say that I was traumatized would be an understatement. I was more worried after our conversation than before, but laughing about it eased my mind.

I stood to grab another bowl of stew when I bumped into a sturdy chest. Turning around, I found Cassius, alone this time.

He wore a confident, sultry smile. "It seems you've swept my fiancé away, Charlotte. Would you be so kind as to return her to me?" he asked with a quirk of his lips.

My breath hitched at that moment, the possessive words making my heart leap in my chest. I couldn't help the nervous twitch in my hands, yearning to touch him, so I averted my gaze to the floor, unable to look into his warm eyes without jumping onto him.

"I surely wouldn't mind. As long as you keep your hands to yourself." Charlotte raised a judgmental, yet provocative eyebrow.

I looked at her as if begging her to pull me back into my seat. I couldn't be left alone with Cassius. She reminded me seconds ago that, as a lady, no matter my current station, I vowed to save my body until marriage. It was hard enough not to lose control this past year and a half. Cassius was a fever. He swept over me quickly, without notice, taking hold of every function of my body. He left me restless, yet unable to move. And that's how I felt right now. My feet were planted in the ground, as though nailed into the floorboards themselves, and my shoulders were tight as I held my gaze on the grains of wood beneath my feet.

We were so close. Our wedding was in two weeks, and then I could finally have him in the way I wanted.

I took a step forward, moving to leave the hot, sticky room, and his penetrable gaze. So, I found my way out into the hall, leaning against the wall to catch my breath as he trailed behind me.

But the empty hall, and the privacy if offered was too close for comfort. I needed to be far away from this man if I intended to keep my promise. Forget worrying about whether I would satisfy Cassius the way he'd been satisfied so many times before. Now I was afraid of enjoying it so much so that I wouldn't be able to stop. My mother had always warned me of such things. And Cassius was no exception. Above any other man who had attempted to court me, Cassius was different. I loved him, and that made him dangerous.

"Look at me," he ordered, leaning casually against the wall without a care in the world.

I kept my eyes trained on the wall to his right.

"Not at the wall." He stepped in front of me, tilting my chin toward him. "At me."

I closed my eyes, shrugging out of his touch. "I don't feel good, Cas. I think I just need to go to bed." I dismissed myself and turned abruptly on my heel.

Before I could make it very far, he grabbed my wrist and pulled me back so quickly that I crashed into his chest. He leaned into my shoulder and pressed a kiss to my collarbone, his breath coming out quickly, as if he'd been waiting for this all day.

I shivered underneath him at the thought.

"You're shaking. Talk to me," he drawled, his lips now on my neck.

"I can't," I breathed out, words being too difficult with him this close.

Suddenly his confidence wavered, and his eyes fell in concern. "I'm to be your husband, but before that, I'm your friend. And I'd like to think that I know you well enough to know when something is wrong. Tell me." He paused briefly and gently moved my hair off my shoulder. "Was it my interruption in your fitting today?"

Because of my hesitation, he grabbed my sweaty palm and led me to his bedroom.

I followed absentmindedly, unable to do anything else. The muscles in his back contorted rhythmically and his stride was long and confident. Time passed too quickly, and before I knew it, he was shutting the door behind him and turning to look at me.

"What's going on?" He seemed to grow more nervous by the second. "Juniper Rose, you've never failed to speak your mind. Do not give up on that."

When I finally summoned the courage to look him in the eyes, playfulness was lingering within them. My jaw trembled lightly as I opened my mouth to speak. "I'm scared," I admitted.

Cassius turned serious, and he sat me down at the foot of his bed, kneeling before me. He ran his hands up and down my thighs, trying to soothe my nerves. "I'm afraid too. But what is it that frightens you?"

He gently prompted me for answers, not invasive or prodding in any way. He'd become more understanding and patient with me, and the least I could give him was my honesty. I took a deep breath before explaining myself, "I'm afraid to be close to you."

His eyebrows shot toward the ceiling.

Surely that wasn't what he was expecting to hear. And the hurt in his eyes made me reach for his hand. "Not because I don't fancy you. Quite the opposite," I huffed out a laugh. "I want you so much that I'm afraid I can't wait until our wedding to have you entirely."

He smiled lightly, before nodding in agreement. "I'll admit, it's been the most difficult thing I've ever done…staying away from you," he clarified. "I think about it every day—what it will feel like."

His words did something to me, and a tingle started to spread low in my core.

"I'm a vulgar man, I have no doubt of that," he continued. "But you're different than the others. You're about to be my wife, and even though I'd like to lay you down and take you now, I understand that you want to wait until we're officially wed."

My heart beat faster and my hands itched to touch him at that comment. Take me now? Could I just forget my promise to God and myself? Could I just jump into the waters now?

I felt sorry for putting this on Cassius. "But I don't want to make you wait. No one else has."

"But you're not like the others." He shook his head, making his curls bounce on his forehead. "I don't care how long I have to wait. If this is important to you, then it's important to me."

His answer eased the ache in my chest. It must have been so difficult for him—the waiting—but the fact that he was willing was something I'd never forget.

I smiled, laughing lightly. "Look who's in charge now."

He rolled his eyes and laid his hand across my thigh, heat blooming through my leg. "Don't let it get to your head. That won't be the case when I have you in my bed."

His confidence made me gasp, but by the look in his eyes, I could tell that he wanted more from me.

So, I asked, "Until then, how am I to be in the same room as you?"

He seemed to have an answer when he stood to his feet. "If it's so troublesome to be in my presence…" he drawled with such haughtiness it made me gag, "then try to imagine what our first time will be like. Maybe that might help you anticipate it instead of dreading having to wait." He held out his hand.

"What do you mean?" I followed him over to the bed.

He gently removed the thick wool covers and allowed me to slide in. Crawling in next to me and propping himself up on his forearm, he traced the ridges of my ribs. "Think about how it feels when I touch you." He moved his hand down and spread his fingers across the flat plane of my stomach.

I couldn't stop my breath from hitching.

"Imagine when I touch you everywhere." His fingertips grazed up my arm to my collarbone, making me quiver under his touch and close my eyes. He pressed a kiss to the base of my neck, and I lifted my chin to give him more room. I felt hot and dizzy, and I never wanted it to end.

But suddenly, he pulled away and that beautiful sensation drifted into nothing. "Until our wedding night, just imagine how amazing it will feel to have everything at its fullest, and remember that I love you."

It was the first time he'd said those words—words I'd been aching and longing to hear. And those three words were fit for his mouth—it was so obvious in the way his tongue touched his top teeth, and those same teeth punctured his full, lower lip.

"I love you too." I sank into his warmth, my body fitting so perfectly with his.

Chapter Forty-Two

This week's performance was special. I was engaged to Cassius Plume after all, and the world deserved to know.

We'd made our rounds through the northern kingdoms in the past few months, coming to Isleburry—the kingdom by the sea, known for its delicious port and savory cod.

As our train came to a halt in the small city beyond the beach, the circus prepared for quite the performance.

"Where is the lovely couple?" Mr. Monte shouted backstage, his voice carrying in the vast chamber.

"Right here!" I squealed, dragging Cassius behind me.

Mr. Monte didn't waste a second before launching into a lecture, "Remember what I taught you. Smiles of adoration, looks of passion, and tangible, undeniable love. That's what we give the audience."

Cassius and I nodded once and were beckoned to the red and white curtain of the tent. After months of performing on lavish stages and in grand opera houses, we were back to our roots. And after years of battling the killer, we were ready to come together where it all began. The tent loomed above our heads, the tip touching the stars. I smiled as I heard the full crowd begin to hush, and listened to the cracking of peanuts and the steady munching of popcorn as children filled their mouths. Footsteps walking across the stadium seats began to quiet just as the lights dimmed.

I blinked, trying to get my eyes to focus in the dark, when I felt Cassius's hand slide into mine. I smiled, even though he couldn't see it, and pressed a kiss to his cheek.

Brushing back the flaps of the tent, I let go of his hand and walked alone into the arena. My feet brushed through the coarse sand, my toes sinking into the grains. I could vaguely spot the leather mat in the center, acting as a stage, and the aerial ring hanging above it, waiting for me.

And when I grabbed hold of it, the candles were lit in sequence, rolling down the aisles between seats. Shadows were cast over surprised faces, the whites of their eyes glowing in the dim light.

I hoisted myself onto the ring as it climbed into the sky, and when it stopped near the top, I fell back and let the bend in my knees catch me, opening my arms to the crowd as the lights overhead flared.

I lifted my hands back onto the ring and flipped my legs over my head, and as I hung there limply, the audience gasped and craned their necks to see. With one swoop of my leg, the ring began turning, and when I locked my ankles together, making my body as tight as possible, I spun faster and faster. I tucked my chin and watched the world spin below, the crowd's cheers echoing even as the ring slowed.

At that point, the ring began to lower, and I circled my arms as though wading through water.

As I drew closer to the ground, Cassius suddenly burst through the curtain and leapt onto the stage, grasping the ring to pull it down.

Hopping off the steel ring, I laid my hands lovingly on his chest, where I could feel his heart beating rapidly beneath his black vest. I wondered if he was afraid of what was to come—of what the audience might think, but despite the possible nerves, he slowly sank to one knee and retrieved a little box from the pocket in his breeches.

The crowd gasped and the women stood to their feet at the most anticipated surprise of the year.

"Oh my God!" a woman shouted, which made others follow suit before the room hushed to a faint whisper, eager to hear what was being said.

"Juniper Rose, I love you," Cassius began.

The crowd leaned forward, almost falling out of their seats. Hearing those words, even though I'd heard them before, still made my world spin—everything I dreamed of was right in front of me.

"You're more than I ever hoped for. You've made me a better man and I'm excited to love you for the rest of my life. I can't tell you enough," Cassius paused and looked at the crowd, their hands pressed to their hearts, before resuming, "that you've taken my breath away."

I heard someone in the crowd crying, which made my heart warm. I had no idea how complete it would make me feel to share our love with the rest of the world—with our fans.

"And that's why I'm here today asking if you would do me the honor of becoming my wife." Cassius looked up to me with round, hopeful eyes, as if he didn't already know my answer.

The man kneeling before me, who wouldn't have considered giving up his throne a year ago, was now asking for my hand. And he was the love of my life.

So, I clasped my hands in front of me and shouted, "Yes!" I nodded until I'd lost my sense of direction.

Cassius leapt up and placed the ring on my finger as the crowd jumped out of their seats, filling the room with applause. I grasped Cassius's shoulder and brought him to my chest, curling my hand into his hair. He wrapped his arms around my waist, and in that moment, I felt attached to him in a way I couldn't explain.

A tarp at the top of the tent suddenly unhooked and a sea of rose petals fell from the ceiling and rained down on us. Looking to the sky, laughter filled my lungs as petals fell around me. When I looked to Cassius, I found a big smile pulling his cheeks back. I'd never seen him look so happy.

The crowd screamed with joy as children raced to pick up petals around their parents' feet. Meanwhile, Cassius and I raced for the back of the tent and out of sight as the dancers jumped onto the stage to leap and kick amongst the fallen petals.

"Amazing! I knew what I was doing starring you two as the lovers from different worlds, didn't I?" Mr. Monte praised his accomplishment, receiving a nod from us both.

"That you did." Cassius smiled.

It was strange to think about how long ago that was—how much we'd resented the idea—resented one another.

Look at us now.

Mr. Monte clapped once and moved on to the next subject. "Juniper, costume change. You're on stage after the dancers!"

I gasped, having almost forgotten, as I ran for the changing rooms in the back. Drawing the curtain closed, I quickly slipped into a tight, silver leotard covered in diamonds that looked like flecks of snow floating dreamily through the sunlight on a crisp morning. As I pulled thick leather gloves over my wrists, I noticed that this was the closest thing to a wedding dress the audience would see.

I pulled the curtain back and quickly stepped into a pan of chalk, rolling my heels and toes in the mixture to keep my feet dry. Stepping out, I exclaimed, "Will someone zip me up?"

Flint, seeing I was about to be late, jogged over and zipped up my leotard.

"Hands off my wife, you *rake*. You had your chance." Cassius pushed him away and finished the job himself, buckling the clip at the top to secure the leotard.

"She's to be your wife. I have no intention of stealing her from you. But I don't doubt that I could," Flint said haughtily.

Cassius huffed out a laugh and clapped him on the shoulder. "Oh, that's rich. Keep thinking that, buddy."

This continuous spatting of theirs was amusing more than irritating, but I'd be late if I entertained it any longer. Rushing to the opening of the tent, I spotted the dancers nearing the end of their performance. The flame throwers assembled by my side; their bare, toned chests covered in a sheen of oil. Their scraggly bears complemented the bright tattoos scrawled across their bodies—images of naked women, mad hatters, and golden keys appearing in intricate detail along their ribs, torsos, and pecs. The men looked like gods.

"Ready to go?" Hugh asked at my side, his bald head glowing in the light.

I nodded and he knelt by my small frame, grabbed my ribs, and easily lifted me onto his shoulder. Kai, reaching about 6'1, came to stand on my other side, sticking my bum on his shoulder. The two men walked slowly to the edge of the tent, followed by the group of flame throwers behind them.

I couldn't help but think we looked like an army—a unit.

And I was their queen.

When we emerged into the light, with my small body atop two hulking men, the audience jumped to their feet wildly. I crossed one knee over the other and waved gently at the crowd. The other flame throwers followed closely behind with long torches hanging at their sides, their tips covered in a bright lemon flame.

As we approached the audience, they took a large glug of lamp oil and filled their mouths. Turning against the wind, they placed the torches to their mouths and expelled a plume of fire into the air. The audience gasped as hot flames exploded, dissipating into clouds of smoke. Over and over they did this until the room was drenched in heat.

My legs were beginning to stick to Hugh and Kai, and I breathed out slowly, attempting to remain calm while I practically burned alive. I couldn't imagine what the fire breathers were going through, fire coming within inches of their faces. I was suddenly intrigued, hoping one day I'd get to learn the art of fire breathing, but for now, I had to focus on my performance.

When we reached the center of the stage, Hugh and Kai offered me their hands. Holding on tightly, I lifted my feet onto their shoulders, and they held my ankles in place as I raised my arms high into the sky. A rope had been lowered so I could reach it from this height. I grasped onto the coarse material and pulled my hips against the rope as the fire breathers gathered beneath me. They continued their routine until the flames bloomed toward the rope itself.

I grasped the rope tightly and kicked my legs back and forth, gaining momentum until I could flip over it. I spun in a circle while the crowd watched in a trance, completely unaware of what was happening below me. Mr. Monte instructed us to carefully distract the audience—to give them something to look at other than the glowing flames.

And when they slowly got tired of watching me spin, they finally focused on the firebreathers. Expecting this, Mr. Monte sent out the cyclists to ride around in front of the audience and lure them into their spell. Next came the riders, galloping around the edge of the stage to hide the fire breathers. Finally, the dancers entered, slowly moving their hips, and pulling the audience in with their lazy movements.

And before the audience noticed, the entire circus had come to say hello. They were so distracted they didn't realize the plumes of fire had begun to scorch the rope, tearing it with each new burst. Loud *pops* and *cracks* began to fill the room as the rope burned on either side, spreading to the middle. My feet were extremely hot, but I'd perfected a series of flips to keep myself off the rope as much as possible. The audience leapt out of their seats in worry, and began to shout for me to climb down, but I remained on the rope, flipping lazily across, as though I didn't notice.

As I landed a front flip, the rope broke in two, and I began to fall. Suddenly, I reached out and grasped the two pieces of the rope and held on tight. I was suspended in midair, the fireproof leather gloves protecting my palms from being burned. And when my body begged me to let go, my arms straining to hold me up, a lion roared. I bobbed up and down as Abbas's loud cry filled the chamber, making the guests gasp in awe.

Cassius slowly emerged from the back, walking Abbas on a leash made of chains. Bedecked in his usual onyx attire, with a small red handkerchief hanging out of his vest, he looked the image of authority. He strutted confidently to the middle of the stage where I hung, the muscles in my shoulders pulling excruciatingly, and just when I thought I couldn't take it anymore, Abbas lined up beneath me, and I breathed a sigh of relief. I let go, earning another gasp from the audience, and landed on top of Abbas's back. Fixing the gloves on my hands as though

I had done something simple, I watched the women in the audience physically melt when Cassius placed a hand on my thigh, the look in his eyes claiming that I was his.

The rest of the circus spun slowly on their heels toward us and bowed deeply to their king and queen. And when every head fell to the floor, the lights diminished.

At the conclusion of our performance, Mr. Monte stepped out from behind the curtain, earning a wave of applause. He settled them with a humble hand, and they quieted for his speech.

"Although our performances are mere acts, tonight was the exception. I want to congratulate our newly engaged couple, Juniper Rose and Cassius Plume!" Mr. Monte intended to continue, but the women in the crowd screamed. Actually screamed.

"It's real?" a woman shouted, placing a hand over her mouth in surprise.

Mr. Monte chuckled. "Yes, it's real. And we're so happy that all of you were here to celebrate with us. This will be the first wedding the circus has ever had, and we can't wait. Please join me in congratulating the soon to be Mr. and Mrs. Plume." Mr. Monte raised his hands and began to clap.

I dismounted Abbas to stand at Cassius's side, who was placing a hand over his heart. I couldn't control the smile that spread across my face, and when I looked into Cassius's eyes, I saw something there. Pride. By the gleam in his eyes, it was clear this is what he'd been looking for—respect. And he'd gotten it alright.

Chapter Forty-Three

Every paper in every kingdom wrote of my engagement to Cassius, predicting it would be the wedding of the year—an accomplishment to be compared to the array of wealthy couples joining hands.

But me and Cassius were different.

Our wedding would be simple, and we'd live a long and happy life together, continuing to perform for our audiences and never enduring the publicity others might receive, which was what peaked so much attention across the country.

Regardless of the world's opinions, it was the night before the wedding, and I was too excited to sit still. The bridesmaids' dresses were finished, but Valetta was working tirelessly to complete the last details on mine, sewing through the night in hopes of getting it done in time.

To distract myself, I searched for Mr. Monte to see how the preparations were coming along. Peeking into the dining room, I spotted a head of brown hair behind a tall pillar of flowers.

"Mr. Monte?"

He popped out above a sea of white tulips wearing a proud smile. "Ah, Juniper!" he exclaimed, coming to stand on the other side of the floral arrangements. "The florists are getting a pretty penny from us, that's for damn sure." He chuckled, a hint of worry in his tone. "The dining room is currently being transformed for the reception, and hopefully the weather looks up for tomorrow's service." He pondered over a checklist in his hand while biting the edge of his cheek.

"I know there's much to get done, but thank you for making this happen so quickly."

Mr. Monte smiled lovingly. "You're welcome, dear. I think Cassius is rather nervous. I saw him talking to himself this morning."

I laughed at the thought of Cassius pacing around his room, giving himself a pep-talk.

"Go check out the arbor. I'm sure you'll be impressed." Mr. Monte grabbed my shoulder and ushered me out of the room.

I was on my own because of the many things that still needed to be done, so I ventured out of the train toward the field. It was only the beginning of spring, which meant it would be a little nippy for a wedding, but at least it wasn't snowing. We wouldn't have green grass or flowers, but the decorating crew more than made up for that.

"Up!" Cassius grunted, joined by three riders, who hoisted the wooden arbor off the ground. The magicians, assisted by ladders on either side, carefully fastened white silk curtains that blew delicately in the wind, and a vine of ivy across the top with leaves descending beautifully.

Peeling my eyes away from the arbor, I noticed Cassius looking across the field in my direction. He shielded his eyes from the last rays of the setting sun and smiled gently, a sheen of sweat on his temple. I smiled in return and giddily sprung my own duties, feeling behind. My wedding was tomorrow after all, and there was much to be done.

"Shhh!" Charlotte hissed, pressing her ear to the door of the dining room. "Do you hear anything, Finley?" she asked.

Finley, the woman with her lips sewn shut, shook her head back and forth. Since she couldn't use her voice, her hearing had improved beyond what was considered normal.

"Let me try!" Scarlett pushed to the front of the group of kneeling girls and peered through the crack in the door to spy on the men inside.

It was my bachelorette party, but without the wild energy of the men who were preoccupied with Cassius's party, we didn't know exactly what to do. Spying on them seemed about our only option.

"Cassius's shirt is off!" Scarlett exclaimed.

"Let me see!" I pushed to my feet and peeked through the crack in the door. Cassius was indeed sitting in a wooden chair with his shirt off, and the men were seated around him. "What the hell is going on in there?" I whispered.

"What is it?" Evelyn huffed in a gruff voice.

I held up a hand to silence them while I listened closely.

"What's your first move, man?" Kai began, straightening his back and puffing out his chest.

Cassius deliberated seriously. "I'm thinking slow and sensual. Make her comfortable."

The men nodded in agreement while contemplating.

"What about the lights? Dim, dark, or on?" Gus twisted his mouth, as if this would make or break the experience.

"Hmm." Cassius looked to the floor in earnest, thinking hard. "On. I want to see her."

"Atta boy!" Hugh clapped him on the back, and the other men began to *hoot* and *holler*.

"Oh my gosh!" I exclaimed in a horrified whisper, turning to the ladies.

"What? What are they saying?" Olive exclaimed.

"They're talking about—" I looked at Evelyn, making the old woman clap her hands over Olive's and Piper's ears. "Me…in bed." My eyes widened in embarrassment.

"Oh, we'll give them something to talk about!" Charlotte exclaimed, pressing me up against the wall. "Juniper, don't worry, it's small!" she yelled far louder than she needed to.

If she kept it up, they'd overhear us, so I began to hush her until she urged me to join in. She *wanted* them to hear us.

"What do you mean?" I shouted.

"Small…as in it won't hurt!" Scarlett contributed.

And indeed, all noise on the other side of the door ceased.

"Oh, thank the Lord!" I swooned. "But how small are we talking?" Then I thought of something that would really make them mad. "Tell me when to stop." I placed my hands about a foot apart and slowly drew them closer together. It was such a vulgar game, but I knew it would get to Cassius. "Here?" I asked, my hands about eight inches apart. "No?" I asked when my hands were five inches apart. "You've got to be kidding." I let out a huff of a laugh just as three inches neared.

Suddenly the door ripped open, and Cassius stood on the threshold with his eyes fuming and his nostrils flared. The other men's jaws hit the floor when they spotted my hands only an inch apart.

"About that small." Daisy nodded with a pitying look.

"Is that so, Daisy?" Cassius puffed, turning to her maniacally. "How about we talk about the mole right next to your—"

"Okay! That's quite enough!" Charlotte yelled, stopping him before he could say something that'd make us uncomfortable.

"I don't think it is," Cassius said in a low voice as he grabbed my waist and slung me over his shoulder.

"Help!" I screamed to the girls, and they raced in after me before being taken by the other men.

Flint grasped Charlotte from behind and lifted her against his chest, while her legs flailed back and forth.

"You're disrupting our bachelorette party. No boys allowed, remember?" Charlotte screamed.

"You ruined our bachelor party by *spying* on us!" Cassius spit.

"Calm down, it was just a game!" I complained, continuing to pound on Cassius's back in protest.

He slowly pulled me off his shoulder and onto his waist, forcing me to hook my legs around his hips. "A game huh? Why don't we play another game?" He leaned forward, and his lips crashed against mine as he swirled his tongue in my mouth.

His headiness made me gasp, but my lips had never moved faster. I was so eager to taste all of him that I could barely wait for tomorrow.

"Hey!" Olive shouted below us, slapping at Cassius's legs and making him jump. "Don't ya even think about it!" she scolded him.

Cassius looked down at her with a confused smile.

"Don't you give me dat look! I know what your filthy mind is thinking." She squinted, as if peering into his soul, and poked him with an accusatory finger.

He set me down reluctantly and put his hands up in the air, caught by the little girl.

Charlotte raced over to me looking disheveled, with her hair teased above her head and her dress shifted across her body. "This is getting out of control!" she yelled over the voices carrying in the room.

She was right. Every woman was on the lap of a man. This wasn't what I had expected to happen, and one look from Cassius made it clear he hadn't either.

"Ladies!" I announced.

"Gentlemen!" Cassius proclaimed. "Tomorrow will be a celebratory day where this revelry will be completely encouraged. Restrain yourselves." The look on his face was full of disgust.

The men were a riot, sure, but I was supposed to spend my bachelorette party with the ladies, so I was grateful when they rushed to my side.

"Let's grab some drinks and talk more gossip about how big that might—" I quickly glanced down to Cassius's groin before his hand flew to cover my mouth.

He glared at me, daring me to continue. Slowly removing his hand to replace it with his lips, he kissed me softly. But before I could get lost in his touch, I pulled away and followed the women out of the room.

Just then, Charlotte whipped her arms out of her robe, revealing two bottles of whiskey. "Stole it from the boys," she said, in answer to my surprise. She raised a bottle in salute as she said, "To your last night as a free woman!"

"And to a lifetime of regret," I joked, clinking my bottle against Charlotte's and tipping my head back.

Chapter Forty-Four

Many years ago...

"Daddy!" A little girl with dark tendrils curling around her ears and a little bow on her temple ran to the large man standing in the doorway.

"My little Juniper!" Setting down his briefcase, he scooped the little girl into the air and set her on his hip.

She wrapped her arms around his neck and hugged him tightly. The way her little body molded into his arms made it seem as though it might be the last time.

"My, my, what's gotten into you?" he asked gently.

Juniper took after her father, with his dark curls, wide smile, and pale skin.

"I met a boy today," Juniper commented haughtily, pushing the curls out of her face with sticky little fingers.

Her father swayed back and forth, unwilling to her go. "Ah, I see. And is this man worthy of your attention?" he inquired with an arched brow. "Is he kind, loving, and devoted?"

For a little girl, these were rather in-depth questions. Juniper squirmed in his arms and bit at her lip, deep in thought. "Well, yes. I seem to think so!" She came upon the conclusion suddenly, with a sure nod. "I'm going to marry him!" she triumphed.

Her father let out a huff of a laugh that resounded deep in his lungs. "My dear, you will marry many years down the road, when you are ready. You must be patient, but when that day comes, I will be right by your side," he whispered and kissed her on the cheek.

Juniper's father was a gentle soul, present when her mother couldn't be, which was often. She loved her father dearly and dreamed of the day she would walk down the aisle with him, her arm linked in his. But her father's promises that morning would never hold true, because that was the last day she ever saw him.

As morning dawned, the practice tents flapped in the brisk breeze, and a quiet calm set over the idle train. The rising sun shined on the growing grass, slick with dew, and warmed the air as the performers awoke for a celebratory day.

As the birds began chirping sweetly, my eyes fluttered open and I glanced around my bedroom—something that had become so foreign to me. I hadn't slept in my own quarters for quite some time, but I was following tradition in not allowing Cassius to see me until the ceremony began.

As I was dreaming about the excitement of the day, Charlotte and Valetta burst through the room. Valetta was breathing laboriously, her chest heaving up and down as though she'd run all the way here. And laying across her arm was my dress, the contents concealed in a white bag.

"I stayed up all night, but it's finished," she said through gasps.

I couldn't seem to move as I imagined stepping into that dress and walking down the aisle on my most special day.

But Charlotte took the liberty of ripping the sheets off my body. "Well don't just sit there! We've got lots of work to do." She twiddled her finger at my sleepy figure, and I eagerly hopped up, ready to begin.

"Take this, you're going to need it." Gus offered Cassius a glass full of ale.

Cassius took it with shaking hands and downed the contents, ordering Wilman to grab him another. He was a wreck. He'd stayed up all night thinking about the morning's festivities. The circus had never hosted a wedding, but it was more than that. Never in a million years, did Cassius think *he* would marry. He'd been thrown into a life he wasn't prepared for, and even though he'd found comfort in the circus, he also feared being alone.

When Penelope passed, Cassius worried he'd never be happy again, but the possibility of making Juniper his family made everything feel right again. He'd have a friend by his side through everything—and not just any friend—one he hadn't been able to get out of his head since the moment he laid eyes on her.

Wilman walked over with another glass of ale, which Cassius slowly sipped this time. Finally taking his eyes off the floor, he nodded at Hugh, who retrieved a plain black vest and opened it so Cassius could fit his arms through.

Pulling it over his shoulders, he began fastening the buttons with shaky hands. Gus moved to help him don a bowtie while Flint carried over a pair of shiny black shoes. Within an hour, Cassius had readied himself, only to be interrupted by more important matters.

"Stop primping your hair like a girl and get to writing your vows." Mr. Monte pranced into the room, already dressed in a fine waistcoat.

With a scoff, Cassius snatched the small piece of parchment from Mr. Monte. Sitting down, he grabbed a quill and let it hang over the piece of paper. Having written nothing, he threw it in irritation and watched it clatter across the table. "What the hell even is a vow? What am I supposed to write?"

"None of us have done this before. Why are you asking us?" Flint scoffed.

Mr. Monte paced back and forth with a finger to his bottom lip, trying to figure out how to explain it. Turning to Cassius he said, "A vow is a proclamation of love. And you don't have to be sappy, but you both had a difficult journey. Talk about that—losing each other, comforting each other in times of need, and learning to love each other."

He curled his fingers into a tight fist and closed his eyes. "I'm not good with words."

"That's why we're here to help." Hugh came to sit next to Cassius. "What do you think when you see Juniper?" he implored.

Before he knew it, the group of men sprung forth with a multitude of questions to help him craft his speech, and for the next hour, Cassius wrote feverishly to get the words onto the page.

After he finished, he made one last stop before the ceremony began. Walking briskly down the corridor of the train, his heart beating out of his chest, he noticed that despite the help of his friends, he was entirely too nervous. When had he changed his mind on the idea of marriage? Ever since he could remember, he'd thought promising yourself to someone for life was foolish. And now, he was changing every preconception he had for a girl.

She's not just any girl, a delicate female voice whispered to Cassius as soon as he reached the threshold of Penelope's chambers.

Pushing through the door, he was welcomed by the familiar scent of dust and the ghostly white sheets splayed across every surface, clotting the memory of his sister. "No. She's not," he spoke aloud, closing the door behind him. He could feel his sister's warmth in the air, smell her perfume as though she were standing next to him. He looked up to the ceiling with his hands on his hips. "But you know how this goes for people like us. We begin to feel happy…safe even, and then it's torn away. How can I let that happen?"

You are misled, brother. People like us *are not only subject to unhappiness. Many things in life happen for a reason—some good, some bad—but they lead us to where we're meant to be.* She paused for a moment, the echo of her voice filling the room. *Do you believe that you're where you're meant to be?* The pitch of her voice raised into a question before it faded once again.

Eager to hear her voice—to not lose her, Cassius answered almost instantly, "Yes."

Hmm, she hummed. *Then it seems you have nothing to worry about. I'll be right there with you, Cas.*

Her voice faded once and for all, making Cassius leap into the middle of the room. "Penelope?" he asked desperately, needing more of her sisterly advice, but she was gone.

"Take a deep breath," Charlotte cooed, urging me to relax.

I let my shoulders fall and breathed in through my nose. Standing behind the train, fitted in my gown with a bouquet of flowers in hand, I listened to the rest of the circus take their seats. And Cassius was just on the other side waiting.

"I'm going to take a seat. But when you hear the music, just start walking. When you see Cassius, everything will be okay." She held onto my arm as though I might fall over, before leaving me.

I shook my sweaty palms, but before I could even think about my worry, the band struck a low chord. This was the rest of my life—a lifetime with Cassius and with the circus. I didn't have to ponder how big a commitment it was. I wanted this. I wanted *him*.

I took a deep breath, blinked away my fear, and lifted the edge of my dress. My heels sank into the dirt, and as I curved around the side of the train, everyone came into view. The entire circus stood to their feet and turned over their shoulders to look at me, gasping.

Valetta had done a beautiful job. The top of the gown was fitted with a sweetheart neckline, and small, transparent sleeves fell off my shoulders, billowing romantically in the wind. With an A-line silhouette, the skirt fell from my waist to the floor delicately. The fabric was made up of Charmeuse, a type of silk with a glossy sheen that made it glisten in the sunlight. A line of buttons trailed down my back, all the way to the end of the train that flowed several feet behind me, and a lace veil sat at the crown of my head with flowers woven into the tulle.

The performers were dressed in their finest clothes, men in colorful suits and bowties, and ladies in floor length dresses of varying designs. Meanwhile, the field was just beginning to bloom a bright green with the warmth of spring on its way. White chairs were arranged in rows, with fresh strings of ivy placed on either side of the aisle, and a long strip of white silk was laid down to serve as a walkway. At the very end, a wooden arbor stood high, the sun lighting the strings of ivy draped across the fixture, and a priest stood waiting with his hands folded over a bible.

At last, I saw Cassius, with his eyes wide in awe and a sweet smile pulling his lips apart. He wore a fitted white shirt and a double-breasted waistcoat with two rows of buttons lining his chest. Around his neck was a dark blue cravat, tucked into his shirt. He stood confidently, with shiny leather shoes donning his feet and his hands folded behind his back.

As I stepped onto the aisle, I paused. I was really doing this. I was getting married.

I will be right by your side, my father's warm voice filled my head, and I closed my eyes to remember him. But no matter how hard I tried to summon him, he wasn't here to keep me from falling.

Looking to my right and left, I began to panic, searching for someone to help me down the aisle. My father was supposed to be here, but he'd given me away a long time ago. It hadn't mattered to him to stay, and his promise to be by my side on the most important day of my life had been a lie. My knees became weak, and my feet felt heavy in my heels. How would I make it down the aisle on my own?

Sensing my worry, Mr. Monte slipped out of the crowd and rushed to my side. He linked my arm through his and held my hand tightly, and looking at his gentle smile, I didn't feel so alone. My lip trembled as I tried to thank him, but he only tipped his head at me, the hair curled behind his ears rippling in the wind.

"I've got you, my dear," he whispered with a pat of my hand.

I've got you. It seemed that was all I needed to look toward my future husband and smile, so excited to begin our life together. Step by step, comfort and safety settled over me, and I was happier than I'd ever been.

When we reached the end of the aisle, Mr. Monte gave me a tight hug and took his seat.

Charlotte and the rest of the dancers stood at the altar, including little Olive clad in a lavender dress. And on Cassius's left were some of the riders and firebreathers, the most surprising being Flint in a dapper suit.

My heart pounded out of my chest as I handed Charlotte my bouquet, but she only smiled, crinkles forming under her eyes as she mouthed, "You got this."

Cassius extended a hand, his palm open and steady. Electricity coursed through my fingers when I touched him, and just looking at him made my nerves vanish. He giggled, his cheeks a similar nervous pink.

"Thank you all for gathering here today to join Cassius Plume and Juniper Rose," the priest began formally. "Cassius, you may begin sharing your vows with Juniper."

Cassius blinked rapidly and I squeezed his hands to reassure him. He looked up to me then with a pause, something so sure flickering in his eyes, and began. "You all know I'm not good with words, but I'm going to try my best." He cleared his throat, and his eyes darted around quickly as he tried to remember what he'd written hours ago. "Juniper, when I first met you, I loathed you."

The audience laughed, remembering our disdain for one another.

"I thought you were a prude, but you surprised me when you stayed in the circus, despite my every attempt to force you out. You showed diligence and perseverance, and…perfection," he stumbled over his words. "I first fell in love with you because of your kindness toward us. You were never ashamed of us, and that meant the world to me." He took a breath to steady his wavering voice before continuing, "When you left, I lost a part of myself, and I didn't realize until you were gone how much I needed you." When his eyes began to water, I started to shake at the honesty of his words. "You were always there, understanding me for who I was, and never quitting when it got hard, and I can't say that many people have done that for me." He took a moment to think over his next words, before quietly saying, "The circus has been the only home I've ever known, but when I…when I'm with you…that's where I'm truly at home. I am so excited to know you for the rest of my life," he finished.

Tears trailed down my cheeks, and the back of my throat burned.

"You loathed me, but that night I boarded the train, I was afraid of you. You were a mystery, but that only made me want to learn everything there was to know about you. And it was difficult. You pushed me away time and time again, when all I wanted was to be close to you—to really know you. Sure, I hated you sometimes." The crowd chuckled once again. "But it was impossible not to fall in love you, because after everything that happened in your life, you're more passionate than anyone I've ever met. You make me feel safe and protected, and you love *hard*." I smiled and took a breath. "You are half of me, and I'm certain I cannot live without you."

He wore a proud smile, tears welling in his eyes.

"You have found a love like no other," the priest commented with a smile. "Cassius, please repeat after me."

Cassius nodded promptly, not taking his eyes off me as he recited the priest's words. "I, Cassius Plume, take you, Juniper Rose, to be my wife. To have and to hold from this day forward, for better or worse, for richer or poorer, in sickness and in health, to love and to cherish, until we are parted by death."

Those words seemed to break something inside of me. To be with someone in every way humanly possible, through every trial and every celebration, was something I'd yearned for and feared I'd never have. And here he was, the man of my dreams, vowing to never leave me.

I then followed the priest's instruction and repeated his words, crying through them, but meaning them with every ounce of my being. The ceremony was short, but the distance between us seemed to go on forever…I just needed to hold him and cry for a moment.

And finally, the priest motioned to Cassius. "I now pronounce you husband and wife. You may kiss the bride."

The audience leapt out of their seats, clapping and shouting with jubilation.

Meanwhile, Cassius grabbed my face in both of his palms, closed his eyes, and pressed his lips to mine. The cheers faded, and all I could focus on was the boy holding me so tightly—how his hands cupped my cheeks, wiping away the tears, and how his lips brushed over mine like a whisper. He would be by my side always—to comfort me, to love me, and to challenge me. And I would do the same for him. We were one now, and neither of us would ever have to suffer the pain of being alone.

"Ladies and gentlemen, it's my pleasure to introduce Mr. and Mrs. Plume!" the priest exclaimed, and the entire circus leapt onto the stage to congratulate us. I hooked my arms around Charlotte, who squealed in my ear and shook me back and forth. I couldn't have been more grateful for her.

The crowd suddenly parted, and Cassius arrived, holding two of the firebreathers like brothers, his arms strung around them. "Who's ready to get some drinks, huh?" he shouted, the whites of his teeth almost blinding as he smiled.

Chapter Forty-Five

I paid a reporter to photograph the ceremony so we would have something to remember it by, but also because I wanted it published in every newspaper. It delighted me that my mother would finally understand that she failed and that I was happy.

"Can I have the couple stand in front of the altar?" the reporter asked, a chunky camera hanging from a brown leather strap around his neck. He was a slim fellow with sandy hair that fell in front of his eyes sloppily, and his clothes were rather disheveled, perhaps because he'd been traveling all day for work.

The performers had already gone inside to begin setting up for the reception, which meant it was just us two. I sidled up next to Cassius and placed my hand on his chest to showcase the beautiful ring on my finger.

"A little to the right." The camera man centered us under the arbor, with the ivy strands hanging above our heads. Lifting the camera to his face, he squinted against the thick mechanism, and *snap.*

"Perfect!" he proclaimed, already stuffing the camera into his bag. "The report will be in the newspaper in a few days, and I'll send a few copies your way."

"Thank you," I said, watching as he made his way across the field back toward the city. I turned into Cassius's chest then and nuzzled into him, not ready to go inside just yet.

He seemed to read my thoughts when he said, "It'll be fun to celebrate with everyone, but I won't lie...I can't stop thinking about being alone with you." He kissed my forehead gently, letting his lips linger.

I watched his lips separate as he pulled away to look at me, his golden irises focusing.

"Me too," I responded, my stomach already twirling at the thought. I pulled on his waistcoat, straightening the lapels over his chest. "But until then, let's go have some fun."

When Cassius and I entered the dining room, my breath was taken away. The tables were adorned with small bouquets of flowers and tealights. Strings of faerie lights hung from every wall, showering the room with endless bits of light. While Wilman worked behind the bar, sending out pint after pint of ale, platters of roasted chicken paired with pails of potatoes and vegetables were served. It was the finest feast the circus had enjoyed in a long time.

"Welcome, Mr. and Mrs. Plume!" Mr. Monte announced, and when he did, the dancers turned around in their seats and showered us with rose petals.

We both laughed as Cassius turned to pluck petals out of my hair. Of all the times I'd looked at him, I'd never seen him so full of joy, so content. When he caught me gazing at him, he looped an arm around my waist and pulled me close for a kiss.

Facing the performers after our kiss broke, I asked, "Can we eat something now?"

The entire crew eagerly grabbed their plates to dish up, and after everyone was seated, I approached the bar and grabbed Wilman's hand. "Take a break for a while. We can manage to grab our own drinks tonight." I pulled him out of the bar and offered him a plate of food.

"Thank ya, miss." He nodded his head decidedly before hurrying off.

Wilman was the one to help me board the train almost two years ago—the one that introduced me to everyone and helped me to fit in, despite how scared I was. He led me to Cassius. Suddenly, a wave of nostalgia swept over me. If someone told me I'd be marrying Cassius a year ago, I would've laughed in their face.

Stories of Cassius and me were passed around as we ate, and I caught Evelyn slapping Cassius across the back of the head after hearing the things he'd said to me. The men attempted to hide their chuckles behind large fists, but I laughed along with them, none too bothered by what had happened in the past.

The laughter ceased and every head turned when Flint clanged a fork against his glass, standing to raise a toast. "To the newlyweds!" he exclaimed with a dip of his head. "Juniper, you have always been a close friend. You are kind and passionate, and you know what you want. Although I don't understand why you would want that *oaf*," Flint looked to Cassius with a confused look before continuing, "I support the two of you, and I hope that you and I, Cassius, can come to be friends."

"That's never going to happen, big guy." Cassius shook his head and downed his drink.

Flint just rolled his eyes. When I tried to change Cassius's mind, he launched into an emphatic argument about Flint's audacity, but I listened intently, never tiring of it.

"It's time for cake, I think!" Mr. Monte exclaimed, moving to the back of the room to retrieve a two-tiered cake.

Cassius looked up in wonder, his eyes widening and his mouth quirking as though he'd never seen the delicacy.

I grabbed his arm and whispered, "You look like a little kid on their birthday."

"I never celebrated my birthday growing up," he said nonchalantly, but not in a depressing way. "I've never had cake before." He almost sounded embarrassed.

My jaw dropped. "Never?" How could a child never have a birthday party, let alone not be acknowledged for *having* a birthday?

He shook his head, but he looked excited to try the sweet cake. As is tradition for the wedding couple, I offered him his first bite. He looked confused, but opened his mouth gently and closed his lips around it. He closed his eyes as it melted in his mouth, but whipped back in surprise when I smeared more frosting along his chin. He was unphased as his tongue flicked out to gather the excess frosting from his bottom lip.

I turned my head to laugh with the others, but when I looked back at him, he had a handful of cake waiting for me, and he made sure to get me back in good fashion.

After wiping our faces clean, we watched the other performers devour their slices, talking amongst themselves about the rich flavor. Soon enough, the tables were cleared away to open the dancefloor. Without any prompting, everyone was hopping and skipping to the beat of the drums. It was a little difficult for me in my wedding dress, so Cassius and I danced slowly in the center like no one was watching.

"I forgot to mention how beautiful you look," he whispered in my ear as I laid my head on his chest.

"Thank you," I whispered. "You look like quite the gentleman yourself."

"And I'm uncomfortable," he scoffed, messing with the cravat at his neck. "How do noblemen wear this all day?"

I wiggled the cravat to loosen it. "Maybe suffocation is why they turn out to be pompous assholes."

Cassius and I giggled together before Charlotte snagged me out of his arms with a big smile on her face. "It's time!" She giggled excitedly.

Following her exclamation, Hugh and Gus struck Cassius on the back firmly. "Let's get moving!"

They pushed him forward, and in a moment's notice, Cassius was whisked off to his bed chamber, and I to Charlotte's room. It was tradition to primp before such an intimate evening between a man and his wife.

Charlotte slammed the door shut after the dancers flooded into the cramped room, and when they took off my dress, she led me to the sink and lifted my arms above my head, grabbing a small knife on the counter.

"What are you doing?" I screamed and scurried away.

"Don't worry, I'm not going to hurt you. It's a technique the ladies and I have learned. You can shave off the hair on your arms and legs, making your skin soft!" Her eyes widened in excitement.

The dancers behind her nodded their heads in confirmation. A wave of nausea swept over me as I looked at myself in the mirror. I wanted to be perfect for Cassius. So, with that, I let them have their way.

Charlotte began scraping the hair from my armpits and my legs, and when she finished, Raelynn and Raegan oiled them to give them a glossy sheen. Evelyn then took out the many pins tying my hair up and brushed out the curls to let them fall on my shoulders. Charlotte grabbed a tiny set of undergarments, so tiny they would barely cover my intimates.

My shocked expression led her to say, "Tonight you will give Cassius everything. Don't worry, they'll be off before you know it."

She was right, but why did it make me so nervous, thinking about laying bare before Cassius? I tried to remain calm as I stepped into a pair of silk night shorts trimmed with lace. Charlotte then strapped a matching bralette across my chest, its cupped lining lifting my breasts. She tied the straps on my shoulders in two delicate bows and draped a blue silk robe across my shoulders.

"All done!" she exclaimed, stepping away with pride.

I let out a shaky breath. Yes, Cassius and I were married now, which meant I could trust him with every part of me, but I was more nervous than I had been walking down the aisle.

Charlotte grabbed my shoulders with a knowing look. "You and Cassius will learn together, and you'll find things that work well for both of you. You don't have to get it right the first time." She shrugged her shoulders before turning me toward the mirror at the end of the room. "You look beautiful."

And I did. My hair flowed freely, framing my face, and my bare legs poked out from under the robe, glowing in the candlelight. The little ensemble I wore accentuated my thin waist, the roundness of my hips, and the fullness of my breasts. I looked…sexy, and I was excited for Cassius's reaction.

"Have fun tonight," Evelyn said, her wisdom calming me. "Show that man what he's got!" She spanked me on the bottom, making me yelp.

She was right. This was supposed to be fun. But when I opened the door, the ladies' reassurance vanished because all the guys stood waiting for me. Instinctively, I tightened the robe around my waist.

I found Cassius in the middle of the throng, being pushed around violently by the other men. He wore a happy smile, clad in breeches and a loose shirt. I froze when I saw him with his suspenders tight across his chest, accentuating his muscles.

He walked confidently toward me with his lips parted and his curls hanging in front of his face. His eyes trailed down my body, lingering on my bare waist and the curve of my breasts. I couldn't help my cheeks from heating as he snaked an arm around my waist, his fingers tickling the small of my back.

"Alright, alright!" Cassius stopped the cheering with a raised hand as we stood in front of his room. "You can all continue to celebrate elsewhere, but if I see any feet peeking under the door, I'll come out and beat you." He raised his eyebrows, daring them to question him.

The men rolled their eyes as if their night had been ruined, before trudging off to the dining room, while the women followed behind, winking at me on their way out.

Cassius pushed open his door, and the familiar sight of his bed, the rugs covering the floor, and the oak dressers put me at ease. I'd been here before. I was comfortable here. I had nothing to worry about.

"Finally, I can hear!" Cassius exclaimed when he closed the door behind him.

My ears were still ringing from the constant noise, but the quiet seemed almost *too* quiet. I didn't know what to do with myself—how to stand or what to say. So, I stood there awkwardly, hoping Cassius would pick up the conversation, but even he appeared nervous.

He paced the length of the room and motioned for me to take a seat at the foot of the bed. "Do you want a drink?" he asked, not meeting my eyes.

"Yes," I responded quietly.

Our hands grazed as he handed me my drink, sending tingles up my arm. "This is weird, isn't it?" I asked, hoping to relieve the obvious tension.

"Yes," he laughed. "I've never had to wait before."

"Of course, you didn't. You're Cassius Plume. You get what you want," I commented, not knowing why. There was no point in making him feel bad about the past.

But he surprised me by saying, "I do, don't I? I got you."

I smirked, grateful he hadn't taken offense. I loved when he spoke so confidently about us because it meant he wanted me as I'd always wanted him. Voice shaking, I said, "I'm scared. I've never done this before."

"There's nothing to be afraid of." Cassius rose from his seat to stand in front of me, snaking an arm around my waist and rubbing at the soft silk.

"That's what Charlotte told me," I huffed, taking a small sip of my drink. Comforted by his touch and the warmth of the drink as it traveled to my stomach, my nerves were beginning to calm.

"You spoke to her about it?" Cassius laughed.

"What was I to do?" I whined, my cheeks blooming a nervous pink. "I'm new to this!"

"I'm not scolding you; I only think it's cute." Cassius leaned forward and pecked me on the lips unexpectedly, and when he pulled away, he almost seemed embarrassed.

He took a step back, but I grabbed his shirt and pulled him closer to me, kissing him in return. I had been waiting for months, years even, to feel connected to someone in this way. I'd been playing it out in my mind for months...the feel of his skin against mine, giving into our raw instincts and being totally satisfied, with nothing left to need or want.

"I want you," he admitted, gently kissing my cheek down to my jaw. He hummed as he tasted the residue of icing on my skin. "You taste sweet." His voice vibrated on my throat, making my shiver.

I took a step forward, forcing him back, and step after step, we inched closer to the bed. Finally, I took his drink and set it down. We'd waited far too long for this and there was no use in delaying it. I needed him.

When we reached the bed, his eyes didn't leave mine as he loosened the tie of my robe. His calloused fingers brushed it from my shoulders, and he watched as it fell at my feet. His eyes roved over my body as he inspected every inch of skin.

Suddenly feeling embarrassed, I crossed my hands over my stomach, which prompted him to squint in concern. This was the most Cassius had ever seen of me, and I had no idea what he thought. But he grabbed my hands and placed them on his chest, allowing me to grow comfortable in my own time.

"Relax," he encouraged with a rhythmic nod of his head.

He kissed me once again, his tongue moving slowly in my mouth. My head was fuzzy with his hands on my bare waist, and a fire spread over my skin. Without thinking, I removed the suspenders from his shoulders, slowly sliding my hands across his shirt until they dropped down to his waist.

"There you go," he encouraged me with a low, husky whisper.

I smiled against his lips, and slowly drew my fingertips down the bit of his chest that was exposed under his open shirt.

"Take it off," he whispered.

With his instructions, I could do this. And I liked it, being told what to do—being under his control. I hoped one day I'd feel confident enough to make my own decisions in our bed, but until then, I needed his help.

I followed his command by grabbing the bottom of his shirt, untucking it from his pants, and lifting it over his head. He took a step back and kicked his boots to the side hastily.

It was as though I was seeing him for the very first time. His chest was golden in the candlelight, the ridges in his torso were like mountains and valleys, and the muscles in his shoulders were rounded and firm. Suddenly my eyes caught on his pants hanging low on his hips, revealing the lines pointing to his groin. He was strong but soft, and I couldn't help reaching out to run my hands down his chest.

He winced at the cold touch of my fingers but allowed me to continue, studying my eyes, then my mouth for what seemed like an eternity, before moving to my breasts. They didn't appear as attractive when suffocated under my leotards every day, but seeing them in the light, suspended by the bralette Charlotte loaned me, made his eyes darken.

Something primal seemed to awaken in him then, the need to ease an ache that had been festering. It was as though electromagnetic waves were pulling us into each other. His lips crashed onto mine at the same time his hand cupped my breast, kneading the pliable, soft skin.

But it wasn't enough. I needed him to touch every inch of me. As if he'd read my mind, he pulled the bow on my shoulder loose and watched the strings fall, letting out a breathy sigh as my breasts came into full view, my nipples peaked against the cool air. His wide eyes held a dangerous promise as he looked up at me and pinched my nipples between his calloused fingertips, gooseflesh trickling up my arms at his brazen movements.

Every thought eddied out of my mind when he grasped my jaw and moved it to the side to send a trail of wet kisses down my neck. I was a writhing mess when he nipped at the sensitive skin behind my ear and pulled back to lick at the small hurt. I grasped his shoulder hard, silently asking for more than these tantalizing touches.

He seemed to understand my plea when he unfastened the buckle on my back and tossed the bra to the floor. With our bare chests pressed together, we stood there for a moment with no inhibition.

He stepped back, and I stood tentatively as he gazed at all of me. It must have been minutes that he took it all in, but when he moved to me, I grabbed at the belt on his waist and eagerly undid it. He looked at me like I was a different person before a smile came over him.

When he slid one finger into the waistband of my shorts, I groaned. "Stop teasing." I grabbed his hand and forced him to pull down my night shorts.

He returned my confidence by grabbing my hips and spinning me around quickly, so my backside was pressed against him. The air left my lungs when I felt a rise in his undergarments, something firm pressing into me. I had the urge to lean into him further—to feel more of him—and warmth blossomed in my core as he spread his hand across the flat planes of my stomach, pulling me into him.

He let his head fall into my neck and sighed in pleasure, his chest contracting behind me, as if he'd been deprived of this for far too long.

"Every day you pass me, I can smell you," he drawled lazily. "You smell sweet, like vanilla and cinnamon."

I was surprised he paid such close attention to me. I'd memorized his smell from our first conversation—musky, like mahogany, yet fresh like pine.

He kissed the base of my neck and I grabbed at his hair, eager to hold onto something. The tedious touching and lingering were making me tremble.

With such apprehension, I couldn't wait any longer. When I spun around to face him, he was already urging me onto the bed, so I laid flat on my back with my body open to him.

This was it. This was the moment I'd yearned for. I was with the man I loved, and nothing would be hidden between us. It began with our bodies, but it transcended into something deeper. Starting today, I would be his and he would be mine.

I looked up at him with hopeful eyes, pleading with him to do something.

Cassius's chest heaved up and down before he leaned in and kissed me gently, as though he was afraid of being too rough. He grabbed my hips tenderly and I felt like I was melting before him. And if I did, I wouldn't care. I would be consumed in his fire if it meant that I could belong to him in every way.

"Are you okay?" he asked, his eyes glossed over.

"Yes," I whispered. Taking his hand, I locked our fingers together and opened my legs beneath him. "Have me. Have all of me."

Chapter Forty-Six

I grasped the sheets below me and clung to the curls on Cassius's head, the black whisps locked within my fingers as his head disappeared between my legs. His quick tongue made my thighs quiver, and I tilted my head up to the ceiling, trying to contain the noises that were desperate to escape. The delicate sensation of his soft tongue was so tedious I nearly came undone, but still, I grabbed his hair harder to move his head faster.

And when he snickered below me, the low timbre of his laugh hummed against my center. When my legs began to shake, Cassius crawled over me until his face appeared above mine, his mouth wet and covered in *me*. I grabbed his jaw and brought his lips to mine, shoving my tongue into his mouth and arching my back into his body.

But it wasn't enough. Our sloppy kissing and our wet tongues darting around in this drunk dance wasn't enough.

I needed all of him.

I reached for his undergarments and pushed them down his hips, and what little air I had left vanished when he was completely bare before me. I stared at it for a moment, unsure of what to do. I hadn't expected it to be that big, but before he could say anything, I reached down to touch it.

Grabbing it gently in my palm, I stroked it up and down a few times, earning a sigh from Cassius, the hard muscles in his back contorting.

His glazed eyes locked on mine pleadingly when he said, "Honey, you can grab it harder. You're not going to hurt me."

He chuckled, but I could see how worked up he was—how much he needed this.

So, I swallowed my nerves and tried again, my hands moving tentatively. I wanted to make him feel good, but I wasn't sure how.

And sensing my anxiety, Cassius put his hand over mine. "Don't be nervous," he encouraged. He kissed both of my cheeks, but instead of asking me to continue, he opened my legs and laid between them.

I looked down at my body, wondering what he was thinking. Did I look sexy in this position? Was he angry that I couldn't please him? But before I could become too insecure, Cassius gently grabbed my jaw and made me look at him, and the sparkle I found in his eyes made me loosen up. I needed to relax. I needed to just *feel*.

As he attempted to slide inside of me, I took a deep breath, the warm tip feeling too big already. He pushed further, but the pain prevented me from feeling any pleasure, and when it became too much, I grabbed at his arm. "Wait."

By the sweat gleaming on my forehead and the nail marks in his arms, he quickly pulled out. I sighed in defeat, hoping this wouldn't be the course for the rest of the evening.

"Let me try something," he said, looking at me as if asking a question.

I nodded my head vigorously and closed my eyes, expecting the same burning sensation I felt a moment ago. But suddenly something small and warm filled me. I opened my eyes to find Cassius's fingers inside of me, moving slowly, in and out, curling to touch the most sensitive spots. The pain was gone, and I could feel that tight knot in my core beginning to unfurl.

Looking up, I reached out for him—for something to hold on to. He found my hand and grabbed it tightly as a moan escaped. My stomach tightened and my center felt hot around his fingers—like I might burst if he added any more pressure.

"Please," I pleaded, to stop him from continuing.

He nodded his head before lining up with me once again, and this time he entered me easily. I watched in wonder as his hips connected with my thighs. Every stroke was smoother, and I could feel myself slowly falling apart as I clutched his back.

He bit his lip as his chest heaved up and down and his hips moved in a rhythmic, circular motion. His eyes were glossy as he watched me pant, and he lowered his body over mine to kiss me. I moaned into his mouth as my body buzzed with electricity.

"Faster," I begged him between kisses.

He smiled and drew away so he could pump his hips faster. With the distance between us, he drew his hands up my breasts and began to massage them, rolling my nipples in between his fingers.

"Cassius," I blurted, my legs beginning to shake.

He took this as a sign and slowed down so that I felt every move he made, every part of him—so that I could savor all the sensations at once. It was euphoric to feel so full and complete and alive, and I grabbed his forearm to hold myself together just a little while longer.

"I want to see more of you," he said, pulling out to lay on his back. Grabbing my hand, he pulled me on top of him, and I gasped then, my eyes flaring at how deep he was inside of me. He kept his hands on my hips and moved me back and forth. Seeing that I was exhausted and out of breath, he leaned up so I could wrap my arms around his shoulders.

"Holy shit," Cassius groaned in my ear and slammed into me.

"Keep going." I let my head fall into his shoulder as I grabbed at his back, my nails digging into his skin.

I was close to crying it felt so good. The knot in my center had grown tighter, ready to pop, and as I drew back to look at Cassius, the sight of his mouth wide open and the damp curls on his forehead did me in. He nodded his head, as if allowing me to finish, and all at once the pressure in my center exploded. Everything went quiet suddenly, and when I closed my eyes, all I could see were stars. He pressed me to his chest and slowly rolled his hips while I rode out my high. Meanwhile, his face twisted, and his mouth popped open, and before I knew it, he was pulling out and expelling a stream onto my stomach.

Seeing the sweat dripping down his brow, I felt so accomplished. I giggled excitedly and looked up at him with a gleam in my eyes. He looked exhausted with the heat in his cheeks, but a smile pulled at his mouth regardless.

He let his body fall back as he looked up at the ceiling. "Come here," he ordered, opening his arm so I could lay with him.

I rested my head against his chest and felt the drumming of his heart slow. There we were, lying naked with one another, our limbs tangled together. I felt complete, connected to Cassius in a way I could never have imagined.

I closed my eyes happily, my entire body still wriggling with energy.

Cassius moved to rest a hand against my stomach, and I curled into his chest. Before I knew it, we were asleep.

Last night was a dream. We had continued until we no longer could, only resuming in the early morning when our naked bodies touched in the darkness. I thought my yearning would lessen once we laid together, but it only seemed to grow. Now that I knew what it felt like, I never wanted to stop.

Cassius rustled next to me, and slowly peeled open his eyes. With a big yawn, he turned to me. "Shall we go again?" he whispered in my ear, with notes of sleep making his voice gruff.

"Again?" I exclaimed in a whisper, my voice feeling raw.

He huffed out a breath and laid his head against my breasts, his eyes fluttering closed.

But before he could fall asleep completely, I asked a question that had been burning through me all night, "How was I?" I turned on my side.

He snickered under his breath and looked at me out of the corner of his eye. "How do I put this nicely…"

"Don't be rude!" I screamed, slapping at his arm playfully.

He laughed harder then, resting on his lower arm so he could look me in the eyes. "I'm just teasing. You were perfect." Cassius tilted his head and tucked a strand of hair behind my ear.

We managed to get dressed without ripping our clothes off again, before making our way to the dining room. I stuck to his side, not wanting to drift too far from his heat and the scent that always lingered on him. He wrapped an arm around my waist to secure me to him and pushed open the dining room doors. The performers welcomed us with cheers, some smiling deviously at what went down last night.

"Look at you two love birds," Charlotte cooed, coming to give me a hug. "Sorry Cassius, but we need to take Juniper for a little while." Her smile was ingenuine as she pulled me away. Once we were in the clear, she whispered, "Details. Give us every detail."

"Not so fast!" Mr. Monte entered the dining room suddenly, opening his arms out wide. "I congratulate our newlyweds, but this is the circus, and we can't afford to dilly dally. I need the tents strewn up, the animals fed, and supplies picked up in the city." Mr. Monte instructed with a brisk nod before shuffling out of the room.

I guess the festivities were over. We'd had our fun and now it was time to get back to work. But how had it happened so quickly? And now that it was over, life felt…normal, but different all at once. We were husband and wife, but we'd hardly had the time to enjoy it. A little part of me wished we could have had a couple days to really soak it in.

I shook the thought away as I followed the crowd outside, where we gathered around the heap of red and white leather. Grabbing the ropes, we pulled as hard as we could, the tent rising higher and higher with every stroke. The sun warmed our skin until we were damp with sweat, but it was nothing compared to the unbearable heat of summer.

The men moved to secure the risen tent, pounding stakes into the cold, frozen earth, and they were thoroughly sweating by the time they finished. Cassius was the first to strip off his shirt and the other men followed suit not long after, but the ladies weren't upset over the fact.

My stomach twirled when I saw Cassius's chest covered in a sheen of sweat. His tanned skin was glowing under the sun and there were shadows in the lines of his abdomen. There was a distinct roundness in his shoulders as his defined muscles contorted every time he raised his arms. I watched hopelessly, my stomach coiling, and turning to the others, I realized I wasn't alone. Charlotte was practically drooling as she watched the muscles in Flint's torso stretch as he unshackled a car to let the animals loose, while the rest of the women floundered over the mix of half-naked men. It was unfair—torturous even, that we were stuck looking at them all day long.

Thankfully, we were put to work helping Cassius with the animals, while the others went into the city to pick up supplies. He'd set up the pens outside to let them roam, and an assembly line of sorts had formed to feed the animals.

I didn't know how Cassius kept track of which animal received which feed, but after years of practice, it seemed like second nature to him. He had the dry foods separated into twenty different buckets in what must have been five minutes, before moving to a cooler to fetch the meat for the birds and larger mammals.

Sauntering up to the peacocks, Olive began flicking small handfuls of grains, seeds, and cubed pieces of meat, which they pecked from the ground with a snap of their beaks.

While overseeing the feeding of the animals, Cassius grabbed a hose from the side of the train that had been hooked to a water line and began filling metal tubs.

I skipped over, eager to help in some way, and coming up behind him, I asked, "Can I help?"

He smirked, knowing I'd been watching him the entire time, and grabbed another pail of red meat. He handed it to me without even a glance and said, "Abbas is hungry."

I frowned, suddenly confused, wondering why he was being so sparing with his words, but I bit my cheek and accepted the pail. As soon as I stepped toward Abbas, the lion seemed to remember me as an old friend and stuck his large nose over the top of his wooden pen to nuzzle my cheek with his whiskers. I giggled and closed my eyes, scratching behind his ears where he liked it. His fur was hot from its time in the sun, his eyelashes tickled my hairline, and by fooling me with his snuggles, he was able to dip his head into the pail by my feet.

"Sit," I scolded him for his impatience, raising a closed fist as Cassius had taught me.

Abbas's eyes sank to the floor shamefully and he sat in the dirt, pawing at the ground excitedly like a little dog. I chuckled and threw a piece of meat, which he caught effortlessly. Over and over we did this, until the pail was almost empty.

As I tossed another bit into his mouth, I felt a cool spray hit my skin. I leapt back and turned to look around me. Cassius was focused on the water bin at his feet, while the other performers were hard at work. I thought nothing more of it and continued to feed Abbas until I felt the spray once again on my ribs. I dropped the pail at my feet, prompting Abbas to lay on his stomach and stick his nose into the remnants, slurping at the blood like a cat drinking milk. I turned around once again, this time finding a faint smile playing on Cassius's lips.

That bastard.

If that's how he wanted to play, then I'd play.

I picked up the pail, and walking up to Cassius, poured a stream of blood on his shiny black boots. I patted his bare shoulder, but as soon as I turned my back, he sprayed my head, almost drenching my hair completely. I swiveled my head while wiping the water off my face and found Cassius smiling.

"Don't you dare." I pointed a finger at him and braced my feet apart, prepared to run for my life.

But he only shrugged his shoulders smugly and grabbed me, pulling me into his chest. I screamed when he lifted the hose above my head and drenched me within seconds. When he made no sign of stopping, I stomped on his foot and snatched the hose out of his hand, spraying him in return. He yelled at me to turn it off, but I didn't drop the weapon until he was soaked, and I burst out laughing when I saw a mop of black hair covering his eyes. He wore a dangerous scowl, but he let out a small giggle as the rest of the circus began to laugh at him from a distance.

In a matter of seconds, his smile disappeared and was replaced with a glare, his eyes glimmering from under the shadow of his eyebrows. He shook the wet hair out of his face before he grabbed my hand and pulled me to the train. Coming around the back and out of sight, Cassius didn't waste any time before pressing me into the wall and slamming his lips against mine. I opened my mouth invitingly, the taste of him swimming on my tongue. His hands traveled aimlessly, as though he couldn't touch enough, and I ran my hands across his open chest. His lips roved over my jaw and down my neck, where he nipped at the tight skin, making me yelp.

But when he grasped the lining of my shirt and began pulling it up, my entire body locked up, despite how much I wanted him. "What are you doing?" I yelled in a whisper.

"I want you." He smiled innocently and leaned in to kiss me again.

I drew away further. "And I want you, but not for everyone to see," I scolded him, slapping at his hand when he grabbed at my shirt again.

"I couldn't care less if everyone on this damn field hears you moaning my name," he groaned, his hand slyly moving to grasp my breast.

My breath hitched, and I almost let him continue trailing his lips down the column of my throat, but for selfish reasons, I didn't want the others to imagine what Cassius was capable of doing to me, or the sounds he might make. Cassius was mine, and mine alone.

I lifted his jaw and placed a firm, quick kiss on his lips. "Later," I said, and sauntered away to join the rest of the crew.

Cassius whipped his wet hair back and yelled out, "You're going to regret that!"

I turned over my shoulder and smiled. "Oh, I hope so."

I walked away with a goofy smile, already anticipating another night to explore Cassius.

"Juniper!" someone screamed, ripping me out of my thoughts and into panic.

The sound was shrill and full of warning, and I picked my head up to find the dancers standing in the middle of the field, pointing toward a spot in the distance. When I followed their line of sight, my heart plummeted into my stomach.

My mother, in all her grandeur, was headed straight for us. She was bedecked in a long spring gown, the pastel colors washing out her pale face, and she wore a small hat on her petite head, the lace fringe covering her eyes as though she were a rare commodity.

She was anything but. She couldn't have looked more out of place.

An array of Axminster's finest guards formed a line behind her as she approached us, accompanied by Mr. Young, Colette, and Joseph. He walked with trepidation, which made sense, since I had up and left him without warning. I took a moment to look at his freshly pressed waistcoat and his gelled blonde hair, suddenly feeling guilty for betraying his kindness.

I knew they would come for me, and I didn't feel the slightest fear about having to return home, not after marrying Cassius, but seeing them here, in this magical place—the place that had become my sanctuary—made my stomach turn. My mother ruined everything she came in contact with, like poison rotting the earth and turning it grey and dull. I wouldn't let her taint the one place that had survived her.

I stood there with my feet planted in the earth, too afraid to move. The other performers ceased their work to see what the fuss was about, simultaneously joining in the middle of the field like an army, prepared to march into the heat of battle. The sun suddenly felt too hot, the growing field and its flowers too bright, almost blinding. I closed my eyes, as if I could pretend none of this was happening. As if I could imagine the night Cassius and I would share later and not feel like my family ruined every happy moment.

There, in the darkness, I felt fingers lock between mine and squeeze, willing me to open my eyes. When I did, I found Cassius standing next to me, proud and unfaltering.

When he turned to look at my family, the glare he leveled at Joseph made it clear this would only go one way. With me by his side. And that comforted me enough to push forward to join the others.

Mr. Monte stood on the front lines with his hands folded graciously over a dark cane embedded with gold strands, like marble. He turned his head up as my mother stopped before him, as though she was beneath him. "Lovely afternoon is it not, Ms. Rose?" he inquired kindly, completely disregarding Mr. Young, who scoffed at his inattention.

"It'd be more comfortable in the confines of my warm home, although, you must not even know what a home feels like," she said, as if this spring day was even too cold for her liking. "I'm curious, how do any of your performers survive the winter months? I could provide you with a new train altogether, with lavish bed chambers, food prepared by culinary artists, and an actual heating system. At a cost, of course," she remarked with disdain.

"Dare I ask what that cost might be?" Mr. Monte asked with great humor, already aware of her terms.

My mother took a step forward and explained with her hands, "My daughter, of course. She has intentions of marrying a nobleman who will take care of her. I do not need to explain myself to a band of misfits on the run," she criticized, flicking a piece of hair out of her perfectly powdered face.

"Oh, Diana." Mr. Monte skipped the formality of her last name, which made her press a gloved hand to her heart in surprise. "You should know by now the circus never runs. That's why you're here today after all. Because you know you've lost. You know you'll never get your daughter back, and it scares you. But for a wretched woman such as yourself, I can't find it within me to forgive or even pity you. It's over." Mr. Monte turned his back, prepared to walk away, and I felt victory surge up in my chest.

I'd never had the confidence to speak to my mother in that way, but maybe, with the help of my friends, I finally could.

"It is over when I say it is over," Diana Rose exclaimed, slapping her palms against her overly large dress, as though she were pouting like a child.

Colette shuffled uncomfortably next to her, not knowing what to do.

I took a deep breath, my heart pounding. I had to put a stop to this. "No, mother." I finally stepped out of the crowd to face her.

It was scary, knowing that after this I may never see her again. She may hate me for the rest of her life, and I'd always resent her for what she did, but I hated the thought of leaving my mother and sister behind. But no matter how much it saddened me, it had to be done. I had a new family now and I wouldn't allow my mother to threaten that.

"You have no power here. You tried to destroy the circus, but it didn't work. And do you know why?" I asked in frustration, balling my fists at my sides. I didn't give her the time to respond before explaining, "Because the circus has something you will never have. Love."

I found it impossible to avoid Joseph's gaze and the palpable awkwardness between us when I said those words. Love was the one thing missing between us, but by the quirk in his brow, it seemed he understood.

I turned back to meet my mother's eyes. "And we do what we love, even if it makes us the poorest, least respected people in this world. The circus gives a family to those who never had one."

I hadn't been abandoned as the other performers had, but there was always something missing—the tender touch of my mother, the security of a happy home, and all the times she should have been there to support me.

"For thirteen years I stood dancing on a stage, looking for your face in a crowd of smiling parents. And I felt defeated every single time I didn't find you. I felt abandoned." I cleared the lump in my throat, hating the tears that sprung to life.

She looked appalled, as though it was wrong to blame her for such trivial things. "You know we had other obligations to attend," she said condescendingly.

I wanted to scream at her or shake her to make her understand, but it was useless. My mother would never apologize and would surely never change. There was no use wasting my breath. "All you need to know is that the circus has given me a family that I'm proud to belong to. It's made me happy—happier than you ever could have. My friends make me feel cherished instead of ridiculed. Mr. Monte has protected me when my own *mother* wouldn't. And Cassius loves me for *me*."

I turned to look at Cassius, his small smile prodding me to continue. "I couldn't have asked for anyone better to spend the rest of my life with. And I know you don't understand why I look for love—you stopped caring for it after father left because all that mattered to you was security." My voice wavered. "And I feel sorry for you because love is the greatest gift anyone can be given. I truly hope you find it someday."

My mother looked at me in disbelief, her jaw quivering. I hadn't seen her cry since the day my father left, and today would be no exception. "You think getting engaged will fix everything? You have obligations to another man." She motioned to Joseph, who was staring at me with a hint of a smile, as if saying *you did it.*

I was unable to hide my chuckle then. "Not engaged, Mother. Married." I placed a hand on Cassius's chest where my wedding ring glinted in the sunlight.

My mother's face fell then as it dawned on her. She glanced down to my hand, finding the delicate wedding ring on full display.

"You married a bum who cannot provide for you. You will be unhappy; I promise you that," she spat.

"Do not speak of him in that way," I said with my head held high. I wouldn't tolerate her treating him as less after everything he's been through—after everything *we've* been through.

"I will speak of him however I wish because I know what's best for you. You might hate me, and I can live with that because I am your mother, but I will always fight for your future."

"You will never know what's best for me." I shook my head before turning to Joseph. "I'm sorry, Joseph, that you've been caught in the middle of this. I never meant to hurt you."

He nodded then, his eyes so understanding and kind. Perhaps he was proud of me for standing up for myself. Perhaps he'd even be encouraged to do the same.

"There's nothing you can do now. Cassius and I were officially married yesterday, and if you attempt to ruin this marriage, *you* will be ruined. After father left, it took years for the church to accept you, and another divorce in the family would be the end of you. You taught me best, Mother." I smirked, revenge feeling so sweet. I knew my mother. She loved her image more than anything in the world.

Cassius hadn't taken his eyes off Joseph since he arrived, making his point that I belonged to him.

My mother, on the other hand, stood in utter failure as the wind whipped her dark hair in front of her face. The shock in her eyes was worthy of a painting, and I wish I could have captured it in that moment.

"You will regret this," she scoffed. "You will tire of this life and of him—of not being supported, always fighting to survive, always being one step behind. You will regret not having the means to sustain a family. The circus will become dull, and you'll want to settle down, but this choice of yours will make it so that you cannot. I hope you understand that. And if you do, it would do you well to return with us." Her voice shook at the thought that this would be our final goodbye, but she already knew my answer.

And that's why Mr. Monte spoke for me. "It's time for you to leave, Ms. Rose. You are never permitted to return."

It wasn't often that Mr. Monte was so emphatic.

Mr. Young scoffed at him. "You will not speak to your superior in that way." He then turned to me with disgust written in his features. "I don't know what I was thinking, attempting to marry my son to such an ungrateful whore." He spit on the ground.

Joseph turned to his father to reprimand him, but Cassius was already removing his arm from my waist. In two strides, Cassius had reached Mr. Young and punched him in the face.

"Don't you ever speak to her like that again," Cassius said, returning to tuck me into his side.

I almost laughed at Mr. Young. His words meant nothing to me. They were simply the showing of a small man. He'd gotten what he deserved. Meanwhile, my mother remained silent, and I was reminded of a man's power to say what he wished without punishment or consequence. She wouldn't defend me even if she wanted to…she wasn't allowed to.

"Leave. Now," Cassius ordered.

When Mr. Young turned his back, the guards followed accordingly. Joseph glanced my way, almost unnoticeably, before joining his father. My mother looked sidelong at me, hoping I'd change my mind and come with her, but I only raised my chin higher in defiance. She took that as her cue and began trailing behind Mr. Young.

Colette looked back at my mother's retreating figure, unsure of what to do. She opened her mouth as if to say something, but then closed it.

Such an obedient daughter, I thought.

My blood began pumping faster and faster. I loved my sister, but I wouldn't watch her be stifled under my mother's control any longer. So, I looked to her and said, "I suggest you find your own voice, instead of following her for the rest of your life."

She nodded promptly, tears falling down her cheeks. "I'm going to see you again, I promise."

I didn't expect her to keep her promise, but I sincerely hoped she would. My sister wasn't to blame here, she was simply caught in the middle and unwilling to move.

"I know," I reassured her. The memories of my sister and me growing up together, laughing together, and crying together, seemed so far behind us now.

Finally, Colette walked away, and my heart hit the floor. She was the only one I had ever really trusted—my closest friend. I clenched my jaw while watching them leave. I shouldn't have been sad, but I was. They were my family. They were the ones I'd shaken every Christmas morning to open presents with, the ones I baked sweet treats with in the summertime, and the ones that, despite our quarreling, had tried to love me. I quickly blinked away the tears that began to fall, and took a deep breath through my nose, but I was unable to control the sobs that filled the silence around me. And when their figures faded from view, I wept even harder. Were it not for Cassius holding me to his chest, I would have fallen to the ground, but he pressed me to him tightly, his hands locking me in place. Regardless of the warmth Cassius provided, I felt numb.

Chapter Forty-Seven

After my family left, I busied myself practicing with the dancers for our next performance. I was grateful for some alone time with them since I hadn't gotten the chance to tell them about last night. That, and it was a good distraction from the events of this morning.

Charlotte was the first to speak up as we sat in a circle and stretched our limbs. "So," she started. "How was last night?"

The other girls sat up straighter and nodded their heads excitedly. So, I told them every motion, every sensation, and every tender moment.

"He was sweet," I summarized. "But I didn't know it would hurt as much as it did!"

"Mhm," Raelynn hummed in agreement.

"Ah, yes, I remember my first time," Charlotte added, looking up to the peak of the tent as if it had been centuries ago. "But Cassius isn't too rough. It'll go away soon, I promise."

I promise. Behind her eyes I could see images of her time with Cassius unfolding, and I couldn't seem to put out the embers of jealousy threatening to burn me. I'd put the past behind us, so why did the thought of him with her make me want to crawl into a deep dark hole?

"Let's get to work!" I jumped up, eager to distract myself.

Our next performance was in Dangarnon, a rather small city by the sea, but the city most affected by the circus's influence. It was important to impress outlying kingdoms, because if news of the circus traveled from Dangarnon to Hewe—home to the biggest entertainment industries—then the news was important. So, every year, we made it a point to impress them so that word traveled, and this year was no exception. The lovers from different worlds had just gotten married, the circus had defeated their enemies inside and outside their midst, and it was time to show everyone our victory.

Mr. Monte had something special planned for the audience, which had me working with the dancers. It was liberating and shackling all at once. I was glad to be performing with my closest friends, but I yearned to be on the rope. Dancing was safe, but walking a thin line was thrilling.

"Come on, ladies!" Mr. Monte yelled, clapping his hands to the beat. "After years of being crushed by the elite, we're here to show them we have come out victorious! After being held down by the killer, we've found peace. I want you to portray beauty and ease."

I kicked my legs and swished the torn skirt hanging from my hips until my legs were sore and aching.

"This is our chance to show them that we're worth watching."

The ladies nodded smoothly and took a moment to rehydrate as Mr. Monte pulled me aside.

"You'll join the dancers, disguised as one of them, but when it's your turn to walk the rope, you'll control the audience. You will be the marionette, twisting the puppets' strings."

After he briefed me, I skipped to my room. Cassius and I barely slept last night, and I needed to rest before our performance this weekend. When I arrived, it was obvious he had the same idea. He laid in bed with a book folded open in front of his face, but when he heard the door close, he moved it aside and cracked a smile.

"Join me," he offered by patting the sheets next to him.

I undressed willingly and changed into a thin, silk nightgown, hopping into the warm sheets and curling into him. Humming with relief, I laid my head against his chest to listen to the drumming of his heart.

"You aren't going to bed, are you?" he asked quietly, throwing his book aside and scooping me into his arms.

"I'm tired," I whined.

"Oh, I'm sure." He winked in reference to last night's activities. "But I warned you I'd punish you for what happened earlier."

Despite how tired I was, the simple fact was that I hadn't stopped thinking of him either. Now that I knew what it felt like to be his—completely his—I would want him every moment of every day. So, I ran my hand under his shirt and pressed my cold fingertips to his stomach.

He winced, before placing his warm hands on top of my own.

This man was mine forever, and that realization was so overwhelming that I crashed my lips onto his. Climbing on top of him, I quickly unfastened his shirt, which he pulled over his head with similar impatience. My toes curled when he ran his hands up my bare thighs, and before I knew it, my nightgown was thrown over my head and onto the floor. My breasts peaked in the chilly air and Cassius eyed them as though they were works of art.

He grabbed my ribs, moving to flip me over, but I placed a hand on his chest to stop him. He understood exactly what I wanted, and positioned himself below me, allowing me to take control. I rolled my hips as our breathing became quickly matched, and when I came undone, the sun had already winked out of the sky.

Chapter Forty-Eight

The night of the performance...

"This is a special day for us, my love." Cassius rubbed his calloused hands up and down my arms, spreading warmth down my spine. "Let's show everyone that we're in this together. That we've found peace."

After all, peace was the theme for tonight. Valetta had designed pastel costumes to illustrate simplicity after a long two years. This seemed to be the final step—revealing our victory to show the crowd that we were undefeated.

"I must dress." I pecked Cassius, and the softness of his lips sent butterflies through my stomach. It was strange that he still made me this nervous and excited.

"*Must* you?" he drew out the word, making fun of the proper way in which I spoke.

Even after all this time, I hadn't lost the diction I was taught in Axminster. It would take time to develop the idiolect of the performers.

"I heard Valetta prepared *quite* the costume for the rose of the circus," Cassius continued.

"We'll find out soon enough. Now, stop teasing and get dressed." I pushed him away and went to the back of the tent where the dressing rooms were located.

Closing the curtain behind me, I noticed Valetta already seated on a small stool, ready to help me get into costume. She didn't waste a second before notifying me about tonight's order. "This is the first time you'll have a costume change. You'll enter the stage accompanying the dancers, then you'll have to quickly change before walking the rope. No dallying unless you want to miss your entrance," she reprimanded with a pointed finger.

I nodded to confirm that I understood her instructions. She offered me a small white leotard with flowers cascading down the sleeves and a skirt to tie around my waist. I looked like a flower, innocent and delicate.

When I heard Mr. Monte's voice booming throughout the tent as he welcomed the audience to the show, I knew it was my time to go.

"Don't be late!" Valetta yelled as I raced out of the dressing room.

I waved in acknowledgement, quickly sidling between Autumn and Daisy as the line of dancers formed. Olive and Piper, the smallest and youngest pair, tied off each end. I smiled down at the little girls then straightened, just as the flaps of the tent were pulled back and light swept over our faces. I smiled at the crowd and sprinted forward with the group, swishing the skirt around my waist. When we reached the middle of the room, we kicked in unison and a wave of sand flourished in the air.

Separating into a v-formation, we opened our arms and pirouetted, spinning once, twice, our synchronization moving the audience to clap.

Charlotte took the lead and kicked her leg up while we circled around her. The rush of the dancers created a strange illusion, putting the audience into a trance of sorts. Too many bodies were moving to focus on just one until we stopped and raised our arms to bow.

And just like that, our performance was over. It was a lighthearted opening to what we hoped would be a lighthearted show.

Quickly, I shuffled with the rest of the dancers into the back before being pulled into the dressing room by Valetta. I ripped off the leotard, almost tearing the seams in my haste. She shuffled a dress that resembled a wedding gown under my feet, opening the neckline for me to step into. When she hoisted the fabric over my hips and up my arms, I flattened it over my stomach and took a minute to look at the details.

The top was made of tulle, completely transparent, with a lace bralette fastened underneath to conceal my breasts. Just below that, a porcelain corset constricted my waist, diamonds running down the panels and shimmering beautifully under the light. A white collar wrapped around my neck while blooming sleeves of tulle fell to my wrists. Lastly, a white skirt ruffled out below the corset, spilling widely over my hips, and reaching high above my knees. It was short, and it was sexy, expensive, and delicate all at once.

Valetta held in a small giggle as I ogled her work.

I sprung with joy and bounced on my toes, prepared to show the audience Valetta's creation. I jogged to the flaps of the tent, where just beyond, the crowd had gone quiet, and the lights had dimmed. A soft violin began to play, filling the room with serene chords and the light plucking of strings. I stepped through the curtain with a bouquet of flowers in hand, padding along the path of sand toward the middle of the tent, where a light was ready to shine like a halo around my figure.

I gently tossed the bouquet into the crowd, which made the ladies scream as they scrambled over each other, and reached above my head to the ring that was positioned there. I performed a few of my signature moves, my body twisting effortlessly, as though I was void of control and simply dangling there. When I glanced around the room, I noticed a few audience members who appeared rather unimpressed. They seemed bored even. And boredom was Mr. Monte's worst fear.

So, to excite them, I lowered my body off the ring, pushed my legs back and forth to gain some momentum, and leapt. The rope wasn't that far off, but the audience was taken by surprise, not having seen it before.

I'd gained their attention once more.

Just then, Cassius came stumbling into the tent, dressed head to toe in black, a top hat shadowing his eyes. His wavering steps made him appear drunk, and when he looked up at the crowd, his eyes were red and the bags under them had been painted darker.

"My love!" I gently proclaimed from the rope, and Cassius looked up at me immediately.

His eyes filled with hope and a smile formed as he climbed the ladder to the platform without apprehension.

When he reached the top, I extended my hand and urged him to follow me, which made him take one dangerous step onto the rope. When it trembled, he looked up to me in terror, extending his arms on either side to show his struggle.

The audience clapped, encouraging him to continue, and he straightened his back and took one step after the other, finally coming to join me in the center of the rope. I grabbed his hands and smiled as he bobbed on the rope. This was a story for the audience as well as for us. We'd made it through the worst of the year, through the trials that befell us, and we'd come out together. I slowly moved my hands to the buttons on his midnight coat and unfastened them, all the while ensuring that Cassius and I remained balanced. Stripping him of the coat that fell to the floor below revealed his white poet's shirt and cream-colored vest. He had turned from darkness to light, as all of us had. We had been saved by one another.

We turned in unison to the crowd, raised our hands into the air, and leapt off the rope. Tucking our knees into our chests, we flipped once before twisting onto our backs, and landed on the net safely, with the crowd roaring in approval.

We rolled off the net together as Mr. Monte arrived with the rest of the performers at his heels. The firebreathers expelled glowing orange flames and lit the path for the group, and the cyclists rode around the tent, waving their arms in invitation and drawing the audience closer. Mr. Monte halted the performers a few feet away from the audience as Cassius and I joined him at the front.

He cleared his throat before beginning, "Our hope is always to offer you a magical experience, but that has been disrupted for two years now by the efforts of Monroe Beringer."

The audience gasped, recognizing the man as one of our own.

Mr. Monte continued regretfully, "Monroe Beringer led Penelope Plume to take her own life almost seven years ago and returned when Juniper arrived. He sought out our tightrope walkers because of a personal vendetta." Mr. Monte then nodded his head to me, encouraging me to step forward.

I took a deep breath, this being the first time I would speak openly about this. "Monroe threatened me for two years, targeting me during our performances. I was injured on multiple occasions, but what hurt even more was not being able to perform at my best for all of you." I continued, my voice shaky, "Recently we put an end to his efforts, and it is our joy to announce that he is now permanently behind bars."

The audience clapped and stomped their feet, the sound resembling the beat of a drum in the heat of battle. It was a cry for victory.

I then looked to Cassius, who stepped forward and said, "We've loved performing for you, and even more so sharing our stories, our trials, and our joys with you. My sister Penelope should never have suffered at the hands of that man, and I'll miss her every day, but by the grace of God, we were able to save Juniper, my wife," he added, looping an arm around my waist, "from meeting the same fate."

The crowd went absolutely wild when Cassius snuck in the part about me being his wife. The women began screaming, as fans would only do for stars—with a hint of jealousy that the handsome lion tamer was now unavailable.

But Cassius only quieted them by raising his hand. "Juniper has helped me through some of my darkest times and has been an amazing partner to perform beside." He gently took my hand, speaking directly to me. "I love her with all my heart, and I am hoping you can love her like I do, even though she came from a different world. Because she's the one who showed me that *that* world may not be so different from ours." He gazed at the crowd of dirty bums and pristine men and women sitting alongside one another. There used to be a barrier separating rich and poor, but that had slowly begun to fade.

"It's time we forget our differences and come together as equals," Mr. Monte proclaimed, just as the fire breathers released their flames into the air.

All around us, the echo of cheering and clapping filled the room, drowning out any other noise. This was our dream—to bring together those who had suffered through poverty and those who had relished in their wealth. And it was just beginning to come true.

Chapter Forty-Nine

"Cheers to a crew that can survive anything!" Mr. Monte proclaimed that night after our performance.

Everyone raised their glasses into the air, and I listened to the delicate *clink* resonate through the room before the tables were moved and the dancing began. When I arrived at the circus, I felt awkward dancing without restraint. I was used to holding the shoulder of a partner and remembering specific footsteps. It was orderly and perfected, while dancing in the circus was wild and free. I was terrified at first to let myself go and *really* dance, but I'd come to love it—when the lights turned down low, the stomping began, and the merry stringed instruments played. But more than anything, I loved the laughter of those I now called family.

I wiggled into the center of the group and threw my hands into the air, letting every terrible thing from the past two years glide down my arms with the sweat. And when the song picked up, I found Charlotte rubbing her rump against Flint, and I clapped and cheered with the others as Flint's eyes practically rolled into the back of his head. Charlotte and Flint were a good couple—Flint had a sweet, smart side to him, while Charlotte had a wild and free soul. They were opposites, but they complemented each other perfectly.

Their closeness made me search for Cassius in the crowd, suddenly feeling lost without him. After scanning the room for quite some time, I spotted him in the back with Piper on his hip. By the crease in his forehead and his downturned lips, it seemed he was giving her a rather serious lecture. I watched her eyes dart to his mouth, but over the raucous music, she couldn't hear him, which led her to lean in so that he could speak into her ear.

My heart melted as I pictured what kind of father Cassius would be. He'd be kind and gentle, but strict. He'd teach our children to have fun—to not take life too seriously. I didn't know whether he wanted children, but surely his love for Piper and Olive was a good sign.

Just then, Olive ran up to him, begging for his attention. He lifted her up so that both girls rested on his hips, and they began to banter back and forth, his head darting right and left while he tried to mediate their argument.

As the music died down, switching from one song to the next, I heard him shout, "I'll drop you both if you don't quit your bickering!" And when they didn't listen, he jolted them down his hips until both girls were screaming.

I laughed out loud, and he turned to find me across the room. He smiled gently and set the girls down, who ran off to convince Wilman to finally give them a glass of ale. Cassius walked across the room with a sense of purpose, and when he reached me, he slung an arm around my waist and pulled me into his chest.

An upbeat song began, and all the performers jumped and danced around us, but Cassius just kept swaying. I tucked my head into the crook of his neck and breathed in his warmth. "Those girls have taken a liking to you," I whispered in his ear.

"Mmm," he hummed, no doubt with his eyes closed.

"Do you think you'd ever want children?" I asked, somewhat afraid of his answer.

"Maybe…someday. I hadn't thought about it until now. Until you," he admitted shyly. "I think it'd be wonderful to raise them in the circus." He pulled away then to look at me with excitement in his eyes. "I could teach them about the animals, you could teach them how to walk the rope, when they're old enough of course, and they'd have an entire family to love them and protect them."

My heart burst with joy. I could picture it so clearly—telling our children stories of how we met. I could visualize them trying to walk the rope and sharing the same fear I once had. And I could see Cassius lifting their hands to touch Abbas's golden fur.

"Then again, they're grimy creatures," he interrupted the picture I created in my head. "They're hands are always sticky, and all they do is whine and complain. And don't get me started on the amount of shit that comes out of their small bodies," he ranted.

My body shook with laughter, his bluntness catching me off guard. "You're right. They can be rather disgusting. And it'd be a first for everyone. The circus has never taken care of an infant before." I giggled, looking down at my hands. "But we've got plenty of time. We'll think about it."

The day after our performance passed the same as any other. Mr. Monte had left the tent up because it had gotten far too late to haul it back to the train. So, today, we ventured into town to pick up our equipment before we set on the road again. Our next stop was in Penketh, and then we'd travel through Axminster and Culchester before summer arrived.

Taking multiple trips from town back to the train was quickly wearing us out. It was spring now, and a light breeze filled the air, but it was growing warmer day by day. When afternoon came, the circus went to rest for a while in the cool train.

Mr. Monte stayed in town to pay for the plot of land we used for our performance, and as soon as he returned, we'd ride through the night for Penketh. Sleeping on a moving train was a strange feeling, like returning from a day at sea, still feeling as though you're bobbing in the ocean. It was soothing, rocking back and forth while the dull sound of the tracks lulled you to sleep, but it could be disrupting. If the train jolted from a sudden turn or a bump in the tracks, it sent you sprawling awake. But it was exciting, knowing that when you awoke, you'd be in an entirely different place.

Before the train set off, I spent some uninterrupted time with Cassius. The past few days had been hectic, and we were rarely allowed time alone, so we had to make every moment count. We laid in his full bed, our legs spread out across the soft fur blanket as I stroked his shoulder. When I closed my eyes, I visualized the overwhelming sensation of our bodies pressed together…our first night as man and wife. During the busyness of the past week, we hadn't talked about it, and I was worried he hadn't enjoyed it.

"Our first night together…was it all you hoped it would be?" I was ready for any answer he might give because there was no risk. This was forever, and I felt safe.

"Juniper, it was everything I hoped, and more." He turned to face me then, knowing how nervous I'd been. "If it makes you feel better, I was nervous too. I haven't ever slept with a woman I love, and I didn't really know how to. I was worried I'd hurt you."

"You could never hurt me. Not even if you tried," I whispered.

His eyes fell suddenly. "I did last year, though. Time and time again, I hurt you."

I nodded my head slowly. "Yes, you hurt me last year, but it helped me understand who you are." I wrapped him into a tight hug, pressing him into me, hoping he would see himself as I do. "I forgive you," I whispered. "And I'll continue forgiving you for the rest of our lives."

Cassius wrapped his arms around my back and pulled me closer, curling his head into my neck. When he pulled away, he just smiled. "Thank you…for being so patient with me."

I smiled, feeling at ease about everything.

His demeanor turned playful when he offered me a wicked glance. "And when it comes the bedroom…you don't give yourself enough credit. You know exactly what you're doing. Especially with those hips." Cassius pulled me forward suddenly to rub against his lap.

He chuckled, and moved to stop, having had his fun, but I leaned forward and pressed my lips to his, grabbing his jaw to make him stay. When I pulled away, his expression changed from lighthearted to one that was full of need, the rolling of my hips making soft moans fall from his lips.

My shoulders relaxed and the blood seemed to rush through me faster, like the spread of a forest fire. He slowly trailed his calloused fingers up my thighs, deepening our kiss, and in that moment, I didn't want to rip off his clothes. I wanted to savor every lingering touch because we had all the time in the world.

But before we could even begin, we were jarred by the door slamming open. I gasped and turned over my shoulder, practically leaping off Cassius when Gus entered the room.

Gus turned his head to shield his eyes. "I'm so sorry!" he yelped, his breathing frantic, as if he'd run the whole way. "I don't mean to interrupt, but you need to come quickly!"

Cassius glanced over at me with worry etched in the lines of his forehead and sat up. "What's going on?"

"It's Mr. Monte," Gus commented dimly.

In a split second, Cassius had jumped off the bed and laced up his boots. "Is he alright?" he demanded while following Gus out of the room.

"He was in the city, paying the realtor when he found something." His voice wavered as he marched ahead.

Cassius's mood flipped like a switch and before I knew it, he grabbed my hand and raced out of the train. Mr. Monte was the closest thing he had to a father, and if he was in trouble, Cassius would do anything to help. I prayed deep down that Mr. Monte was safe, not only because of my own affection for him, but because of the man at my side who was racing fervently to the center of town. Cassius needed Mr. Monte.

Gus screamed through the hall of the train to gather the other performers, and they followed closely behind him as he led us to Mr. Monte. Our tent was still standing after last night's performance, positioned squarely in the middle of town, which looked odd among the stark brick buildings and homes. It almost seemed symbolic, the way it flapped freely against all the structures cemented in place.

When we made it to the tent, we spotted Mr. Monte, safe and sound, and I released the breath I'd been holding. Cassius sighed deeply next to me and raked a hand through his hair, but when I looked above Mr. Monte, my heart sank once again.

There was an enormous poster hanging across the entirety of our tent. It was made of leather, flapping in the wind, and it read in fanciful letters:

There's a new circus in town.
Christophe's Spectacle from across the sea presents to you:
A Night of Dreams.

"What the hell is this?" Cassius stepped up next to Mr. Monte to get a closer look.

"We've got competition," he said morosely, his chest rising and falling quickly. An angry fire was blazing in Mr. Monte's eyes as he stared dead ahead.

The night breeze sent a chill down all our spines. Summer was approaching, but it couldn't stop the cold dread from filling our bones. Something was coming—something we couldn't have expected.

A gust of wind created a shrill cacophony, and I could hear Monroe's words quietly whispering to me.

You can't escape what's coming.

About the Author

Emma Gilman was born and raised in sunny Colorado. She spends much of her time in pursuit of her rhetoric and writing degree but continues to write for pleasure as time allows. A love for redemption has inspired her to create characters that are bruised and broken but deserve a little bit of magic, and what better place to start than the circus? When she isn't writing, she's likely to be lost in a romance novel, rooting for the bad boy.

www.ingramcontent.com/pod-product-compliance
Lightning Source LLC
Chambersburg PA
CBHW021932120726
47992CB00001B/30